Dale Gunthorp was bor
and has lived in Londo
writing fiction in the late
short stories, *The Flying*

Georgiana's Closet

DALE GUNTHORP

A *Virago* Book

Published by Virago Press 2000

First published by Virago Press 1999

Copyright © Dale Gunthorp 1999

The moral right of the author has been asserted

A CIP catalogue record for this book
is available from the British Library

ISBN 1 86049 798 5

Typeset in Cochin by M Rules
Printed and bound in Great Britain
by Clays Ltd, St Ives plc

Virago Press
A Division of
Little, Brown and Company (UK)
Brettenham House
Lancaster Place
London WC2E 7EN

In memory of
Catherine Rae Arthur
1937–1991

Part I

1

Saturday, 21 October, Georgiana's party

In 1989, the Wheel of Fortune took a great lurch. Perhaps, with hindsight, we shall think of that year as the real end of the twentieth century. It was the year the People's Army ambushed a generation in Tiananmen Square and left 3,000 dead, while another People's Army put Nicolae Ceaucescu, and his wife Elena, up against a wall and shot them. But in Berlin, the wall against which thousands of people had been shot was pulled down by naked hands. In 1989, Gorbachev began to dismantle the Soviet Empire, de Klerk took the first steps towards dismantling the apartheid empire, and John Major, tremblingly, defied Margaret Thatcher, and history began to dismantle the Iron Lady. It was the year the *avante garde* slipped quietly back into the ranks, leaving modernism, socialism, radical feminism stranded, and Salman Rushdie at the mercy of the ancient savagery of fundamentalism.

In that same year, Lucy, a 26-year-old woman with few friends and an insecure job, found herself at the fringes of the small and very private world of Georgiana's parties. And so, on Saturday 21 October, in 1989, that year of many endings, another dismantling began.

❋

Georgiana never bustled, or made any show of wanting things
to get moving, but on that evening, at about 10 p.m., she was
briskly topping up half-full glasses when a taxi screeched to a
halt in her forecourt. Georgiana's cheeks puckered in a replica
of her once-famous smile, but she righted the bottle while
Ulric still stood with his glass politely extended. 'Wonderful,
darling,' he murmured, in time with the throbbing of the taxi
and contrapuntal tinkling of Georgiana's windows.

Georgiana watched the bubbles subside and the wine rise
to the level of Ulric's ringless ring finger. The taxi signified the
arrival of Toby, or – if they had for once wisely decided not to
drive – Fiona and Co. If it was Toby, he was an hour less late
than was his wont, so something had curtailed Jezebel's
walkies on Hampstead Heath and Toby would bring a welcome touch of drama. The prospect of the alternative caused
Georgiana to view Ulric's glass with a frown. If it was the only
other party not yet accounted for – Fiona and her appendage
Lorraine, plus their new friend – they had compounded their
crime by swanning in after the crowd but before the settling
down, in that crucial second half hour when everybody had
360 degree hearing.

Female voices rose in Georgiana's courtyard: it was the
alternative. One voice was magisterial; the other slow, uncertain, androgynous, slightly nasal and questionable as to class,
uttering, at intervals, 'Oh', and 'Ah'. So Toby and Jezebel
were still sniffing the scents of the night, and the Fiona
ménage had arrived. Worse, it had arrived unabashed – since
Lorraine was now exhibiting to the new friend – as proudly as
if she'd made them herself – the three windows of Georgiana's
drawing room.

'Wonderful, darling,' repeated Ulric, modestly raising his
half-empty glass: 'Just what it takes to rinse a ghastly day out
of my hair.'

Georgiana's smile was as gracious as before, but she didn't
pursue the invitation to inquire into Ulric's day. She was listening. She heard, in Lorraine's resonant delivery, the now
classic comments on her windows: 'They're too elongated

even for Georgian, too consciously proportioned for Regency, and more monumental than anything Victorian. They're the precursor of post-modernism, early Mussolini camp.'

Georgiana had no need to turn to confirm the details. It was for precisely that prospect viewed twenty years earlier from the running-board of a taxi that Georgiana had bought the middle first-floor flat of this mansion block in a trafficky corridor through St John's Wood. She had since devoted much thought to perfecting it. For Georgiana, no artefact expressed elegance and order better than its simple arrangement of three sash windows – draughty, yielding to rot and impossible to open, but a perfect group – ten feet tall, the wider central window surmounted by a carved pediment, the outer ones adorned with faux stone balconies; each divided by slender astragals into panes of touchingly imperfect glazing. Sombre curtains, which were never moved or cleaned and so had developed sculptural lines, enhanced the effect. These were looped back to show, at the side windows, clusters of little parchment-shaded lamps hinting at cabals of cardinals, and, at the centre, the huge glittering chandelier which had once been part of a set for *The Cherry Orchard*. Its glass icicles answered the vibration of the windows, throwing sparkles of light into the flaking remains of gilding on the senatorial ceiling mouldings. This metaphor of the slow attrition of time had been achieved through years of work with *papier mâché* and bulbs of ever-lower wattage.

The flat was the one inspired relationship of Georgiana's life, and it redeemed many others. Georgiana's acting career had followed her gazelle-like youth into extinction; her marriage, to a would-be leading-man, she had abandoned when it became clear that he was consuming her small inheritance as quickly as all their other assets; her one pregnancy had ended quietly at a small private clinic; her lovers had been numerous but regrettably neither distinguished nor reliable; the modest achievements of her other investments paled beside the horror of one rash entry into the market for platinum futures, and her

second career at Sotheby's had failed to take her beyond a
cluttered desk behind the auction rooms.

But the flat had paid off. It was more than a home; it was an
identity. Georgiana's career now was Georgiana's parties, held
for select friends on the third Saturday of each month. The
pattern was varied only for the Biarritz season (so August
was partyless) and December. Then, to avoid any connection
with the vulgarity of Christmas, it was held a fortnight early.

This room, with its three great windows, was the magic
ingredient. For this room Georgiana could endure stoical
economies over heat and food, so that her budget would
stretch to one lavish delivery of canapés from Prue Leith. It
was of no great significance that the flat comprised, beyond its
magnificent drawing room, only a slit of kitchen, a bathroom
crammed with wailing pipes, and one dark, poky bedroom,
about half the size of the lobby. This flat was Georgiana's love
and Georgiana's triumph. Georgiana felt the terror of death
only when rumour threatened an increase in the annual service charges.

'Talking about hair,' continued Ulric helplessly. He found
himself now facing Midge. Georgiana and the bottle had
moved on to replenish other glasses en route to the door, with
timing carefully judged to intercept Fiona and Co before they
could slide into the company, their new friend unvetted and
unexposed.

Georgiana did not invite outsiders to her parties. In twenty
years, the guest list had been modified only by *force majeure*.
Two names had been dropped – one former friend, never now
mentioned, had been convicted of fraud, the other had com-
mitted the equally unmentionable act of being found dead at
Victoria Coach Station. One name had been added. A decade
back, Georgiana had admitted Lorraine, cohabitation having
made her liaison with Fiona impossible to ignore. Lorraine
was still not quite one of the crowd. Considering what she had
done to this party, she never would be. Only she could have
the temerity to telephone, out of the blue, to say: 'Fiona and I
have discovered someone we'd simply love you to meet . . .'

As the gates of the lift clanged and Lorraine's commentary echoed through the corridors, Georgiana assembled that smile of hers and opened the door wide: 'Darlings – you made it. Fiona, my love. Lorraine.' These greetings were punctuated by brief but audible kisses.

'And this,' Georgiana reached out to the duffel-coated figure hovering behind, 'this must be your little friend. I've heard so much about you, Lucy dear.' A girl as mousy as this Lucy should never, but never, let anyone cut her hair short and spiky, a style that was possible, if at all, only for someone with superb bones and bags of personality.

Georgiana stepped back to give her friends a full frontal on the arrivals. Conversation faded as gently as if she had turned a dimmer switch.

Midge peered around Ulric's enormous chest-cage to see whatever was going on. Midge was every bit as pale as Lucy; her hair, in a greying Eton crop, was almost as severe and, barely reaching five foot, she was of even lower stature. But on Midge, such failings were cloaked by history: Midge had, at various times between the prime of Judy Garland and the death of Marlene Dietrich, been to bed with almost everybody in the room. References were veiled, but Midge, though herself non-orgasmic, rated as a marvellous lover. Midge was supple, subtle, tireless, romantic, energetic and hungry, a perfect slave: her instincts took her directly to everyone else's need and she had none of her own. Midge was at anybody's disposal. Midge was the 'mental cruelty' cited by Georgiana's ex-husband's lawyer in the counter-file for divorce.

As a result of these activities, everybody's secrets were shared with Midge. It had been revealed only to Midge that, for Ulric, *It* was all internal, that Toby owed his sensitive jaw to a face lift, and that the bone-hugging black satin gown Georgiana wore that evening had been remodelled out of the costume of a drag artiste.

Secrets were safe with Midge. Not because she was discreet. She wasn't: she had a woolly head. Though not stupid, she was always a little slow to take the point, which she forgot immediately afterwards. Her friends saw this as guilelessness. Midge feared it was the consequence of thirty years of serious social drinking.

Such fears had become habitual with Midge but, on the third Saturday of the month, she forgot them. Midge loved Georgiana's parties. The pouches under her own eyes filled her with shame, aversion and rage, but in similar indications of mortality under Ulric's eyes she found beauty that moved her near to tears. In these ravaged faces, she saw the wreck of her dreams. And the finality of it, the waste, the sudden glimpse of the cruelty of God, gave her a sweet, sad pleasure, the desire to embrace all these dear, dear friends in a huge hug of oblivion.

Unfortunately, before the end of each party, and a little earlier each time, oblivion returned in its more familiar form. But, somehow, Midge always found her way back to the draughty house in Kilburn and somehow when she, rather nervously, phoned Georgiana next day pre-armed with her thanks and if necessary apologies, Georgiana never had anything worse to say than 'So glad you're safe, darling; it scares me to death that you walk home alone through these mugger-buggered streets.'

Dear Georgiana, dear proud Georgiana of the slightly shaky hand. A memory of Georgiana of twenty years before, the thongs of her thighs tightening around Midge's ears, rose ghostlike before her and Midge quite missed whatever it was that Ulric was saying – something about hair. 'What's that kerfuffle at the doorway, Ulric dear?' she said, creating a diversion.

Ulric stepped aside to give Midge a clearer view. 'The arrival of Fiona and Lorraine accompanied, it would appear,' he replied, 'by a representative of the caring professions.'

Ulric was a singer, well over six feet tall and full-chested though slender. His achingly soulful bass voice was still good after fifty years on this planet, hundreds of productions of

The Messiah and the desertion of his clergyman lover. But often, during Ulric's solitary meditations, his voice lodged like a stone in his throat. He grieved not for Father Peter, but himself. Ulric could never surrender himself to the rough, warm, animal bonding of men. Often, on holidays, he had sat in cafés, his emotions wrenched by out-of-tune guitars or balalaikas into a craving to join in the dancing of Greek, Turkish or Russian men. He had never done so. He had never swayed in the arms of his brothers on the terraces, even when they were themselves swaying to the unashamedly bullish and sentimental recording of 'Jerusalem' he had made for them. These joys were impossible for Ulric because men in the mass persecuted him. The fans loved Ulric's voice, but when they were gathered in packs around Arsenal Stadium, any glimpse of his person aroused in them the instincts of the hound. Fortunately, as a youth, Ulric could run like the wind. Now, except when he was safe among friends, a cold, prissy mask hid all but his voice.

Yet even his whisper still raised hairs on the arms and would carry through Georgiana's circle to exactly as many ears as he sent it. Half a dozen people heard his remark, peered at the stranger escorted by Fiona and Lorraine and tittered. Some forgot the Third Natural Law of Parties (that each codicil to a moderately successful joke is feebler and more spiteful than the last) and guessed the new arrival to be some current Aunt Sally. 'You've all got it wrong,' concluded Steven-John, whose sex-change from female to male emboldened him to assume chairman's rights, 'it's the bailiff.'

Steven-John's remark did in fact end the discussion, not because the controversy had been settled but because Steven-John had, as usual, put his foot in it. Ulric laughed – which he was obliged to do, since Steven-John was his friend. But Sophie, darting out from under Sarah's wing, snapped: 'Don't be nasty, Stevie.' Sarah glowered in the general direction of anyone who would cast aspersions on Georgiana's financial stability or provoke Sophie into opening her mouth.

❖

Tim and Thelma, standing beside Sarah and Sophie, glowered in parallel. Superficially, the two couples had little in common. Sarah and Sophie were always being taken for somebody's lost aunties, while Tim and Thelma were pillars of society – married, parents and members of the Rotary Club. As if to emphasise this, though it was Saturday night, Tim wore a dark suit with waxed seat and elbows, and Thelma a green linen two-piece which reproduced faithfully the creases of her corsets.

Yet, at every party, the two couples gravitated towards each other and spent the first hour rediscovering their identical loathings of the M25, social security scroungers and the tripe on television. On other subjects they did not compare notes, but neither couple would have joked about the bailiff any more than about compulsory early retirement or heart disease.

Chelsey had been hovering about the two couples but, being as bean-pole tall as they were rotund, seemed to belong to a different element. She bent her head to make an entrance and said, in her breathy Vanessa Redgrave whisper: 'Steven-John may have a point. Fiona and Lorraine look pleased as people with a new puppy, but I doubt they've checked its pedigree.' When nobody responded, she added, 'I sense trouble ahead.'

Chelsey was an authority on behaviour and its consequences, having spent the 1970s in analysis and, the cost of that having become prohibitive for a frequently resting actress, the following decade in serial imbroglios with women therapists of the interactive persuasion. Later, she found clairvoyants to be cheaper and as effective: and now a pack of Tarot cards and her advanced relationship with the spirit world sufficed.

Nobody took up Chelsey's point. Although her remark was at least as offensive as Steven-John's, Chelsey was allowed to say anything, because what Chelsey said didn't count. Inside every group is an outsider, a special inside-outsider allowed to say cranky things because the crankiness attaches to her person, not her ideas. This was Chelsey's role. Chelsey never sought allies, and didn't want them. She guarded her loneliness and her Cassandra voice. At times it seemed to her that her outsiderness arose from a deeply solitary nature, at others that it came from pain or cynicism or some inverted need for attention. But most times, Chelsey attributed her loneliness to the crass insensitivity of the world.

Yet Chelsey was one of the stalwarts of Georgiana's circle. She said rude things about everyone, but wished no real harm to anyone except Fiona (about whom she said little). It was Fiona, Chelsey believed, not herself, who was the snake in the garden. Chelsey could call Ulric a spinster, Steven-John a phoney, Lorraine a diesel dyke and Midge Sergeant Peanut, and cause no permanent damage, but Fiona's unspoken scorn could shrivel the entire crowd into a fossil of the English class system.

With a toss of the mass of her still fire-red hair, Chelsey watched the people who were her only friends drift away from involvement with the problem at the doorway: Steven-John to consult Ulric about some deeply masculine matter; Sarah-Sophie and Tim and Thelma to wind themselves up into ever greater outrage at whatever had most recently occurred; Midge (of course) to get another drink, and nameless others merely to escape Chelsey's presence.

'Midget, hi!' Midge spun round as Lorraine grasped her shoulder. 'Meet Lucy.' Lucy's trailing hand was grabbed with equal ferocity. 'Lucy, this one's Midge, Margaret Winters.'

Midge was a kindly soul. 'Hello, dear,' she said, as Lucy's limp and chilly fingers were thrust towards her. 'So this is your first visit to Georgiana's?'

Lucy withdrew with the awkward shuffle of a boy escaping the embrace of a great-aunt. 'Yes,' she said quietly.

'We aren't as fierce as we look, my dear.' Midge put her hand in her pocket.

Lucy looked around the room and then at Midge. 'No.'

Midge caught a glimpse of huge, round, puzzled, honey-coloured eyes under skimpy new-moons of brows. Her mouth – like the eyes, several sizes too large for her child's face – was unsmiling, but had fallen slightly open, vulnerable. 'Long battles with the world have given some of us troopers' manners; don't let that bother you, my dear.'

Lucy nodded solemnly.

Conversation thus launched, Lorraine took off to find Lucy some gin (since Georgiana was unlikely to have cider, vodka or diet Coke). Within seconds she had been waylaid by excited exchanges, more or less the same as the exchanges of four weeks previously, with various of her dozen most intimate friends.

Lucy waited with the air of a dog tethered outside a shop, but for Midge the evening was putting out its first pale tendrils of pleasure. If there had been a chair within sight, she would have offered it to Lucy. If there had been a dragon, she would have slain it. 'In fact, you'll meet interesting people here,' Midge said. 'No doubt you recognise Georgiana? No? Of course you're too young to have seen her on stage. That's Ulric, Ulric Rolle, the tall chap – you interested in music, um, classical music?'

'I don't know a lot about it,' Lucy said, peering through the crowd at nobody in particular.

'Well, he's a singer, though his sort of music is rather old fashioned. But – look – over by the window: that's the actress Chelsey Chamberlain.' The blankness of Lucy's face caused Midge to add, in a doubtful tone, 'But I suppose she hasn't had a lot of work recently.'

'I wouldn't know. I don't go to the theatre.'

Midge was astonished.

'I like films,' Lucy added hastily. 'But plays, they're so, well, artificial, amateurish, they're somehow embarrassing. But, don't mind me; I come from Lincolnshire . . .' Lucy trailed off: her pale face was suddenly a furious red.

Midge watched the blush spread to the roots of Lucy's hair, flush the lobes of her little ears and spread patches on her throat. Yes, I know what you mean. But then . . .' Midge struggled against the urge to book this deprived child to see every show in London.

From the now quiet windows-end of the room, Chelsey noted that Fiona, having acquired a drink, was slouched against the kitchen doorway and in conversation with Georgiana. Steven-John, in the centre of the room, had turned his attention to Lorraine. She, nodding furiously and hopping from foot to foot, was no doubt desperate both to escape Steven-John and to rescue the new friend from Midge, who appeared to have launched into her usual number.

Lucy the name was. Chelsey had caught Lucy's glance in her direction and noted its indifference. Chelsey returned the compliment. This Lucy looked like every other anorexic young female at the bus stop. Chelsey observed the close-cropped baby-round skull, the toothpick body. She glanced discreetly at the owlish eyes, the pale macrobiotic skin, nervy nailbitten hands, the floppy backpack, the black schoolboy shoes worn with baggy trousers, navy pullover and a grey thing (perhaps a collarless shirt) underneath. Then Chelsey caught a gesture of helplessness exchanged between Lorraine and Lucy, and pursed her lips. Not *quite* any girl at the bus stop.

This Lucy was clearly the youngest person present though, taking into account a certain incipient scrawniness about the neck, already past playing Juliet and, with that thin skin, not likely to wear well. Probably not too far off 30 but able, after a heavy night, to pass for 40. That would make her some fifteen years younger than Lorraine, twenty younger than Fiona and as much or a bit more than the rest. If this Lucy had been cute, she could have been a toyboy. If she'd been expressive and fashionable, she could have been a student of the old sort, searching for experience. If her name had been Tracy or Dale or Sheila she could have been a temp at the office or some other aspirant picked up by Lorraine.

As she was, Chelsey sensed that this Lucy was lonely and

craved attachment to something powerful. Greenham
Common, lesbian separatism, Women Against Pornography,
the Unification Church, the Animal Liberation Movement?
None of those; Chelsey knew that Lucy was, like herself, an
outsider, one of the dispossessed. Chelsey narrowed her long
green eyes and called on her spirits. They gave her Lucy
hunched over a telephone. Though this vision came without
an audible soundtrack, the tingling along Chelsey's neck told
her these were defamatory calls, Outing them all: Ulric, the
suppressed queen; tweetie-pie Sophie; Midge, always struggling to see the bright side; Toby, whose scorn for the *hoi polloi*
press thinly masked his terror of it. Then Chelsey's vision had
her Outing Georgiana – Georgiana.

Chelsey turned her face to the window. Fractured images
of a new vision appeared in its irregular glass panes: of
Georgiana Outed a quarter century before, by a wild young
woman, desperately in love and more dangerous even than
this Lucy. In the vision, Georgiana did not look any younger,
but that was because, to Chelsey, Georgiana had never aged.
Yet things were different:

Georgiana is back in the theatre, touring *A Doll's House*. She
plays the lead – Nora, the brave, innocent, credulous wife.
Chaotic digs, ecstatic local reviews, wine at dinner, a script
full of righteous rage against husbands, a rattletrap van that
throws the players into each others' arms every time it takes a
corner, things untoward, cause Georgiana to want an affair.
With a casual glance, she takes the company's recent recruit
from the Webber Douglas Academy of Dramatic Art, the
leggy Celtic redhead who understudies her and plays the
maid. The tour takes the company to the highest heavens.
But it returns to London and its end, and so does the affair.
Because, waiting in London is the company's new freelance
prop-maker, a student jeweller, the divine Fiona.

Chelsey clutched at her throat as in the panes of Georgiana's
windows she saw the jilted lover run, screaming, almost

knocking the decorator off his ladder, out of Georgiana's flat. Not this flat – not this church hall, this stand-up brothel, this clock at Victoria Station – Georgiana's real flat, the one with black candles and big feather bed smothered in satin and damask, above the saddlery in Drury Lane. Chelsey saw the desperate redhead run blindly up the street; saw her stop, think, look mildly pleased, return to Georgiana's flat, grab the decorator's paintpot, shin up his ladder and in scarlet paint dripping like blood, scrawl LESBIAN BITCH over the wall and window.

As Chelsey wiped the fogging of her breath from Georgiana's window, her fingers remembered the slippery, paint-covered glass of that other window. She closed her eyes, and saw the mirrored but windowless dressing room where so short a time before that dreadful end, Georgiana had taken her hand saying, 'Now pay attention, because I'm going to teach you something very, very special.'

Of course Georgiana had not forgiven. There could be no question of forgiveness. After an appropriate exile, Chelsey had been allowed back as if nothing had happened. And Chelsey knew that now, for Georgiana and everyone in the crowd, nothing *had* happened. The thing had ceased to exist. There was nothing to forgive.

But for Chelsey it was not over. Now, it was Chelsey who could not forgive. In the acid of her anger, Chelsey's passion for Georgiana was preserved for ever. But now its ferocity was so dimmed by years without hope and eventually without dreams, that it could express itself only in a thin pain of jealousy. The pain had in it something of sweetness as Chelsey turned once again to note that Georgiana's attention was still focused on the kitchen doorway, and the elegantly *louche* figure of Fiona.

Fiona's glance, slow as a submarine emerging after long immersion, rose to meet Georgiana's. She did not smile – Fiona rarely smiled – but her huge pale grey eyes softened, causing Georgiana to catch her breath. 'There's no point in asking me what it's about, Georgie,' she said in her soft Highlands burr. 'Lorraine thinks this Lucy person knows something we don't know.'

All Georgiana's friends were handsome; even Midge, on a good day, recovered her urchin charm, and Chelsey, despite the toughening of her features and the awful colour she put on her hair, was still catwalk material. But only Fiona was beautiful, beautiful in the soul and in the bone. For this, Georgiana loved her. 'Whatever it is, best let the person keep it, darling,' she replied.

'Oh, I don't know.' Fiona's tone was abstract, as if the subject was not worth her whole attention. 'We're a timorous lot, women. I see it in myself.'

Georgiana, recalling Fiona's famous adventures of the couch, raised an eyebrow.

'We say "No" before we've seen what's on offer. The boys do better. They confront things – not aggressively, with insouciance.'

'Really? Ulric *confronts* danger while Midge *timorously evades* it?'

Fiona waved this away. 'You know very well what I mean.'

Indeed, Georgiana did, but she wanted to keep the debate open, not to fence with the ideas – Georgiana's ideas were undebatable permanent verities – but to find out what was going on in the Fiona ménage. 'It depends on what you're confronting, my love.'

'Oh, this and that. The used-upness of things. The way you get the stone before the high. That it's all so much effort.' Though Fiona's tone was as even as ever, Georgiana recognised the need out of which she took a gulp of wine. 'I guess you could say I'm confronting middle age, and I've yet to learn to do that with insouciance.'

Georgiana was well acquainted with middle age, being herself close to leaving it for something worse. She had, over the past year or more, been watching it begin to spread its slow obscuring film over the exquisite clarity of her friend's features. She was not angered by the desecration – what was inevitable, one took on board – nor did she seek to hide from herself what she saw. But she could not curb the weakness of wishing that Fiona did not see it. 'Perhaps, darling,' she smiled, 'a new object of desire?'

Fiona answered gravely. 'I don't lack an object of desire; I lack desire.'

'Desire,' Georgiana's smile turned mischievous, 'comes with the object.'

'Objects need maintenance and servicing – work.'

'Perhaps, darling, you've been working too hard – at suppressing the seven-year itch.'

Fiona laughed. 'Wouldn't that be nice, even if three years late. We've talked about it, Lorraine and I. Lucy's attitude is refreshing. It astonishes her that anyone could think an exclusive sexual relationship was valuable, or even healthy.'

Georgiana nodded. A threesome in view? She glanced across at Lucy, who looked as if she might explode if someone did not instantly release her from Midge. 'If it's what you want, darling Fifi. I'm sure she's intelligent and all that. Midge certainly likes her. But she looks, well, anaemic and rather underbred: would you have any fun?'

Fiona spluttered. Don't ask me, for Christ's sake. Talk to Lorraine.'

So, not a playful threesome, but Lorraine messing about and hurting Fiona. Georgiana looked at Lucy with a colder eye. 'In that case,' she said, 'tell your Lorraine to be wary of people who are really hungry. First they eat the food out of your hand, and then they eat your hand.'

'Poor little Lucy!' Fiona spluttered. 'Georgie, you don't have one drop of Christian charity in your veins.'

'I don't suppose I do,' said Georgiana absently, running an uncharitable eye over the assembly. She noted with satisfaction that Lorraine had escaped Steven-John only to fall into the even deeper trap of Tim and Thelma. Ulric was at the window, tapping his ear like a woodpecker as he talked to Chelsey. Dear Ulric, who tried to be inconspicuous, but couldn't help being an actress even more theatrical than

Chelsey. Georgiana briefly contemplated rescuing Lucy from Midge – for the opportunity to put a shiver of the fear of God into her. That wouldn't of course get her off Fiona's back, but it might be useful to remind this Lucy and her ilk who really ran the world. She turned back to Fiona. 'I've always thought the Good Samaritan gave a very bad example – any sensible person, seeing a man lying at the roadside, should take him for a drunk or a decoy.' Georgiana spoke flippantly, showing that she was deadly serious.

The ticking of another taxi in her courtyard informed Georgiana that Toby had arrived, and her crowd was now assembled. Georgiana was, in fact, the only member who didn't call it 'Georgiana's crowd' – or angels or gang – or by any collective noun. These were her friends, people who had known each other for a long time, who knew discretion to be the First Commandment and loyalty the Second, who gave generously but did not lend, who constituted, for each other, the human race. For a few seconds, she indulged herself by running her eyes over the cast: Fiona, Ulric, Midge, Toby, Chelsey, and so on – beautiful people, her people.

2

Sunday, 22 October, Kilburn

In the hallway of a tall, narrow Victorian house in Kilburn, a telephone was ringing. The sound penetrated the stiff door of the parlour, where it dissolved in horsehair, antimacassars, Turkey carpets and the fireplace where spiders had knitted together the ashes from old Mrs Winters's last illness. In the dining room, it set off tinklings in the china cabinet and splintered the reflection in its glass of Colonel Winters's portrait. In the kitchen and scullery, the sound was diffused among take-away cartons, doggy bowls and spills of refuse.

The ringing gathered momentum as it mounted the stairs. It bounced off the solid door of the marital bedroom (shut and locked now that neither Colonel nor Mrs Winters had any use for it), lost itself in the dressing room still crammed with old woman's furs, but clanged like a fireman's bell in the big, bare room at the top of the house, where Midge sprawled flat on her belly, pillow clamped over her ears.

But Raffles, Midge's little Yorkshire terrier, was distressed. She burrowed under the pillow and scratched.

'Chuck-chuck, girlie,' muttered Midge after several attempts to dodge the claws, 'it's nothing to do with us.'

Raffles understood the phenomenon of wrong numbers.

With a sigh, she snuggled down, and Midge absently patted her belly, springy as new dough. 'Unless it's the police,' she muttered. 'I have this awful feeling somebody went over the top again last night.'

Raffles's ears took on an intelligent perk and a soft sliver of tongue wiped Midge's wrist.

'You've got to pull yourself together, Miss Raffles. It's so obvious, it's got to be easy. Just *do* it: turn up your snout against the demon drink.'

Raffles clawed at Midge's hand, which was slowing over its belly-patting. Midge smartened up, but other preoccupations were wafting into her consciousness. Memory came with little spasms that gripped her lungs in a vice. Georgiana's face, sculpted with disapproval, rose before her. She folded her hand over her eyes, but flung it from her at the first whiff of her fingers, which smelt more than doggy, having spent the night curled up in her crotch. Later, much later, when she could brave the dizziness of heaving herself to her feet, she would stagger downstairs to make tea, delicious, life-giving tea, the only drink truly created by God. Then she would telephone Georgiana to discover what she needed to offer in the way of apologies. How long, O Lord, how long?

The frozen silence of the house pushed to a far distance the sounds of the day – traffic kept in order by lights at the cross-roads; a man washing his car with the encouragement of its radio, Irish families gathering their broods in voices still full of music from 11 o'clock High Mass.

Consciousness began, mercifully, to ebb, but again the telephone tore through the house. Raffles whimpered. This was serious. Midge thought so too. She threw a blanket over her shoulders and, tugging at the strings of her pyjamas, stumbled downstairs to confront the screaming monster in the hall. 'Winters,' croaked the ghost of her voice.

'Hello? Oh, hello, is that you, Midge? Lucy here.'

Lucy? Who on earth was Lucy?

'Midge, I want to apologise for upsetting you last night.'

Midge's stomach dropped to her bowels. This had something to do with Georgiana's party.

'Midge, are you there? – I've rung for something else too.' There was an awkward pause, then the voice said, very formally: 'I must ask you to accept that I really do not want to do sex with you.'

Out of a dry mouth, Midge whispered, 'I accept.' So that was why, all through the night, waves of shame had battered her.

There was a silence, as if her accuser didn't know quite what to make of Midge's reply. Midge struggled to bring her brain into action. From her years of experience in the classroom, she could recognise the resolute yet nervous tone of a prepared statement. 'I must have been' – the icy blast from under the door was now making Midge's teeth chatter, but politeness kept her at her post – 'a pes-st. Most awfully sorry. Won't bother you again.'

'You aren't angry with me?' The voice was now uncertain, even rather childish, and Midge began to remember: Lucy, the girl with a rucksack.

'Angry? How could I be? It's decent of you to phone.'

Midge was by now desperate to end the call, but Lucy wasn't picking up the signals. 'I'm also ringing,' she added, after another painful silence, 'to say I was really pleased that you wanted us to be friends. But of course, after what I've just said, I'll quite understand if you change your mind.'

Midge was still puzzled about what was going on, but replied firmly, 'Not at all. I would be honoured.'

'Because you said,' Lucy's voice hardened, 'you'd take me to lunch at St Katharine's Dock; you said you'd "motor" over to pick me up at noon. But,' her voice trailed away to a mumble, 'I'd quite understand if you didn't really mean . . .'

'Gosh; I seem to be running a bit late.' Midge hoped that the rising pitch of her response came across as eagerness, not a poor attempt to conceal her panic. For Midge hadn't the faintest recollection of any such arrangement. She also knew that she was in no condition to drive, and she had no idea where this Lucy lived, even if she could remember where St Katharine's Dock was.

A soldier father – and years of caring for a sick mother – had given Midge a redeeming discipline. 'Afraid I'll be at least another half hour. Remind me of the details.'

An unemployed schoolmistress prone to self-doubt, barely five feet tall yet packing nine stone of planetary volume, Margaret Winters wasn't someone most people would take for a Don Juan. She was so out of touch that she still presented herself to the world in a greying Eton crop and a pair of horn-rimmed spectacles, and sported outfits from the camp fashions of the 1960s and 1970s. Yet Midge had had success with women (and in her younger days also with men) that other Don Juans might envy.

Midge fell in love every time, but her conquests were not lasting. After a night, a week or a fortnight, the other felt so much better, thanks to Midge, that she (or he) was determined to make a go of whatever had driven her (him) to Midge in the first place. Midge would be inconsolable for a month, then there would be someone else.

A few hung on to Midge, at least until they had no further need. Those affairs mutated into long, confessional, hand-holding sessions. This aspect of Midge's life appalled Georgiana. When she – sadly many years ago – last invited Midge to stay over, she'd said, 'Cheer me up tonight, darling. But let me throw you out before you can herd me into your collection of lame ducks.'

Midge's ducks had also been gathered from her professional life. As a teacher, she had always had problems over classroom discipline, yet she had opened new ways of seeing to numerous boy children till then sunk in despair and rage. She had played with them, loved them, smacked them (while it was still legal), been herself outraged by the things that outraged them, and poured them into a boy-scout mould similar to her own.

Several of these former pupils she still saw from time to

time at Kwiksave or the No 16 bus stop. They, still wearing a Number Two up the side but now successful motor mechanics or refrigeration engineers, introduced their own children to Miss Winters. Though the little ones were puzzled by her old-fashioned inquiries into their health and ambitions and often hid behind the trunks of their father's grey flannels, on parting, they usually responded to Midge's finger curling and uncurling farewells.

Midge had never aspired to beauty, but she did think of herself as personable. Time had been kind to her, until she reached 50. Overnight, a mask loose and grainy as the skin on her morning porridge attached itself to the gamin face that had been her principal signifier of selfhood since the age of 12. Her bouncy boy's walk stiffened into parade-ground snappiness. Alcohol affected her in new ways. She had always drunk rather a lot, rather quickly, and seen wine as something that enhanced her natural exuberance. Now it loosened before it heightened and hid from her awareness of how much she had taken.

Fiona was distressed by her menopause, but Midge had hardly noticed her own. Other losses had diminished her life. Colonel Winters, so spruce that he'd seemed immortal, dropped his *Daily Telegraph* tactfully over his face as he sat in his chair at his club one day, and died. Midge had adored her father, but avoided intimacy with Mama, who tended to find fault. But Mrs Winters became an invalid when she became a widow, and Midge was all the support there was. Midge's life became hard.

One particularly hard day, when Midge was thanking her lucky stars that she still had school as an escape, the headmistress called in the staff and asked three noble souls to volunteer for redundancy. Without any willed act on her part, Midge's hand rose. Within a week the narrow Victorian house was the whole of the real world, and tending Mama the whole of her function.

Now that too was gone. To her surprise, Midge missed her mother painfully. It came to her that it was possible to live

without love, but not possible to live without duty. But Midge
was a survivor, an opportunist, a gambler. And today something – good or bad but something – was going to happen
apropos of this Lucy.

Within fifteen minutes, Raffles had been fed and watered,
Midge's body washed in the essential places and dressed in a
suit of Paddington Bear tweed, and they were both packed
into Midge's ailing Mini.

Was it the state of her head or of the planet that all the
lights on the zigzag route across north London from Kilburn
to Dalston were against her; that the Mini's pouncing clutch
was in particularly ferocious mood, so that every other take-
off threw Raffles off the passenger seat? Midge's anxieties
twisted and turned. Now her great worry was not over last
night's crime (whatever it was) but that Lucy may not have
been warned that the 'motor' amounted only to these four
pram-wheels and a rattling exhaust. Unfortunately, when
Midge was in her cups, the Mini took on the appurtenances of
the lovely old Jag she had once co-owned with her father.

For all the preoccupation with shame, at moments during
the journey, memory emerged from its stupor and Lucy
acquired an identity: formidably questioning eyes, new-moon
brows, shapeless clothes, anonymous haircut, the acquired
Inner London accent. Midge didn't need Georgiana to point
out that this young woman's presence was devoid of style;
Midge understood that it was designed, like a nun's habit, to
extirpate it. Yet, unlike Georgiana, Midge did not see this as
plainness. For Midge, beauty lay not in classic lines but in
small secret things – a fieldmouse glimpsed through corn-
stalks, a child in the park, struggling to smile while a dog
made off with its lolly-ice. Or, in this case, the way Lucy
habitually bit her prominent lower lip, leaving it damp and
toothmarked, signalling a vulnerability her gaze denied.

How disgraceful of Midge to force herself on this innocent
young woman. In spasms of self-disgust, Midge banged her
fist on the steering wheel, causing the Mini to lurch as if

afflicted by hiccups, as she vowed for the umpteenth time that never again would she be deluded into believing that the power which drew her to the small and helpless was benevolence.

Yet, at other, quieter moments, different words came to Midge, so clear they could have come out of the dashboard, words spoken in a low, quiet voice: 'You aren't angry with me?' 'I was really very pleased that you wanted us to be friends.' Lucy's condemnation of whatever tasteless pass Midge had made last night was complete, yet she appealed for Midge's friendship. Lucy was not only forgiving, she had the rare gift of being humble in her forgiveness. Might it be possible that Midge might one day become worthy of this friendship? The woozy sweetness of hangover, like dreamy music, gently wafted Midge's imaginings in the direction of introducing Lucy to the theatre, kitting her out in elegant, ego-enhancing clothes, exchanging confidences in the half-dark. Friendship; perhaps more?

Although self-disgust kept repeating on Midge like a bad meal, by the time she reached Lucy's housing association flat, Midge was not only relatively sober; she was letting her feelings slide towards that familiar delicious passivity which would make her able, at the first encouragement from the other, to fall, for the thousandth time, in love.

But Midge had not allowed for the sheer clumsiness of the mechanisms of reaching out to another human being. Midge, though forward, was shy, and Lucy, though determined, was reserved and decidedly gauche. Midge did not at first recognise the figure, backpack at her feet, waiting on the doorstep with the patience of a refugee. For her part, Lucy stood by and watched Midge park the Mini between two cars on blocks – a Punch and Judy scrap between Midge and the clutch, which filled the narrow air of the street with clonks, grunts, engine roar and black smoke – and then climbed into the car. Midge began the shoulder-wrenching process of getting the car out again.

'You've brought a dog', was Lucy's first comment, made as she turned her face away from Raffles's wet greetings. 'They aren't allowed in restaurants.'

'She'll stay in the Mini while we eat. But I thought we might work up an appetite with a stroll along the river first.'

'Well, okay,' Lucy glanced up at the louring skies, 'but you will keep it on the lead? Dogs know when people are afraid of them.'

Midge pointed the car towards Tower Bridge and left the choice of route to autopilot. Lucy's head rocked backward and forward as the car leapt into gear. Georgiana was refusing to travel in the Mini these days – 'Offer me lifts after you've taken out insurance against whiplash, dear heart.'

It was a grey day with a chilly breeze that flecked the Thames with scum and shook the straggling buddleias and Michaelmas daisies down to their moorings in brick and tar. Lucy's face disappeared into the hood of her duffel coat. Raffles led them away from the marina, along the narrow road towards Wapping. On their right, a barge laden with scrap iron laboured upstream. They paused to watch it through the high fencing. Midge struggled unsuccessfully to think of something to say about it. On the landward side, cranes hung idle over a muddy crater. This fascinated Raffles, but for Midge it was heavy going. She remarked that she'd always wanted to swim in the Thames, then corrected herself on remembering that the water was polluted. Lucy, preoccupied, made no attempt at conversation. Midge allowed her thoughts to wander: at how easy it was to communicate with young men (via chat about football, model railways, or the various routes from London to Slough), while young women were so very complicated and difficult to reach.

Then, without preliminaries, Lucy stopped short and said, in her nervy prepared-statement voice: 'I ought to tell you I had an ulterior motive in dragging you out today. I want to ask you to help me.'

'My dear?' prompted Midge, with quickening interest.

'I'm not sure it's right to do this, because I'll be talking about your friends, but I haven't anyone else.'

The nerve-ends in Midge's brain stood up like hairs on her neck. 'You can trust my discretion.'

Lucy nodded. 'Sometimes I think,' she said vaguely, 'that I ought just to walk away. People say you can only get hurt by mixing with rich bitches. But I have only one life, and this may be my one chance.'

Years of listening to problems had taught Midge that the best advice is conveyed by sympathetic silence, but she was also human enough to want to know what was going on. 'Mixing with whom?' When Lucy didn't respond, she added: 'You mean Georgiana's crowd?'

Lucy gave a faint nod.

This was making Lucy *desperate*? Midge frowned. 'Rich? They're church mice.' This wasn't true. Accuracy was important to a teacher. 'Well, Toby has family money. And Sophie and Sarah are career girls. And Fiona and Lorraine have a lovely home. But "rich bi—"?' In Midge's language, 'bitch' was a very rude word indeed.

Lucy released her lip, which curled in a bitter little smile. 'It's them: Fiona and Lorraine.'

Fiona and Lorraine were doing something to hurt Lucy? They seemed so fond of her. Midge would trust Fiona with her life, of course; they'd had an affair some twenty years back which, though sadly, curtailed by a Persian prince, had left Midge feeling honoured. But she hadn't known Lorraine above ten years, and only briefly in the intimate way, since Lorraine had abandoned her at first sight of Fiona. Older, sophisticated women could be dangerous. Though what danger Fiona and Lorraine could represent, she found hard to envisage. Their values were a shade materialistic, but Fiona was a sincere artist. Lorraine was a great egoist, but had a generous heart. Something maternal and possessive didn't fit with Midge's idea of either woman though she knew herself to be perfectly capable of it. The most likely answer was that the couple had turned Lucy's head, giving her the taste for pleasures that enlarged her imagination but were beyond her pocket and diminished her appreciation of her own community.

This, in fact, was exactly what Midge was herself endeavouring to do. Having bundled Raffles (muddy paws and all) into the Mini, she guided Lucy to the smallest and most expensive restaurant, La Renarde Rusée. Any resolution of the mystery of Lucy's desperation would have to wait.

Midge had failed to book a table, so slipped the maître d' a large and premature tip and pointed to an elegantly laid table overlooking the marina. He led them to it with all the dignity of one who had descended to a low-class bribe. To Midge's satisfaction, he drew up a chair for Lucy, flicked the seat, and squeezed her in, tight to the table. He unfolded her napkin and laid it lightly at her breast, quite *comme il faut*. He then watched Midge seat herself and, with an ironic 'M'sieur', handed her the wine list.

Midge drew out her spectacles and glanced without interest at the appellation mineral waters. She paused at the house red but, catching again the maître d's ironic glance, pointed to a monstrously overpriced Château Somethingorother. When he withdrew, Midge realised that she was trembling. But the wine arrived promptly, Midge nodded approval on tasting and, after the first big slug, her hangover evaporated, and the planet, and Lucy's pain, had manageable dimensions. As the waiter turned away, she reached forward to cover Lucy's limp hand with her own. 'Cheer up, my dear,' she said with a grin, 'food is half the answer to any problem.'

Lucy stared at Midge's veined and brown-spotted hand.

'At your age, one should be free to make friends, a diversity of friends, including even rich, ah, bitches. It's a great big exciting world. Experiment.'

Lucy's hand moved slightly in Midge's.

Heart leaping, Midge tightened her grasp. 'Georgiana's crowd must seem ancient to you, but we're a decent lot — more or less. Fiona and Lorraine, now, ah yes, Fiona and Lorraine?'

'That sleazy waiter,' whispered Lucy, 'he called you "Monsieur".'

'Did he indeed?' Midge raised a disingenuous eyebrow.

'You know he did.'

'It's all part of the game.' Midge spoke lightly, but she withdrew her hand. Midge had enjoyed the gentleman treatment. For a few moments she had not exactly forgotten but been able to lay aside the knowledge that she was a middle-aged unemployed schoolmistress, without either the presence or the purse to suit the style of the restaurant. Where she had seen in the maître d's deference the insouciant conspiracy of two frauds, now she saw only mockery.

Well, Raffles, done it again! Fallen for it. Lucy had not come out with Midge to weave her indignation over a pass into something that might encourage another. Their assignation had, in fact, nothing to do with Midge's person. Midge refilled her glass and emptied it. Though there was disappointment in such knowledge, it was in its way comforting. This was familiar territory. Sympathy over the behaviour of third parties was what everybody wanted from Midge.

But she knew that whatever she had said or done to compromise herself last night had now been compounded by a waiter she would loathe throughout the meal but lack the courage to deny another ludicrously overlarge tip. So, what did any of it matter? Midge was so loose-headed with hangover that she had already forgotten where she had parked the Mini. There was no magic in the young woman opposite her; there was no magic in anything. Midge reached again for the bottle, and added another drop to Lucy's almost full glass.

Menus were thrust under their noses. Even the lightest starters were well over a fiver. Midge exhaled hard and recommended the oysters.

'Eat them – alive?'

Midge stopped herself short. She couldn't bring herself to eat them either. 'Well, in that case; now let's see . . .'

The arrival of the first plates put a touch of colour into Lucy's cheeks, and turned conversation towards general channels.

Lucy ate well; she ate everything on the menu that didn't contain creatures (alive or dead) or chemicals beginning with E. Midge noted this with pleasure until it crossed her mind that this child might be starving. 'Do you have a job, my dear?' she asked gently.

'I work at a small business advisory centre, nothing much.'

'Oh, you help people set up as potters, wood-carvers?'

'*I* don't. I did the mailings, leaflets on tax, that sort of thing. But small businesses are all going bankrupt these days, so they're closing the place and we don't do anything except have meetings about our redundancy terms.'

Redundancy was a subject close to Midge's own heart. 'I went through all that a year ago,' she said. 'It's a terrible blow.'

'That's what the union says. But I just want to take the money and run. Though I don't know where to.'

Midge's jaws paused in mid-bite.

Lucy's gaze was fixed on the choppy water of the marina. 'I don't belong anywhere,' she said quietly. 'Nobody needs me or wants me. There's nothing I can do that will ever make any difference to anything.'

Without a sound, Midge laid down her fork.

'I don't know why. It's been this way all my life. I don't know why I was born.'

'None of us knows that, my dear.'

'But they don't feel so – so useless. Other women my age are having fun. I've done that. But, next morning, what's it worth?'

'Everything has worth,' Midge looked at her plate, 'if you have someone to love.'

'But I DO,' cried Lucy, suddenly animated. 'That's the problem. I do. I have a lover who treats me as trash. And that makes me and everything in my life into trash.'

'I'm so sorry.' Midge slowly raised her eyes. Lucy's brilliant blush was flooding her entire head and neck; her eyes had the staring brightness of a creature in shock. The helpless child of Midge's imagination had become something wild and fierce. 'I don't know how I can help you. But I'll do anything I can.'

In the silence that followed, Midge didn't even think to drink her wine.

Eventually, Lucy spoke: 'Could you get Lorraine to be honest, about me?'

Midge's thoughts had been running along quite different lines. She looked up and the room spun. Lorraine who? Of course, Fiona's Lorraine, who had briefly been Midge's. 'In what way is Lorraine dishonest about you?'

'You didn't pick up on it? Lorraine and I are in a relation-ship.'

Midge lacked Georgiana's appreciation of the more com-plex human connections. 'How can that be? She's with Fiona; they've been together – it must be six or seven years.'

'Ten. I shouldn't have asked. This is a stupid idea. Stupid.'

'No, no, please.' Midge's hand moved as if to reach out to Lucy but instead was raised in gentle admonishment. 'I didn't mean to interrupt. It's just that – all of us in Georgiana's crowd adore Fiona, though I haven't known Lorraine long enough to – well, to say truth, I did rather think the two of them were making rather a good job of –'

'Please, just leave it,' muttered Lucy.

' – which goes to show how fuddy duddy . . .' Midge ground to a halt. Midge was grieved, but also shocked. Lucy was not shocked at all. Midge found herself doubly shocked in consequence. Lucy, a generation younger than Midge, was at least a generation more worldly wise. In silence, Midge watched Lucy's big nocturnal-animal eyes narrow into slits of anger and pain.

'I got it wrong,' said Lucy. 'Please forget the whole thing.'

'Oh no, no.' This time Midge's hand did reach over to Lucy's. I'm a bit slow and terribly old fashioned, but I do want to help. Now, let's see. You're having an affair –'

' – a relationship –'

' – a relationship with Lorraine and you want her to be honest about it. How, exactly? Do you want her to leave Fiona?'

'No-way, no!' Now Lucy was shocked. 'She must *tell* Fiona,

so that Fiona can accept the relationship, and I can have a place in Lorraine's life. I wouldn't ask you to do anything unethical.'

Though she still didn't grasp the logic of the situation, Midge was relieved that ethics had a part in it. She also didn't want to look the fool by asking too many simple questions. So she tried to keep them short and to the point. 'If you have a place, what place will Fiona have?'

'We'll both be having a relationship with Lorraine.'

'Where will she sleep? Lorraine, I mean.'

Lucy looked at Midge blankly. 'Wherever she liked.'

'So some nights she'll sleep with Fiona and some nights with you?'

'You mean do sex?'

'I suppose that's what I had in mind.'

'She can do sex with whoever she likes whenever she likes. But I'd expect her to be honest about it and tell me; and I'm sure Fiona would want that too.'

Midge was appalled. But she was also impressed. It was good to be honest. Wasn't it better than playing the game she had herself played with various members of Georgiana's circle over the years?

Take her liaison with Sophie. This had had its beginnings in Sarah's flirtation with Steven-John, who had not yet entered the less aesthetic later stages of his sex-change. It had ripened through Midge's chivalrous attentions to the neglected Sophie. The leather-scented Jaguar had encouraged developments that were, as Midge recalled, rather sloppy couplings, Sophie being a particularly wet sort of woman. After a week, certain similarities in the grunting reminded Midge of her earlier brief thing with Sarah, and she had to acknowledge that Sarah had excited her rather more than Sophie. After a few more weeks, she mislaid Sophie's work telephone number and was only a touch disappointed to discover that Sophie had done the same with hers. The affairs became, as Georgiana might have said, things that had never happened. They became, in fact, nothing – gone, lost, without value, like so many of the connections of Midge's life. Midge looked up at Lucy, and saw a formidable integrity.

Lucy seemed to sense the change in Midge. 'See what an opportunity this is, Midge, for them and for me. They'll be able to *trust* each other. They won't have to fantasise about people they daren't touch, they won't have to *hide*; they won't have to feel *bad* about themselves. They'll be able to accept that human beings aren't designed to do sex just with one person.'

'Well.' Midge scratched her head. To say truth, there did seem to be something a little too emphatic and stagey about Fiona's and more especially Lorraine's show of the perfect marriage. 'You do have a point.'

'I want to respect Fiona; how can I when I'm lying to her? And I want her to respect me; how can she, if she's looking at a liar?'

Midge looked up boldly. 'I'll do it,' she said, 'I'll go to Gospel Oak this evening, and confront Lorraine. I'll say her secret is out, I'll tell her . . .' Midge trailed off: Midge had never in her life found the nerve to challenge any person on this planet, least of all a roarer like Lorraine.

'No, don't,' said Lucy, suddenly pale. 'Lorraine would just ditch me.'

'All right.' Midge let out a small sigh of relief. 'Perhaps I should talk to Fiona. She thought. 'No, I couldn't do that.'

'No,' said Lucy.

Midge loosened her collar and puffed out her cheeks. 'All right then. Action. I'll go to the top. I'll talk to Georgiana.'

Lucy thought for a moment. 'Yes, that's good. People respect Georgiana.'

Though pleased to have struck the right note, Midge felt obscurely insulted, and her uncertainty returned. 'She'll take it up with Fiona, you know; they're very close.'

Lucy nodded. 'I know. I saw that last night.'

'But would it be better,' said Midge carefully, 'if you told Fiona yourself?'

Lucy sat back in her seat. 'I thought of that,' she said

quietly. 'And once told Lorraine I was going to do it. But I didn't. If I did, she wouldn't hear what I was saying for her anger against both Lorraine and me. But I'm sure Georgiana understands these things, and I think Fiona will listen to her.'

Midge nodded. How very clever of Lucy, on so brief an acquaintance, to have picked up so many nuances. She did not need to ask why Lucy did not at least cut out one step by herself approaching Georgiana. Because even though this was all so honourable and above board, there was something just out of view which wasn't. It was scarcely possible to imagine Lucy making an approach to Georgiana; but if she did, it would be all too easy to imagine the response. Georgiana might well understand these things, but Midge sensed that she would – with a look if not actual words – reply: 'You little rat!'

'I'll put it to her very tactfully,' said Midge. 'You'll have to brief me.'

Midge had quite forgotten her anger at the maître d' when she paid the bill. Something else was nibbling at her hungover brain, some sense that something wasn't quite right about this very righteous arrangement.

3

On that same Sunday, around the time Midge was roused by
the telephone, at a house some two miles to the east, another
dog was whimpering. This house was not a tall sooted-brick
edifice with its front shut tight against the street. It was a
whitewashed 1920s semi in fashionable Gospel Oak with big
airy windows that seemed designed to waft the strains of
piano music over its cottage garden, and out to the village
street lined with plane trees of the same age as the house.
And the dog was not a ratty little terrier; he was a cartilagi-
nous brown hound with a hide like a slippery wetsuit. He
was usually defined as something of a boxer, and answered
to Bonzo, Bobo, Bonze and (with especial eagerness)
Bonsko-witztableski.

Bonzo, however, was whimpering, with his teeth clamped
tight to let as little as possible of the sound past his lips. A light
whistle escaped, seemingly through his ears, though they lay
flat. Bonzo's mistresses were tussling in bed, and Bonzo knew
enough about human amours to make distinctions.

'Oh leave it,' snapped Fiona, throwing herself onto her
other side.

Lorraine's hand reached up to cup Fiona's shoulder, graceful as ever although her arm was clenched tight as rigor mortis against her ribs. 'Best way to ease a hangover.'

Fiona sighed. 'Georgiana's wine isn't as good as it used to be. The only thing that could ease me would be a couple of aspirins, so long as they aren't the fizzy sort that make all that noise.'

'If I bring you a quiet aspirin, will you give me a fizzing kiss?'

'God's sake, Lorraine.' Fiona's long legs threshed the bed. 'How can I get it through to you that I am not in the mood?'

The few seconds' silence that followed showed that this had now got through. 'Yeah, yeah,' Lorraine said in a different, flat, tone. 'Receiving loud and clear.' She sat up sharply, pulling the covers around her and leaving Fiona with the protection only of her aged pyjamas. 'When are you ever in the mood, as you with such sparkling originality call it?'

Fiona curled up tight and pulled the pillow over her head. 'Would I be right in thinking that it could be a month, maybe two?'

'Lorraine: I am going through the menopause. I regret that this should coincide with a time when you feel particularly sexy. But I do not. I feel lumpish and ugly. I get giddy. My gums itch. My womb feels as if it's pumped with bitumen. No, I don't feel sexy. I don't even feel sexless. I feel positively anti-sexy.'

'But what about me?' said Lorraine plaintively. 'I'm not going through the menopause. At least not yet. Are you expecting me to go through it twice?'

'You, Lorraine,' said Fiona in a small warning voice, 'are not listening. You're not making up to me. You're pestering me. You want a reaction? What you'll get, if you don't give me some space in this bed – all you'll get is – oh God, I don't even have the energy to want to thump you.'

'Oh great, the great British Sunday morning ritual! At this precise moment, in every other house south of Watford, one half of a couple is trooping downstairs to mix an aspirin for the other half.'

Fiona grunted.

'Marriage! A sacrament ordained to ensure that dogs get fed.'

Bonzo edged up to the bed and gingerly placed a paw on Lorraine's bottom.

'Well, you can't beat City Hall.' With a sigh, Lorraine pushed the dog aside, rolled off the bed, picked Fiona's silk dressing gown from off the floor, flung it over her shoulders, and padded heavily downstairs.

Fiona recaptured the duvet, curled herself into a ball, and zonked back to sleep.

Lorraine paced between kitchen and hall like a caged animal: red and black quarry tiles, stripped floorboards scattered with rugs. Her steps took her from the sink (where she ran the taps over the stacked dishes then turned them off again) to the telephone. This squatted, white, immobile and very silent, on its little antique oak table, leather-cased notepad beside it and National Gallery calendar hanging above. At each passing, Lorraine put her hand on the receiver, then removed it. Lorraine was not angry with Fiona, nor even with herself for causing that little spat: she had already forgotten about it. Through her head now ran another desire – to press the magical numbers. But this was not possible. Lorraine had failed to unplug the extension in the bedroom.

Bonzo scratched at the kitchen door, momentarily recalling her, and she let him out. Then she gave his bowl the merest rinse and heaped it up with whatever leftovers in the fridge hadn't yet grown whiskers. All the while, the telephone remained gloomily silent. The boiler purred, then itself fell into silence.

A thought came to Lorraine. If she timed things carefully; if she dialled just as the boiler kicked back into flame, then the clicks of the call would be masked. Again she prowled. Lorraine picked up the receiver, but the boiler roared before she'd pressed the first number. 'Damn!'

But that small action had roused her. A flame, hot as the jets of the boiler, burnt in her crotch. Now she was desperate to phone. She prowled. If she turned down the thermostat, which could be reached from the phone, and turned it up just before she pressed the last number, if she, if she . . .

Bonzo scraped louder, reminding her that between him and the dog dish lay a closed door. She let him back in and wiped his feet. Like a ghost, the telephone hovered at the edge of her vision. She watched Bonzo slurp up the mash of broccoli, squashed potatoes and chicken curry. Bonzo could ingest the remains of a three-part meal in as many seconds. She could race him, taking up a cup of tea, checking that Fiona was asleep. But that would risk waking the sleeper, and ruining everything.

Ruin everything? Ruin what? This was Lorraine's house. Lorraine's telephone. She could phone anyone she liked. Of course she could. She could do it. She did. With great care, she pressed nine of the eleven numbers and then turned up the thermostat. As the heating system exploded into action, she dialled the last. The response came to her, clear and loud – the engaged signal. She dropped the receiver with a clang. 'Bloody hell!'

Lorraine glowered at Monet's water-lilies, smirking at her from the calendar. Bloody flowers enamelled by slow-speed Ektachrome, bloody gardens, houses, possessions, dogs, monogamy, chains. Then she marched upstairs with the now overbrewed tea and two well-dissolved aspirins. She laid the tray down with care and leaned over to kiss the top of Fiona's head, but this time her pulse quickened only at the sign that her partner was deeply asleep. If she wasn't asleep, she was pretending, and deception deserved to be met in kind. Quiet as a thief, Lorraine unplugged the telephone extension beside the bed.

Downstairs once again, she didn't try the phone immediately. She paced the hall and living room, viewing with increasing discontent the dust on the blinds, the doggy cushions and half-read books, the squashed and misshapen Tully's

sofa. She flicked through the mountain of dreary LPs —
Bronski Beat, Joan Armatrading, Vangelis, Janis Joplin,
Manhattan Transfer. She paused at the mirror over the fireplace, fingered her hair into spikes and prodded the bags
under her eyes. She looked about 90. No wonder, when Fiona
was working so hard to make her an old woman. But — she
climbed on the footstool for a fuller view and turned from
side to side — while nobody could call her beautiful and some
had called her funny-looking, she had her points — plus and
minus — didn't she?

'How do you rate, Face?' She stuck out her tongue at it,
and it did the same to her. No help there. She took it item by
item. The eyes were tawny, even, to a kindly view, intelligent-
looking, apart from the bags, but the nose was a botch job,
which she likened to a Jerusalem artichoke. The skin was a
strong clear olive (though sallow now, after the party), and
there was plenty of thick, strong, dark, wavy hair, lots of it —
far too much of it. The eyebrows had authority, but they met
in the middle and only tweezers stopped them from crawling
down the nose. This face was quite well shaped, with broad
cheekbones and a chin that wasn't flabby, but you couldn't
actually see much of the outline with all that hair. And, what
else did this creature have to commend it? There were ears,
one on each side of the head. Oh damn! Lorraine began again.
Her body was strong and athletic — she had a lighter step
than Fiona — but her arms and shoulders were heavy, and
wasn't that a spare tyre forming in the place that used to be
her waist? She passed over the breasts. She could have liked
them if they'd been half their size, a tenth of their weight,
and hadn't developed a tendency to collect cheesy sweat
underneath. But, for all that, she was sexy; at least to other
people. Fiona had said she was sexy. She had the style — didn't
she? — of a Maltese pirate. Lorraine screwed up her face and
gave its reflection a pirate's growl with twisted mouth.
Lorraine did not admire the flesh in which she was encased.

But she believed she had something. There was evidence:
beautiful people had lusted after Fiona, but Lorraine had got

her. Because Lorraine was a sport; she was a doer; she could give herself and her companions a good time. She wasn't particularly clever (and this grieved her more than the plainness of her face), but she could make things happen. Lorraine was a photographer, and usually considered herself a good one. She seldom took a bad picture though, when she saw other photographers' work, she knew she'd never taken a brilliant one. Perhaps, Lorraine thought, if she had anything special at all, it was energy. She had a lust for life; wasn't that beauty of a kind, and equal – or somewhere near — to being a lovely object of contemplation?

Lorraine turned away from the mirror. What she had, she would keep: she was not going to crawl into the bunker of old age – not now, not ever. A beautiful woman could languish, and still be beautiful. But if Lorraine, who did not have beauty, allowed her energy to be swamped by Fiona's depression, she would be nothing. Lorraine, at 45, saw herself as passionate and young. She was ready to fight to be that way for ever. Her heart whammed at her chest as a phone rang, then sank as she realised that the sound came through the party wall. Well, at least the neighbours had friends who bothered to phone them. This was Death! Say No to it!

She said No. Marching firmly, Lorraine seized the telephone and pressed. This time, the ringing tone. She almost dropped the receiver. Two rings, and then, in the magical voice, came an unusually brisk 'Hello.'

'Lucy, a quick call before —' Lorraine's sense of herself withered as she heard her voice echo with the hollowness of someone who'd been in a dungeon for years.

Lucy seemed taken aback. 'Good god; it's Lorraine. Well, this is an honour. Fiona given you permission to phone?'

Lorraine was rather afraid of the sharp side of Lucy. 'I tried earlier, but you were engaged,' she muttered.

'Perhaps I was. I've been trying to get hold of Margaret Winters.'

'You mean Midge?'

'Yeah. She's stood me up on lunch.'

Lorraine felt suddenly chill. She had, indeed, taken Lucy to meet Georgiana's crowd, but hadn't planned on Lucy forming independent and possibly dangerous connections. 'She probably fell in a hole on her way home last night,' she said coldly.

'Hey, come on,' said Lucy, 'Midge is a dear. I was hugely flattered when she tried to get it off with me last night.'

'She what?' Lorraine was now utterly unconcerned about how far her voice carried up the stairs. 'She bloody WHAT?'

Lucy's reply was soothing, but Lorraine's feelings had moved beyond the voice that gave her goosepimples. She wanted to smash somebody's teeth in. Midge had been monopolising Lucy – in Lorraine's reckoning driving Lucy up the wall – half the evening, while Lorraine was struggling to square things with everybody, to make sure that Lucy would be favourably received by her (well Fiona's) friends. Seems Lucy had done more than enough work on her own account.

'I really liked her,' continued Lucy. 'She tried to make me feel at home. She was the only one who did.'

Lorraine, now acutely uncomfortable, was unable to reply.

'They've got under my skin, though. I can't stop thinking about them. They're weird. They don't seem to do anything except relate to each other. They go round and round, uttering little witticisms, having little "affaires", acting like they're the centre of the world.'

'I know exactly what you mean, but —'

'— They aren't glamorous and powerful like I'd imagined. That Toby said he almost fainted when Outrage marched into the Foreign Office. And, under those ancient rugs, there are holes in Georgiana's carpets. They're cold, used-up snobs, and they made me feel like the housemaid. Yet, somehow, I'm still impressed. Just don't know why.'

Lorraine took a deep breath. 'Lucy, I rang because I'm missing you horribly. I wish I could take you to lunch myself. but —'

'But you can't, I know. Well, that's the way it is.'

It came to Lorraine that she could just, gently, without fuss, without explanations, put the phone down. Lucy was bullying her, and so was the wretched dog, now at her feet making that awful guilt-inducing whistling noise. She could put the phone down. Then she could smash all those disgusting LPs, she could crash out to the van and drive to Dungeness or Land's End or Marseilles sous Hell or wherever she bloody well liked. But Lorraine wouldn't, couldn't, do anything of the sort.

'I so want,' Lucy said, ending the pause, 'your friends to like me. I so want to be accepted. But how can I be, when I'm a dirty little secret?'

The dreadfulness of everything seized Lorraine. The heat in her crotch evaporated, leaving a sizzling pain. 'You're not a dirty anything. You're my lifeline.'

'Then admit it. There's only one world, and it's got Fiona, and me, in it. Tell Fiona. Tell Georgiana. Tell that Queen Toby. There's nothing to be ashamed of.' Lucy paused. 'I've got to tell you,' she said in a low voice, 'that I'm going to tell Midge.'

'Please, no; not yet.' Did Lorraine imagine it, or were there moving sounds from upstairs, as of someone crawling out of bed to listen at the stairwell? 'Give me a few days. I can't tell Fiona right now; I can't be so cruel.' Her voice fell even lower. 'Fiona's ill.'

'It's not illness, it's nature; it's the Change, new beginnings. Fiona is just as trapped as you are. Give her freedom; she needs a lifeline just as much as you do.'

There were moving sounds. It was real. Fiona's voice sounded crossly from upstairs: 'Lorraine: those aspirins were flat. And I thought I heard the phone.'

'I've got to go,' muttered Lorraine, and without waiting for the reply, she replaced the receiver as quietly as her shaking hand would allow.

Lorraine laboured up the stairs. The magic in the number had evaporated, and left her with a horrible feeling of shame.

What was it that was happening to her, to Fiona, to Les Biches?

They had been together for a decade. Not any ordinary decade. When they got together was the beginning of the world, and when they parted would be the end. This was real.

So what, then, was Lucy? Lucy was also real. So was the amazing transformation of herself that Lucy had made in her – almost three weeks before.

On that day, she had seen and stared at a pretty young woman. This had happened before. But this time, the young woman looked back at her, with big round tawny eyes saying 'try me'. With the suddenness of a blow on the head, Lorraine knew what she was looking for, and a madness swept her, gathering force like fire through a dry forest. She hadn't planned to have an affair, but with the first kiss she was attacking Lucy's clothes. It was Lucy who'd said they'd better find somewhere private if Lorraine was *that* fast, and Lucy who now wanted this private act made public.

Lorraine couldn't do it. She crumpled under Lucy's logic, and promised to tell, but when she faced Fiona, the words were impossible to utter. Yet, she assured herself, Fiona gained from the affair. The sweetness of Lucy softened Lorraine, made her love Fiona better, helped her endure Fiona's moods with saintly patience. Lorraine was not – she was sure she was not – in love with Lucy. She couldn't be: she was in love with Fiona, that was the central fact of her life. If she stopped seeing Lucy, within a few weeks, this fire would die, and Lucy's power would fade away. But so would her own youth, her energy, her lust for life. The game she was playing was a dangerous one: Lorraine knew that. Two prominent British politicians had ruined themselves this year through affairs which ran out of control. But she would keep hers under control; she would do her best not to harm Lucy; if it became the right thing to do she would tell Fiona, and she would keep the affair short. These things were solemn promises. Entering the bedroom on quiet feet, she crept up behind Fiona and kissed the back of her neck. 'Sorry I've been such a brute. Next time I'll dissolve the aspirins in a glass of ice-cold chablis.'

Fiona's hand reached up and limply stroked Lorraine's ear. 'You could make it a bucket.'

Lorraine laughed. She felt, just then, like Judas might have felt.

4

Although Midge's life was confused and Lorraine's heading towards the chaotic, most members of Georgiana's crowd lived, or tried to live, by order, method and regular habits. One regular ritual, held each Tuesday morning, involved Ulric, Steven-John, and in due course Toby's Irish wolfhound, Jezebel. This occasion was important for both men. Jezebel appeared to take it as a matter of course, which was perhaps to be expected since, in her pampered old age, life seemed to be all ritual.

On Mondays, Wednesdays and so on, Ulric coached promising singers at his flat. On Tuesdays he went further. As other mature singers passionate about technique had done before him, he took on the opinionated, truculent, philistine world. In the afternoon of that formidable day, he led the senior singing class at the Guildhall School of Music. Ulric would fight to the death for voice delivery that came out of the bowels, not the chest. He had declared war on the Pavarotti bellow, then sweeping the student body like a virus. His Tuesday afternoons were, in consequence, demanding. The mornings he devoted to a ceremony which steadied his own bowels: tea with Steven-John and then a stroll through Regent's Park, the company augmented by Jezebel.

Ulric had need of such steadying. Increasingly of late, the vacuum of his solitary hours had been filling itself with anxiety that distracted him not only from the beefy bellow but even the preceding student virus, the Peter Pears rhinitic whine. Ulric worried about his growing tendency to hypochondria, and sometimes even that he might in some real way be ill. He was troubled by a succession of tedious complaints that took an immense time to fade away. Steven-John's homely company did him good. Steven-John listened; he sympathised; and then gave freely from a stock of wholesome advice about early nights and the benefits of massage.

The gay community was much preoccupied with health, for obvious reasons, but these were not Ulric's. Ulric didn't know what the gay world was thinking, because he wasn't in it. He considered himself far too private a person – private and sensitive. He had met that society of course. And had found the encounters bruising and repellent. Toby's casual promiscuity appalled him. So did the assumption of so many men encountered at the fringes of public places that Ulric was femmy, and so anybody's.

He wasn't. He was nobody's. But his body let him down. Ulric was tall and high-waisted with narrow hips, so that his thighs semicircled each other no matter how stiffly he walked. His long fingers, in their nervous endeavour at distancing gestures, suggested the actions of a spider, or a drag queen. He had so curbed the agitation of his features that he had the icy countenance of a duchess. When he wore his hair long, it was floppy and Rupert Brookeish; when he had it cut short, it gave him the peeled, red-eyed look of a clone. His only defence was his frigid manner. This did not fool men on the prowl, nor did it deceive his own hungry nature. Yet he remained nobody's, because within seconds of a first flirtatious glance, Ulric could see only the beast beneath. Then his longing was no longer for the rough camaraderie of the changing rooms but to be allowed to join an order of contemplative nuns.

Ulric believed, none the less, that the poverty of his sensual life brightened the small coinage of his friendships and enhanced his real wealth, his work. Ulric loved music, and he loved the power that he had to deliver it. He loved the authority, severity and order of music, the total submission it demanded of him and, when it came, the release which was so deep that he recognised not sound, but the energy of the universe flowing through him in a torrent that left him exhilarated, exhausted and utterly cleansed. The strongest expressions of passion in Ulric's life had come not from Peter's embrace, but from standing in a row of four beside the conductor with the chorus at his back, at that moment when, at the conductor's nod, he let it go, the great voice that, like a circus elephant, would lift soprano, tenor, mezzo and chorus on its back.

Teaching gave a humbler pleasure. As a teacher, Ulric was cold and demanding, and hardest on the students he loved – those with real art in them. These students feared (and sometimes mocked) him, but under his tutelage, they sang as they had never known they could. That was Ulric's reward.

He also had a few friends, all, apart from Steven-John, musicians, women and older than himself. His friendship with Steven-John was an oddity. But when the two men were together, something happened that brightened his view of the world. Ulric hadn't given much thought to this friendship, beyond defining it to himself as wonderfully mundane. His friendships with women were mildly camp and so more demonstrative, although he was secretly repelled by a coldness that he detected at the heart of the female psyche. In all females, that is, except his mother, with whom he had enjoyed a love that was, on both sides, unconditional. But Ulric's mother had died of cancer when he was 16, and he had never, except between the ages of 38 and 40, been free of the pain of that loss.

For those two glorious years he had been the darling of his sporty Anglican priest, Father Peter. But this, like his mother's love, was in the past. A decade back, Peter, whose only fault was an attraction towards evangelism, had responded to God's summons to set an example to his diminishing flock by equipping himself with a wife and (God willing) children. Ulric had departed from the vicarage, with his personal possessions. These he would have left behind, since they were all that redeemed the place from aesthetic puerility, but Peter had done the packing.

Since then Ulric had lived in Marylebone, alone in a handsome flat, but a bare and echoing one, since most of Ulric's lovely things were still in Peter's boxes. Ulric's heart was among the unpacked objects. He had never again loved, and he was celibate. Apart only from one single encounter, arising out of a moment of almost unendurable loneliness, and so brief and superficial that he hoped, in all conscience, he could ignore it. In respect of health risk, there could surely have been none, since his bodily fluids had leached into his own shirt-tails and his unknown partner's left no more than a slick on Ulric's thigh.

But he worried. Now, when music was falling into the hands of promoters who had come to the classics via Simon and Garfunkel, and his agent no longer telephoned him on his birthday, he worried about everything. On this Tuesday, he worried about a dull soreness in his left ear.

For Steven-John, the meetings were the highlight of the week. They mattered in part because Ulric was the only man who accepted him without question as an equal, a friend – a fellow. Unlike Ulric, Steven-John was fascinated by people and an active participant in the life of anyone who allowed him to be. Earlier this morning, for example, he had spent 1.5 per cent of his weekly income at the telephone box, trying to sort out the mess Georgiana's girls were getting themselves into. This had given him the satisfaction of doing his duty, but not the deeper satisfaction he gained from his relationship with Ulric. With Ulric, Steven-John was liberated from the chains of gender. He had endured hideous surgery to join the brotherhood, and had to dose himself daily with androgen to remain in it, yet felt a joy close to ecstasy when he found himself, with Ulric, neither male nor female – only soul meeting soul. Steven-John loved Ulric.

Ulric was not the only man with whom he had tried to bond. Toby had been first choice. The relationship had begun well; one night it had almost, if Steven-John was reading the signs aright, seemed as if might develop into something deeper. That night Toby, coming home late from an embassy reception, had reached out and stroked first the dog and then Steven-John's hair, curly as sun-dried tobacco. But after several months of effort, Steven-John realised that he was making no progress in getting closer to Toby's inner life. Toby never had time to visit Steven-John at home. Toby never inquired about the health of Steven-John's blackbirds. Toby didn't read the books Steven-John regarded as seminal. Toby was always exactly the same: friendly, breezy, open; but emotionally at precisely the distance he had been at the start. Eventually, Steven-John had come to accept that Toby had found his curls tough as couch grass; that Toby couldn't endure emotional bonds; and that, at 42, Steven-John was just too old to delight Toby.

A relationship had developed, but in another direction. Steven-John had, by degrees, become Toby's servant. Now, he did for Jezebel at £3.00 an hour, lunch and walkies, Monday to Friday. He also made himself useful around Toby's flat. He didn't do any cleaning, of course. He acknowledged the limitation of his skills in that area; it would, anyway, have taken a far braver man than he to invade the territory of Toby's char. Instead, though Toby repeatedly told him not to bother, he took in the mail, tidied up loose papers and dealt with phone messages. Steven-John had had to admit that, as a bosom friend, Toby was one of his failures. But, over the past year or so, Ulric had more than made up the lack.

With Ulric, there was not only love. There were other, more practical rewards. Steven-John had come down in the world. Ten years earlier, while Ulric was still Peter's princess, Steven-John had been Sheila-Jayne and Chelsey's cute little diesel dyke. Chelsey's flat had allowed him (then her) to live in the chilly elegance of Frognal, and Chelsey's occasional TV jobs had funded holidays to the sunspots of Spain. But now his castle had shrunk to a bedsitter over a Caribbean grocery shop in the Kentish Town Road. Ulric's visits stimulated him to clean up the place as best he could, and to coax the ancient gas cooker into producing Karma-strengthening biscuits of buckwheat, wild oats and sesame paste. For Ulric, he would turn on all three bars of his buzzing electric heater. It was for Ulric that he had covered his curtainless windows with cutouts in coloured film, and for Ulric that he had run his sleeping bag through the launderette's washer-dryer, taking his chance on the bag's survival against its tendencies to exude clotted fluff and stuff of a curious grey colour which arose in part from car-fumes and the emanations of Steven-John's body, but mainly from the droppings of blackbirds.

Steven-John would have loved to have an animal, for preference a dog, for total perfection, Jezebel herself. A man was incomplete without a dog. Steven-John was never able to forget his hunger for one. He slavered over Bonzo (a proper dog), and even ratty little Raffles tempted him. Pet-shop windows were torment. Worst of all was the local Wood Green Animal Shelter charity shop where, on any night but especially in the weeks after Christmas, he might pass, tethered to the door, a shivering puppy with a note tied round its neck. But benefit allowances for a single man and £30 a week from Toby were barely enough for Steven-John's own small needs. So he consoled himself with the friendship of a pair of arthritic blackbirds, who shared his food and, when they chose, his minimal heating.

The birds were one of several pleasures this room gave him: the birds, the space, and the freedom from Chelsey. Steven-John would have loved to live in a draught-free mansion block, like Ulric did, and he pined for a telephone. But he had the attic under its mansard roof, five storeys up and west facing, with enough wall-space to hang all his mantras, and a long concrete window box. In the corner of this, he had built a dolls' house for his blackbirds, and at nesting time they moved in. So even if he now had the opportunity of a holiday abroad, he could not have taken it, because the blackbirds ate their breakfast, lunch and supper from his hand and sang their thanks from the gable over his head. He had named the male Rufus and the female Aurora. When fledging time came round, he discouraged the chicks from taking over the territory of their aged parents by feeding the young only with wise words about finding one's way in the world. Rufus and Aurora were company; because he was involved with their life-cycle they were also a process. As a Buddhist (or Gaian, or adherent of a combination of various religious philosophies), Steven-John believed that process was the only aspect of truth comprehensible to a creature bound in time. Gossip is, of course, the pure expression of process.

This was a subject on which Steven-John, who had a theoretical bent, liked to discourse, but Ulric was uneasy about any discussion which began with Steven-John's birds. He was repelled by their unlidded stares and scaly claws, and the sudden panics of fluttering feathers if he imitated Steven-John and stretched out to stroke one. So this morning, Steven-John had his window well shut.

At precisely 11 a.m., Ulric rang the bell, urgently, several times, as a rough-looking youth had been hovering around Steven-John's doorway and was now, half hidden among the shop's racks of yams, papayas and cut flowers, watching him. The door opened. Steven-John, almost of a height with Ulric when he stood on the doorstep, met him with a hearty clasp at both shoulders and an unflinching eye-to-eye gaze. 'Ulric,' said Steven-John, with a surge of manly emotion.

'Steven-John,' replied Ulric in kind.

The predatory youth took the point; Ulric caught the movement as he consoled himself with a hand of bananas and melted away.

Steven-John's big, irregularly proportioned and sparsely furnished room always gave Ulric a quiet pleasure. Despite

the perpetual pounding of traffic and the inefficiency of
Steven-John's dabs at the dust, it was a centre of peace. It was
scented with old incense and Steven-John's herbal roll-ups,
and a pleasant nutty aroma escaped from the cooker. Ulric
presented, as he always did, a two-litre bottle of claret, with
his usual remark about needing to lubricate his gorge before
throwing it to the dogs of the singing class. Steven-John
uncorked the wine with the back end of the can opener
Chelsey had taken as a souvenir from a hotel in Malaga,
remarking, as usual, that such a big bottle would last him all
week.

This litany was not without meaning. Through it, the two
friends slipped effortlessly through the awkwardness of finding their ease with each other, and could begin where they had
left off at their last meeting. It opened the way for Ulric to say,
casually, 'I've got this ear thing, old man, and it doesn't seem
to be getting any better.'

'How does it take you?' asked Steven-John putting a
brimming tumbler down on the floor, beside the mattress
where Ulric was now splayed, apparently at ease, though the
angles of his limbs suggested a stick-insect impaled on a thorn
by a shrike.

'Well,' Ulric shook his head slightly. 'There's a burning sensation and, I suspect, inflammation. This morning, I had a
spell of dizziness while doing my voice exercises.'

Steven-John was a slow mover. He poured his own wine
and shuffled himself into an ancient beanbag before continu-
ing with: 'Had it long?'

'It started to bother me last week.' Ulric was aware that the
condition was older than his consciousness of it. 'I might have
mentioned it to you last Tuesday, but I was concerned, then,
about swollen glands and even more about my weepy eye.'
Ulric would not have been able to utter so womanish a term
as 'weepy eye' to his doctor. But Steven-John's commonplace
attention took the horror out of many things.

Steven-John heaved himself up on an elbow to peer at
Ulric's face. 'Your eye looks much better.'

Ulric pursed his lips in partial agreement. 'It's still crusty when I wake in the mornings.'

'Been bathing it?'

'Indeed. In salt water, as you suggested.' Steven-John had in fact recommended seawater from the Hebrides, but admitted that a mix made up from a pack of Safeways cooking salt would be acceptable.

Steven-John nodded, as if this was adequate. 'Which ear?'

'Left one.'

'Ah,' said Steven-John softly, 'negative energies. You might try soothing it with honey.' He rose to his feet, and began rooting about in the overflowing cupboard above the sink. 'I have some Scottish heather honey. They don't use insecticides up there on the moors. Try this.'

'Thank you,' said Ulric, taking the sticky jar. 'Do I use a spoon or tip it in?' He wasn't quite clear if he was supposed to apply the honey to his ear or eat it.

'You could tilt your head up sideways, and drip it in off your finger,' said Steven-John with a smile.

Ulric wrapped the bottle in his handkerchief and put it into his bag, between the sheaves of musical scores. He did not in the least mind that Steven-John's tone was patronising. Steven-John's confidence made him feel secure. So did the medications. Though he only partly believed in their medical efficacy, his ear felt better already.

'I had, actually,' said Ulric, 'already consulted someone about my ear.' Ulric didn't need to explain that this someone was not his doctor. Steven-John knew that she was the person from whom Ulric was most anxious to conceal any weakness. 'At Georgiana's party, Chelsey said I was holding my head rather oddly, so I told her a bit about it.'

Steven-John grunted.

'She was concerned.'

'I'm sure she was,' said Steven-John, with a touch of bitterness, 'and no doubt wanted the full story to chew over endlessly with her fifty best friends.'

It was a poor pleasure, particularly as that was exactly

what Steven-John was inclined to do, but Ulric was flattered
that Steven-John was jealous of his confidence. He laughed a
little, and took a sip of wine, and pressed an escaping wisp of
fluff back into the sleeping bag. Then, taking a breath, he
continued with: 'She said – I think her exact words were –
that I ought to get myself "tested".'

Ulric had now made the statement that he had all morning
been preparing himself to make. He waited for Steven-John's
response.

Even for Steven-John, this was slow in coming. Once
again, Steven-John got to his feet. This time he went over to
the window where one of his wretched blackbirds was scrab-
bling at the glass. He raised the sash, and the bird hopped
onto the big square table and then onto the open pages of
Steven-John's beloved book of chakras. It squawked and
then, when food was not immediately forthcoming, squitted
on the book. Tutting to himself, Steven-John first extracted
the biscuits from the oven and broke one into crumbs which
he fed to the bird, and then dug into his pockets for something
to wipe the book.

'Maybe, old chap,' he said, his back still to Ulric as he
returned the wad of crumpled lavatory paper to his pocket,
'you could try the honey first.'

5

Tuesday, 24 October, lunchtime, the Savoy Hotel

'You WHAT?' The tray, glasses and chablis went flying as Lorraine leapt off the bed and turned, red-faced, to Lucy. 'You did *what*?'

Lucy righted the bottle, then carefully dismantled a mitred napkin and dabbed at the spill. 'I told Midge.' Her voice was sullen, like a child expecting to be slapped but standing her ground. 'I told you I would.'

'And you said what?'

'I asked her to let Fiona know about you and me. She said she'd tell Georgiana.'

'Jesus wept!' Lorraine, still wearing shirt, socks and knickers but minus her trousers, flounced over to the window, yanked it open. The grey wind-chopped surface of the Thames flew up at her, as if through the barrel of a zoom lens, and her lungs filled with petrol fumes. She slammed the window. 'That's really done it.'

'It hasn't, unfortunately,' said Lucy in the same low tone. 'If you'll let me finish —'

'I suppose you'd better.'

Lucy, now sitting cross-legged on the bed, poured what was left of the wine into Lorraine's glass — her own having rolled under the bed – and took a sip. Lucy's face was hot red, but her movements were controlled. 'Well, Georgiana didn't tell Fiona, and isn't going to.'

If this was a mercy, it was such a small one in the scale of the disaster that Lorraine felt little relief. She flung herself on her back at the foot of the bed and covered her eyes. The room was so small even the mingy bed seemed to be bursting the walls. This was really turning out to be some anniversary!

This happened on Tuesday, two days after Lucy had lunched at La Renarde Rusée, and the day of her and Lorraine's third anniversary – of their third week, that is. They were spending the afternoon at the Savoy. Lorraine had meant this to be a very special treat. Lucy had never been inside the place and had probably never expected to – until Lorraine told her that she and Fiona had spent their first night together there. After that, it had always seemed to Lorraine that Lucy's feet dragged if they passed that bit of the Strand in their lunch-time searches for somewhere to be alone. The tariff was £199 for a single room overlooking the river. That was a lot of money for a photographer, even one on a civil service payroll, particularly as Lorraine's hotel bills now totalled many hundreds of pounds, and only the B&B in Norfolk could be slipped in with her expenses.

Now they were here. Lucy had followed Lorraine demurely down the long, carpeted corridors smelling of wax, old cigars and inadequate ventilation. They found their room. Within minutes, a steward, with superb indifference to the situation, brought and poured the wine. Then, during the first kiss, Lorraine discovered that Lucy was wearing the gift of their previous anniversary – satin chemise and knickers. The image of Fiona, lonely and unwell at her workbench, faded, and Lorraine was a child at play. She pressed her fingers into the coarse fabric of Lucy's jeans. The slippery slither of satin beneath raised goosepimples on Lucy's bottom and ran tingling shocks up Lorraine's arm. This was what Alive meant. This was completeness; this was being in possession of one's body and soul, the only thing that was.

They had the whole afternoon and nothing to worry about. Nobody would be interested in Lucy's absence from the small business development centre – no meetings were planned for that afternoon and nobody kept records any more.

For her part, Lorraine (staff photographer at the Foreign and Commonwealth Office, and envied for the privilege of working under the debonair Head of Protocol, The Honourable Toby Hume) was often on the road. She had, in any case, told colleagues that she'd be out all day. This was plausible. Lorraine had dutifully spent the morning covering the State Visit of the new President of Malawi. But the afternoon entourage did not include her. The President had an interest in flower gardens and wanted to visit Kew. Kew being in one of its less photogenic moods, Toby had not included the photographer. So there was absolutely no reason for any anxiety and no need to hurry. Just one kiss to take the heat off.

The kiss had the opposite effect. Lorraine lifted Lucy off her feet and onto the bed. 'Let's get you out of these impedimenta.' Lucy, splayed against the headboard, her limbs wide and loose as a doll's, looked up at Lorraine with open, hungry, timid eyes. Lorraine leapt up onto the bed beside her. She stripped open the buttons of Lucy's shirt. 'God, I've missed you.' Her fingers whipped over to cup Lucy's breast. 'You smell, you feel, like peaches. Oh, skin, skin.' Lucy's nipples, wonderfully responsive to rough handling, rose in her hands. Lucy slid lower into the pillows, and Lorraine anchored her there with another kiss. The sweet sharp liquor of pleasure ran all through her body, into her breasts, into her toes. 'It's been three whole starving, empty days of longing for this.'

Lucy grasped a handful of Lorraine's hair and tugged until Lorraine lifted her head. 'Starving?' she said, peering close into Lorraine's eyes, 'I know you, you rabbit. You've been at it with Fiona.'

Lorraine was indignant. 'You have absolutely no reason to think anything of the sort.' A shadow of Fiona's caress – when was it – Sunday? – crossed her mind. Lorraine brushed it away. 'Absolutely none.'

'You want me to believe that?'

'Of course. You're the one who makes such an issue of honesty.' Lorraine's voice was prim. 'What's the point of demanding honesty from me and then disbelieving everything I say?'

Lucy pushed softly at Lorraine's breast. 'If you really mean to be honest, why don't you tell Fiona about us?'

Lorraine sat up with a sigh. 'Here we go *a-gain*.'

'Well, this time we go a bit further. You see, I did tell Midge.'

'You WHAT? You did what?'

Lorraine lay flat on her back at the foot of the bed, her body now burning with a fire of quite a different kind: Lorraine was frightened. The room had become strangely quiet, except for a mousy sound: the wretched loose-tongued woman was fiddling in her backpack. Lorraine winced as she thought of Fiona, mouth wide, eyes blank, Fiona saying: 'How *could* you? How could you do this to me – to us?' Lorraine asked herself the same question and was as dumb as before. Lorraine was married. Lorraine loved Fiona. Fiona was ill. Fiona needed Lorraine. Fiona was the one person who was always on Lorraine's side. Without Fiona, there was no order in the universe. What was Lorraine doing, messing about with this delinquent? She raised her arm a few inches to see her watch – it was still horribly early.

'Midge did talk to Georgiana, and Georgiana called me, like I said,' muttered Lucy into the silence.

'And?'

'And I taped the call.'

'You WHAT? What kind of person are you?'

'Georgiana knew I was doing it,' Lucy said indignantly. 'I told her. I wanted you to know exactly what I said, what she said. How otherwise could I be sure I'd given you the whole truth?' There was a rustling as Lucy pulled something out of the bag. 'Here's the tape. I also brought my Walkman, but there's a cassette slot in the console thing here by the bed.'

Lorraine sat up. 'I don't want to hear it.'

She was too late, the tape was already running.

A click and then Georgiana's voice, sounding upper-class to the point of parody, filled the room: '. . . but you're not too surprised, I don't doubt, under the [with emphasis] circumstances.'

'No.' Lucy's voice sounded very loud on the tape, though in life it was a mere whisper compared with Georgiana's. 'It's best you called me first.' Lorraine recognised from Lucy's measured delivery a firmness of intent she had learned to fear. 'I hoped you'd want to hear the full story, and Midge only knows what I told her.'

'Midge is an ass.'

The Lucy on the tape tittered, though the Lucy at the far end of the bed was solemn as an owl. The sound sent shivers down Lorraine's spine.

'Midge is a fool to have allowed you to say what you said, and a greater fool for approaching me. I told her so.'

'I expect you did.'

Lorraine, dumb with shock, could at this point register only that one did not speak to Georgiana as Lucy was speaking.

'And most foolish of all to imagine that I could ever be party to your machinations.'

'Machinations? That's a very posh word for wanting things put on the level.'

Lorraine flung an arm over her face and groaned.

Georgiana did not reply for a moment. 'I have few enough words of any kind for you, my girl.' A long and menacing pause followed, then: 'Only these: get off: go.'

There was silence from Lucy.

'You hear me? Or do I have to make myself even plainer?' Each of Georgiana's words was uttered with equal stress, each nipped off at its end. 'By saying "bugger off!"'

'I don't think you can say that to me,' said Lucy quietly, 'I'm in my own home, where I have a right to be.'

Georgiana did not reply, but her breath was more than audible.

Lorraine had never known Georgiana to be upstaged, ever. Despite the gravity of her own case, a wan smile came to her lips.

'Lock yourself in, if you like. Or go —' Georgiana's voice dropped to a low growl. 'Go wherever it pleases your little gold-digger's heart to go.' (Georgiana's phrases were now punctuated by pauses so regular that she could have been taking them from the prompt box.) 'Except anywhere near Fiona Douglas, my dearest friend.'

Lorraine leapt to her feet. 'Switch that thing off. This is disgusting.'

But Lucy's voice interrupted her. 'I don't think you quite understand. I'm not doing anything to Fiona. Lorraine is. I want to save Fiona from getting hurt.'

Georgiana's laugh, her most Ascotty neigh, set off the console's vibration register like miniature fireworks.

'Also please remember,' added Lucy in the same level tone, 'that I wanted your help to clear up a lie, I'm not asking you to run my life.'

There was a sharp intake of breath. Lorraine had never known Georgiana to be so roused. 'All right, Miss Lucy, Miss Lucifer. I can do as you wish. I can approach Fiona. You think that would increase her happiness? Or advance your interests? Want to know what I would say? I would inform her that her precious Lorraine has been rolling in the gutter.'

There was another silence before Lucy's voice sounded, now with a tremble, 'I can't let you say that. I can't allow you to denigrate me.'

'"Denigrate!" You know posh words too, it seems. But, my dear, you can't dictate what I say.'

'If you won't be civil, I can put the phone down.'

'It would not greatly surprise me if you did.'

'I'll tell Fiona myself.'

'I would not advise that, my dear.'

'I'd tell her the truth.'

'So would I. So would Toby. So would everybody else. Do you think, my dear child, that afterwards you, or Lorraine, would be left with many friends? How sweet then, would be your stolen kisses, your secret assignations, your little plots? Eh? When Lorraine finds that things she's taken for granted as part of herself – a lifetime partnership, a house, dog, her friendships, even her class – are at risk, do you think she'll then be in the mood for dalliance?'

A longer silence followed. Lorraine would have broken it with a cry, but her throat was paralysed.

Then Georgiana spoke again. 'Good.' The word had the soft thud of a marksman's rifle. 'I think you begin to take my point.'

The tape wound slowly onwards.

Lucy's voice broke into the silence. 'I've never asked Lorraine to give anything up for me. I've done nothing wrong, nothing.'

'No?'

'No!'

Give yourself time. Think about it.'

'I've thought. Tell everybody. I've got nothing to hide.'

'I'm very pleased to hear that. But do bear in mind, my dear, that, however innocent we may think we are, our judges are other people, not ourselves. No man, as they say, is an island.'

Lucy reached out and switched off the tape. 'You don't need to hear any more. She called me a "little rat".'

'No more.' Lorraine shook herself, suspecting that she might be feeling sick. But it wasn't nausea that was troubling her, it was shame: she would never be able to face Georgiana again. Worse, some mean little nerve in her brain was pulsing with relief that Georgiana's appalling cruelty to Lucy was her protection, at least giving her time to work something out. 'Destroy that tape.'

'Oh, I won't,' said Lucy, shocked. 'I think Georgiana

wanted you to hear it. And I might need to play it to Fiona one day.'

A laugh like a belch escaped from Lorraine's throat. 'What do you mean? Are you playing Georgiana's game now; are you threatening me?'

'No,' replied Lucy carefully. 'I do want Fiona to know about us. It is her right to know. And it might help her to know what her friends are really like.'

'Oh my God.' Lorraine once more stretched herself along the bottom of the bed, and rocked her head in her hands. 'What on earth is this all about?' Lucy made a minimal move towards her. Lorraine pulled back.

'You can't handle it, can you?' said Lucy savagely. 'You play tough and independent but you're shivering in the ghetto with the rest of them. Georgiana's right. She's only got to set her precious angels against our relationship, and you'll run like hell.'

'I will not. I've given you my word.' Lorraine edged herself to the floor and fumbled under the bed. She emerged with the glass and, still on her knees at the foot of the bed muttered, with the asphyxiated gasp of someone who had breathed the air of a thousand illicit copulations, 'God, this is ghastly.'

'You hate me for it, don't you? And I did nothing; I did absolutely nothing wrong.'

'I don't hate you; I'm shocked.'

Lucy took hold of Lorraine's forelock and forced her to meet her gaze. 'You're *shocked*. You don't know what shocking is. You don't know what *ghastly* is. You don't know what it is to be lonely, and poor, and to have nothing in your life but a lover who treats you with contempt.'

'Please, Lucy, please. This is our anniversary.'

Lucy tugged at the tough, wiry hair: 'Do you understand that if I can't have a real relationship with you, I don't want to know you at all?'

Lorraine shook herself free. 'Let's leave this alone for a while.'

'You're shivering,' said Lucy. 'You think I'm polluted. You don't want to touch me.'

Lucy was right. Lorraine, at that moment, shrank from Lucy. This aversion was not new; it was deeply entwined in her whole response to Lucy, feelings that were frequently succeeded by a powerful sexual need. At this moment, Lorraine struggled against it, knowing that it was she, not Lucy, who had behaved shabbily. 'Truly, I love you.' Lorraine reached out her quivering hand. 'I know you've done nothing wrong.' Lorraine pulled herself onto the bed. 'I won't let Georgiana bully you.'

Lucy folded herself into Lorraine's embrace. 'I was very upset by Georgiana,' she whispered. 'I don't know why, but they hate me; they really hate me.'

'It's nothing personal.' Lorraine stroked the skinny, vulnerable little shoulder. 'They don't like me either. They are a different class with different rules. But next time you want to play political games, don't take on Georgiana and her Mafia, okay?'

Lucy sank her head onto Lorraine's breast. 'I just wish,' she muttered, 'I could trust you.'

Lorraine's nerves, stripped bare by Georgiana's voice, responded with a rush to Lucy's touch, till every inch of skin, every organ, was roaring with desire. 'Give it a whirl. Trust me,' she whispered. 'This is our anniversary. Let's not let Georgiana wreck it. Guess who's got you an anniversary present?'

'You did? I get the Savoy and a present on top?' Lucy, excited as a child, pulled herself out of Lorraine's arms. 'Let me see.'

'No, guess what it is!' Lorraine reached over to her jacket and extracted something small from an inside pocket.

Lucy, struggling in vain to prize open Lorraine's hand, so much brawnier than her own, eventually said, 'Oh, I can't; you'll have to give me a clue. Is it shiny yellow?'

Lorraine shook her head.

Lucy, in a slightly disappointed tone, asked: 'Is it silver?'

Again Lorraine shook her head.

'Not even silver like that little purse of Fiona's that I like so much?'

'I'm not giving any clues. You've got to guess right.'

'That's not fair.' With a cry, Lucy flung herself onto Lorraine and they were rolling and struggling and laughing on the bed until the small package was in Lucy's hand and Lucy's satin chemise was under the bed with the re-abandoned wineglass.

They were dressing to leave, doing it by inches. Lorraine had wobbly legs and a warm ache in her abdominal muscles, her body's most characteristic post-coital signifiers. More significantly, her entire system was still quivering from a sexual charge of such ferocity that she could truly say to herself that this passion was beyond her control. How ridiculous to think that something so god-given could be wrong or do any harm. These things put a soppy grin on her face.

Lucy's face, on the other hand, was wistful. 'I hate going home after being with you,' she said quietly. 'The flat feels so empty.'

'You'll be glad of a bit of peace and quiet.'

'No.' Lucy laced up her shoes. 'I won't have peace. I'll be torturing myself thinking of you and Fiona.'

'For heaven's sake. There's nothing to think about. I'll be zonked out, and Fiona will – well, if she hasn't a headache she'll be spending half the night in her studio, melting bits of glass or something.'

'It's not that, it's not sex that worries me. It's that she'll cook for you, or you'll cook for her, and you'll sit together talking to each other and the dog, and I won't exist.'

Lorraine pulled on the rest of her clothes. She washed her hands and splashed her face, dumped the empty chablis bottle on the tray, and grabbed her camera bag. 'Shall we go before you get back onto your favourite subject?'

'But you are going to tell her?'

'I told you. Of course I'll tell her. Now that Georgiana knows, I haven't exactly got much choice. But I can't and won't tell until she's ready for it. And right now she is not. Why do you think Georgiana refuses to tell Fiona? You think it's because she hates you? It isn't. Georgiana knows Fiona couldn't handle it. If you hadn't tried to drag Fiona into all this, she wouldn't care whether you were alive or dead. That's how she'd like to feel about me. But she has to notice me, because I married her adored Fiona.'

'I hate it when you talk about your marriage. It's so phoney; it's so totally phoney.'

6

Tuesday, 24 October, Gospel Oak and Regent's Park

Tuesdays were bad days for Fiona, in a specifically Tuesdayish way. Fiona was an independent jeweller, a home-worker. The emptiness of time couldn't be hidden – by the chat, flirtations, jealousies, power politics and other distractions of an office – from someone working at home, alone, in silence.

Monday had the compensation of relief from Lorraine's Michelin-Man bounce, which became exhausting by the end of a weekend. Wednesday wasn't reliable, but when it delivered it was Fiona's best working day. Thursday, with any luck, could be a continuation of Wednesday, and Friday, of course, opened onto the by then pleasurable anticipation of Lorraine's bounce. But Tuesday was a day without shape.

Fiona could make the most exquisite tiny pieces, with layer upon layer of fine gold or silver thread, inset with half-hidden rare stones and enamelled with glass. They were birds, or scaly insects, or a landscape where, between the tiny trunks of trees, lurked an infinitesimal horseman or Diana with her bow.

Fiona also – what financially speaking was more to the point – made brilliant lavish rings, tie-pins or netsuke that carried the label of a very famous Italian designer, on commission from buyers who paid in Swiss francs and preferred to remain anonymous. It being Tuesday and a day of low creative energy, Fiona was working on one such, a lumpish thing based on a Greek urn which would be used to fasten a toga-like garment. Bonzo snoozed at her feet, one ear half pricked in case the magic word 'walkies' should penetrate his dreams.

The phone rang. Fiona made no move to answer. It was probably Lorraine, momentarily released from attendance on her visiting President. Fiona wondered vaguely what jewellery a President of Malawi would wear. Lorraine wasn't particularly observant about such things, but she might notice her President's embellishments, as she'd seemed unusually conscious of jewellery that morning. After dashing out to the van, she'd dashed back again to put on the Russian wedding ring Fiona had, years ago, made her. She'd been quite wrong, she'd said, to think it might scratch her camera lenses. Fiona found it strange that jewellery, which on her bench often seemed useless trash, was so significant. Significant of what?

The voice on the answerphone caused Fiona to start with pleasure. 'This is a message for you, Fifi my darling.' The voice was Georgiana's. 'What are your plans for lunch today?'

Fiona picked up the extension at the edge of her work-bench. 'Georgie, what a surprise.'

They agreed to wrap up well and meet in the rose garden at Regent's Park, then have a cup of tea at the park café. This was, in fact, one of the few possibilities. Even the closest friend in the world didn't visit Georgiana's flat between parties. Fiona was too tactful to suggest a restaurant, knowing that Georgiana would want to pay, having proposed the meeting. Fiona's house, with its litter of Lorraine's presence in every room, caused pain Georgiana preferred to avoid.

So they walked, two tall, slender and elegant middle-aged women, one stiffly erect and verging on elderly, side-by-side through the spiny relics of red, pink and white roses. Sparrows chittered, a blackbird was spiking the wet earth, and a thrush ran, head low, before them, more confident now that the swallows had left on their long flight to southern Africa. Bonzo trotted at Fiona's heel, his lead rattling in his mouth. Georgiana was accompanied by an animal too, but hers was long dead, an ancient fox fur draped shamelessly over the collar of her beaver coat.

'I feel a tidge worried about you, darling,' said Georgiana.

'There's nothing wrong with *me*, Georgie, just with this and that.'

'Start with "this".'

'This period in one's life where the most tempting vice is not sex or drink but sleep.'

'It passes. The "that"?'

'That passes by definition. The Change.'

'Oh "that".' Georgiana waved *that* away with a sweep of one kid-gloved hand. 'It isn't necessary to loathe it. Midge was having a bad time in other ways but enjoyed the event – seeing the back of those insanitary periods and acquiring a dinky little moustache. I was indifferent on the whole, though rather pleased to notice that one develops rather less body smell. Now I can wash because I like to wash, not because I have to camouflage my carcass.' Georgiana briefly laid her hand on Fiona's shoulder. 'But you, my dear, you're someone who takes things hard. Why not have a word with the family doctor? Get him to give you some happy pills. I've taken them for years. So much cheaper than alcohol, thanks to the good old NHS.'

'My doctor's a her. And she doesn't believe in happy pills, though she has proposed pills, hormone replacement therapy.'

'That fad! Made out of horse-piss. You'd be as well off with eye of newt. And switch to a man doctor, my dear. One can be firm with men, and they're less cranky.'

Fiona laughed and, long after the joke had worn itself out, she went on laughing. Suddenly, as if a swallow had returned to swoop over the grass, she was lifted up by a peculiar sensation, something long forgotten: her dog and her dear friend beside her on this fresh autumn day, Fiona was suddenly aware of being carried out of herself, by pleasure. 'You don't need a doctor, Georgie, you need St Roch of the Plague, the Patron Saint of Hopeless Cases.'

Georgiana seized Fiona's ice-cold hand and gave it a squeeze. In unspoken agreement, they began, again, to clip briskly along the path.

'Actually, there is something particular I'm worried about just now,' added Fiona, surprised at herself for saying this: Fiona was not someone who confided. 'It's Lorraine.'

Georgiana, consummate actress, struck the pose of perfect astonishment. 'She's well, I hope?'

'Oh yes, she's fine. Except that she's not. I'm giving her a hard time. I just can't keep up with her these days. I'm gripped in the jaws of the Black Dog. It's driving her mad. I'd rather hoped the HRT would liven me up.'

'Oh pish! What you need to do is give that Lorraine a little more rope and see what she hangs in it. Then you'll get a bit of peace.'

'Meaning?'

'Let her wander a bit. Let her pick up some floozy who'll wear out her high spirits. She's hitting 45. She won't have them for much longer. Give her a last fling. She'll be happy soon enough to curl up with you by the fire.'

Fiona laughed again. 'You make it sound such good clean fun that maybe I'd best ginger up and take over the floozy myself.'

'I think, dear heart, you have too much taste to go for the sort that takes her fancy. But why not get one of your own? How about a nice boy from one of the more closeted regiments, a fellow who still languishes after his governess and cuts himself with his razor.'

Fiona didn't answer. She knew that she wouldn't, couldn't do anything of the sort. Nobody had magic for her these days, and when she could steel herself to look in the mirror, she could see no residue of the old magic in herself. She had been faithful to Lorraine for a decade, but she remembered well how very dangerous loose sex is. 'Women can't play the game the chaps play,' she said in her low drawl. 'Women get involved.'

'Of course. But it's temporary. You have to be brave enough to wait till the thing passes and your turn comes round again.'

Fiona gave one of her rare, sad smiles. 'If Lorraine got involved with someone, I don't know what I'd do. I think I might kill myself.'

'Oh stuff!' Georgiana shoo'ed aside a clutch of pigeons with leprous feet who'd drawn closer now that the two women's perambulations had slowed almost to a halt.

'What else could I do if she left me?'

'Fifi darling, things far tougher than passion do the real work of holding relationships together. They're called a house, investment policies, having someone who's always on your side, being able to sleep through someone's particular snoring, plus, in your case, a slobbery individual answering to the name of Bonzo.'

Bonzo pricked up his ears and at the risk of dropping his lead produced one of his idiotic grins. 'See what I mean?'

Fiona shook her head. If she let her mind shift out of fear that she might lose Lorraine, she came closer to a worse one: that she was losing herself.

The day, too was slipping away, growing darker and colder, with squally winds. Fiona buttoned up her camel-hair coat, Georgiana wrapped the fox tighter with a vicious twist at its tail, and they headed towards the café, where the women could have tea, but Bonzo would have to wait in weather that was on the verge of turning to rain.

Bonzo didn't have to wait long. The café was a public place, very.

As they approached the dog-posts outside, Bonzo gave a squeal of pleasure at seeing a friend already tethered there: Jezebel. Forgetting his doggy obedience classes, he leapt at her, and they sniffed, from head to wagging tail, Bonzo in between casting pleading glances over his shoulder for Jezebel to be let loose.

Fiona, with sinking heart, patted both dogs to encourage

patience: where Jezebel was, at a time when Toby would be engaged with the President of Malawi, the dog-walker could not be far behind. 'Well,' she said to Georgiana, 'looks like a social occasion.'

Georgiana was standing stiffly beside her. 'You know how much I abhor crowds,' she replied, 'and I remember now, this place has sunk to teabags. Bridle the hound and let's be away.'

They made off with dignity but not fast enough, for Steven-John, dabbing at his moustache with a paper napkin, caught up with them. 'I say, girls,' he called, 'I was waving like mad through the glass, and now I've had to abandon my breakfast. If you'd been just minutes earlier, you'd have met Ulric. Georgiana, hi!'

Georgiana snorted.

'Fiona.' Steven-John's voice dropped an octave as he gallantly took her hand. 'I'm just so terribly sorry to hear your news.'

'Steven-John,' said Georgiana with severity, 'Fiona and I are engaged in a private conversation.'

'Of course. I won't crash in. I just wanted to tell you, Fiona, that if you ever need a shoulder to cry on, or anything, anything at all —'

Fiona watched with puzzlement while Georgiana shook Steven-John's sleeve and said in a harsh whisper: 'Get lost, boy!'

'Hold it.' Fiona didn't like this at all. 'What's going on?'

Despite Georgiana's parrying, Fiona insisted on hearing Steven-John's story. It was this: While doing for Jezebel yesterday, Monday, Steven-John had, as was his custom, taken in Toby's mail and played his phone messages. He'd then telephoned Toby to report what he'd found.

'Which was?' said Fiona, irritated that Steven-John was taking so long to get to the point.

'There was a postcard, with a picture of junks in Hong Kong harbour and some washing hanging up somewhere, from someone called Tommy, who is planning to visit London in December. I read it out to Toby.'

'What's that got to do with me?'

'Absolutely nothing!' snapped Georgiana.

'That is true.' Steven-John shook his head as if he'd been saying the opposite.

Fiona's heart began to pound. 'And?' she roared.

'There was also,' stuttered Steven-John, 'a telephone message. It was, as a matter of fact, a message from Georgiana.'

'What sort of message?' Fiona looked from one to the other.

'Absolutely none of your business and certainly none of this foolish boy's.' Georgiana reached for Fiona's cuff.

Fiona shrugged free.

Georgiana, looking daggers at Steven-John said: 'It was about Midge, for heaven's sake. I refuse to be interrogated.'

'Well, you tell.' Fiona turned to Steven-John.

He shuffled. 'I'd rather not if Georgiana doesn't want—'

'But I *do* want,' insisted Fiona.

Looking alternately at Bonzo and then Jezebel, he said awkwardly, 'I can't remember the exact words. To be honest, I've been rather taken up with another friend's problems lately, ear trouble, you know the sort of thing – but I think Georgiana said – is this correct, Georgiana? – that Midge had told you something worrying about, um, a couple, and you needed Toby's help.'

Fiona remained silent, so did Georgiana.

'So,' continued Steven-John with the shamefaced manner of someone reduced to explaining a joke, 'I played the message to Toby and asked him what it meant. He didn't know at that stage, so I called him again from my callbox before Ulric came round this morning. He was vague, though he admitted that you, Fiona, could be in for a spot of bother.'

Georgiana was now striding ahead and possibly just out of earshot. Fiona walked slowly, with a hand cupping her mouth. Menopausal symptoms were manifesting themselves in warm waves of nausea.

Steven-John laboured towards the point. 'Well, I was worried about you, Fiona, and I couldn't leave it at that. So I rang Midge immediately after. She sounded foul – I guess she really hit it last night – but she told me the whole story. She took a funny line, I must say. She kept saying that it was Lucy who was being hurt, and Lorraine was the one who should get the hell out.'

Lucy, the queer little fish who'd been hanging round them for weeks? 'What's Lucy got to do with anything?'

Steven-John was deeply engaged in checking the setting of the stones in Jezebel's jewelled collar.

Lucy? Lorraine doing a number with Lucy? It wasn't possible. The girl was sexless as a rag doll. 'It's not true,' said Fiona.

'Of course. I got it all wrong,' responded Steven-John hotly.

Lucy: with almost no body, no personality, no colour, no hair, no form, just a jumble of half-baked notions and a great hungry mouth. Fiona saw the mouth, and knew at that moment that it was not only true, but that she'd known it for weeks. 'You didn't. It is true.'

'It is?' Steven-John was confused. 'I'm heckova sorry. I'm really sorry I blurted it out like that. I wanted to help.'

'Well, you did help. Now I know. That makes me a bit less of a fool. Thanks for telling me.' Fiona was getting horribly close to the point where she might start retching.

'I'm glad you're taking it like this,' said Steven-John, 'You want to do so much, but feel so useless, at times like this. But I've got support going. Chelsey is always busy on Tuesday mornings, but I rang Sarah and Tim and Thelma. We all, each and every one of us, want you to remember that we're all one family, and we'll do anything, anything . . .'

It caused Fiona no perceptible pain at all that everybody knew. The world was spinning. A bench loomed nearby. She dropped onto it and was sick.

'Georgiana, I say, Georgiana! Come here a mo. I think Fiona's not feeling too well.'

7

Fiona and Lorraine

The decade-old partnership of Fiona and Lorraine had not been sanctified by the Church or recognised by the State, but it was as a couple that they were a pillar of their small society. To every member of Georgiana's crowd, it was, for better or worse, the centre of both their lives. Though everyone knew that such structures were fragile, and several had personal knowledge of their failure, the prospect of such collapse evoked fear second only to the terror of death.

Fiona and Lorraine's partnership was regarded as equal and parallel to those of Tim and Thelma, and Sarah and Sophie – with minor variations. Tim and Thelma defined themselves as Other Halves. Sarah and Sophie began each sentence with 'We'. Fiona and Lorraine took a more aggressive approach. They spoke, Lorraine loudly, about their 'marriage'. This had at first caused some embarrassment. It suggested claim to a particular status in the world at large; and one of the unwritten laws of Georgiana's crowd was that in the wilderness outside it, one made oneself invisible.

But old friends accommodate each other's eccentricities, and nobody cringed now when Lorraine talked of anniversaries. They'd got used to several things, including the connection itself: only Georgiana still flushed with anger that Fiona hadn't aimed higher.

So when Steven-John had concluded his round of telephone calls reporting that Lorraine was carrying on with that bailiff person she'd brought to the party, the reaction everywhere was shock, and fear for Fiona. Sarah and Sophie — each of whom was frequently unfaithful to the other — were outraged: Lorraine should be horsewhipped, the girl exiled to Patagonia, and Fiona courted like an offended deity until it would be appropriate for Lorraine to crawl back into favour. Steven-John sought the same outcome though he favoured softer means — counselling, conducted by himself. Tim and Thelma said little, but looked at each other with wide frightened eyes. That night they lay close and did very tenderly whatever it is that heterosexuals do to entertain each other.

Lorraine's preoccupation in these most intense ten years of her life had not been art, or truth, or making a career. It had been relating to Fiona. First to win Fiona's love, and then to hold it. Lorraine strove anew each day to earn her place in Fiona's life, to extend herself till she could fill Fiona's field of vision.

Fiona's concerns were different. She knew Lorraine loved her, and she knew she loved Lorraine. But the road that Fiona trod did not have the firm surface of Lorraine's; it was of a slippery disintegrating material. Fiona, whose face and form had defined her, since her teens, as a heavenly creature was, by the time she met Lorraine, afraid — of change, of age, of failing. Lorraine, who was in one sense her strongest defence against these fears, was also a cause of them. Lorraine expected too much of her.

These differences aside, their shared conviction that what lay between them was something extraordinary, and their ever-renewed delight in sex that never failed and conversation that could still find fresh channels, had for years given them long nights of pillow talk about this marriage that they could still find mysterious and wonderful.

*

Of the many starting points leading to discussion of this subject, the role of Chance gave the best results. Their meeting had been the product of so many chance occurrences that the odds against their ever getting together were – they reckoned – five billion to two. Fiona found this scary: it could so easily not have happened. Lorraine found it magnificent: proof that their conjunction had been written in the stars.

Chance came from both sides. It had been on the merest impulse that Lorraine (a humble research assistant's assistant at the Foreign and Commonwealth Office with no distinction beyond papers from the wrong kind of university) had signed up for a night-school course in photography when the course on European integration was abandoned for lack of sufficient applicants. Chance had then given her the opportunity to snap the crazy tilting of the Royal Coach as the massive Queen of Tonga mounted it, and through further chance the Honourable Toby Hume – youthful, enterprising, then heir-presumptive of the Protocol Department – was in the canteen when the picture circulated, and was amused.

When Toby succeeded to the Headship, the empire of the Protocol Department expanded. The several new establishment posts included one for a photographer. 'This is Tonga Lorraine,' said Toby to the interview board, and Lorraine got the job.

Another chance came a few weeks later with the State Visit of Kenneth Kaunda, then President of Zambia and one of Africa's Big Men. He wanted to see not just tiaras and weaponry but to study the mechanism of what he believed to be a functioning Welfare State. This threw the Foreign Office into confusion. Toby – a gifted improviser and one never reluctant to make use of his friends – stepped into the breach and set up visits to the hospital where Sarah was deputy matron and Sophie senior radiographer, and the school where Midge redeemed the wayward. He tagged the new photographer onto the party.

Lorraine took to Midge. She promised her a print of the shot showing her shaking hands with one of the great heroes of African socialism, and brought it round to the school that evening. It was a delightful picture, Midge looking up at the giant Zambian as a child might look at Father Christmas, Midge's boys arrayed like toy soldiers around them. Midge was thrilled. They went off to the pub in a state of exhilaration, and enjoyed each other so much that Midge offered thanks in the only way she knew how. That was Lorraine's first experience of sex with a woman, and she was unusually fortunate in the partner fate had tossed her.

Midge found Lorraine to be forward at the first moves, and later wanting her fears rushed in a rough, muddled, noisy and not totally sincere charge. Midge obliged but, natural teacher that she was, added, with a delicate touch, a few sensory marginal notes which Lorraine's nerve ends remembered. Lorraine returned, in thoughtful mode, for more, and was better able to receive. Midge took her under her wing. At the weekend, strolling on Hampstead Heath with Raffles, then little more than a puppy, they met Fiona.

Fiona too was directed by chance: she had put herself into its hands, because her own government of her life had led it so sadly astray. On that grey afternoon, she was walking on the Heath trying to convince herself that chance might, at the least, come up with a new direction. She was at an unmarked crossroads, and afraid. Over the previous months things had happened that made the future obscure and possibly dreadful. Her partner (not in Georgiana's crowd and of simple-minded values) had walked out after finding her in bed with Sarah. Each day she counted it less likely that he would come back. His bank account still paid one half of the mortgage; his wetsuit and flippers still hung in the wardrobe; old girlfriends still phoned for him, but he had disappeared from her life. Fiona felt his absence with an intensity she had never felt for his presence.

Further, in the confidence that came from his encouragement plus his financial security, she had not long launched herself in the only business she wanted to pursue. But the

Fiona Douglas Jeweller-Artiste enterprise was, at the age of six months, a sickly infant. Commissions poured in, but cheques did not. The bank was kind; its interest rates were cruel. Fiona had never been in debt before. She did not find the condition comfortable.

Third, and this anxiety possessed her particularly on that day: it was her fortieth birthday. She had never before spent a birthday alone. Worse, she had never before seriously considered that she might one day no longer be young. Fiona was hoping, but not hoping for any particular thing, unless it was that she could wake up and find the previous three months, or three years, not to have happened.

She saw Midge, the dog and Midge's new girl before they saw her. She drew back into the bushes and watched. They were laughing, swinging their hands, so happy, so young. She decided to remain concealed. But Raffles recognised the hidden figure and leapt into Fiona's arms. Fiona emerged with an embarrassed greeting.

In this way, fate threw Fiona and Lorraine together. What occurred was not absolutely instantaneous, but very nearly so. Each claimed that she had given the first signal; each, contradictorily, that she'd been first to respond to the other's. But what neither could remember was exactly what happened as they stood there in a shower of sparks, Fiona with the excited puppy in her arms, Lorraine knocking the mud from her boots, with Midge – nobody could remember Midge's part, except that it was she who suggested that they move on to the Freemason's Arms. That night they parted in three separate directions, but Lorraine had Fiona's telephone number scrawled on the back of a barmat.

What is 'in love'? Lorraine believed it to be a divine state in which she could see into each particle of the universe, and see it glorified. Fiona considered the same condition to be dangerous insanity, yet surrendered with as little struggle.

They agreed within a day to become lovers, but spent weeks planning the event. Lorraine was nervous about her lack of experience, her only appropriate training having come from Midge (who had also, of course, bedded Fiona). Fiona was afraid that the shell might crack and she might find herself bored.

They forced themselves to it. They booked a room at the Savoy for this specific purpose. There they confronted each other, naked and ashamed of their bodies, and both so nervous and full of wine that they crossed the great barrier blindfolded.

It was the next day that the full ferocity of the change in them struck. This left Lorraine raging to possess Fiona totally and for ever, Fiona afraid that they were travelling so fast they might take a wrong turn and plunge off the edge.

But fate was kind. Their lunches grew longer, and nobody seemed to notice, at work, or in the crowded pubs where their feet made love under the table while Lorraine talked and Fiona's long fingers played with her little antique change-purse of fine silver mesh. Each day, Lorraine begged to be allowed to come that night to Fiona's flat, and Fiona sometimes said, after hesitation, 'yes', and sometimes she would plead fatigue or another engagement. On the afternoons of such refusals, she would find herself compelled to phone Lorraine to say that she had bought a beautiful amethyst, or a loaf of bread, or that she had seen a jay in the garden. Then somehow the conversation would turn until it came round to agreement that Lorraine had better, after all, come that night to the flat.

They talked endlessly about love. Fiona wanted their love kept secret out of fear of the envy of the world; Lorraine wanted to announce it from the housetops so that all of humanity could share in their joy. But it was less through talk than through touch that they learnt to know each other. They were full of sensation, and this overflowed of itself to the other. They met, now, every day and most nights, all the while getting skinnier, more excited, and totally oblivious to anything except themselves. Within a month, most of Lorraine's clothes had migrated to Fiona's flat.

About domesticity, they were gauche. They still didn't eat,

but they drank a great deal of soft German wine and, over and over, made love. Lorraine enjoyed her work as she had never done before. As she herded her dignitaries into photogenic clusters, sporting with them in a freedom Toby would never allow himself, her joy swelled simultaneously with the fore-taste of a good picture and the aftertaste of Fiona's breast on her mouth.

After two months, and a long and serious discussion, Lorraine wrote to Fiona's ex-partner, offering to buy him out of the flat. From about that time, they spoke not about their 'affair' but their marriage, and a new seriousness, and with it tenderness, entered their lives. They had not the slightest doubt that no two people had ever been so in love.

Nearly ten years later, they had moved on. Fiona's little flat was now a romantic memory, and the house in Gospel Oak, with its demands of garden, drains and good neighbourliness, the reality. Bonzo had slunk out of the Wood Green Animal Shelter and into their lives. Georgiana's circle opened a crack to admit Lorraine. The Fiona Douglas Jeweller-Artiste enter-prise now paid half the mortgage and all the improvements to the house. Lorraine still talked about the future, but Fiona played less often with her little change-purse, and they kept their feet to themselves.

Their lovemaking was still of excellent quality, reliable and very efficient, though less compulsive and frequent. They were also less experimental. Various bits of gear acquired on visits to New York gathered dust in the cupboard. They seldom played at their fantasies – Fiona of becoming one small part of her body and concentrating all sensation into that ankle or hollow under the collar bone; Lorraine of them being plough-boys rolling in the hay. They slithered apart when the telephone or doorbell rang, and became expert at the Saturday morning quick-fuck, scaled down to get them to Waitrose's before the worst of the crowds.

Sometimes they worried about the leach of romance from their life, but they didn't think to worry that sex was their only sure way to find each other. They seldom quarrelled, but when they did, it was shocking – Lorraine raging in a terrible articulateness which possessed her only at such times and caused her to say things afterwards much regretted – Fiona ice-cold and unable to forgive. When they could, they forestalled quarrels by making love until the anger seeped away and the problem could be marked down as one to be avoided.

But though, as the years passed, quarrels became even rarer, moods did not. Fiona's were, for someone with a cat-like tread, noisy, even clumsy. She would crash and bang about the house, muttering curses at the kettle, workbench, any inanimate thing, turning on Lorraine only when Lorraine whined to know what she had done to offend. Lorraine's foul moods were of the ranting order – impassioned (and to Fiona utterly boring) speeches about the state of the nation.

For all that, they were still in love. Fiona, at 50, was still beautiful, though she now wore her shorts only in the garden, and began to suffer the assaults of the menopause. Lorraine, at 45, was thickening about the upper body and she talked too much, but she still had a killer serve at tennis and could be relied on to say something provocative enough to bring the dullest party to its feet. They didn't admit that they were older. They were still Les Biches, who envied nobody because there was nothing anywhere better than what they had. Yet sometimes, when a mood was brewing, they looked at each other and wondered if this really was all that human life amounted to.

8

Tuesday, 24 October, Frognal to Kilburn

Fiona's was not the only calendar on which Tuesday was marked for a day of unease. Chelsey suffered too, and by sunset, would be fending off despair with irony, possibly a more dangerous drug than the whisky from which Midge, at around the same hour, would be taking her first evening dose.

On Tuesdays, Chelsey was battered by the mischief of the spirit world, due to a vision received by a highly regarded medium. On one Tuesday, probably before the sun reached its zenith, a thing winged like the seed of a sycamore would fly to her, lodge in her throat, and then carry her, on a low moaning wind, to a field littered with stricken and headless angels. Chelsey, seemingly alone in this aftermath of some dreadful battle, would throw open her long cloak and speak. Not words but beautiful flowers would come out of her mouth.

The medium found the message puzzling, but Chelsey, the mostly resting but always very restless actress, had no doubt about the meaning. She was wild with excitement. She urged the medium to scour the spirit world for clearer voices, but the only answer was the boom of cosmic tides. The spirits were unresponsive when asked if this meant that Chelsey would be a greater actress than Georgiana in her prime, and positively churlish when asked if Chelsey would star in one of Georgiana's plays – *The Cherry Orchard*, *Separate Tables* or *A Doll's House*. The medium ventured that they rejected Chelsey's suggestion of a great tragedy, likewise any social drama. With hesitation, she backed Chelsey's guess that it could be a comedy, perhaps even a farce. But she did agree that it seemed certain that one day Chelsey would triumph.

Consequently, on Tuesdays, Chelsey was yoked to the telephone. By the time of the rise of the Evening Star, she could no longer keep her fingers off the dial. But the telephone at the Hodgson-Brookes Theatrical Agency was always answered by Iolanthe (Rupert Hodgson-Brookes was too important to answer the phone himself) and Iolanthe always said, in her pert little Roedean drawl: 'Nothing on deck that's absolutely right for you today, darling, um, Chelsey, but you know we're always on the lookout, especially for you.'

Chelsey took herself regularly to the theatre, entering humiliatingly through the ticket doors. She saw dozens of comedies with parts that would have been absolutely right for her; several of these had been placed by Hodgson-Brookes.

This was Tuesday lunchtime, not long after Georgiana's voice had bypassed Chelsey's apartment on its electronic route to Fiona in Gospel Oak and Lorraine and Lucy had shut themselves into their hotel room. At Hodgson-Brookes, the great Rupert would be doling out the booty of desperate calls from producers whose stars had overdone their liquid brunches. Chelsey, warming her hands around her mug of thick black coffee, was struggling not to stare at the phone (in deference to the watched kettle principle). So she looked around her apartment, though this was distressing enough.

They were large rooms at the bottom of a very large house, perched on one of the most gothic and precipitous slopes of that exclusive corner of Hampstead which prefers to call itself Frognal. These rooms were shaken by subsidence and painfully expensive to heat. There were many long mirrors, but it distressed Chelsey to catch sight of herself hunched in an old man's cardigan and long woollen socks, so several were draped. No decorating had been done since Chelsey and Sheila-Jayne moved in a decade back, and Chelsey's glance now ran along the cracks in the walls. She debated, for the umpteenth time, painting the place. She had selected the colour, a cool deep moss to contrast with the red in her hair, with black lacquered woodwork to frame her form as she stood at the windows.

But there was a hindrance, a serious one. The flat belonged to Chelsey's brother. And his productivity had regrettably extended beyond property. He had also generated a son, and this egregious sprog intended, when he graduated from law school, to move to London. Chelsey had been informed, gently but firmly, that, while there could be no question of throwing her out, she would, of course, put the lad up. The lad had a voice as loud and lordly as Laurence Olivier playing Henry V, the finesse of Robbie Coltrane playing Bottom, and lavatorial habits which indicated a natural affinity to Sir Toby Belch. When the nephew came, Chelsey would have to go. She would leave cracked and un-repainted walls behind her.

If the phone had rung just then, she would have taken anything, even a commercial for detergent. The sound that filled her ears was so shocking that it took her almost a second to recognise it.

She pounced on the telephone. 'Yes?' then, remembering to inject a relaxed and sensual note into her voice, 'Chelsey Cham-ber-lain. Hel-lo.'

There was a little awkward sound, the tenth of a laugh. 'Chelsey! You answered before I'd even finished dialling.'

A pause followed; Chelsey was struggling with a falling feeling. She touched ground and knew the gravelly tone on the line for the gender-enriched voice of her ex-lover. 'Steven-John, how often must I remind you that I must keep my line free on Tuesdays.'

'I remembered, or I would have phoned this morning. I'm in a phone box in Regent's Park.' A pause to the value of at least three pence followed. Others might have suspected this to presage some very sombre announcement indeed. Chelsey took it for Steven-John's normal tortoise pace, until he followed with: 'There's bad news, I'm afraid, about Fiona.'

'Oh my God,' Chelsey clutched at her throat as her psyche flashed up a shocking vision. 'Is she all right?' she added feebly, already convinced that Fiona was dead.

'I'm afraid she's not. She's being sick on a bench.' Steven-John paused again, as if the words cost him pain. 'Lorraine's got involved with that Lucy woman.'

Under the circumstances, this was an anti-climax. 'Oh that,' replied Chelsey, 'those two are well suited. Dog will sniff out dog.'

Steven-John emitted another of his fractional laughs. 'I know Fiona's not your favourite person, but we're all going to have to rally round. She's a loner, but somehow we must get her out of that house and involved with people.'

Chelsey's answering laugh was a mocking 'Ha!' Fiona had never condescended even to call at her flat; Chelsey had, of course, not invited rebuff by asking her to.

Chelsey was jealous of everybody – even at times of Midge – but her jealousy of Fiona was of a different order. When she thought about it (much less often than she felt it) she envisaged it as a red-hot wire piercing her entrails. Yet nobody better understood Fiona's sufferings or was more conscious of her powers than Chelsey. Fiona had been the cause of Chelsey's greatest misfortunes. That Fiona was the unconscious cause of them merely emphasised for Chelsey the indifference of the world to her pain. Chelsey hated Fiona. Fiona, young, had always been more beautiful than Chelsey, although Chelsey's features were superior. Fiona, in middle age, had acquired a remote, Garbo-ish air of spiritual depth; Chelsey's looks were turning leathery. Worst of all, on the third Saturday of every month Chelsey had to learn again the hard lesson the weeks between helped her to forget: Georgiana simply adored Fiona.

Struggling with rage at the certainty that this drama would absorb all of Georgiana's energies, and equally with excitement at the thought of her enemy laid low, she listened while Steven-John rattled on. Yes, she could quite appreciate that they had all to join forces to support Fiona. Yes, of course they should keep up her spirits until Lorraine returned to her senses. Yes, Chelsey's nephew was indeed almost a lawyer, though she doubted that he would be the man to call on if Lorraine and Lucy took over Fiona's house. Yes, of course there was no question that Fiona had prior rights to the dog. And yes, Midge did indeed seem to be playing a curious role in all this. Chelsey even heard herself agreeing that the best person to get hold of Midge and stop her from meddling would be Chelsey herself.

Chelsey was familiar with disappointment. Life had given her a long string of them. The brother, born when Chelsey was an angelic two-year-old, became the passion of their mother's life, and Chelsey's earliest pains had included consignment to the wrong end of the bath. At school, she was the shy, skinny older sister of the captain of the junior football team. Chelsey's small successes on stage had been eclipsed by massive family celebration when the brother was called to the bar; and the beautiful men she used to fill the gap in her life seemed to have a lot more fun when the brother took them off to the boozer. Then came the devastation of Georgiana. Chelsey had never before been attracted to a woman – she hadn't been strongly attracted to anyone, in fact, though she liked to flirt. But after Georgiana, men lost their glamour. In place of the scent of the leather interiors of sports cars, she was conscious only of their less pleasurable odours – breath smelling of whisky, armpits smelling of mice, semen of mouldy mushrooms, and feet of cheese. The partnership with Sheila-Jayne could have worked, while giving neither of them quite what she wanted, but the process of transformation into Steven-John had taken far too many years of squeamy and eventually boring surgery. All the phases of Chelsey's life had begun with promise, and then petered out. She hungered, lonely, and now deeply envious, for power.

So when Chelsey put down the receiver, her languor was gone and her brain was whizzing as if the coffee (her fifth that day, it being Tuesday) had suddenly become 100 per cent caffeine. She pulled the telephone closer and dialled.

She got Iolanthe.

'Chelsey Chamberlain here,' she said brightly. 'Anything come in for me?'

Iolanthe seemed taken aback. 'Not right on deck as yet, darling, um – but we're always on the lookout for something especially –'

'Good. Put them on hold will you? I'll be *hors de combat* for much of today. I'll get in touch at my very soonest.'

Then, without further ado, Chelsey kicked off her socks and cardigan, picked up her coat and purse. Stuff the cost, she was going to take a cab.

Midge, Raffles in her arms, stood at the window of her attic bedroom, abstractedly rocking the little dog like a baby. Midge had another heavy hangover, but was forcing her brain to work out how she, who meant so well, had gone so terribly wrong. How had she not seen, until Steven-John put it so clearly before her, how much harm she was doing to Fiona? Yet, how could she be doing harm? She had set out to help Fiona: to bring the truth to her; to liberate her from deception; to give her control again over her own destiny. All these things Midge had understood, when explained by Lucy. Midge had been deeply moved by Lucy's account. And now she was deeply moved by Steven-John's. Midge worried about herself. She believed that she had a strong moral sense yet, somehow, it always seemed to have its roots in the other person. Was something missing from her frontal lobes? If so, the cause could not possibly be in her genes; both Colonel Winters and Mama had the clearest, firmest, most unshakeable ideas of right and wrong. It couldn't be the drinking. Midge was visited with wonderful moral clarity in that visionary phase between the fourth and sixth glass. It had to have to do with that obscure area in which Midge knew that she was, congenitally and predestinately yet unquestionably through her own fault, a Bad Person.

Midge longed to see Lucy again. She had phoned the small business development centre on Monday, but nobody answered. When she called Lucy's flat, she got the answer-phone, at 3 o'clock, 4 o'clock and 5. By the time Lucy answered in her own person, at 6, Midge was near sick with worry. But Lucy sounded neither worried nor sick, just off-hand. Today, Midge had not dared to phone.

Yet she had to see Lucy. Her own need aside, Lucy was in danger. Georgiana's crowd was baying for her blood. And Midge, stupid, clumsy Midge, had caused this to happen.

She watched a taxi draw up and a tall gawky woman, under a great bush of red hair, emerge. The figure turned towards her door. Raffles's ears pricked. So, at that signal, did Midge's. It was Chelsey Chamberlain.

Midge opened the door and Raffles launched herself into Chelsey's arms in a fulsome greeting. This contrasted with Midge's somewhat formal welcome. Though, after various parties during the sixties, they had ended up in Midge's attic bedroom, the two women were not close. Midge respected Chelsey as clever and feared her as devious. She believed that Chelsey regarded her as a nonentity yet retained a cool inter-est in her, if only because Chelsey was always interested in failure.

'I'm not dropping in,' began Chelsey. 'I'm charging in. I have to talk to you immediately about something important.'

Heart sinking, Midge knew this was to do with the Lucy business. She led Chelsey into the parlour but, noticing how cold it was, transferred to the kitchen. Messy and (alas) drain-and-dog smelly as it was, the kitchen was more comfortable than the dining room and less disreputable than Midge's bed-room.

'Tea?'

Chelsey asked for coffee, which Midge was not able to supply, as the half-jar of Sainsbury's Instant left by Mama's home help had calcified.

So they settled for tea, Indian, brewed strong and red, and Chelsey held her peace while Midge clattered in search of teapot, clean cups and the like.

Then, without preliminaries, Chelsey launched forth. 'I know about Lorraine and that Lucy girl, and that you approached Georgiana, asking her to plead Lucy's case.'

Midge's mouth opened and closed. 'Well, yes, well, no.' Midge would have given years of her life to have a sharp edge like Chelsey's. 'What you say is, of course, completely true, but still not quite what it was about. I asked Georgiana to show Fiona that the affair was not dangerous and to help her be open-minded about it.'

Chelsey nodded briskly as if satisfied with that, far as it went. 'Why?' she added in an innocent voice. 'Why did you bother?'

This, too, struck Midge as an astonishingly percipient question, touching on another disturbing problem. Midge simply could not judge how far her actions were led by concern about Fiona, how far by her desire to please Lucy, and how far she was mechanically following the 'I've started so I'll finish' principle.

'Well, I found out what was going on,' Midge began awkwardly, 'and it seemed to me that Fiona ought not to be deceived. So I decided to approach Georgiana as the most appropriate person to break the news to her.'

'My dear Midge,' said Chelsey, stretching out her long legs, 'you *have* changed. You've done a bit of deceiving yourself in your time, wouldn't you say?'

Midge's head sank low over the teapot. 'I was young and foolish,' she muttered.

'Maybe.' Chelsey extended a hand to take her cup before Midge could add dollops of milk and sugar. 'But I'm not aware that any great harm was done.'

Midge looked up quickly, caught the flash of Chelsey's ironic green eyes, and dropped her gaze.

'And,' Chelsey smiled, 'it was fun at the time, wasn't it?'

Startled, Midge looked up again, but the green eyes escaped her.

They fell into silence. Raffles, who had been ignored through this exchange, trotted, claws clicking, over to Chelsey and looked up pleadingly. Chelsey scooped her off her feet and settled her on her lap. Then she leaned down and placed a little kiss on the dog's head, her great red bush mingling momentarily with Raffles's rat's-tail fur.

Midge looked on in mixed pleasure and puzzlement. If anyone's bothering about this business was a mystery, it was Chelsey's. There was absolutely nothing in it for her, and dispassionate action was hardly what one associated with Chelsey. Strange about Chelsey, she had so much, yet had made so little of it. She'd started well: from RADA, straight into rep, where she'd been lucky enough to work with Georgiana and other actresses almost as exciting. About town, it was she who caught the eye of photographers from *Country Life* and the like, and was reliably to be seen with men of the right sort in tow. Then she'd got into films, in Elstree's last days as a great crucible of British cinema. Television programmes on the death agonies of yet another great British cultural institution often included clips from Chelsey's films. One commentator cited her as an example of the up-and-coming talent that would surely now be lost to Hollywood. Chelsey, young, had given the sense of someone poised, waiting for something really big. She was still waiting. Raffles turned to Chelsey, eyes awash with adoration. Chelsey smiled back. Raffles favoured Chelsey above Midge's other friends (apart from Steven-John of course); Midge believed her dog to be an excellent judge of character. Surely Midge was at fault in being, these days, so hard on the lovely, disappointed Chelsey. Wasn't she neglecting an opportunity to ease her own loneliness by easing the loneliness of an old friend?

'This tea': Chelsey looked up, 'is just begging for a shot of something to liven it up.'

That was exactly what was missing. Midge hadn't yet made her daily trip to the off-licence, so there was nothing in the kitchen livelier than the latest empty bottle beside the bin. But she didn't question her next move. She picked out the key of Colonel Winters's cabinet from the bunch in her back pocket, made her way to the dining room, and returned with an exceptional 50-year-old single malt. For Chelsey, Midge could break the taboo against taking her father's drink: it had been Colonel Winters's belief that Chelsey was a goddess.

The whisky brought a flush to Chelsey's pale cheeks, and brought to Midge a flash of memory – of Chelsey stifling Midge's giggle with her cool hand as a brisk military voice called up from the half-landing: 'Now don't you girls disturb Mother by gossiping all night.' A pang of grief that Chelsey (one of Midge's few achievements admired by dear Pa) was something she'd been unable to share with him, was quickly replaced by the weird, wobbly, delicious, utterly familiar, yet new feeling. This came so unexpectedly and with such sweetness that Midge took it for a gift from the ghost behind an exceptional single malt.

Chelsey peered past Raffles's ears to give Midge a lazy smile, 'Gesundheit, old chum,' she said. 'Today, I am escaping from myself, and what a relief that is.'

Midge was still puzzled by Chelsey's attention, but her chair inched closer. 'Do you remember,' she asked, 'the first time I brought you here, after one of Georgiana's parties, as I recall.'

'I remember your father. I thought of him when I saw the label on this bottle.'

'He was fond of you.' Midge spoke coolly, trying not to show that she was fishing for praise of someone she loved to hear praised.

Chelsey grinned. 'That dirty old man.'

'Surely,' asked Midge, alarmed, 'you found him upright?'

Chelsey was still grinning. 'They're the worst.'

Chelsey's cynicism always had a numbing effect on Midge. Had her father felt anything improper about Chelsey? Surely not. All of humanity, apart from Midge, had a capacity to channel strong feeling into the upper body. Only she was so weak in discipline that she couldn't lift it above her bodice. Even something as transient as the sound of a marching brass

band made her heart swell with emotion expressible only in
tears or a clutch at the nearest creature. She turned her gaze
to Raffles, who was now licking the fine red-gold hairs on
Chelsey's wrist. Chelsey had a very long, slender wrist; she
turned it to give the dog the delicate underside with its vulnerable ridges of tendon and vein. Midge's tongue became a
slippery wetness in her mouth.

This small silence was broken by crashing at the door.
Chelsey raised her head in surprise, and Midge made another
rush for the door and opened it wide. 'Good God: Lucy! Are
you all right?'

'No!' Lucy mounted a couple of steps. 'I've come here
straight from the Savoy Hotel. Georgiana's trying to black-
mail me, and Lorraine won't help.'

Like a lion, Chelsey bounded up from behind. 'What did
you say?' Raffles, following close after Chelsey, emitted a
muffled growl.

Lucy backed down the steps again and stared at Chelsey
and the dog in horror.

'Come inside – Midge, pull her in for heaven's sake; we
can't have things like that said in the street – come inside and
then, my girl, you'll repeat what you just said about
Georgiana, and you'll justify it.'

Lucy took herself into the house unaided, though she did
allow Midge to go down to fetch her backpack. From under her
lowered brow, she studied Chelsey. 'You were at Georgiana's
party on Saturday,' she said, 'but we weren't introduced.'

'So sorry, my dear.' Midge put down the bag and shuffled
closer. 'Chelsey, this is Lucy. Lucy, this is my dear old friend—'

'Oh, stuff it, Midge. Lucy, you have some explaining to do.
Come with me into the kitchen.'

Lucy was, if possible, blushing more furiously than ever,
but a fire of pure will shone in her eyes. 'I came to see her.'
She gestured towards Midge.

'First, let's have a drink together,' said Midge, rubbing her
hands. 'Then we'll be more relaxed and I'm sure it'll all get
sorted out.'

Chelsey, with a bow, gestured Lucy towards the kitchen. Lucy, looking about her with the air of someone noting landmarks against a future escape, went in with an attempt at a saunter and sat in the chair recently vacated by Chelsey. She folded her small, nailbitten hands on the table before her. Midge poured her an enormous neat whisky.

Nobody seemed in any hurry to start. Chelsey, sitting bolt upright on the wonky bench, Raffles in her folded arms, stared at Lucy in open hostility. Lucy took a slug of her drink, coughed, rushed to the sink for some water, then returned, red-eyed but still unspeaking, and drew patterns in the whisky she had spilled on the table. Midge was afflicted with waves of panic. She felt impossibly obligated to both women and shocked at herself for what she had felt for (and perhaps shown to) Chelsey only moments before. And to think that had happened while Lucy was desperate and trying to reach her. On Sunday and Monday, Midge had been in love with Lucy. Today, she had started to fall in love with Chelsey. Midge was, Midge decided, a toad. She hadn't even got up to bang Lucy on the back when she was choking with coughing.

But whatever she was, there was a crisis, and she had to do something. Midge hated being one of three. Even in the most casual grouping, there was always a two and an other. Midge's instinct was to avoid causing hurt to whoever was the other by taking on the role herself. She racked her brains to introduce a subject on which Lucy and Chelsey would be in agreement and on which she could take an opposing line and so draw the fire to herself. After thought, one possibility presented itself. 'Steven-John,' she said, 'has been most public-spirited about this whole business.'

'Balls,' said Chelsey.

Lucy looked up with puzzled brow, then down again at her doodles.

Midge realised that, even if Lucy remembered who Steven-John was, she was unlikely to know about his intervention in her drama. She tried again. 'I hope you're both getting on all right with this awful whisky.'

This time Lucy ventured a reply. 'It does seem a bit rough,' she said. Chelsey responded with a mocking laugh.

What was left, apart from 'lovely weather for the time of year'? Midge gave up. 'Do you two want to talk?'

'We do,' said Chelsey.

Midge looked at Lucy. Lucy, her golden eyes misted, looked at Midge and then the dog. 'Okay,' she said uncertainly.

'Right.' Midge got to her feet. The whisky rushed her and she steadied herself against the table. 'I'll be upstairs if anyone wants me. Riff-raff, come here, old girl.'

Midge tried hard to exchange a look with Lucy, but her head was bent low as with deep concentration she neatened the outlines of the labrys doodles now fencing off her corner of the table.

But when Midge came down again, about an hour later, Lucy, head still bowed, was talking in a low drone, and Chelsey, her minimal breasts rising and falling under heaving breaths, was stroking the almost-colourless soft fur at the back of Lucy's head. The whisky bottle was near half empty. Chelsey caught Midge's eye and gestured, with a flick of her chin, towards the door. Midge retreated through it and, though it was barely six o'clock in the evening, went back upstairs and for the want of any other occupation, unhappily to bed.

9

In Regent's Park, earlier that same afternoon, the other temporary threesome broke up. Steven-John, pleading male aversion to blood and suchlike viscous eruptions, left the scene of Fiona's embarrassment, dragging Jezebel, who was as fascinated as he was repelled. Conscious of the duties of friendship, he then telephoned Chelsey from a nearby phonebox, and crept back to within sight of the bench, to make sure that things were under control. Then he walked Jezebel home. He was very sorry for Fiona, and undefined anxieties about Ulric's ear kept rising in his consciousness, but these worries couldn't keep the lightness out of his step: Toby was taking the President of Malawi to Edinburgh that night, and Steven-John would have the rare pleasures of telephone, heating, carpets and, best of all, a dog on his bed.

Georgiana did have the situation well in hand. She had Fiona pinned to the bench and was wiping her face with a scented lace handkerchief moistened in the pond.

Chin butting like a child's, Fiona submitted to being dabbed at the corners of her mouth and around her brow. But after a few minutes she edged away. 'Thank you, Georgie,' she said, 'but I'd like you to go now.' There had been no further discussion of Steven-John's revelation.

Georgiana straightened her back. 'Are you sure, darling? I'd far rather stay, or drag you home with me for that cup of tea.'

'I know that.'

It wasn't necessary for Georgiana to insist. They both knew she would do anything that could be done in this world to help her friend. Without farewells, she handed Bonzo's lead to Fiona and left, her heels clipping the path with a stately measure. She didn't look back.

Nor did Fiona look after her. But when Georgiana was out of earshot, she dug her nails into her hair and moaned out loud, 'Oh my God, Oh my God.'

Darkness had closed over by the time Fiona and the dog, wet and cold after hours of walking through parks and streets she no longer recognised, got back to Gospel Oak. Fiona paused at the gate. Light streamed from the cottage windows and splintered on the path and garden. On the other side of the glass, the living room glowed like a jewel: the art nouveau mantelpiece surmounted by a mirror framed with painted lilies, the walls covered with watercolours and small oils, the low, rosy lamps, the faded patchwork quilt tossed over the back of the Tully's sofa. Fiona had made this beautiful room. But tonight it mocked her: the burly figure of Lorraine paced back and forth, and sentimental crooning sounded from the stereo.

Fiona hesitated, but for Bonzo home was home. He lifted the latch on the gate with his nose, romped up the path, pressed at the incompletely closed front door, and reappeared in the living room, leaping up to nuzzle Lorraine's neck. Fiona heard her greet him – 'Bonskowitztableski, dat dumb Bobo' – in a voice that gave no sign of recognition that the world had collapsed. Slowly, Fiona made her way inside, locked the door, unbuttoned her coat with dead fingers, and hung it several hooks away from Lorraine's.

Fiona heard a board creak and sensed Lorraine's presence at her back. She moved her camel hair one hook further down the line. She heard Lorraine clear her throat, sigh, shuffle her boots. Fiona, half buried in the heap of coats, busied herself with moulding them into a semblance of tidiness. Lorraine sighed again, then began to sing softly along with the stereo, still droning in the background. Fiona loathed Lorraine's way of singing blues, in a slurred cowboy drawl that welled up like bubbles in syrup. A sudden swipe of claustrophobia broke through Fiona's inertia. In fear that this would bring on another bout of nausea and leave her vulnerable to some hideous, cloying mothering from Lorraine, Fiona pulled free of the coats and pushed past, to the kitchen. Georgiana had recommended tea. Fiona would have tea.

But Lorraine followed, and leaned, now, against the kitchen door. She was silent, but the singing dribbled on, and Bonzo clattered in after. Fiona focused all her strength on the act of making tea. She poured water into the already rather full kettle, half emptied it to around the level it had held before and switched it on. Shoving Bonzo aside, she reached up for tea. The caddy slipped in her hand, and teabags scattered on the floor. Lorraine gathered them up, then laid them neatly on the table. Fiona moved forward and swept the little pile into the bin. Not a word had been spoken.

Fiona rinsed one mug, dug into the lower reaches of the caddy for a surviving teabag and dropped it into the puddle of sinkwater at the bottom of the mug. Mercifully, that soppy song had come to an end, though the speakers faithfully delivered into the kitchen the sound of the needle dropping back into its cradle and then the hum of the now idle hi-fi. Fiona rinsed the dog dish. She didn't fill it; to reach the tins of dog food she would have to turn towards the woman in the kitchen.

'So.' Lorraine's voice sliced across Fiona's nerves. 'I guess that's so.'

Fiona grasped the chilly edge of the sink.

'So. I guess – well – I guess you know.' Now Lorraine's voice was deep and rumbling as if recently disinterred.

Fiona concentrated hard at pouring the boiling water into the mug and not over her hand. 'I guess I know.'

'I had meant to tell you myself.'

The fridge was also in Lorraine's direction, so Fiona decided to do without milk. She fished out the teabag and took a sip of scalding brew. She still had her back to Lorraine.

'I've been wanting to tell you for some time. It was just never the right moment. Fiona, you must know this. It's not serious. It doesn't mean a thing.'

Fiona put down the mug. 'Please go away. Please leave me alone.'

'Give me a minute. Fiona, let me explain.'

Fiona realised that she had burned her mouth. Yet she needed the strength that came from tea. Georgiana was right. Tea was good, clean; it gave strength. She splashed cold water into the mix. 'There's no need. I know.'

'Fifi. Please, darling.' Lorraine put a tentative hand on the edge of Fiona's sleeve.

Fiona jumped. 'Don't touch me!'

'Sorry.' Lorraine stepped back.

There was another long silence. But Lorraine had broken the icy grip which kept Fiona at the sink, staring only into its seamy depths or at the blackened glass of the kitchen window. Fiona could now busy herself with getting the dog's supper ready. She made her way to the larder. Bonzo abandoned Lorraine and came over to Fiona. Lorraine tried to become involved, hauling the can-opener out of the drawer. Fiona ignored the offering and opened the tin instead with the blunt spiky thing they had, in their days of innocence a thousand years ago, used to make jagged tears in cans of beans when out camping.

'Fifi, please just say one thing. Who told you – was it Georgiana?'

Suddenly Fiona was galvanised. 'How could it matter who told me? You've destroyed my life. That's what matters, at least to me. But since you think it worthy of thought, you might at least have sensed that Georgiana wouldn't dirty her mouth with a message of that kind. Steven-John told me. And I thank him for it.'

'Steven-John! How did it get to that gossipy old bag?'

Fiona breathed hard. 'Perhaps you'd better ask him. I can't be bothered to go into all the sleazy details of how your little drama has Georgiana's crowd completely agog. Do you mind moving, so that I can go to bed?'

Lorraine slid aside, making way.

'And put this muck in the dog's bowl, will you.' Fiona handed over the can. 'But don't send him upstairs. By alone I mean alone.'

Later, around the time the rest of the world was watching *Eastenders*, Bonzo padded quietly into the room and pushed his wet nose into Fiona's neck. So Lorraine had, after all, sent her go-between. Fiona shoved him off and pulled the covers up tighter. Bonzo, with a sigh, lay down on the rug beside her. She ignored him. She made futile efforts to force herself to sleep.

Minutes later, Lorraine followed. Fiona lay on her side, knees bunched tight, covered up to the ears. Like Bonzo before her, Lorraine reached out to touch. 'Do you mind?' she muttered.

Fiona did, but she was too exhausted to explain that, or anything. She merely said, in a tone that sounded dreary even to herself, 'I hope you remembered to switch off the stereo.'

Lorraine chose to interpret this as an invitation to stay. She crawled in behind Fiona, plucked at a corner of the duvet and pulled an inch of covering over herself. Then, picking out words as if they grew among thorns, she began once again to explain herself. Fiona was too weary even to block her ears. Though she was barely conscious of Lorraine's story, Fiona registered that Lorraine was deeply moved by it for her voice thickened with tears.

'Now you're weeping,' said Fiona drably. 'I should be weeping. I'm not. I'm just completely wiped out. Don't waste breath justifying yourself. I don't blame you. I've had this coming to me.'

'No, darling, no,' cried Lorraine, drawing closer but not touching. 'You've done no wrong. It's me. I've been a complete fool, and it's been over nothing. It's finished. I'll end it with her first thing in the morning.'

A small flicker of feeling rose briefly somewhere in Fiona's belly – not anger, not pity, certainly not love for Lorraine – a curiosity that it now mattered not one jot whether Lorraine ended it in the morning, or ever. Absolutely nothing was the centre of it, for absolutely nothing mattered.

'Better still, I'll go straight downstairs and phone her. She won't be surprised.'

Fiona groaned at the thought of all that fuss. 'Do what you like.'

'I just need to work out whether to tell her to get lost, or to admit that I've made a terrible mistake, and have now come to my senses.'

'Do what you want to do; it's nothing to me.'

'Okay, I'll phone.' Lorraine made a move to rise. 'It'll be better all round if I make it absolutely unambiguous, don't you think? I'll just say I never want to see her again.'

'For heaven's sake: don't try to *tell* me. I won't hear another word about this sordid business.'

'My mistake.' Laboriously, Lorraine rose, picked up her shoes and, seating herself at the furthest end of the bed, began to fiddle with the laces, undoing and redoing the knots.

'Before you go downstairs,' drawled Fiona, 'perhaps you had better tell me just one thing – not about your inner anguish, but what's been going on.'

Why had she said that? Was she, in some awful sadistic part of herself, wanting to squeeze a little more contrition out of Lorraine or a little more anger out of herself? Finding herself infuriated by what Lorraine had to say before she had even opened her mouth, Fiona made ready to stifle her ears with the duvet.

'Um.' Lorraine now had the shoes on her feet and the laces

in her hands. She began to smooth out the kinks in them. 'I found I sort of fancied Lucy. I don't know why or even quite how it happened, out of the blue. I don't know what got into me. I certainly wasn't looking for anything.'

'Don't tell me *why*. I know *why* you fancied someone, even if the choice doesn't give me a high opinion of your taste. Tell me this: have you been to bed with her?'

'Well, she seemed sort of needy, and I, I guess, somehow I kissed her. Later I sort of . . .'

'*Sort of* fucked her?'

'Well, sort of . . .'

'How many times?'

Lorraine moved uncomfortably. 'I don't know. Maybe two or three.'

Fiona doubled, trebled, quadrupled the figure. 'Was it *sort of* good?'

'No. She was clueless.'

'But it was exciting?'

'Exciting?' Lorraine seemed to find the word obscure. 'I suppose.'

Fiona threshed at the covers. 'Shit!' She seized the pillow, thumped it and pulled it over her head. She kept very still. So did Lorraine.

Then, inching the pillow aside, Fiona drawled: 'Did you touch her screw her ride her or suck her?'

Lorraine's reply was a whisper. 'I don't want to say.'

'Say it, damn you, say it. I don't need you, or anyone. But I need to know.'

'The sex wasn't important.'

'You're lying. The sex was hugely important. I can smell it on you.' Fiona lifted a corner of the pillow to look at Lorraine. She had her shoelaces wound tight enough around her fingers to cause gangrene. 'Or perhaps it wasn't,' added Fiona in a small cruel voice. 'She wouldn't compromise her radical feminist principles just for cute little Lorraine, would she?' Fiona stared in hostility at Lorraine's hands. 'Penetration would be off the menu, being, in her words,

'male imitating". That must have left you – to coin a phrase –
high and dry.'

'Fiona. Stop it.'

'Or maybe you didn't mind. Maybe you go into one of your
stone butch acts with her. I hope not. They're seriously
boring.'

'We did nothing much. And I was seriously boring.'

'That's not true! I knew it. You *are* lying. You're a creepy
wormy slimy liar; even now you're lying to me, with your
good little girl, tiny mistake act.'

'I'm not lying. I was – I don't know what – somehow lonely,
and she seemed, like I said, needy.'

'God, can't you see how much worse that makes it? You're
involved with her; you're emotionally involved. You're in love
with her.'

'I'm not. I'm absolutely not. I fancied her for a moment.
Now I never want to see her again. And that's what I'm going
to tell her.'

Fiona didn't reply. Another silence fell. Lorraine, very
secretly, slid along the bed. Her hand crept towards Fiona's
shoulder and touched. With a spasm of rejection, Fiona threw
it off. Then, again lifting the pillow a fraction, she snarled:
'Did you come?'

'No.'

'Did you try to?'

'No.'

Fiona lay still. Of course Lorraine didn't; at that stage, she
wouldn't have needed anything so common and physiological.
The feel of Lucy's breast under her hand, the closeness,
warmth, smell, the rhythm of heartbeat and breath of their
lovemaking, and – worse than what they did with their
bodies – what they did with their minds, struck Fiona with
new waves of nausea. She fought them, struggling again for
anger, to make one fixed point. 'Did *she* come?'

'Fiona, this isn't what it was about. It was momentary,
trivial; it's over. It doesn't change anything, anything between
us.'

'I asked a question. Did she?'

'No.'

Fiona laughed. 'So you're incompetent as well as cheap, as well as cowardly, as well as faithless, as well as – Shit! – get out of my bed.'

Lorraine, sobbing now, rose to her feet, but only to reach for the box of tissues. Then she sat again on the edge of the bed. They still had their backs to each other. 'Fiona, I love you. You're my life, my lifeline. I've never loved anyone, ever, like I love you. I didn't come alive until I loved you. I've been so stupid, so terribly stupid. But, truly, when it first started, it seemed good for us.'

'Really? So you did this thing for us, out of pure kindness to me?'

Lorraine again picked up the laces and looped them, in a noose knot, around her neck. 'No, I can't say that, but it did liven me up. I didn't get so upset – well for a while I didn't feel upset at all about – about –'

'– about my foul moods.'

'Well, yes, I do understand; I know you're having a hard time –'

'But I'm dragging you down.'

'No!' Lorraine started. 'No, of course not.' Then she seemed uncertain how to continue. 'Once that business had sort of spruced me up, you see, I loved you better; I was a better lover, too. Remember Sunday afternoon, after we'd been quarrelling? You said you felt healed. That was only two days ago.'

'Oh my God.' Fiona's head once more disappeared under the pillow. 'It was. You came to me when in your mind you were going to someone else. How stupid; I had no idea at all that you were giving me something fraudulent.'

They talked until late. At certain moments, Fiona almost forgot what trouble it was that kept them talking. Their talk became elliptical, reaching out to include memories of the unborn lives they had lived before they met each other. At one point, Fiona confessed to Lorraine that she too had fancied someone recently, just before her menopause began. But she had not pursued. She had allowed herself a couple of weeks of fantasy, and then she had let the feeling die of lack of action. All that remained of regret was the knowledge that, because she was a married woman, she would never again have the excitement of going to bed with someone for the first time. Perhaps what they ought to do, she said then, was both to have a bit on the side, like the boys do. But let them do it together. Let them first revise their marriage code, draw up new rules with great caution so that whatever followed could be contained within their shared life. Let them vet each other's affairs; let them choose people who were not dangerous; let it be a fun thing – not this Lucy, this clever serious solitary young woman from another world.

But such moments were brief. Lorraine, sharp as a lawyer in launching at any soft spot into which she could drive her argument, was too bold, too nakedly fighting for a 'not guilty' verdict. Despite herself, despite her wish, for all the horror of the present, to give the earth a chance to return to its normal orbit, Fiona could not give this to her.

They ended in each other's exhausted arms, with nothing resolved. Lorraine did, indeed, repeat her promise to give Lucy up first thing in the morning. Fiona said that was irrelevant. What had been broken could not be put together again: never again would she be able to trust any human being.

10

*Marylebone, Tuesday night, 25 October, to
the weekend*

That Tuesday night, while Fiona and Lorraine faced the terrible fragility of marriage, and Midge, sleepless because sober,
was assaulted by distrust even of her closest friends, Ulric
flew into a panic about his health.

All evening, the buzzing in his ear grew louder, till by midnight his most acute fear was of an electrical explosion. He
tried to rinse out the honey (in case it was host to hyperactive
bees), and his whole head felt as if it was bursting into flame.
Reeling with panic, he reached for the telephone, desperate
enough now to call his doctor. Sudden inspiration came:
Steven-John was within reach; he was spending the night at
Toby's flat. Ulric dialled and within two rings heard Steven-
John's gravelly 'hello'. Within the next minute, Steven-John
had written off the delights of Toby's bathroom and insisted
on dashing over to Marylebone. Another twenty minutes and
he had arrived: Ulric had paid the taxi; Jezebel, whining with
indignation, had been confined to the lobby; and Steven-
John, exuding the calm of someone who had been in
meditation for hours, was seated at Ulric's bedside, on the
petit-point footstool embroidered by Ulric's mother.

Ulric, enrobed in a purple gown and with a towel knotted about his ears, now lay flat on his back on the vast bed, giving a striking resemblance to a recently expired monarch.

At the appropriate time, Steven-John inched off his bottom and loosened the towel. He peered into the ear, touched it, tutted, and then did a little laying on of hands. Ulric opened an eye. He began to feel more comfortable. 'Perhaps the honey is helping after all?' he said pathetically.

'Ulric, old chap' – Steven-John straightened his spine – 'how about me giving a quick ring to your doctor-fellow?'

'No!' This came out in a wail. 'Oh-o-o' replied the echo in Ulric's head.

'Okay'; Steven-John sat down again. 'I guess it's a bit after hours.' Then he leapt to his feet. 'Maybe a quick word with Sarah and Sophie?'

'What?' Ulric opened an indignant eye.

'Well, they're nurses, and everybody knows it's nurses who really understand things – not doctors, those pill-pushers.'

Ulric shuddered. 'Nurses are needle-pushers.'

Steven-John sat down. 'Okay.' But within a minute, he was again on his feet. 'I'll ring for a taxi.'

'No-o!' Ulric was now overwhelmed with horror at the thought that Steven-John might be planning to abandon him.

'Just a short run, no more than a couple of quid's worth, to take us to Casualty, let someone have a recce round your ear and whatnot.'

'Waiting for hours in a mob of drunks and howling babies? No!'

'Okay.' Steven-John sat down again. 'I take your point, but you do get a better class of drunk at the Royal Free Hospital in Hampstead . . .'

Fifteen minutes later, they were in a taxi and Jezebel's howling was resounding through the Marylebone block. The 'quick recce' turned into two hours of queuing to see a junior doctor, followed by several hours wandering the long corridors waiting for the regular medical staff to arrive in the morning, then several consultations, a visit to the

Haematology Department and finally to the terrifying Oncology Department for a further consultation and more tests. They returned to Marylebone thoughtful and very tired, although Steven-John charged up the stairs as soon as they came within earshot of the dog.

Steven-John took Jezebel – now snapping at people in the lift and generally determined to display her outrage – home in yet another taxi. He consoled her as best he could, and left a note for Toby saying that there were serious worries about Ulric. Then he collected the hospital's prescribed ear ointment from the chemist and returned to his post at Marylebone. He and Ulric spent a quiet day, the start of the long wait for test results from the hospital.

Evening came. Steven-John, still posted on the footstool, watched the evanescent halos of car headlights swell and fade around the interlaced birds of paradise embroidered in the fabric of Ulric's bedroom curtains. He listened to the tides of external sound – starlings settling into the eaves for the night, the roar of the rush-hour, police sirens – city noises. Occasionally, he heard a rumbling from his stomach, and thought about food. He thought about Jezebel and his blackbirds. At some moments, he thought about the transience of life; at others, he allowed himself a brief catnap. He wondered about the efficacy of prayer. He did not think about the descent of the hospital consultant's tone into an awful solemnity when he looked at the blood test report.

Ulric too was listening: to the thump, thump, thump in his ear, which had reacted badly to the experience. His thoughts were angry. He was awash with disgust and shame. When he was sixteen and his mother had been the patient, he had been quelled by Hospital. Then it had seemed not so much a locality as a condition combining the solemnity of church with that of courtroom and morgue. Now he found everything about Hospital abhorrent and demeaning. All that poking and prodding. How underworld pale everybody was, and friable, like sweating cheese. How shamelessly the inmates walked about,

more than naked with so much of what belonged to their
insides exposed on the outside: bags of urine dangling at their
knees, teeth on bedside cabinets, wounds oozing through
dressings. How they shuffled in queues, quiet as lambs being
loaded onto abattoir trucks. Mortality was most hideously
conveyed by the odours: the nicotine breath of the porter; the
menstrual breath of the nurse; the acid-stomach breath of the
doctor; the whisky-under-mouthwash breath of the consultant
– smells sprayed into the face then dissolving into the envi-
ronmental smell of blood, vomit, pus, faeces and drains,
blended and preserved in the saccharine stench of disinfectant.
How disgusting the place was; how futile its ambition; how
utterly without hope or grace were the medical professionals.
A body was well, or it was ill. Either way, it was the business
of God. But for better or for worse, the hospital had put his
ear on the agenda, and nothing would ever be the same again.

At the time Steven-John was searching for a delicate way
to raise the subject of supper, Ulric asked the necessary question: 'How do you think it went?'

Steven-John looked up mildly.

Ulric was patient. 'How do you think the biopsy went?'

'I was hugely relieved when they agreed to let you know
the results by telephone, and first thing on Monday.'

'Since I refuse ever to go anywhere near that germ-ridden
sewer again,' responded Ulric stiffly, 'their choice was to give
me the results by phone or not at all.'

'Yes.' Steven-John paused. 'Though I have some doubts
about the way we played it. I wonder if we ought at least to
have considered letting them keep you in for a few days.'

'Consistency, Steven-John,' Ulric raised his head an inch,
'never was your strong point. At the time they were trying to
bully me into getting into one of their disgusting beds, you
fought even harder than I. You insisted that you could look
after me best. You called yourself my "partner".'

Steven-John, slow and calm as ever, said: 'I was angry
with them, and that stopped me seeing that they were trying
to help. I was wrong.'

'You were right; and I enjoyed your act, playing it so butch while being so maternal.'

Steven-John rose to his feet: 'Camomile tea with rice crackers, mashed banana and Branston Pickle,' he said in his butchest growl.

'Just tea, please. But only when you've told me how you think the tests went.'

Steven-John shook his head.

'Okay, if you won't say it, I will. I'll give you the test results, right now: we don't have to wait till Monday.' Ulric pressed his hands together in the attitude of prayer inherited from the good Father Peter, and stared close at the tips of his bony fingers. 'Their first thought is that I'm developing AIDS.'

'You aren't, of course.' Steven-John's reply came fast.

'Correct. I am not.'

Steven-John nodded uncertainly.

'They also admit the possibility,' continued Ulric, 'that I might have a bacterial infection, perhaps from some member of the staphylococcus tribe.'

'Very likely,' snapped Steven-John.

'Unfortunately not likely enough; that doesn't cover the swollen glands, weepy eye, repeated colds and the lassitude. What I do have is what they investigated at my request. I don't know why I asked them to do it; perhaps only to show how dumb they are.' He shook his head clear of the towel. 'Or maybe I did want them to prove something. I am full of doubt. I am equally full of fear: of pain, of deafness and of losing my voice. But now I know. I really know. That last test will be positive. I have what my mother had. I have cancer.'

Steven-John started: 'I can't let you jump to conclusions like that. It could be any of many things. You have to wait for the hospital to give the results.'

'Why? I know. Those scruffy white coats, ragged finger-nails, cryptic notes scribbled on pads of Bronco lavatory paper confirmed what I've known for years but hadn't allowed myself to think. I've known it was waiting for me and would take me when I was the age she was when it got her. We both knew. I was then sixteen. She was fifty. Now I'm fifty. I didn't need the tests.'

Steven-John made a throaty sound. 'You're in an unsettled emotional state. I can't believe your mother knew – or thought – anything of the kind.'

'She didn't say it, but she knew.' Ulric unpaired his hands and stretched them out. 'I remember exactly when she passed this knowledge on to me. It was when she'd been dead about fifteen minutes.'

Steven-John looked uneasy. He believed in ghosts as he believed in everything, but preferred not to cultivate their acquaintance. 'We must stop this talk. We just don't know.' In a firmer voice, he added, 'Anyway, men don't get breast cancer, at least hardly ever.'

'I didn't specify the variety,' said Ulric mildly. 'And if I had a choice, it would certainly not be that; my preference is for something of the elegantly wasting order.' He smiled. 'It should deplete one's strength sufficiently for leisure to be a necessity, but not so much that one doesn't have energy to think. It ought not to be painless, since without pain one would lose the immanence, but the pain should be varied and interesting. And its progress should be sufficiently slow and predictable for me to complete my work. I'll go for leukaemia. Would that be consistent with my symptoms?'

Steven-John looked at his feet. 'I won't have any part in this speculation. We must wait.'

'We'll wait if you want to wait,' said Ulric, now almost gaily, 'but how long do I have to wait for my tea?'

Steven-John shot off to the kitchen. The light was snapped on and a vigorous clattering ensued.

Ulric noted that he was teasing and embarrassing his friend, and gave him Brownie points for courage. Then, the brightness in his eyes fading, he turned away. The last consultant they had seen, a fellow who was too pretty to be regarded as a fool, had glanced at Ulric's blood test and then, without hesitation, agreed to Ulric's suggestion of a biopsy. Ulric knew, of course he knew. But he needed another human also to know in order to believe. How strange that this should be a necessity; how odd that one can know something, yet be unable to make it part of one's consciousness until another creature as fallible as oneself also knew it. Ulric stared at the far wall of his bedroom. Intermittent illumination from the passing headlights showed that it was lined, floor to ceiling across some 16 feet, with big square cardboard cartons. Column by column, Ulric traced the boxes. Each was labelled in Father Peter's neat hand: 'Smaller Chinese vases', 'Tapes of *The Messiah*', 'Spare pyjamas', 'duplicate scores', 'Teddy bears', 'File copies of recordings', 'Spode and Minton pieces', 'Documents and awards'. His history, pre-packaged, was ready for the archive, and he would leave behind a record typical of any genteel queer. What was he, if anything more? How had he allowed his fifty years to slip so casually through his fingers? If it was all over, why did he still have a good voice? Why did he still want to be admired and, more, loved, and more still to produce music that he knew to be in him but never yet expressed?

Down below, in Old Marylebone Road, a car was approaching. Into his sick ear came the sound of its engine, so like the swell of applause, from the first nervy clapping to the passionate roar. No such sound in the archive. That was a place of silence, immobility, timelessness. Ulric's person would shrink to a handful of ashes and his only solid presence in this world would be this wall of boxes – these things that he, in ten years, hadn't even bothered to unpack. Ulric's adam's apple rose towards his jaw, then slid back.

Perhaps, after all, it was the staphylococcus. The thought brought first relief and then the dull weight of anticlimax and depression.

Steven-John padded in and laid the tea (from the scent liberally doused with honey) on his bedside table. Depression gave way to irritation at Steven-John's pussy-footing. 'Is this,' he said savagely, 'what they give you on Death Row?'

'It'd be nice to think they had something so comforting.'

'I don't want comfort.' Ulric turned to Steven-John. 'I want you to needle me into making some sense of this transient state ludicrously labelled "life". I want you to stop patronising me.' Ulric was aware that he was unfair to Steven-John. He didn't care.

'Seems to me', Steven-John repositioned himself on the footstool, 'that you're needling yourself well enough.'

'But not getting the point.' Ulric laced his long fingers over his face in his familiar clerical gesture.

'Try to wait: for the results of course, but more for the voices that will speak to your mind.'

'Oh,' Ulric shook his head slightly, 'I'm hearing them all right. Every single damn one gabbles something different.'

Steven-John's hand, reaching over to cover Ulric's bony knuckles, seemed soft, small and powerless as a girl's.

Ulric endured this light embrace for a moment before shaking his hand free. 'This whole business smells of fraud to me,' he said in his old prissy tone. 'I can't bring myself to accept that that clapboard laboratory could produce any momentous truth.'

Tutting, Steven-John placed the porcelain cup of cooling camomile tea in Ulric's hand.

'Do you know,' continued Ulric, with a critical glance at the saucerless vessel, 'when that haematology technician was scribbling on his pad of lavatory paper, I could swear I saw dirt under his fingernails.'

'They do make mistakes,' said Steven-John.

'I've no doubt they do.' Ulric nodded. 'Unfortunately, I doubt if I could believe them whatever they said. Uncertainty is my life condition. Doubt, scepticism; that's my nature. I want to forget all about that damn hospital. It's from some other starting point that I've got to needle my way into this thing.'

'Let your mind go quiet; don't try to direct your thoughts.'

Ulric did this, or something of the like, while Steven-John's chin sank gently onto his breastbone. But it jerked up sharply when Ulric spoke again:

'I can't say I'm ready to die, but I'm as ready as I'll ever be. This has to do with my mother. The whole of my life is bound up with hers. Even when she was dead, she was my mentor. For so many years, whenever I was losing, I could comfort myself with her presence, her being there, waiting. Even when Peter was around there were times I believed she was the only person I could love. There's that verse, know it? —

> *"My love lies underground,*
> *with her face upturned to mine,*
> *and her mouth unclosed in the long last kiss*
> *that ended her life and mine."'*

Steven-John nodded. He had heard these lines from Ulric before, during that first terrible year after Peter.

'But now that I really believe that I will die — insofar as I believe anything — I feel I'm letting her down. My faith has gone. I can't believe this is the real thing. It's too drab; it's tedious. I don't even feel sick enough. I'm fed up with it already.'

Steven-John summoned a jovial tone. 'All we know for certain is that you have a sore ear. When we get the results, things will become real; we'll know what to do. Whatever they say, it'll be better to know.'

With a fastidious move, Ulric laid the tea, as yet untasted, on the bedside cabinet. 'Steven-John, your philosophy is delightful to me when you're talking about blackbirds. But I'm talking about death, my death. I've seen death and thought I knew it, but I can't get any purchase when I try to think of my own. I feel stupid, and when you say things that are banal and expect them to give comfort, I feel angry as well as stupid.'

'Let's try to wait.'

'I am waiting. I am ludicrously engaged in waiting for what that hospital has to say. Yet I don't believe that it has one single thing to offer me. The only time I could take them seriously was when at the very end that clown in the white coat said I should prepare for some possibly very momentous news.'

Steven-John knew that Ulric had, in fact, been impressed by this 'clown', the oncologist they had at last become important enough to see. Steven-John, however, had been so stricken by jealousy of this handsome and athletic man that he took a poor view of his medical capabilities.

'So what do you think I've got?' said Ulric, accusingly.

Steven-John half smiled. 'That's the same question as you asked me before. I said then we should wait.'

'What's your feeling?'

'My feeling isn't worth anything till we know.'

'I only want to know your feeling, not its worth.'

'I don't know myself what it is.'

'You do. You feel that I've got – what? *Say* it. Say the word.'

'I can't. I don't know.'

'You do.' Ulric was angry. 'At least *I* know what you feel. And I insist that you say it.'

Steven-John sighed. 'You think that I think – which I insist I do not think – that you have, um –'

'Um what?' roared Ulric.

'Cancer.'

'Cancer. Thank God you said it. Cancer! I don't *think* I have cancer; I *know* I have cancer. Cancer. Cancer. And my hope is that it will be kinder to me than it was to her, and give me time enough to finish my work.'

Steven-John's whole body surged forward into an embrace with the slippery skirts of the purple gown. This, being silk, spread the girlish tears that flowed onto it all over Ulric's knee.

Steven-John stayed over on Wednesday night, making a bed of the chaise longue in Ulric's music room. On Thursday morning, he subjected Jezebel to a brisk run round the park, which left him with a stitch in his side and her in a state of high dudgeon about the skimping on protocol. Later, he went out with Ulric's shopping list. Each time, he was away for little more than an hour, but Ulric awaited his return in fear, lest it did not happen.

Over the weekend, Steven-John's absence was more prolonged; to Ulric, it seemed very long indeed. He went back to Kentish Town to feed his blackbirds and the villainous youth who had now taken up residence in his doorway. He returned with flowers (acquired by the youth) and his little book of Buddhist meditations. In between, he spread his presence over the prim flat, covering the stainless steel surfaces of Ulric's kitchen with scatterings of wild rice and the creatures that crawled out of his organic vegetables, and making liberal use of the telephone extension in Ulric's music room.

By Monday morning, Ulric felt so much stronger that he got up to clean the washbasin after Steven-John's incompetent efforts at shaving, and decided not to cancel his teaching engagement for the afternoon. And he was beginning to think that – after the phone call for which they were both waiting – it would be time for his dear friend to go home.

His ear had so much improved that the piercing shriek of the phone, when it came, shocked him into paralysis. Steven-John answered. 'Hello,' he said in his slow gravelly rumble.

The bell-like clarity of the voice of the Honourable Toby Hume filled the room. 'Ulric, that can't be you?'

Ulric took the phone.

Toby continued. 'I hear you're a tidge under the weather, old girl.'

'A tidge.'

'Not the old immune system, I hope?'

'Isn't it always the immune system?'

'What a bugger.' Toby's voice swelled with sympathy. 'But you can take it from me, it's not the end of the world.'

'I am not familiar with the way the world ends,' replied Ulric stiffly.

'Nor am I, thank God, but it's in my thoughts. To say truth – it's been a closely guarded secret till now – I've got the same problem. I was flattened by the news at first, but now, six years down the line, I'm still fit as a flea, and keeping Malaysia's economy booming with my consumption of latex.'

'I'm glad for you,' said Ulric coldly.

'So am I, my dear. There's something to be gained from being able, each day, to look your last on all things lovely.'

'Look on what?' Ulric's glance caught Steven-John's furrowed and sweaty brow.

'Give yourself time to deal with the shock, until the condition seems almost normal. Then look at what remains of life: amazing. Each day opens like a miracle; every challenge is a game. For me, the biggest problem is to get the bats of the AIDS industry out of my hair. They want everybody to mingle in some New-Age maypole dance. Gruesome, my dear.'

Ulric frowned at the telephone. 'You're talking about dedicated people who do an excellent job.'

'Oh yes, you do get the odd Princess Diana type. But those clinics and therapy what-have-yous are crawling with worthy lesbians. And you know me. I do my maypole dancing deep in the hedges.'

Ulric's face turned stony. 'I think I'd better put you straight.' He wrenched his glance away from Steven-John's brow. 'I'm not infected with HIV or any virus as far as I know.'

'Oh?' Toby's voice paled.

'I've got an ear infection. I appear to be hosting bacteria called staphylococci which are giving me a deal of bother but will, in due course, yield to antibiotics.'

Steven-John, his mouth open, stared at Ulric's averted face. Toby's face was hidden from them, but his shock was clear from the silence that followed. Eventually, the voice on the telephone said, 'Well, I appear to have been misinformed. Apologies.'

'Who was your informant?'

'Oh, one of the Georgiana crowd.'

'Chelsey?'

'As a matter of fact, yes. What a bugger. I'm going to have to reconsider my faith in her psychic sense.'

'Psychic garbage.'

'So it would seem.' Again Toby paused. 'But I'm pleased and relieved to be corrected. Get well soon.'

When Ulric put the phone down, Steven-John, now stiffly upright and with one arm thrust into the sleeve of his anorak, said: 'Why did you lie to him? I believed you were serious about trying to make sense of life, and death.'

Ulric faced his friend coldly. 'Yes, I am. But it'll be my sense because it's my life. Not Toby's, not even yours. My maypole dance will be a solo.'

Steven-John shifted his feet. 'I don't really mind about the lie; but how could you be so mean when Toby was so generous? He gave up this important secret just to help you; what do you think that cost him? Why did you have to be so cruel?' He thrust the other arm angrily into the sleeve. 'And you're wrong about Chelsey. She does have a psychic sense, a real one. Its weakness is that she can only see the bad.'

'Steven-John,' said Ulric with an evident fraying of patience, 'your theories come out of an admirably warm heart. But I don't owe Toby one damn thing; I didn't ask him to sacrifice his dignity. Nor do I think any clairvoyant sense led Chelsey to this. I think it was your gossip.'

Steven-John sat down again, abruptly. 'You know I rang everybody when you needed friends. It wasn't gossip. It was concern.'

'That is the problem precisely stated. You'll have everybody concerned and involved, everybody steering my life in every direction. I haven't got time to comfort my comforters. Not even you.'

Before Steven-John could reply, the telephone rang again. Ulric picked it up himself, and nodded in response to the inaudible drone.

'That will do well enough,' he said, 'just the results please. I don't need to know how sorry you are to have to give them to me.'

Ulric's face was marble, as the voice, inaudible to Steven-John despite his best efforts, droned on.

'Yes thank you,' said Ulric. Then, after more mutterings on the line, he added: 'Since you have no cause to suspect spread to the throat or the lungs, I have no wish to take chemotherapy, nor to make any further appointments. I will inform my GP myself, thank you. Would you like me to reimburse you for the cost of this telephone call?'

He put the phone down.

Steven-John looked hard at him.

Ulric stretched flat on the bed, and pulled up the covers. 'If you don't get back to your dratted blackbirds and derelicts pretty soon, I'm going to start charging you rent.'

'What did they say?'

'I told you last week what they'd say.'

'Did they say you had – um?'

'I have um and um and um, and there's no damn sense in any of it.'

Steven-John fell on his knee beside the bed. 'There's your singing. Don't forget you have so much more to do.'

Ulric turned away. 'There'll be no more music from me. I've got nothing to say.'

'Oh Ulric,' Steven-John restrained himself from throwing himself on his friend, 'you have, you have so much.'

'If I do, I'll do it when I'm alone. Now go. For Christ's sake, Go.'

'I'll go, but will you remember, anytime, anytime at all; whenever you need me . . .'

'Thanks. I'll bear it in mind. And you bear in mind that, whenever your hormones thrill at the sound of a telephone, I would most earnestly beg you to keep your rosy lips shut.'

As Steven-John made for the door, Ulric called after him: 'Do me one more favour will you? Phone Toby. Say something consoling: say I've got staphylococci on the brain – or something more imaginative if you can bend your high principles to it. And then, clear out.'

✻

The pavements Steven-John trod as he made his way from Marylebone to Toby's flat at Regent's Park, were barely recognisable through his tears. Steven-John was terribly afraid for Ulric and, though he couldn't say why, for himself. He was wounded. Though large in love, he was limited in experience. He didn't know that it is probably not possible to face death with any durable composure.

11

At lunch-time of the day after Fiona had found out, Lorraine set off to St James's Park determined to end the liaison, cleanly and firmly. As soon as Lucy arrived, she blurted out her statement: 'Lucy: Fiona knows. Steven-John told her yesterday. I'm sorry, but it couldn't develop as you hoped, and now I have no choice. I have to stop seeing you.'

Lucy didn't react as Lorraine expected. She gave Lorraine a socking great kiss, in view of half the British civil service. 'Don't worry; we'll sort it out with Fiona. This is terrific news.' She shook Lorraine's hand wildly. 'Now we can be honest women, all of us.'

Lorraine managed, with difficulty, to dissuade Lucy from charging round to talk things over with Fiona, but nothing could convince her that the affair was over.

That evening, Lorraine assured Fiona that she'd end it the very next day. Fiona, pounding metal at her workbench till late, didn't even pause to listen.

On Thursday Lorraine revised the breaking-up speech. 'Lucy,' she began, as they walked along the trafficky perimeter of the park, the part least favoured by the civil service, 'I've *got* to end it, I can't do this to Fiona.'

This didn't work either. Lucy, her face bright red with anger, replied: 'Well, you can't do it to me either. Fiona isn't stupid, and nor am I. I'll finish with you when it's over, but it isn't. You haven't given Fiona any chance to hear my side of it.'

At the Gospel Oak cottage that night, she told Fiona she had already ended it. It wasn't, she thought, exactly a lie, more an advance on the truth. Because on Friday she would definitely, definitely do it, unilaterally if Lucy wouldn't co-operate. All evening, Lorraine hovered over the phone, in a state of lively terror that Lucy might call Fiona.

Lorraine *had* to do it. But honourable withdrawal was dif-ficult. Lucy would fight. This could be very public and very unpleasant indeed.

Lorraine set off to work on Friday, threshing about to find some way to resolve the dilemma. As she sat stewing in the traffic, the thermometer of her tinny van rising towards the red, she found the problem more complicated at every turn. Lucy *had* improved her life. With Lucy in her blood, instinct led her to ways to calm Fiona – not her old clumsy attempts not to notice rebuffs, not the false-sounding effort to treat rudeness as some kind of joke. Lucy had given her the strength to move a little apart, and when the moment came, to be tender.

There were still moods, but not all the time, not hopeless, involuntary, chasms of miscomprehension that neither of them could bridge. Sex too had improved. In the year before Lucy, this had only happened after a quarrel or a movie. It had been hard, dry sex: Lorraine anxious; Fiona, ice in the head, flame in the crotch, coming quickly to a heartless orgasm; both falling asleep without pillow talk after. Lucy made it possible for them to be real lovers again.

Why, Lorraine asked herself, couldn't she be allowed to nourish her love for Fiona by feeding it from Lucy? Why couldn't she take Lucy in measured doses, like a tonic? Why couldn't she keep Lucy in some safe separate place? If Lucy could only be persuaded to be discreet, she could be true both to Fiona and to Lucy.

When she reached the official car park in the Horse Guards Parade Ground, Lorraine was beginning to think that perhaps she owed it to Fiona to keep up her liaison with Lucy. For Fiona's sake, she needed to keep herself alive and giving. Georgiana's snobby crowd knew how to deal with these things. You did what you had to do, but you did it with decorum so as not to frighten the horses. *That* was the message to get through to Lucy.

It was 10 o'clock on the morning of Toby's 9.30 meeting to discuss the results of the visit of the President of Malawi. The Protocol Department would have completed the pleasantries and be looking for a scapegoat for whatever had gone wrong with the world in the past half-hour. Lorraine sauntered towards the Disneyland towers and domes of Whitehall. She didn't care. She had at last reached a decision about breaking it off: she would do it and not do it.

She muttered the usual apology as she slid into her seat.

'Ah,' said Toby, with one of his sardonically impish grins. 'The traffic your way was, I presume, diabolical?'

That settled it. The world of propriety was so much junk. At lunch-time today, Lorraine would tell Lucy that the liaison could continue, for so long as Lucy acknowledged that secrecy was necessary and that Fiona came first.

The meeting rattled on, developing into the usual exchange of poisoned darts between the Principal Protocol Officer and his immediate junior (who was somebody's son, was treated as Toby's heir, and was venomously hated by the Principal). The Principal was relaying news that the President had invited a gaggle of British MPs to visit Malawi's nature reserves, to see that its government was concerned not only with human beings (proliferating like vermin) but also with (that sacred word) the Environment.

His junior proposed adding a few AIDS hospitals to the schedule to forestall press insinuations that the MPs were on safari at the taxpayer's expense.

The Principal (who had of course foreseen this patently obvious trap), proposed instead that the British mission be offered the opportunity to safeguard the taxpayer's interests by volunteering to travel economy class.

Toby found value in both proposals. The Principal was instructed to persuade the MPs to travel with the *hoi polloi*, and his junior to tip off the Malawi Government on smartening up its hospitals. 'Thus,' concluded Toby, 'we satisfy all parties.' The junior smiled, the Principal grunted, and everybody else around the table nodded blandly, as they always did when Toby pontificated. But Lorraine was thinking ahead. In her mind, Lucy had already accepted the new terms, and Lorraine was entertaining her with an account of the meeting which played on Toby's resemblance to Sir Cliff Richard. Unlike Fiona, Lucy could still enjoy Lorraine's stories.

Rain was seeping through the misty light and fell in blobs off the trees. Lucy, half an hour late and stony-faced with determination, marched over to Lorraine's bench. Lorraine's tale about Toby evaporated.

'Have you sorted it out? Does Fiona accept me now?' Lucy plopped down on the wet seat.

'Still a way to go.'

'Is it going to take as long as it took you to admit things to Fiona?'

Lorraine was not amused. For this, Fiona was suffering. Out of such adolescent point-scoring, Lorraine somehow imagined that she drew strength and vigour. She began to wonder if she really did want to end the affair. 'Last night,' she said, 'I told Fiona I had given you up.'

'You didn't!' Lucy turned to her. There were beads of rain or sweat on her brow. 'You couldn't!'

'I did. But I didn't mean it. Not, at least, in the obvious way.'

'What un-obvious way is there?'

'The traditional way.'

'Back to the secrets and lies? No!' said Lucy.

'No?'

'I won't end it, but there'll be no sex till we've got it sorted out.'

Lorraine, embarrassed, laughed. Not being a heterosexual male, she was unfamiliar with terms and conditions.

'You've had three days to sort out what can be done in three minutes. You're messing me and Fiona about.'

'Lucy, it'll take time, a lot of time, for Fiona to believe that my loving you is good for her too.'

'Everything hangs on you. What about her and me? How can she respect me when I'm nothing but your tart? How can I respect her when I'm cheating her?'

'Oh, here we go, haven't we heard this one somewhere before?'

Twenty minutes later, after all the familiar arguments, they came back to the starting point.

'Okay,' said Lucy, 'tell me exactly what you said to Fiona last night.'

'I told you what I said.'

'Not everything. Did you say you'd chucked me, ditched me, junked me?'

'Ended it.'

'Is that truly what you said?'

'Of course.'

'So you lie to Fiona but not to me? How can I believe that?'

Lorraine leapt to her feet. 'Believe what you like.'

'It's not what I like,' said Lucy softly, 'but I'm beginning to wonder if you really do want to give me up. If you do, I wish you'd say it.'

'No!' Lorraine grasped Lucy by the shoulders. Her small pale head seemed, tortoise-like, to be withdrawing into the carapace of her duffel coat. 'Please. I don't want to hurt you. I don't want to hurt either of you. I'm just terribly confused.'

'Why? Nobody will be confused about why you've done it.'

'Lucy, please, I don't want to walk out on you. I couldn't bear it.' As Lorraine spoke, a new thought bubbled up: if she did walk out on Lucy, there would be pain, but there would also be the most enormous relief.

Lucy struggled to her feet. 'You don't know what *you* can bear. You don't know what *you* will do. You. You. You. What about Fiona? What about me? Must we wait until you decide what our lives are to be?'

But I'm *not* going to —' Lorraine stopped herself. She was ready to do what she thought she could not do. She was going to give Lucy up. 'I'm so sorry.' She looked over the top of Lucy's head at the statue of the Duke of York teetering on its vertiginous column. 'But it has only been three weeks.'

'While' (Lucy's voice, by contrast to Lorraine's near whisper, blared) 'you and Fiona have been "married" for ten years.'

Lorraine could feel herself squirm, but she didn't take her eye off the Brave Old Duke who'd marched ten thousand men. How ironic that, at the very moment she was finally ready to give in to Lucy, Lucy chose to let her go. Lorraine was, with Lucy's assistance, giving Lucy up.

'So you lied when you said you loved me.' Lucy's voice was low, but angry. 'You lied when you dreamed about running away with me to the Maldives. Everything you did was false.'

Lorraine was afraid of Lucy's anger. She was particularly afraid of arousing it under the eye of half the British civil service. 'I think very highly of you and do, in spite of what you think, respect you. And it's been wonderful being with you. But I suppose I did lie when I said those things.'

Lucy didn't reply for a long time. She opened her backpack and took out a crumpled, fuzzy paper tissue. She made as if to blow her nose on it, but instead dabbed at her brow and then began, carefully, to wipe her hands. 'There is nothing – you know that – absolutely nothing left in my life if I lose you.' Her small, nailbitten fingers began to poke holes in the tissue. 'I don't have many options, because I find it hard to make friends. I don't know how to crack that shell, and when I do try, I seem to smash the egg, not open it. That's my problem, of course, not yours. But it does mean that when I am able to give my love, it's a very big thing. I've never really loved anybody before. And I wanted to be able to love you both, honourably. I never asked you to give Fiona up, only to share.' Her lips were trembling, but firmly clenched. 'But you don't understand sharing. To you, only possession matters. Perhaps, after all, I should want us to end it.'

Lorraine winced, but the blow didn't strike deep. 'I've been callow, selfish. If there's any way I can help you . . .?'

'You can help me by going to Hell.'

Lorraine, shaken and soaked to the skin but with a bounce in her step, returned to the office, for once before the clock struck three.

Before she could even telephone Fiona, Lorraine was summoned into Toby's presence. She tapped on the mahogany double doors of his office and slipped in. Toby rose from his desk and strolled, smiling, across the Persian carpet, gesturing to her to join him at the conference table in the alcove. 'By what appears to be a miracle, Ms Struthers, you not only avoided offending the Malawian delegation –' (Toby's speeches always started off in the Foreign Office's Johnsonian syntax) '– but have, by the exercise of some charm which is not apparent to me, won their approbation. Do sit.' He touched the back of a chair.

Lorraine sat; things happening all over the place on this good Friday.

'I've had a fax from the President's Office. You're to accompany the mission of MPs. Short notice, but call of duty. They leave on tonight's flight to Lilongwe.'

'Wow!'

'Take a full stock of film. They're doing good work in the primary health sector, so pictures with babies in arms please, equal numbers of Tories and Labour, plus the odd Liberal Democrat. Colour for the wildlife, black and white for the hospitals. Pick up your ticket at Heathrow; you've got three hours to get there; four if they hold up the flight.'

The van whizzed through the traffic like a firecracker. Brilliant news, brilliant. Lorraine could tell Fiona that it was over, well and truly over, with Lucy. And Lorraine would not only have a week in the tropics to get Lucy out of her blood; she would also be adding two powerful lines to her CV. After that, she and Fiona would make a new start. They could, now that the earth was so wet, at last dig up that patch of rough grass and plant a rose garden.

12

Monday, 30 October, Gospel Oak to Dalston

It was late morning – that part of the day Georgiana called forenoon – of Monday. Fiona, barefooted and wearing her ancient striped pyjamas, stood staring at the kitchen table. In the three days since Lorraine had gone off to Malawi, she hadn't been out or spoken to anyone. On the table, half an apple – brown, pulpy and bearing a disintegrating impression of Lorraine's teeth – teetered on top of a pile of photographic paraphernalia. Inside-out garments sprawled on the stools and floor. A shoe, one of a pair jettisoned in favour of sandals, lay in collision with Bonzo's water dish. Everywhere was chaos. Fiona pressed her hand to her mouth, and tried again to focus on one thing, to make a beginning of order. Throw out the apple!

She tensed herself to attack it. It gave back the grin of a shrunken head. She grabbed it and, with a squeal at its clammy moistness, flung it at the sink. She towelled her hand vigorously against a sweater scooped off the floor. The acrid animal odour of wool spread through the room.

'It's okay,' she whispered. 'This is my kitchen. I have not fallen out of the world.' Fiona was all right. She had a spouse who had not abandoned her, who was merely away, doing a job, as people did.

But this kitchen was not Fiona's warm, familiar, dishevelled nest; it was a hostile half-alive thing where taps oozed slime, fridge bred poisonous cultures, boiler licked itself with tongues of hungry flame, and Lorraine's baggage, unbuttoned, unhinged, hanging wide as the teeth of man-traps, had taken possession.

There had been no reconciliation during Lorraine's frantic departure. This Lorraine, bright-eyed with excitement, was not the contrite sinner of Tuesday night. This woman was triumphant; fate had rewarded her for her return to marital virtue. Her crime had been wiped out; there was no need for penance. Shouting: 'Coming, I'm on my way' to the taxi, Lorraine had left Fiona near bruised from the last fierce kiss on her jaw. Leaning out of the cab window to make sure the neighbours knew what a conscientious partner this busy and important woman was, she shouted: 'I'll phone the minute we touch down in Malawi.' Then she was gone: Lorraine, Fiona's spouse. Fiona hated her. But the energy had leached out of her anger.

What was left? Fiona's kitchen, defiled, Lorraine's dumping ground. Fiona took hold of the nearest foreign object on the table, a leather pouch containing camera lenses, filters, what-have-you, with the thought of flinging it out into the wet bedding plants but, assaulted by waves of weakness in her arms, dropped it back onto the table. Fiona told herself, sternly, to treat herself gently. She was suffering something natural, the menopause.

But how could nature be so cruel as to put women through this disintegration? How could God be so cruel as, at this time, to shatter her one dependency – on the partner who had promised to love her in sickness and in health? Why, when Fiona had had three days to calm herself down, had she been unable to work, to eat, to sleep, even to clear up this mess in her kitchen? Fiona swept the pouch off the table and was rewarded, as it hit the quarry tiles, with a muffled crunch.

There came a scraping at the door: she started. It was what's-his-name whom she'd left outside for she didn't know how long. And when had she last fed him or filled his water bowl? She didn't know that either. She let him in.

Raindrops dripped from the end of his sunken skinny tail as he came towards her and placed a paw on her knee. Big soft eyes turned to her. He forgave her for leaving him out in the rain; more than that, he was sad. He was sorry for her. Something weird, warm and wet swelled in her breast, the rudiments of an emotion. 'Poor Bonzo.'

Bonzo's ears pricked and he turned his soulful eyes towards his empty dish.

'Poor neglected Bonzo.' Fiona got to her feet and rooted about in the larder. 'Wicked mother of Bonzo.' She found a tin of gourmet liver, his favourite, apart from table scraps which were not available since no cooking had been done. Bonzo instantly metamorphosed from hangdog to whirling Dervish, and Fiona's heart executed not quite a skip, but a pleasant enough little flop.

Bonzo, slurping and snorting and nosing his dish across the tiles, wolfed his breakfast. Fiona watched: one thing in this world was faithful and true: her Bonskowitztableski. Bonzo caught her look and, rolling his eyes, lay at her feet. She crouched down beside him and he began, delicately, to wipe his chops with his great paws, then to lick his paws, and then give a similar wash to Fiona's feet. As her toes curled up against the ticklish touch of his tongue, other relative certainties came to her. She was alive. When she could calm her heart, she would have quiet. In the three remaining days of Lorraine's absence, she could have the peace she longed for, to create something wonderful, in silver. It would be as lovely as her silver mesh change-purse, the little thing that had folded itself, soft as a tiny kitten, into women's hands over 150 years. It would be small, simple, and so beautiful that it would glow from its own inner light. She would put it in a black velvet box and give it to Georgiana. It would pass from hand to hand at Georgiana's party, evoking such

admiration that nobody could again see Fiona as the wreckage
of a marriage.

But when Fiona tried to imagine the object itself, she could
see only a Greek urn, the ugly decoration for the vanity of a
very rich man that lay unfinished on her workbench. She
could envisage the reaction to something beautiful in the face
of someone who admired it, but she could not see the work
itself. 'I can't do it,' Fiona said out loud. 'I have nothing to say.'

The small reconnection with her art that she'd had as the
gift of Bonzo snapped. Fiona couldn't see art, couldn't see
herself except as a thing paralysed with loneliness and failure,
couldn't see anything except Lorraine's presence – in the form
of things flung about for Fiona to put away. She hated
Lorraine's presence. But Lorraine's absence, too, was everywhere – in the silence, in the erratic and unpredictable
movements of time. Fiona couldn't connect without Lorraine.
Lorraine's absence filled her with fear; the thought of
Lorraine's return filled her with dread. Fiona was too tired for
Lorraine. She didn't want to see her – not today, not ever.

She wanted to be quiet, alone. She wanted to be safe, not
threatened by Lorraine's terrible new power to blow the
world apart. But was she safe here? Once again the tap
reverted to its measured dripping toll; the fridge buzzed with
mating calls of bacteria and fungi. She wanted to be completely alone – to shut out these terrible demands of her
kitchen. She wanted to be dead. 'Oh God!'

Bonzo, his ears cocked questioningly, staggered to his feet
and pressed his muzzle into her hand. She wrapped him in her
arms.

Fiona and Bonzo started as at a shot when the telephone rang.
Normal answerphone procedure was forgotten, and they both
charged out to the hall, Fiona to seize the receiver and Bonzo
to give a ritual bark at the front door.

'Fifi darling!' It was the megaphone voice that had blared
from the taxi: 'It's me, safe and sound in Lilongwe after two
amazing days in the bush.'

Fiona fought the impulse to put the phone down.

'There hasn't been a single second free to phone till now. Those MPs demand attention day and night. And you won't believe the damage they do to Malawi's stock of hospitality champagne. To think we chose that lot to govern us!'

In small flashes, Fiona caught the sense of what she was hearing.

'You know what one of those wallies said at the AIDS hospital? That I was to photograph him with a smiling baby in his arms. I swear to you, "smiling" was his very word.'

'Really?' Fiona wondered how much it cost to phone London from the five-star Malawi Panafrique. 'And did you?'

As Lorraine launched into the next chapter, Fiona's mind drifted off, out of habit. It wasn't necessary to pay attention to Lorraine's stories; Fiona could always get the gist from their repetition at dinner parties.

Lorraine's seamless chatter then ran on to the weather – it was the wet season, the equivalent of spring – and cosmos bloomed in a ribbon of pink and mauve along every track from the forest fringes to the broad colonial avenues of Lilongwe. Fiona didn't know what cosmos was. She envisaged a thick steel cable, enamelled and inset with sparking stones, twisting in the likeness of a snake – electric, dangerous.

Then, her voice dropping an octave, Lorraine said that, foolish and flighty as she was, she loved Fiona to the sum total of her capacity to love.

'Thanks. Watch out you don't step on a sleeping cosmos.'

Fiona put the receiver down, and instantly forgot about Lorraine. She struggled to remember what she had been thinking before the interruption. She had been so close to touching on something that would make everything simple, clear. What was that important thought? Peace had come to her when she thought it. She wandered back into the kitchen and could think only of putting out breakfast for Bonzo. For some reason, the wretched dog wouldn't eat.

She was almost relieved when a new distraction offered itself: the phone rang again. It was Steven-John at his call

box. He delivered what sounded like a prepared statement:
Fiona must please pardon him for being the bearer of bad tid-
ings and remember that she was always welcome to half his
crust and the whole of his ear at any time, day or night. Things
had happened in his life recently which made him realise how
very fragile human happiness was. She was to promise him —
absolutely promise — that before she made any decisions that
might arise out of despair, she would give him some chance to
show that life was worth living. Then his 10p ran out and his
voice gave way to the moan of the disconnected line.

As Fiona listened, tears rolled down her cheeks: strange
that, for she felt nothing.

When she got back to the kitchen, Bonzo had picked the
bits of meat out of his second breakfast. Controlling an incipient nausea, Fiona tossed the meal at the bin. It landed around
Lorraine's shoe, reminding Fiona that spare bread should be
put out for the birds. Hastily, she collected up the bits — not
out of anxiety that birds might go hungry, but in fear of God's
anger against those who allowed them to. The phone rang
again. Again she ran to it, with relief. It was Georgiana.

'I've got a wicked story for you, Fifi my love,' Georgiana
began.

Fiona sighed. 'I've heard it. MPs get drunk if the Malawi
Government is paying for the champagne.'

'That so? You do amaze me.' Georgiana then paused for the
merest second, but Fiona, dull-brained as she was, knew that
was enough for Georgiana to register that her friend was alive
and coping, but barely. 'This tale, my love, concerns you, and
comes from that master of chicanery, the Honourable Toby
Hume.' With perfect timing, Georgiana paused again. 'Even if
the champagne is free, other things aren't. Hear this: Toby
trimmed the budget for the Malawi trip. He bought tickets
from a bucket shop, then got the airline to upgrade the MPs
at its own expense.'

'How fascinating,' said Fiona, bored.

'Then, my dear, he used the savings he'd made to add a
photographer to the party. Why did he do this? To give

Lorraine a week in Darkest Africa, or, to change the metaphor, in the cooler.'

Fiona's heart flipped.

'He persuaded the Malawi Cabinet Secretary to put in a request for a photographer,' continued Georgiana. 'It took some doing, as the Malawians had had enough of the loud woman who kept interrupting meetings, cooing for big smiles.'

Fiona knew this routine from a thousand barbecue parties. The pall over her mind lifted; her belly began to heave, and she belched with laughter.

Georgiana was also laughing, as crazily as Fiona. 'Lorraine, photographer of presidents, my dear, is nothing but a naughty child sent out of the room by Toby.' Struggling for breath she added, 'Let's you and me never get on the wrong side of that villainous Toby, my darling.'

After this call Fiona's state of mind was transformed. The dullness, the miasma had gone; she kept breaking out into hoarse laughter, and in the spaces between this release, was jittery as a fly at a window pane. She needed to do something. She should clear up the kitchen; she should make a cup of tea. She could do many bold things to imitate the action of the living. Better still, she could take Bonzo out onto Hampstead Heath where she could draw the heron that lived on the lakes. Because now she knew what beautiful object she was going to make.

Today, despair could be exiled to Darkest Africa. Today, Lorraine, kitchens, death, even thoughts of Greek urns and suchlike measures to escape the fate of the bag lady, could go hang. She would open her mind to the heron; she would make an image as sinuous and cruel as the creature itself. She would be free.

Bonzo trotted up to her, his tail now wafting gently above his backside. 'Bonzo old man,' she said, patting his sleek rump, 'your patience will shortly be rewarded.' With a lightness of step equal to Bonzo's, she trotted up to the bathroom to wash and dress and swallow her pills and then launch forth onto Hampstead Heath. She'd take her binoculars and charcoals and Bonzo would splash about while she sketched.

Bonzo, who could sense the word 'walkies' even when it wasn't voiced, spun himself round in gleeful efforts to demolish his now wildly rotating tail.

But the phone rang yet again. Fiona would have left the call to the answering machine, but did rather hope it might be Lorraine – to whom, of course, she would not breathe a word about Toby's fix. It was Midge.

'I say,' began Midge timidly, 'sorry to disturb you, but could I have a word with Lorraine?'

'Feel free,' replied Fiona, 'but you'll have to call Malawi.'

Midge made no move to end the call with the usual politenesses. 'In Africa?'

'Yup, that particular Malawi. She's photographing happy children with AIDS. Hotel Panafrique.'

Midge dithered. 'I'm rather worried about something, well somebody, and I rather hoped for her help.'

A sinking feeling told Fiona that this concerned something or somebody she'd rather not know about.

'However,' Midge took a firm breath, 'you've been dragged into this wretched business, so perhaps I ought to put the problem to you.'

Like any other close couple, Fiona and Lorraine had long taken it for granted that couplehood made them twins, a double. Fiona's spirit was deep and dark, Lorraine's wide and bright; Fiona wanted to control her inner self, Lorraine to control the world. Yet they were filled with each other and could be each other, take each other's roles. Fiona registered, with a new sensation of sinking, how wrong they had been. Lorraine always had to know; good or bad, she wanted the facts, wanted a clear light on everything. Fiona preferred, if the facts were dreadful, to be left in ignorance.

But this wasn't to happen. 'I'm worried about Lucy, about her state of mind.'

'That person's state of mind, Midge, does not concern me.'

Midge rushed her reply. 'No, of course not. It's not really my business either, but one has to do something.'

'Does one?' Fiona said mildly. 'One could pass her on to Chelsey. A clairvoyant is next best thing to a priest.'

The pained silence that followed hinted to Fiona that she'd trodden on a corn. 'Sorry, can't help you,' she added, 'whatever I've been dragged into, it isn't going to be this.'

That was a mistake. It allowed Midge to explain, at length, that the problem did involve Fiona. Fiona discovered that Lucy had the highest regard for her; that Lucy had been struggling for weeks to win a place in her life; and that Lucy had discussed these matters in detail with Fiona's closest friends. Fiona felt besieged.

'She tried so hard to get it right for you all,' continued Midge. 'Nobody could have tried harder. So you can imagine how shocked I was when she phoned on Friday to say Lorraine had "ditched" her. I motored over to Dalston immediately. She was in terrible distress.' Midge paused. 'She's so young; she doesn't know how to cope with pain.'

'Well,' responded Fiona dryly, 'we all have to learn. You thought, I presume, of a bottle of Scotch.'

'Vodka. I don't think it helped. She wept even more. There was nothing I could do to comfort her.'

Fiona gave a bitter laugh. 'Nothing? You mean you didn't spend the night?'

Midge answered in a low voice, 'I didn't. She wanted to be alone. Alone to, you know, to . . . to . . . And since then I haven't been able to raise her though I rang and called at her place several times.' In a voice that rivalled Ulric's for its solemnity, Midge added: 'I appreciate that Lorraine has done the decent thing, but I had thought she was a person who would take some responsibility for the consequences.'

The pause that followed suggested that Midge, ever the gentleman, might be giving Fiona an opening to defend her partner. But Fiona said nothing and Midge, her voice now halting and uncertain, concluded: 'Now I don't know whether to call the Samaritans, or break the door down, or what.'

If Lorraine had any real talent, it was in making the mother and father of emotional messes! When Fiona put the phone down this time, she was shaking with excitement. But she was also filling up with a new fear.

Where was Bonzo? Bonzo had reached his own conclusions and deposited himself on the hall mat. He offered her a disappointed sideways glance. She went over to him, and stroked his ears, hoping once again to touch his simple needs, and through them find simplicity in her own. By degrees, sanity returned, and Fiona's thoughts drifted back to the heron. Then the phone rang again.

Four calls in one morning had so conditioned Fiona out of her usual habits that she picked up the fifth without thinking.

'Is that Fiona?'

Fiona's heart stopped beating at the sound of the low hesitant uninflected inner-London voice.

'Fiona, are you there? I'm speaking from the call box opposite your door. Could you come out for a walk: I have to talk to you.'

Mist hung over the Heath. The trees fringing the hill had a spiderwebby vagueness. Clumps of crows plucked at the grassy slopes in search of something dead. Bonzo, subdued by the presence of a human who shrank from dogs, walked, without instruction, to heel. There were no people apart from Fiona and her companion. They walked in parallel, enclosed in separate silences: Fiona with her camel hair buttoned tight and Robin Hood hat tipped well forward; the woman who had cracked her life, casually as she would a nut, half hidden under the hood of her duffel coat.

Bonzo was first to obtain release. A stiff and grizzled poodle, an old chum, emerged from the mist. Bonzo stopped, stiffened, lifted his left paw, glanced at Fiona. At her nod, he emitted a light whinny, made two or three spinning leaps and bounded up the grassy slope. The old dog, at a stately trot, came down to meet him. Protesting loudly, the crows made way. Fiona watched as, with slowly gyrating tails, they sniffed each other from earhole to asshole and then, the formalities over, began to prance.

A warmth that owed little to her excellent camel hair flowed through Fiona's veins, reviving thoughts of the heron. Without speaking to Lucy, Fiona turned to the right and headed up the path towards the pond — not to draw the heron, but to note its position in preparation for her next visit. The heron was not something she could share with this companion.

Not the heron, not anything. Lucy was now laid low, but she was still the disease in Fiona's heart. Yet, strangely, Fiona had agreed to Lucy's request without hesitation. Fiona knew that, this Monday morning, she was not in her right mind. Lorraine's lies and her inglorious exposure had left Fiona without grief but giddy, open in some strange way to suggestion. Today, Steven-John's clumsy affection had warmed her. Georgiana's delight at Toby's villainy had lightened her spirits, and her head. How amazing her friends were: how sweet, clever, ruthless, powerful, and how solidly hers. She could crush this Lucy — whose manner indicated that she presumed to look to Fiona for *sympathy* — she could laugh, the kind of laugh that rocked the theatre when Charlie Chaplin fell over his walking stick. Fiona had come out with Lucy to be entertained. She accepted without shame that the entertainment she sought was to revel in the collapse of the misalliance between this woman and the partner she no longer even liked.

She had half circled the pond before she realised that Lucy was still at her side, at a decent distance, walking in the wet grass since Fiona had possession of the path. Bonzo rejoined the party. He sent many crows to the treetops before anything was spoken. Lucy opened.

'Can we talk now?'

Fiona nodded. They took the path up towards Parliament Hill.

'I need to defend my honour.'

Fiona picked up a stick and hurled it far as she could; Bonzo set off in hot pursuit. 'So you have some to defend, do you?'

Lucy blushed. 'I'm not asking you, as yet, to believe this,' she continued, 'but I did everything I could to protect you.'

'How kind. How pointless. You can neither help me nor hurt me.'

Lucy stopped short. 'You're wrong about that. I could have hurt you very much indeed.'

Something fast and invisible whizzed through the air and struck Fiona in the breast.

'But I never wanted to hurt you. You must understand that.' Lucy spoke on, still without looking at Fiona. 'Before I met Lorraine,' she said, her voice low, but sure of itself, 'I was searching. I didn't know what for, but I knew the life I was leading was waste. Then suddenly, she was there, and the world opened to me. The wonderful thing that happened was not that I found her but that, through her, I found myself. I saw value in me. The women's movement taught me that I had worth, but I didn't feel it until she touched me, and liked it.'

'Yes,' said Fiona coldly, 'I expect she did.'

'I didn't know anything about you at first.'

'No,' said Fiona, even more coldly, 'I expect you didn't.'

'And, as soon as I did know, I tried to make it right between the three of us.'

'It didn't occur to you that the simplest way to make it right would be to fuck off?'

Lucy looked shocked. 'I owe it to myself to make the best I can of my life.'

'I'm familiar with that argument.' Fiona wrestled with Bonzo to get the stick out of his mouth. 'It's used by thieves whose happiness requires somebody else's Ferrari.'

'I suppose it is,' said Lucy vaguely, a gentle warning, which Fiona had to heed, that Lucy wouldn't be rattled. 'But I won't do anything underhand or manipulative to get what I want. I wouldn't force her to choose between us.'

Fiona growled: '*Choose!* You think there is a *choice*?'

Lucy, head low, walked slowly on without replying. The urge to bash the hood of the duffel coat with Bonzo's stick forced Fiona to keep pace.

'I must ask you to believe,' Lucy resumed, 'that I never wanted to take anything from you. I wanted us all to share. You see, what I found with Lorraine was love, the only love I've known. And love is supposed to be about sharing.'

'Bonzo!' Bonzo had disappeared. Fiona turned desperately from side to side, until she saw him bounding up the hill – promiscuous wretch that he was – to sniff yet another canine asshole.

Lucy was relentless. 'You and Lorraine are together again. I accept that. I have lost everything; I have to accept that too. None the less, you have no right to get closer to each other by vilifying me.'

This was a target. In her frostiest tone, Fiona attacked: 'Apart from the merest mention, I don't recall that we spoke of you.'

'Perhaps not yet, but you will.'

A wave of dizziness swept Fiona. Lucy caught her uncertainty through a quick sideways look. 'You will quite soon; as soon as you need something more than relief to make you feel safe.'

After too long a delay, Fiona became able to reply. In a low tone, her 'r's as rolling and 'o's hollow as a Highland crofter's, she said: 'You know *nothing* of what lies between Lorraine and me. You could not understand even if you did. It is something outside of your comprehension. You do not even understand that you have one power – the power to destroy.'

Lucy took a quick breath and turned to Fiona. Her face was now pale and her eyes the huge amber globes of a nocturnal animal. 'I understand more than you think. I've watched you for several weeks now. You had so little thought for me that you didn't even see what you were teaching me. But I know you well. I've been as close to you as I've been to Lorraine; closer in some ways, because you never bothered to notice that I was there.'

Fiona didn't have much choice about the means of bringing this meeting to an end. Lucy was blue with cold, and couldn't

be left at a bus stop. Fiona revolted against the thought of letting Lucy into the house to see the disorder there, and she
couldn't face the strain of sitting opposite this woman in the
pub. To cap it, Lorraine's van was parked right before them.
So Fiona chose to dispose of Lucy by driving her home.

Fiona wasn't an aggressive driver like Lorraine, but she
was bold and fast and had unerring judgement of the nar-
rowest gap into which a small government van could be
squeezed.

She darted into the left lane to occupy a slit opened up by
a cyclist, sliced through the lights an eyeblink after they'd
turned red, called out reassurance to Bonzo as he slithered
helplessly across the steel floor behind her, and sensed Lucy's
fingers clutching at the door handle. This set the style. Fiona
abandoned the main thoroughfares and swung off onto her
most complicated doglegging backstreet route to the east.
She took the humps at 40 miles an hour, and they reached
Dalston in half the time the same journey would have taken
Midge.

'Well then,' Fiona said as they pulled up between the cars
on blocks, 'home safe and sound. I hope you think your
honour's safe too.'

'I think it's more likely to be safe, with you.' Lucy gathered
her scattered possessions together. 'Will you come in?'

Fiona did not know that this offer was a rare privilege, and
had not been extended to Lorraine. She gave a vague
unfriendly grin: 'I'm way behind schedule.'

'I've got some vodka.'

'Oh well, why not? The day was so crazy anything was
possible. But Bonzo had to be left in the van.

After the street, claustrophobic with the yells of children, and
the long, dark, mildew-scented passage, Lucy's flat, a recent
extension at the rear of a looming Victorian house, was a revelation. Fiona was led into a big room – living room with
kitchen recess – looking out onto a shaggy but richly wet and
green garden. The square french windows were softened by

gauzy curtains patterned with gigantic poppies. Brightly painted egg-boxes coated the ceiling. Long drooping shelves lined the walls. These were crammed with books, dried grasses in milk-bottles, coffee-jars containing pastas and pulses, and a tangle of dolls and toy animals. Where the shelving ended, pinned-up postcards and photographs took over. The floorboards were painted alternately lime green and orange and scattered with dhurries and rag rugs in rainbow colours. Two sofas, draped with Indian cottons printed in complicated designs of birds and flowers, faced each other over a red coffee-table piled with newspapers and magazines, on top of which teetered a telephone.

Fiona looked at Lucy and then at the vivid room. She hadn't tried to picture Lucy's flat, but if she had, would have thought of barred windows and a cold tap. 'What a nice place,' she said.

'I love it,' said Lucy. 'I feel safe here. Or used to. But the new family upstairs fights all the time, and their TV fights back. When they're in, it feels like my home is being broken up.'

Fiona, who was sensitive to noise, understood. In Gospel Oak, by unspoken agreement, nobody mowed the grass before noon on Sundays.

'I thought I'd get used to it,' continued Lucy, as she made ready a tray with glasses, vodka, sugar-free orange squash and tap water, 'but it seems louder every day, and now I've started noticing noise from the street and the houses on either side as well.'

This phenomenon, too, Fiona understood. She began to wonder why Lorraine, who took up every cause within earshot and loved to flex her muscles in battles with authority, hadn't done something to help. By degrees, awareness came to Fiona that Lucy had infiltrated Lorraine's life despite Lorraine's play at secrecy, but that Lorraine had either failed or been prevented from infiltrating Lucy's. A germ of curiosity about Lucy was taking root, and Fiona did nothing to curb it. She was now amused by a bitter sense of the topsy-turvy.

This Lucy, a woman who was so plain that there was nothing about her even to criticise, was in her own environment so well grounded. Beside her, Les Biches seemed a tired old music hall number.

By the second drink, Lucy was telling Fiona her life story.

Lucy Rutlege came from Lincoln, the eldest and cleverest, but smallest, plumpest and least loved of four daughters of a schoolmistress and her clergyman husband. She cared to remember little about her childhood, beyond that it was closely regulated and that she hated games, boys, having to share bedroom and bathwater, and the teasing of the children from the industrial estate.

On her seventeenth birthday, she decided to challenge her father's ambition – that she would study literature and one day write a famous treatise on Proust. She joined the Air Force as an administrative assistant, and left the vicarage for the barracks at Nocton Fen. Though only a few miles south of Lincoln, none of her sisters came to visit her there. She didn't miss them; for the first time, she was sought after, and had friends' – real grown-up friends – men. She kitted herself out in stilettos, tight skirts, make-up, and called herself Lucille. She wore her hair long and dyed black and dieted herself down to seven stone. She acquired a taste for amphetamines and raunchy evenings at the pub. Pool was the first game she learned to play – and sex. She had sex first with another rookie, a local boy, then also with his closest friend, later with any of them, occasionally, at a heavy party, with several. There were a few she would have considered marrying, if the question ever arose. She had by then reached her twenties; she was proud of her night-bird eyes and close as she'd ever come to being happy.

But one evening her world collapsed. It was near closing time; she'd been off to the john for a quick slash and was on her way back to join the boys.

She heard her current boyfriend say: 'Don't be so miserable, old man, there's plenty more fish in the sea.'

Another, very particular, friend added: 'You can always cool off with a dip in Lucille.'

To which her boyfriend, in a valiant attempt at laughing this off, replied: 'Well, she does give value for money, you must admit.'

Lucy came up behind them. 'Thanks a lot, fellers,' she said, and left the pub.

She packed a small suitcase and, next morning, caught the 6 a.m. bus for Lincoln and then the train to London. Fearful of being court-martialled for desertion, she had her hair cut and bleached, and set about looking for a place to hide. The pub had absorbed what might otherwise have been savings, but a hostel for homeless youth, somewhere near Lewisham, unable to believe that she was a day over 15, took her in.

It was 1984, when the women's movement gave purpose and identity to many women like Lucy. For the first time, Lucy began to think about her life. For the third time, she redesigned her character: as a child, she'd been afflicted by the kind of paralysing shyness that uncomprehending adults take for sullenness. In the Air Force, she had endeavoured to turn herself into a vamp. At Lewisham, she trained herself to look people in the eye, and to say what she thought. But this new personality did not win her friends. Lucy saw herself as one of the dispossessed and was convinced that, if she was ever to get a place, she would have to break into it. She hovered at the edges of various communities, but was never quite bold enough to break in – not at Greenham Common, nor the Anti-Nazi Movement, the Campaign Against Pornography, or the separatist groups that met at Wesley House. She decided to become a lesbian, but didn't know how to make an approach to a woman, and none made one to her. She waited, feeling excited, disappointed and very lonely. Her first years as a lesbian were the longest period of celibacy she had endured since leaving home. In due course, her struggles won her a job, a flat, a few fumbles under the zip that she preferred to forget, and shifting connections that never grew into friendships.

Then, at the launch of the autobiography of a black South-African policewoman who had been a PanAfricanist Congress agent, a dykey-looking photographer from the Foreign and Commonwealth Office gave her the eye. The irony of their meeting was that Toby had sent Lorraine to cover the launch as a qualified gesture of acknowledgement of the PanAfricanists – Toby was punctilious about levels of representation, and the PanAfricanists rated only a junior officer. This junior officer seemed very senior to Lucy.

Fiona normally turned away from what was painful and grim, but found herself touched by Lucy's story. Yet she drew the line at what involved Lorraine. 'You must have been horribly upset by that incident in the pub,' she said, backtracking.

Lucy agreed. 'I thought I was one of the boys. I'd have known their game if I'd had women friends to talk to, but there wasn't a single one – not my mother, my sisters, no one. I didn't know how to form relationships with women. I couldn't ease up; women backed away from me. Somehow, I was missing the point. I regret that.'

This, Fiona couldn't follow. In any case, she didn't want to. 'Let's have another drink.'

Lucy smiled. 'Yes, let's. Why don't you tell me about you now?'

Fiona demurred.

'Oh, I'm not after hearing how you got together with Lorraine. After what she's done to me, I don't even want to hear her name. But you. You obviously come from Scotland. Whereabouts?'

'A farm in the Highlands, near Braemar,' said Fiona shortly.

'Upper class? I thought so.' Lucy seemed disappointed. 'Grouse-shooting, gatherings of the clan and all that? Must have been a drag.'

Fiona grinned. 'Maybe. But I like Highland cattle and red deer. In June, salmon fight their way up the rapids to the loch above our farm.' With a sudden, unexpected, surge of feeling, she added: 'I had a lovely pony.'

Lucy refilled Fiona's glass, this time with rather more vodka and less of the nickel-flavoured orange squash. 'Bet you did. I can see you, galloping through the heather and the cottongrass.' On stepping back, her hand brushed Fiona lightly on the shoulder.

Menopausal symptoms are capricious. Fiona was swept by a furious hot flush.

Lucy dropped onto the settee opposite. Her own face, too, was flushed, a little nervy smile playing at the corners of her pretty mouth. The room, alive with colours and drooping-headed dolls and rabbits with floppy ears, began slowly to rotate. The yielding Indian cotton seemed to cling to Fiona's arms and legs, like a spider's web.

The telephone rang. Lucy leaned forward to pick it up. There was the faint chirrup of a voice.

'Oh, but I'm fine,' Lucy's reply rang with triumph, 'couldn't be better. And you?' She nodded enthusiastically all through a long whispering reply.

Fiona, who considered it impolite to talk on the telephone with a guest in the room, walked, mildly irritated, over to the french windows. In the garden, two cats were disputing territory in the usual cat way. One sat on a fence post, washing itself and ignoring the other which prowled below in a wide circle. Any minute now, the cat on the fence would spring into action. Fiona wondered if either of the cats was Lucy's.

From behind her, Lucy uttered an 'um' and then an 'ah' and then said, 'There's someone here who'd love to hear you say that.'

Lucy signalled to Fiona and then thrust the receiver into her hand.

'Hello?' said Fiona guardedly.

'Fiona!'

It was Lorraine.

For a moment, Fiona didn't know where she was. Then rage took her. What was Lorraine doing telephoning Lucy, so soon after she was supposed to have 'ditched' her; so soon after she'd discovered how much she loved Fiona? In a small, hard voice, she said: 'Hope you're having a good time with the laughing babies at the AIDS hospital.'

Lorraine let out an awkward laugh. 'Not today. The MPs had lunch with the Minister of Co-operation and Development, and now they're sleeping it off. That's the sum total.'

Fiona was aware of Lorraine's sum totals. 'So you're not exactly hard-pressed?'

'Well, I'll be busy tonight, with a reception for the local bigwigs. More field trips tomorrow.'

'Good. You'll see the cosmos.'

'Yes, I suppose I will.' Lorraine's voice began to shrink. 'You don't think, of course, that I phoned Lucy because, because . . .'

'Never crossed my mind.'

'Look, it's difficult to talk right now. Can I call you when you get home?'

'Better not. You'd waste the taxpayer's money on the answerphone.'

Now Lorraine's voice revealed real anxiety. 'You'll be out late; are you meeting someone?'

'Lorraine, for heaven's sake; this call is costing a fortune.'

'I'll ring midnight, your time.'

'I'll tell the answerphone to be ready for it.'

'Well?' said Lucy as Fiona put down the telephone. 'Did you find her well?'

'Come here,' said Fiona brutally. She grasped the wiry fabric of Lucy's sweater and pulled her close. Then, jerking up Lucy's chin, she leaned down hard and, teeth bared, kissed her open mouth.

13

Three days later, Lorraine, surrounded by bags and packages of Malawian handicrafts, stood in the hall, trying to quieten the thudding of her heart. Nobody home? Surely she'd caught the right flight? She dragged herself upstairs and checked the rooms.

The telephone rang. She raced down to answer.

'Um, hi, excuse me . . .' sounded a slow, gravelly, all too familiar voice.

Lorraine muttered a word banned by Toby from the precincts of the Foreign Office.

The fragment of a titter, then: 'Um, is Ulric with you by any chance?'

Yes, it was Steven-John, queen-bee of the world of gossip. 'If he is, it's without my knowledge.' Lorraine put down the phone and, yanking her big rucksack, clattered up the stairs for the second time.

The phone rang again. Again Lorraine ran to it. But again it was Steven-John. 'Look, I'm obviously disturbing you and I hate to do that,' he began, 'but I can't find Ulric and I'm very anxious to get hold of him.'

Lorraine was suddenly, unreasonably, incensed. 'Are you? Well, I've lost somebody too and—' She broke off. Something, pride perhaps, stopped her from exposing her frailty.

'Sorry to put this on you,' continued Steven-John in his dogged way, 'but Ulric didn't turn up to have tea with me on Tuesday, and now it's *Thursday*, and I'm getting really worried.'

'Have a heart, Stevie,' said Lorraine wearily. 'I haven't a clue who's supposed to have tea with whom. I didn't even know it was Thursday. I've just stepped off a plane from Africa.'

'Um, could I have a word with Fiona?'

'No,' Lorraine snapped.

Steven-John continued in an even slower and more patient voice: 'Can you tell me if she's seen Ulric, or talked to anyone about him? You're the only people I can ask. Chelsey is preparing for an audition, and Toby's in Brussels, and I don't like to distress Georgiana.'

'Steven-John.' Lorraine's voice was cold with rage. 'I told you, I've just hit this time zone. My passport is soggy with wet stamps.'

Steven-John had the persistence of a flea. 'I hate to do this to you,' he went on, 'but I'm in my call box, and this is my last 10 pence. Ulric hasn't been well lately, you understand. It's really rather serious. He has, um, staphylococci in his ear.'

Exasperation seized Lorraine in a spasm of desire to cocci Steven-John somewhere fleshier. 'I'm afraid I can't help you,' she said and, replacing the receiver, extinguished Steven-John's last 10 pence.

The small heat generated by this exchange energised Lorraine. For the third time, she ran up the stairs. She hurled her rucksack onto the bed. Then she ran into the spare room and flung open the window. 'Fee-ow-naaa!' she yelled out across the garden. Rainwater sluiced over the rim of the gutter onto her head. A clutch of sparrows and tits chittered.

Lorraine barely paused. Where on earth was the dratted

woman? Where was she now? Where was she when Lorraine made those expensive and homesick calls to the answerphone? Where was she when Lorraine telephoned from Heathrow, three hours back? Lorraine had scarcely thought of Lucy in six days, allowing for one short duty telephone call. She could now barely remember what she looked like (beyond a resemblance to Rowan Atkinson without the humour); she now found it difficult to imagine what she had ever seen in her.

It was years since the time Fiona used to trudge out to Heathrow to meet her, but Fiona was always home and waiting when Lorraine returned. Wet, and beginning to be afraid, Lorraine searched the house again, this time looking for clues. Bonzo's water bowl was empty. But then it was often so as Fiona was absent-minded and Bonzo anyway had a disgusting preference for puddles. Her mind skipped from supposition to supposition: Fiona was punishing her for that wretched Lucy business; Fiona was shopping, taking Bonzo for a walk, picking up a new commission for jewellery. But none of these had the force of the unthinkable worsts.

Instead of thinking the worsts, Lorraine went out to search the street. Thoughtful now, she noted that her van was not parked in any of its usual places, nor anywhere that she could see. At the local mini-market, a neighbour called to her from the queue at the check-out, a cheery greeting, nothing about Fiona. Why hadn't Fiona at least left a note, after she'd picked up Lorraine's messages on the answerphone. Ah – the answerphone.

Lorraine darted back indoors and checked it. There were two messages from Georgiana, the first asking Fiona for news of her health, the second ironic and mildly irritated. There was Lorraine's midnight call explaining, in an embarrassingly weedy voice, that she had rung Lucy purely out of duty. Then something from Ulric about wanting someone to get hold of Steven-John and ask him to ring; followed by a third, frankly concerned, from Georgiana, and two more from Lorraine. Last was the fruitless call from Heathrow, which enclosed

Lorraine's 'I'm home, darling', in booms and PA announce-
ments that Lorraine hadn't heard at the time. Lorraine wiped
the tape to get rid of her own whippet-voice.

She hovered indecisively over the phone. Something wasn't
right. All Lorraine's messages before her call to Dalston had
been cleared. And Georgiana was worried. The unthinkables
were becoming not only thinkable, but distinct possibilities.
The police, the hospital, or Dalston.

Police: surely then the house would be full of white powder
and bootprints and areas fenced off with tape? Hospital:
surely the neighbours would be crowding round and there
would be a great fuss about Bonzo? A person couldn't just fall
out of the world. It had to be something connected with the
housing association flat in Dalston. Lorraine's mind ran back
to that weird phone call. Why had Fiona been there? What on
earth could she have wanted with Lorraine's ex-mistake? The
obvious was out of the question. Fiona was, to an extent that
Lorraine knew herself not to be, a woman of taste, and someone more than usually sensitive to the mores of class. But, on
that Monday afternoon, three days back, she had been somewhere about the unimaginable inside of Lucy's flat. And Lucy
had been there too, during – though this didn't mean much to
Lucy – office hours. Lorraine's breath came faster. Lucy was
a leech. Lucy wouldn't be able to believe her luck if she could
fasten on Fiona. But this could not happen. Fiona, glamorous
Fiona with admirers from Pole to Pole, could never fall into
the clutches of a runt. Fiona could never be capable of something so – so cheap. Or could she? Suddenly the beautiful,
brilliant Fiona, La Biche, had become someone she hardly
knew. Lorraine wandered around the garden, kicking at
heaps of dead leaves.

What should she do now? The one thing she could not do
was nothing. There was no point in phoning Georgiana,
increasing her concern and allowing her a cruel pleasure in
Lorraine's distress. Toby was away on a mission. Steven-John
had no phone, so she couldn't ring him, even if she could bear
more rabbiting about cocci. There was no way she could

humble herself by telephoning Dalston or, worse, knocking on the door of Lucy's flat.

But she had to do something, something necessary. If nothing else suggested itself, she could take her film in to the Foreign Office and pretend to work.

There was just one small necessary thing she could do. She could, at least, try to get Ulric's message to Steven-John. The van was gone, but Kentish Town was only twenty minutes walk from Gospel Oak. Lorraine decided to drop in on him. She didn't ask herself why this decision gave some slight relief, but sensed that one would be done by as one did, and she did so want something – anything – from Fiona.

Leaving her open bag on the bed to signal her return, she plunged her hand into the heap of coats in search of her ski jacket that seemed to belong to a long-distant past. Her hand sensed things missing: Fiona's camel-hair and Bonzo's lead. Ordinary things, suggesting merely that Fiona was out, as people did go out. Lorraine set forth for Kentish Town Road.

London had looked so orderly – damp and welcoming as an old dog – when the taxi brought her from Heathrow. Now it roared with ferocious traffic and people brushed past her, grey-faced, raddled, grim. It was getting colder, and the sky was dark. Lorraine had no hat or umbrella and the wind nipped her wet hair. Newspapers, impersonating flatfish, flapped in the gutters. Limp sprays of coriander and mould-speckled fruit at the Caribbean shop under Steven-John's bedsitter seemed the corpses of what she had left behind in Malawi. In Steven-John's doorway lay a figure curled up in a blanket. Taking care not to step on what she presumed to be human and therefore dangerous, Lorraine leaned over and pressed the bell.

Steven-John opened the door. 'Oh, hi, globe-trotting photo-artist.' The simple warmth in his gravelly voice showed that he bore no ill-will for, or possibly even recollection of, Lorraine's rudeness on the phone. 'Step inside; I was just about to put a light under the kettle.'

'I can't stay,' said Lorraine, suddenly desperate to escape. 'I dropped by to tell you that, at some time in the last three days, Ulric was asking you to get in touch.'

A flash of joy whipped across Steven-John's face. 'Is that so?' he said mildly. He crouched down and shook the tramp by the shoulder. Shove over, mate. There's a lady here wants to come in.'

Lorraine took a further step back. 'I must rush.'

'You didn't speak to him? No, of course not, you were up in an aeroplane. Did Fiona speak to him?'

'He left a message on the answerphone. He didn't say anything about tea. I picked it up when I cleared the machine this morning.'

'Oh, is Fiona away too?' Steven-John gave the tramp's shoulder a gentle tap then straightened up to face Lorraine: his face showed the dawning of suspicion. 'Then you just must come in for a few homely comforts while I pop over to my phone box – if you'll lend me 10 pence.'

She gave him the money. 'I won't come in, thanks.'

'She was home Monday, when I rang. She gone up to Scotland?'

'No. Yes. She's in Scotland.'

A flicker showed that Steven-John registered the lie. 'Are you all right, and Fiona coping? You've got something there you need to look after, you know. Good marriages really are made in heaven.'

For a moment of weakness, Lorraine wavered over Steven-John's invitation. If you needed to talk, he was a person you could talk to. But a mop of matted hair emerged from the blanket at her feet and a child's voice snarled: 'Shut yer face and fuck off, for fuck's sake. A man's got a right to his fucking sleep, even in this mother-fucking country.'

'I don't have a problem with that, my laddie,' said Steven-John equably, 'but the lady's also got a right to get in the door.'

'Bye, then, bye,' said Lorraine, and fled before Steven-John had another chance to catch her eye.

Half a mile down the road, Lorraine realised that she was heading in the opposite direction, for the West End. She about turned, and began, more slowly, to make her way back to Gospel Oak. Steven-John's door was closed and his phone box empty when she passed this time, but the young tramp, still wrapped in his blanket, had his hands round a basin-sized and crudely shaped mug that could only have been created by Steven-John's encounters with the soul of clay. Warm scents of camomile and honey rose from it.

Nothing had changed when Lorraine got back to the house. More than the absence of Fiona, the lack of any sound of clicking claws seemed to take the heart out of the place.

By one o'clock, Lorraine had checked out new admissions at the Royal Free and Whittington hospitals, and had made an embarrassed and inconclusive call to the police. These produced no information. She made tea, but forgot to drink it. She could now do one of the only two things left: contact Georgiana, or Dalston. She dialled Georgiana's number, but put the receiver down before anyone answered. She did the same after dialling Dalston. Then she did make a call. She phoned for a cab.

She got out a block away from Lucy's street and slowly circled it. Then she crept up towards the house itself. Parked outside was the government media van. Fiona was here. Fiona was alive.

Two or three seconds later, relief evaporated and cold rage engulfed Lorraine. They were in there, talking, disparaging Lorraine. Lorraine felt in her pocket for the keys of the van, but she'd taken them off her ring before leaving for Malawi. She tried the door; it was locked. Even her van was shut up against her. There was nothing she could do except go in. She examined the house. It was a Victorian family mansion, three storeys high and gabled, with a light glimmering through the dimpled glass of the front door. Lorraine didn't know which part of the house contained Lucy's flat, so she scanned them all.

The ground-floor windows were barred and curtained. She crept past the dustbins and peered in through a crack. She saw the blue glow of a massive television screen reflected in an equally massive sideboard. Not that one. From the bay window directly above came the screams of infants engaged in mutual infanticide. Nor that one. The top windows were smaller. One was obscured by a poster. She stepped back to read it. It said: 'The only peace is in Jesus.' Forget that one. Lorraine double-checked the door number: yes, the right house, so the flat had to be something round the back. Sheltered by the little porch, she examined the doorbells. Below one of the buttons was a curling strip of adhesive paper with the surname written in the discomfortingly familiar hand. She raised a finger without intending to press.

A rattle loud as a passing train reverberated through Lorraine's body as a ground-floor window shot up and a woman's voice, with a Bajan accent, rapped: 'You lookin' for someone?'

'Ah, no, yes, actually I was trying to contact, get in touch with the tenant at No 16B.'

The woman's face was expressionless, but her voice turned cold. 'You from the Revenue?'

'No, actually, I'm a sort of friend.'

The woman softened. 'Well, ring the bell. They're in. I took the post less than an hour back.'

Lorraine, trapped, gave the bell the lightest squeak.

'Have a nice day,' said the woman, and was gone.

There was still time to escape.

No there wasn't. Lucy, stern-faced, stood in the now open doorway.

'Oh, hello,' said Lorraine, forcing herself not to step back.

Lucy was silent for a moment. She was wearing Fiona's white satin dressing gown, a Christmas gift from Lorraine. The fabric clung to her breasts. 'What can I do for you?'

'I'm looking for – I'd like to come in for a moment.'

Lucy glanced down the hall as if imagining Lorraine's

bearish passage through it. 'I don't know if that would be right. After all, you dropped me. It's over between us.'

Lorraine took a deep breath. 'I've come to fetch Bonzo.'

'The dog?'

A jet of relief shot through Lorraine's veins. He wasn't here. He was with Fiona, somewhere else.

Lucy looked directly at Lorraine. 'It bit me.'

A brief, shocked laugh spurted out of Lorraine.

'They know,' said Lucy, 'when people are afraid of them.' Lucy extended her hand, showing a semicircle of little red pricks.

Lorraine, her courage disgracefully raised by Bonzo, put her boot in the door and said: 'I must come in – to speak to Fiona.'

Lucy hesitated, then nodded. 'I'll do what I can.' Stepping back from Lorraine's boot, she added, 'I want to close the door. I can't let you force your way in.'

Lorraine withdrew and the door closed, leaving her suddenly suffocated by the closeness of the porch. She was still aware of a presence. She turned to it. The woman from the ground-floor flat was watching through a crack in her curtains. Casually as she could, Lorraine stepped back to the little concrete garden wall and sat on it, in full view of the woman. Then, for the want of a tube of lipstick or worry beads, or Fiona's little silver-mesh change-purse – some plaything to indicate unconcern – she began to whistle.

The front door burst open. Fiona charged out and seized Lorraine round the neck. 'Lorrie! How wonderful! Why didn't you tell me you were coming home today?'

Lorraine pulled back to see Fiona's face: her eyes were sparkling. 'I did.'

'Good heavens; is it Thursday?' Fiona embraced her again. 'I was going to have flowers, and a bottle of something splendid – the very best chablis, I thought, our special wine, so much more interesting than champagne – and, oh baby, I've got so much to tell you.'

Fiona was looking absolutely beautiful. Her eyes were a brilliant violet; her skin glowed deep as ivory over the superb bones of her face; her hair was wild but seemed to have shed its pall of grey and to have again that sheen the Scots call strawberry blonde. Her whole body was effervescent with joy, and warmth for Lorraine. 'Where's Bonzo?' said Lorraine in a hard little voice.

Fiona's breast heaved. 'Oh, he misbehaved, the bad boy. He'll be good now that you're home. He's out in the back garden, being terrorised by two cats. I'll fetch him.'

'Why are you here?' said Lorraine, in the same small voice.

'Oh, I'll explain all in the van. It's just incredible. I've had a total recovery from the menopause. No more nausea; no more dizziness; no more of that grinding fatigue. I still get hot flushes —'

'— I'm sure you do —'

'— but I've solemnly resolved to be much better to you than I was — and I've had some marvellous ideas about new ways to use silver — there's an image of a heron I want—'

'Fetch Bonzo, and we'll go home, okay?'

'C'mon, Lorrie babe.' Fiona draped an arm over her shoulder. 'Remember the game we wanted to play but couldn't, because I wasn't up to it? Well, I've been thinking; life's too short to hang about. I'll give it a go.'

Lorraine held out her hand for the keys of the van. 'I'm tired. I want my dog and my bed.'

'Okay, let's go.' Fiona struck her head with her hand. 'But, there is a complication. I promised to take Lucy out tonight. There's a place, a club, called — oh, there are dozens of them — Diva's, the Ace of Clubs, Louisa's, Venus Rising — Lucy's told me about them.'

'What sort of club?'

Fiona's glance was tender. 'Can it be that someone not a thousand miles from here is jealous?'

'Jealous?' Lorraine snorted. 'No, dumbstruck. What happened to the Fiona who wouldn't even go to the Gateways?'

'Oh that!' Fiona laughed. 'In those days, I didn't want to be

ogled by petrol pump attendants. Now – well – at my age
you're grateful for any attention.'

'So it would seem.'

Laughing, Fiona kissed Lorraine again. 'C'mon, Lorrie.
You've always been a sport. You come too.'

'You go if you're so keen on the idea.'

'Not without you, babe.'

'The only place I'm going is bed.'

14

Steven-John waved Lorraine off, then darted into his phone box. But all he got from Ulric was the most formal of apologies for standing him up over tea on Tuesday.

Steven-John emerged slowly, admitting to himself that the rupture which had torn his life into shapeless fragments could only be healed by Ulric, at the time, if there should ever be such a time, of Ulric's choosing. 'Looks like you could use some tea, mate' he said to the youth, and sadly climbed the stairs.

Steven-John had done all a man could do. He had phoned Ulric repeatedly. His calls had been unanswered or even more curt than this one. He had left flowers (collected from various gardens on his perambulations with Jezebel) at Ulric's door, and at intervals rung the bell. Nobody came.

But Ulric was there, and on his feet. This Steven-John knew. Once or twice, after leaving the flowers, he had sent the lift empty downstairs, and hidden himself at the turn of the stairs. From there he'd seen a hand creep round the door to take in the straggly bunches of bug-nibbled frost-pinched rosebuds.

Meditation, walking, the homeless youth, the goings-on

among Georgiana's crazy girls, nothing could shift Steven-John's thoughts from the plight of his friend and the plight of his friendship. He visited the Chinese herbalist bookstore and read everything he could find about leukaemia; he donated his best sweater (pure cashmere, being a cast-off of Toby's) to the Marie Curie charity shop; he prayed; he wept; he plotted. He called several times at the hospital, innocently requesting confirmation of the time of the chemotherapy appointment for Mr Ulric Rolle of Marylebone: they could find no record of any such arrangement.

He even made brave attempts to extract information from Ulric's GP. He forced his voice down to a bear-like growl and so deceived the receptionist into believing that she was speaking to the patient (somewhat altered for the worse by illness). But the doctor uncovered the impostor and, though she then allowed Steven-John to state his case, medical ethics prevented her from revealing to him what, if anything, she would do. Between Steven-John and his friend was a wall of ice.

That Thursday evening, Steven-John crawled under his disintegrating duvet before Rufus had ended his winter song. Steven-John was seeking warmth and remission from the pangs of hunger; he would have thought it disloyal to Ulric to ask for sleep. But nature took control of his wracked body and gave it to him anyway.

Ulric, in Marylebone, was not so kindly treated. When the starlings had done with their quarrelling, the fretful silence they left behind was interrupted by cars, churning like stomach ulcers. Ulric lay flat on his back, his fingers laced across his breast-bone. After an hour, he ceased to hear the noise: blocking out such ugliness was a skill he had early in life taught himself, to preserve his sanity. Now he did it automatically, without anger. But his eyes were less well schooled than his ears, and they lay wide open, following the shadow-play of headlights. Each pair, as they approached, projected onto the ceiling an image of the birds of paradise so bravely, recklessly, printed on his curtains. He watched their tail-feathers swelling, spreading and then falling away into the abyss of darkness. As the hours passed, there were fewer headlights but, when they came, they shaped the birds into ever stranger and more ghoulish forms. By 3 a.m., this vestige of life too was dying away, leaving only the marsh-gas flicker of red and green from the traffic lights. Beyond and within that, vacancy.

Ulric had cancelled his teaching engagements and, for the first time since his teens, neglected his voice exercises. Instead, he had spent much of the past week in bed – long enough for him to register with an occasional flicker of alarm that the tender points on his rump might be the germ of bed sores. Much of the time he thought of nothing at all. At other times, he was possessed by a blinding rage which he controlled by gripping his hands so tight over his ears or, more often, over his breast, that the joints of his fingers were now swollen and bruises had appeared on his ribs.

This anger would pounce on him at any moment of unpreparedness, set off by some triviality: a neighbour whistling as he waited for the lift to take him off to his day at the office; the flowers left dying to no purpose at his door; the repeated mechanical clack as the postman pushed a litter of advertisements through one door after another; the dark, the rain, the light, the birds, the cars, the fuss of all that pointless activity everywhere; that ignorant, stupid, emotionally gluey boy.

Just once, the anger had caught him off his guard. The telephone did it. Some idiot was trying to call him approximately every two hours. Ulric had switched off the bell but, being unfamiliar with electrics, knew no way to stop the faint clicking of a call. Ulric felt persecuted. At times, he thought it was the hospital, refusing to understand his unambiguous refusal of treatment; most times he was sure it was Steven-John. The thought of Steven-John shivering in his call box with a pocketful of small coins so incensed Ulric that, despite his best efforts at control, anger once pulled free and piled itself on itself until it broke out into a howl. Just that once, he raged at death, which had, like a maddened bear, struck so brutally at his mother, and was now advancing on him; at life, which had thrust him, a creature made tender with love, into a world where the lovers he desired mocked and taunted him; at his friends, who had fitted him into his role of daffy queen; at Steven-John, who, though he loved Ulric, had no conception of the ravenous beast that he loved; of the rage inside him, a rage so contained and controlled and compressed and terrible that it did not burn with a flame but, like a black hole, extinguished everything that smelled of hope.

This outburst caused Ulric to break out in sobs – something foreign to his nature, which caused his chest to ache as if he had been coughing with bronchitis. And the weeping took him to thinking about his mother, at whose death he had not wept at all, through whose dying he had sat like a stone. How had she been so ridiculously brave? Ulric, at sixteen, had had no sense of what she so calmly looked into – her own extinction. He had been awash with fear of being torn away from all that was known and safe, like a child dragged from its mother's skirts by the press of a crowd fleeing a cinema fire.

Young Ulric, sitting quiet and self-possessed by his mother's side, exhibiting an apparent maturity the nurses found unusual and touching in an adolescent boy, had not known her, this person he loved better than he had been able to love any other creature. And she? On the day before her death, she had said: 'Be careful not to overdo your exercises, Ulric. Remember, your voice is still breaking.' And, that evening, she had said, rather crossly, 'Ulric, you haven't eaten your supper.' The next day, the day of her death, when she was vague with otherworld knowledge, she had had little to say. Only once, starting out of unconsciousness when he straightened her covers, she had said, in a sprightly tone: 'Listen to the grasshoppers, Ulric.' The nurse shook her head sadly, but Ulric could hear them: in the rhythmic whirr and click of the electric pump injecting morphine into her stomach. And later, when they told him she was going, and he didn't know what they meant, and the nurse instructed the gangling youth, gently, to kiss her, she had whispered: 'My bonny bonny baby boy.'

When the sobs subsided, Ulric lay exhausted on his bed. Yet, within thirty minutes, he had dragged himself to his feet to get some supper and, though his dry mouth wasn't able to do much with it, when he returned to his bed, new and quite different thoughts began to prickle. Ulric had begun to think about music. This was a matter entirely other than what had to do with his mother, with life, with anything. And suddenly, it was desperately important. It was the only thing that was.

Ulric's work was not complete. There was something he still had to say. He had only to find out what. It would, of course be a song, perhaps a concert aria. To allow for his diminished physical vigour, it would be short, its passion fierce but contained. To give expression to his ironic nature, it would be an anti-lyrical lyric. Whatever it was, it would be perfect. Nothing that he had yet done, no matter how high it had flown, how carefully it had been phrased, had not had something in it that was bumbling, or only half understood, or worst of all, insincere.

His fingers once more joined over his ribs as he moved on to thinking about time, the medium of his art. Close time up into a single present, and all the notes are condensed into one white-hot screech. Stretch time out to near infinity, and there is no development, no beginning, middle or end, no music, just a low perpetual drone. Ulric's tendency was towards the latter state. If he had been a soprano, his desire might have been to sharpen, pile the notes high and urgent. But he was a deep bass; for him temptation was to hold the notes, draw them out long and dark. This the Slavonic and black American basses, men involved with earth, blood, community, had cultivated. Ulric could not follow them. Nor could he follow the majestic and solemn Italian basses. He had a different consciousness, and now he knew what it was. He could sing with the fore-taste of death, the end of time; he would be able to let it go. There would now be no need in him to drag his music down towards any indulgent lengthening of emotion. He would have to fight no urge to slow it or, out of fear of slowing it, to rush it; detachment, non-possession, balance would give him a new art. What the song was was not the first concern. What would matter would be that he could let it float away. This must be what the gods feel each time they create and let loose a butterfly — what D H Lawrence felt when he wrote: 'My love lies underground, with her face upturned to mine . . .'

Yet, what song? Ulric laced and unlaced his fingers with uncertainty. The bass solo from Verdi's Requiem? Too rich. The bass arias in *The Messiah*? Too elevated. The captured king's despair in *Aida*? Too monumental. Mephistopheles's solos in Gounod's *Faust*? Too theatrical. Wagner's Wotan? Too male. It should be a song not of innocence but of experience — of bitterness against death which ends in acceptance of death; a song about rejection, the sterility of revenge. Its music would have that cruel beauty that runs down the nerves in a shiver. What song? My love lies underground, he thought, but her face is turned away from mine. The answer came to him softly as an arrow from a blowpipe: Beethoven's *'In questa tomba oscura'*.

The melody came instantly into his mind, but Ulric quickly shut that out: in his present state, the excitement of singing would seem like an obscenity. So he thought not of the sound but of the lyric, the dead man, seeking rest in the tomb, but unable to rest because the woman he had loved, who had rejected him in life, now pestered his spirit with her futile lamentations — what sweet, poisonous satisfaction, expressed by Beethoven in sounds pure as an orchid. Yes, this was it. Beethoven had made beauty out of the ignoble; and Ulric would reveal the greatness in a minor work.

Ulric would not — could not — give to this song the grief that Chaliapin had given it. But there was something else he could do: he could give it his last — and till the last utterly controlled, hard, coldly passionate and dying anger.

As he thought these thoughts — the song without the music — Ulric's fingers tightened till the joints cracked. Then he allowed some of the musical phrases — *'Lascia che l'ombra ignade, godansi in pace almer'* – to sound in his mind, and the purest of release came to him. Who was the man Beethoven, who could take the darkest of passions, and transform them into the wing of an angel?

So what did it matter if he already had in his collection of tapes, so carefully boxed and labelled by Father Peter, two or three recordings by a self-conscious young bass called Ulric Rolle of the same. At the time he'd made them, he'd thought the emotion he conveyed was transcendent. Now he knew it for trash. Only now, when he looked death in the face, did he know that the most hideous of lies are those statements which approximate to the truth. Pray, just pray, that the disease would deal kindly with his instrument, his vulnerable lungs and vocal chords.

It did not occur to Ulric that there might be, woven through these various thoughts, some injustice, or even cruelty, towards Steven-John. To Ulric, the ultimate things were impossible to share, because they were outside of any connection between one human being and another – even Peter – even, if it came to it, with his mother. Ulric told himself that it was his nature to partition off his various passions, and if this caused problems to Steven-John, they were not Ulric's concern. Because of this capacity, Ulric could think of music as the language of God, and he could think of it as a mathematical puzzle. He did not wish to change himself. Thus, he could think of Steven-John as a little cherub, or a willing slave, or a fool; or he could dismiss him from any thought at all. And none of these conceptions interfered with another.

But, even while he reassured himself on this point, Ulric was aware of a more local and extremely tedious agitation: he couldn't cut out from his imagination the sight of a pathetic figure slinking like a tramp about the stairwell while Ulric took in the flowers. Ought he, ever so slightly, to relent, just by one degree, the merest nod of his head; just enough to stop the foolish creature from freezing his balls off in the draught?

Of course not. Ulric was doing important work which

should not be interrupted. This was a critical period. He was in control and he could think about death, his own death. For some absurd reason, his brain shaped this into an imaginary conversation with the idiotic boy. Ulric thought how he would say that he could understand the necessity of death – because endings are a necessary product of time, and without time there can be no change or growth or art; there can be no music. He would then add that he could see the need; what he couldn't see was the thing itself. What, for someone bound in time, did death actually mean? In its consequences, death made birth possible; it was the manure of all life. But in itself? For the dying, or the dead, what meaning? Since death was necessary, to give oneself to death was a proper and so virtuous act. But to what, in practical terms, was one giving oneself? Despite the scant respect that Ulric had for Steven-John's intelligence, his ears pricked to hear Steven-John's reply. It even occurred to him that he could right now, at four o'clock in the morning, send a message round to Steven-John in a taxi, and know for sure that the boy would be at his side within an hour.

But after the passage of three more ulcerating motor vehicles, this vision too sank and disappeared. Ulric reminded himself that nothing earth-shattering was happening. He was merely dying, turning into a lump of rotten, stinking meat. All these elevated thoughts were about nothing at all.

Part II

15

To miδ November

As winter approached in 1989, that year of many endings, foreboding hung heavily over Georgiana's crowd.

Ulric, through the first two weeks of November, tossed and turned, and did little else. His only real act of will was to mutter imprecations: against Hospital, to reinforce his determination to have nothing to do with it, and against Steven-John, to subdue the womanish weakness which kept putting thoughts of the mop-headed boy into his mind.

Steven-John, for his part, waited, struggling to keep his faith. He did, however, have some comfort from the homeless youth, who was now intermittently lodging in various parts of the hallway. He discovered that, under the fuzz covering his head, the lad had a broad Lancashire face, and that he was Damien William O'Connor Whitehead. But the youth refused to be drawn on the subjects of his age, his parents' phone number and the source of the various items he offered in lieu of rent. For his part, Steven-John said nothing about his grief.

Georgiana, through this fortnight, was generally low. She was tetchy with the local butcher when she had to wait seven minutes for her weekly order of four ounces of bacon and half a dozen small eggs. She lost a whole night of sleep after children accosted her in the street, demanding pennies for their guy. Foreigners, invading Regent's Park in chattering hordes, presumed to ask her the way to the Serpentine and even that epitome of vulgarity, Madame Tussaud's. Each of these encounters left Georgiana feeling affronted, and in some undefined way vulnerable, as if the distance between herself and the press of the human race was imperceptibly narrowing.

More particularly, Georgiana was deeply hurt by Fiona. Fiona's distress on that day of Steven-John's revelation had stoked the engine of Georgiana's love. Georgiana thought about Fiona constantly. She had no great desire to possess her, physically or in any other way, but she wanted to see her, spend time with her, do little things for her, and to know she was all right. Fiona responded to Georgiana's first telephone message – a breezy call saying that she was just fine and looking forward to seeing Georgiana at the next party – and not at all to later ones.

Tim and Thelma, and Sarah and Sophie were also feeling frail. Their problems arose from similar aspects of the economic dynamic. The Thatcher revolution had at first brought Tim's little management training company profitable business in training public servants to save the taxpayer's money. But his first graduates, themselves now important officers, had been so well trained by Tim that they were loath to spend this precious resource on equipping future officers to compete for their jobs. Tim and Thelma had, over the years, spent lavishly on educating their children to face the future. The consequence, as of 1989, was that they had put little away for their own future, and had produced two highly qualified young adults who despised the gross world of commerce: one gave his time to art and the other to growing organic vegetables on her allotment, and neither activity had yet proved materially profitable.

Sarah and Sophie had at first welcomed the clean-up of their hospital. Sarah had been proud to become a Director of its NHS Trust, and had concurred in the appointment of a chief administrator, a clever young man who had won his spurs in the banana export business. But things had gone awry. New money to pay for the improvements had been slow in coming and damp in the hospital's Victorian walls regularly sabotaged the cabling of the new computers. The orderlies, the clerks, the caterers and now even the junior doctors and nurses fretted against changes in the rules, and there was dark talk of strikes. The chief called meetings, at which Sarah's proposals were generally placed under Any Other Business. Sarah didn't know what to do. She and Sophie sat up late, complaining, worrying, and feeling old.

Chelsey suffered from disappointment, but this was her usual condition. For almost three weeks, nothing much followed from the exciting afternoon in which she had won Lucy's confidence. Midge called her every other day, but she knew nothing, and Chelsey told her nothing. Steven-John rang too, with the disturbing news that he'd seen Lucy in the van with Fiona and Lorraine. Chelsey's spirits hinted at strange goings-on in that ménage. But Lucy didn't call. Chelsey waited. Then, advised by the spirits, she swallowed her pride, and called Lucy herself.

Unexpectedly, and a good omen, Lucy answered the phone in person.

For Fiona, life had become chaotic, incomprehensible, exciting and disturbing. Her days were swept in a great dreamlike tide, and almost every night a repeating dream, like an undertow, pulled her back to the beginnings. In this, Fiona was lying under the hedges of the paddock at her childhood home in Braemar, and calling for her pony. The leaves would part above her, but instead of the furry muzzle, she'd see the moon-face of the Cameron boy. Fiona, as a child, had been afraid of the Cameron boy, who couldn't speak like other folk and followed her about, striking at the young corn with his stick. She would try to cover herself with the branches; but the eyes – pale, big and vague – held her with some mysterious magnetism. It was the boy and not the boy; the pony and not the pony. It was the Angel Gabriel.

'You must go away,' she would say, 'I'm an old woman now, and life has soiled me.'

But the angel came closer, until she could feel breath on her throat and hands on her breast, although she could see no mouth or hands, only the eyes. They filled her vision, like hypnosis.

Silently, still holding her with his stare, he would draw closer and closer, a great weight sinking down through the leaves, pressing her against the earth, until she couldn't move any part, not even a finger. Very slowly, his tail, moist and red as the extending penis of a dog, would penetrate her.

While she was dreaming, she always knew this to be a dream, but held on to it until the sharpness of the sensation forced her into consciousness. The first time she dreamed it, she was shocked that her mind had produced something so – she searched for a word – so dirty. When the dream came after that, she woke at the same point, but she was no longer distressed by it and thought only of her body's want of Lucy's touch.

Fiona didn't, through those weeks, feel love for Lorraine – though she felt Lorraine's confusion and unhappiness as a sharp pain – but she knew that she did, when she was in her right mind, love Lorraine, trust her and need her. But Lorraine could not give her the excitement that Lucy now could – not through any failing of Lorraine's but because only for a while can the sex and the lover become one. Fiona regretted that she and Lorraine couldn't do what the boys do – go off and fuck someone, have a great time, and come home happily to their partners. But, she thought, we can't. Women aren't made that way. Sex gets into everything we do and are. Fiona didn't like what she was when sex was dead in her, but when it was alive again, she thought herself to be something bestial.

I've got to stop this thing, she thought, often. It is too wounding, too dangerous. But not just yet, not just yet. This is my last fling. Just one more time. And many such mornings, after Lorraine had left for work, Fiona would dream her dream, then reach over to the telephone and ring Lucy. Then she would have a shower, and go back to bed to wait for the bus to arrive from Dalston.

The weeks passed, and Fiona came no closer to ending it. On the contrary, the sweetness of Lucy seeped into her fibres. She tried to make it right for Lorraine by drawing her in. She was also willing – and so was Lucy – to do as the boys do, and all share in the fun, but Lorraine had turned savage. And every time Lorraine – as she now frequently did – attacked Lucy, Fiona's tenderness towards her intensified.

Lorraine did not recognise her own savagery; through most of that first half of November she thought of herself as confused and very vulnerable.

She had stuck to her guns – at least at that first salvo – and refused to join Fiona and Lucy at the club on the night of her return. Instead she had, as planned, gone to bed. But not to sleep. In the first hour of wakefulness, she acknowledged that she deserved what she was getting; she squirmed at the memory of her many blunders; she felt an utter fool. She planned little speeches that would put everything right again.

In the next few hours, it came to her that Fiona might find more in Lucy than an agent of revenge. She might fall in love. This thought was so terrible that Lorraine could not believe it possible.

By the time she got up to shut the bedroom door against the clicking of claws as Bonzo paced up and down the hall, her thoughts had again changed direction. Now she was desperate to know what Fiona and Lucy were doing at that moment. Fragmentary images kept flashing in her mind – of a look, a whisper, a touch – and each came with a charge like an electric shock.

When, after 3 a.m., she heard a taxi halt outside the cottage, she could no longer trust her self-control and pretended to be asleep. She heard Fiona whisper a few words to Bonzo, then creep in quietly beside her. Fiona's hair smelled of tobacco and cannabis smoke; her breath smelled of wine, and her whole body, almost definitely, of sex.

Fiona was in her studio when Lorraine came home from work that evening. Lorraine brought her some wine; Fiona said Lorraine didn't need to look quite so hang-dog, and the evening Lorraine had planned as the start of a new courtship was consumed in a quarrel. Fiona refused to say what, if anything, was going on between her and Lucy. Lorraine learned only that Fiona thought Lucy 'a sweet thing'.

A week later, Lucy took Lorraine aside: she and Fiona were becoming important to each other, she said, and neither of them wanted Lorraine to be left out. Lorraine felt no shock of surprise, just a dull throb of fear. She asked no questions. Lorraine – bullish, confident Lorraine – was beginning to think that her life was being organised by two people she wasn't at all sure she knew or trusted.

The following evening, Fiona and Lucy went to a rock concert. Lorraine, who loathed rock, went too. She got very drunk. She flirted crudely with Lucy and afterwards insisted that Lucy spend the night at Gospel Oak. While Fiona was giving Bonzo his bedtime walk, Lorraine dragged Lucy up to the bedroom in a state of greater agitation and excitement than Lucy had ever roused in her before. In the days that followed, sometimes she hated Lucy, and sometimes she was in love with her.

It was Fiona who decided that, due to the unsettled state of things, they had better not take Lucy to Georgiana's party.

During this same period, Midge had been endeavouring to remake herself. On the first of November, her windows wide to let out the decay of her kitchen and to let in the cleansing wind, she sat with her first cup of tea, while her stomach churned in bitter remorse over the last night's drinking and the last ten years of wasted life. Suddenly, she was engulfed by quite a different feeling. This had nothing to do with Lucy or Georgiana, or any individual, and arose from a different source: it was All Saints' Day and, from the church at the corner, the organ and the choir burst forth in all the glory of the Blessed Ones in Heaven. Suddenly, a new life, a new Midge, seemed so achievable, so imminent. 'There is another way, Raffles,' she said. Raffles wagged her bottom in enthusiastic agreement, and then demanded a walk. They took a long walk, a very long one, since Midge gave a wide berth to all the Off Licences — and Kilburn is well supplied with them. They returned home as the sky was darkening, but by this time Midge had a wrapped bottle in her coat pocket. It was only for a little drink, to give her courage to plan her new life.

But the day which followed was All Souls' Day, and the church replicated, in a monotonous drone, the sufferings of Purgatory. On Midge's kitchen table, in a scrawl unlike her normal rounded school-mistress hand yet discomfortingly familiar, lay the achievement which had last night sent her to bed in high excitement — her list of noble intentions.

For a full two weeks, this list lay on her kitchen table. And each day she contemplated it, until it became a measure of her despair.

One morning in mid-November, Midge sat glancing at this list as, for the third or fourth time, she picked up the bottle anchoring it to the table. This she again raised to the light in the hope that it might contain enough for a modest hair-of-the-dog. It was still empty. She snapped upright and to attention, then marched the bottle firmly over to the scullery end, where she thrust it into the clank of empties beside the bin. This powerful act of will pleased but exhausted her. She shambled back and collapsed onto the wonky bench. Only one thought could be held with any clarity by her brain, and that came direct from the Tempter: not many days earlier, in honour of Chelsey, Midge had broken the seal on Colonel Winters's best single malt. Could a tiny medicinal sip be excusable under the circumstances of this morning that was so stressful because it was no longer morning? She looked to Raffles for advice. Bright-eyed, the little dog came trotting up. With the resigned sigh of one who was accustomed to

accepting defeat from a strong-willed beast, Midge scooped
Raffles up under her arm and set herself in motion. She made
her way not to the cabinet in the dining room but to the
fridge. She extracted the dish of boiled fowl and doled out a
gluey portion.

This second small act of will reminded her that the day
that Margaret Winters, in solitary misery, rifled her father's
collection, would be the day that she destroyed it – down to
the last drop. It would be the day that she finished with
Planet Earth. And that could not be while Raffles needed
breakfast. She put down the bowl. Raffles, in innocent preoccupation with her own need, thrust her dainty snout into
the mess.

Midge, mug of tea now firmly in hand, sat down – not
exactly to read the list, since she knew it by heart – but to
accentuate her humiliation by once more looking it over. It
ran as follows:

    1 One can only Red Stripe each evening
    2 Take Instruction to enter the Church
    3 Two mile walk daily
    4 Tidy kitchen
    5 Teach at Somali Refugee Centre
    6 Lose weight
    7 One can Red Stripe lunch time; small whisky to
       follow Red Stripe evening; one, note one, only; never
       more than two (crossed out) three (crossed out) two
       (crossed out)

Then the writing ran off the page. Midge pushed aside the
paper, and strove to turn her mind to other things, anything
that was not herself. Lucy. Whatever was happening to Lucy
could only be bad, and Midge could not help her. Lucy had
wanted Midge to know that Lorraine had dropped her, but
most decidedly did not want Midge to comfort her. No matter
how Midge worried about Lucy, her role was to keep away.
This would have been painful enough on its own; worse was

the memory of Lucy sitting right here in the kitchen with Chelsey's arms about her. This image tormented Midge.

Why was she so upset by it? She could scarcely claim to be in love with Lucy, even less in love with Chelsey. She ought to be pleased – and in part of her mind she was – that Lucy had a friend. It wasn't over Lucy that she grieved; it was over herself. She, Midge, was, for any function you could name on the Planet, useless. That touching scene had made clear how sidelined, redundant, superfluous, spineless, stupid, empty, hollow and false she was.

What she felt, Midge decided, was not jealousy. Jealousy was big and hungry. Midge was so depleted that she barely touched the verges of such grand emotion. Midge's feeling was envy – the meanest of self-indulgences. Midge didn't desire Lucy or Chelsey half so much as she coveted their capacity to mesh with another human being.

Yet surely it was to make human relationships that she had been put on this Planet? She hadn't the powers for the highest mode of being – a life of prayer and contemplation – but she had – hadn't she? – made use of the one gift she did have, of human warmth. She had saved many lost children. She had been an unstintingly generous lover. She had been a loving daughter to her father and a dutiful one to her mother. But, in her deepest mind, Midge was convinced that all these achievements were null, because she had not been pure of heart when she did them. And she was now punished with a life in the void, in Purgatory.

While her dog slurped up the remains of the animal she had dismembered while its chilled corpse still smelled of fear, and had then reduced, by a chemical process, halfway to primeval sludge, waves of faintness washed over Midge. Each came up in a swell of desire for the ease she could take from her father's cabinet, and broke over her as she, quite softly, pushed the desire aside, and held to her mug of tea.

The telephone rang. Midge was too ill to deal with anyone, especially anyone who was getting on with life, and she did not at that moment want to communicate even with Lucy, but she knew distraction was necessary. She staggered to the hall to answer it. She wouldn't have done so if she'd guessed who was on the line. It was Chelsey, in her unpleasant sprightly mode.

'What would you think, Midge dear, of taking young Lucy to Georgiana's next party?'

Midge's mind was slow, and full of thoughts that didn't easily turn to parties.

Chelsey must have been bored with waiting for Midge to reply. 'The party this coming Saturday,' she prompted.

What mischief was behind this suggestion?

'It's our best chance, don't you think,' continued Chelsey, 'to get that silly quarrel between Lucy and Georgiana patched up. We'll all be there to explain that neither of them meant any harm.'

Midge was not *that* stupid. 'I'd do it gladly,' she said, 'if Georgiana and Lucy asked me to.'

'Midget, come now. Be realistic. How could they? Consider the tangle they've got themselves into. They need a helping hand.'

'What about yours?'

'My hands are tied. I'm very close to Lucy, as you know; it would be obvious that I had an interest.'

'Lorraine will be there. It would be appallingly tactless to expose Lucy to the pain of bumping into her so soon after their break-up.'

Chelsey chuckled. 'My dear, those three are tight as peas in a pod.'

'Then let Fiona and Lorraine take her.'

'That, of course is what Lucy would prefer. I've just been speaking to her. But – I'm not sure how much of this I dare divulge – but –'

Midge was now all ears.

'They're good friends, true, but Lorraine is the jealous type. She still sees Lucy as her property, and takes umbrage at any closeness between Fiona and Lucy. And Fiona doesn't want Lorraine making a scene in Georgiana's presence.'

'No more do I,' said Midge, who hated scenes.

Chelsey pounced. 'That's the point. There won't be a scene if Lucy sticks close to you.'

Midge prevaricated. 'No, I think this is dangerous. It seems to me like meddling.'

'But if it would make Lucy happy?'

'Of course I'd do anything to make Lucy happy, but – I'm sorry Chelsey, but I would want at the least to ask Lucy if she'd be prepared to face it.'

'My dear, that's exactly what I hoped a true friend would say. She's home. I've just been speaking to her. Phone her. Do it right now, and ask.'

Chelsey put down the phone with satisfaction. She knew that Midge had taken the bait.

16

Georgiana's entire life was, in Toby's view, a pursuit of form –
the highest class of form, of course. Toby respected her efforts
on balance: he credited her achievement of an impenetrable
front, but debited her for believing in the part she had chosen
to play. Toby also adopted a formal pose, but considered that
he had escaped the chains that bound Georgiana because he
believed – or so he thought – in nothing. While he was no
doubt correct in asserting that he did not believe in God, love
or the existence of any inherent moral order, there were things
about himself that he did believe. The most basic of these was
that nobody, apart from his closest friends and the boys in the
hedges, knew he was gay. He was wrong. Toby was probably
the only person in the civil service establishment who hadn't
heard the Honourable Toby Hume described as camp as a
row of tents.

But it would never cross anybody's mind to describe
Georgiana in such terms. Curiously, since her life was so
much more restricted – by poverty, gender, age and the very
small field of her operation – she was above such limitations.
Georgiana was the true Mother Superior. She knew this but,
perhaps because she knew also that it was a fragile persona,

didn't pride herself on it, nor castigate herself if the mask slipped. Unlike Toby, unlike anybody else in her circle, Georgiana, even when, as now, she was low in spirits, was at ease with herself.

Yet Georgiana fretted over parties like any ordinary host. And, as the third Saturday in November approached, she did over this one. The crates of wine arrived punctually, the bill in Toby's name. The canapés and vol-au-vents were perfect. Shadows cast by flowers in her tallest vase masked stains on the wallpaper caused by an overflow from the bathroom in the flat above. Nobody had telephoned to cancel on such allowable grounds as a broken leg or the death of a mother. By 7 p.m., everything was in order, leaving an hour for Georgiana to get into armour.

She bathed in four inches of warm water, washed her hair under the bath tap (easier than bending to the handbasin) then, shrouded in towels, examined herself in the mirror. Georgiana was not looking her best. She could discount the depredations of age, but not the clear signs that she was tipping over from slender to gaunt. She needed to put some flesh on. She made a trip to the kitchen, took out the tin of Nice biscuits and ate two, helped down with the remains of her last cup of tea. Feeling better, she returned to dress her body and her face. Georgiana was an expert at make-up, and the results concealed much. Then she began on her hair.

Georgiana was her own hairdresser, and an expert in that art too. But this evening, the hairpiece she needed to weave inconspicuously into her chignon simply refused to cooperate. She struggled for over half an hour; the last ten minutes of struggle undid most of what had before been achieved. Each minute, her arms became heavier, her fingers clumsier and the stiffness in her neck more painful. If she had been given to cursing or throwing things about, she would have damned the bathroom mirror (positioned at shaving height for a six-foot man) and flung the slippery glass tray of pins, hairnets and clasps into the intestines of the bathroom plumbing.

Instead, as there remained the one friend who could be trusted to fasten the pins, Georgiana's resentment of Fiona's neglect over the previous weeks was by degrees laid aside. As, one by one, she rejected the sharp remarks stored up for Fiona's arrival, more of her body softened with the anticipation of Fiona's touch. After all, tonight was Georgiana's party, and people knew how to behave; Fiona would be herself again. This thought restored Georgiana.

Martina arrived, ruddy-faced from the gym, on the dot of eight. Georgiana left her rippling her muscles at the three long windows, and turned to welcome Hugo. He presented a bottle wrapped in brown paper then, breathy with blood pressure, flopped into his usual seat near the door. Georgiana made her way to the kitchen to bring out the wine. She knew that Hugo, dear old toad, would stay put all evening, noting each arrival and passing on anything of interest. Georgiana struggled with the wires round the cork; in these days of mass-production everything was stiffer and tighter than it used to be. The doorbell clanged, followed by the embarrassedly cheerful noises of greetings. No need to hurry. The celibates always arrived first and could be trusted to amuse themselves.

'I say, Georgiana, may I?' Steven-John was at her back. She swung round, thrust the bottle into his hands, and patted her chignon into place. She'd been caught off-guard. Steven-John was not normally permitted to open bottles since he had the vulgar habit of firing the cork at the ceiling. But on this occasion, he did the job without bravado and Toby's good wine tricked, not a drop spilled, into the glasses.

'Thank you, my dear.' Georgiana swivelled her chin to greet him with the usual peck, but their eyes met in the process, and she stopped short. 'What's this, young Steven? Are you all right?'

Steven-John burst into tears.

Georgiana hated to see a man cry. On this occasion, she probably succeeded in not seeing it, as she switched the conversation to the weather and swooped out with the wine as quickly as possible without further damage to Steven-John's dignity.

Fortunately, Sarah and Sophie walked in at that moment, and the general hoo-ha of their arrival prevented any spread of the drama in the kitchen. None the less, Georgiana felt in her bones that party-giving was becoming hard work.

This party was certainly slow to get moving. Those present did their best. Tim and Thelma and Sarah-Sophie prattled away as usual. But this was 1989, so there was an ominous undertone. Since religion and politics were taboo subjects, nobody voiced the rumours of plots against the Prime Minister, the male priesthood and the marriage of the Prince of Wales. But something about Tim's bearing suggested that he hadn't had much work that month, and Thelma's glances lingered at the corners of Georgiana's carpets, like someone wondering what life would be like if she had to give up her char. Sophie seemed more than usually protective of Sarah and, when the tray came round, ordered her a spritzer. But old companionship soon put them at their ease, and they turned to the proper preoccupations of their class: that the youth of the nation preferred social security to honest labour and even decent districts were being invaded by immigrants.

Steven-John emerged, red eyed, from the kitchen, and hung about at the edge of this conversation. He said little. This was not because he himself lived on social security and so could have no views of any worth, but because he was listening for the sound of Ulric's footsteps. Georgiana, with her good sense of what was needed, put a tray of little eats, each neatly trussed into foetal position, into his charge. Sophie delicately plucked out a cocktail stick on which was impaled a prune wrapped in bacon, while Tim dug into the centre, for a chicken leg wearing a frilly paper bloomer. Steven-John breathed a prayer for the pig and the hen.

There were footsteps. Chelsey strode in, cloak billowing, greeting the crowd with broad smiles and hand gestures:

Chelsey was in one of her jolly moods, an indication that the spirits had foretold that someone would come down on a banana skin. More worryingly, Georgiana's grandmother clock struck the half-hour after nine, and there were still notable absences. Toby, of course, hadn't yet arrived. But neither had Fiona and Lorraine, nor Ulric, nor, most oddly, Midge.

Hardly bothering now about her fraying chignon, Georgiana plied the wine with a heavy hand. And, uncharacteristically, she took a few glassfuls herself. Georgiana did not enjoy inebriation, though she willingly played her part in getting other people pissed as newts. The only effect wine had on her was that she walked with an even straighter back, and kept her tongue in check with more than usual discretion.

So, when Hugo opened the door to Fiona, looking extremely pleased with herself, Georgiana's anticipatory flush of pleasure and relief gave way to a pang of remembered injustice: Georgiana had spent three weeks *worrying* about this woman! Georgiana swanned up to the group and offered to Fiona and then Lorraine, the profile of a cool cheek.

But Steven-John rushed over and flung himself at Fiona. 'I say, Fifi,' he cried, 'you look absolutely terrific.'

Fiona, as if in surprise, stepped back and looked down at her clothes. They were not her usual party gear of silk and soft leather. On her feet were trainers, black velour, designer-stamped and new, no socks. Her long slender legs were wrapped in satiny black tights. She wore a leather bomber jacket, its collar poking into her silvering red-gold hair, now cut elfin short, softly fringing her forehead and fingering her cheekbones. These were more than usually prominent, as she had lost weight. She raised her head: her great soft violet eyes were moist with pleasure. 'I feel fine,' she said.

'Dietrich in her prime,' added Hugo, moving closer. 'But where, darling, are the stiletto heels?'

Fiona, who never smiled, tossed off the jacket with an ironic shrug, to reveal a sleeveless black T-shirt. It was marked, in embossed white capitals, with the legend:

OUT & PROUD
& IN YOUR FACE

There was an embarrassed silence. Georgiana turned on her heel and retreated towards the kitchen, the tangle of the hairpiece protruding from her chignon like the innards of a doll in the mouth of a puppy.

'Oh dear! Georgie doesn't seem to like it.'

'She'll learn to move with the times,' called Tim from across the room, 'and take it on the chin that we're hitting the nineties. From now on, my dears, we'll all have to turn gay. Heterosexuals will be as dull as vicars used to be before they converted Jesus into a queer.'

'Come, Tim. It's *le fin de siècle*,' said Thelma. 'A touch of delicious decadence – for us all, including you and me.'

'Well, I'm postponing the *fin* of everything right now,' said Fiona. 'This is the start – for me, and Lorraine, and um —' Fiona looked about, her face radiant. Her glance encountered Chelsey's, then moved quickly on.

Steven-John cleared his throat. 'Well *I*,' he said gruffly, 'really like Fiona's T-shirt. *I* think it's really original.'

Steven-John was in danger of diffusing the first drama of the evening, and Chelsey stepped in smartly. 'But not exactly unique,' she said. 'Lorraine's wearing one too.'

Lorraine stepped back. She made as if to take off her own jacket, but instead pulled it close. 'It's the same,' she muttered.

'We'll all be decadent tonight,' said Thelma, 'c'mon, Lorraine, flaunt it for us.'

'But – oh all right.' Lorraine took off her jacket, horribly aware that the slogan roller-coasted over her breasts and several letters disappeared in the creases under her arms.

Thelma's look turned gentle as she noted Lorraine's chest. 'It's good to be Out and good to be Proud, my dear.' Then, bending closer, she whispered, 'You mustn't mind Tim's remarks about gays. It's the male castration complex. They bluster when they're feeling down.'

'I didn't mind his comments.' Lorraine hooked a finger through the jacket and slung it casually over her shoulder. 'Anyway, I understand bluster. I've been doing it a lot lately.'

'Oh, have you?' Thelma looked at her closely. 'Is there anything you'd like to tell me, dear?'

Lorraine stopped short. She looked quickly about her – the old habit of reaching out for Fiona's support when she was cornered – and saw her partner and Georgiana making for the bathroom. She could not, of course, run after them. Instead, she ran away from Thelma. Mumbling something incoherent, she slipped off to the kitchen. She poured herself a glass of wine.

Lorraine decided that she did not much like these people – her friends because they were Fiona's friends. Not because they believed her unworthy of Fiona, but because (apart from Georgiana and Toby, who were raised above the mass purely by class) she considered them a bunch of particularly silly and affected people. They did nothing with their lives except – as Lucy said – relate to each other. 'But what?' she thought as she stood at the kitchen window, staring across the well into kitchens just as small but far better equipped than Georgiana's, 'does my life consist of apart from relating to Fiona – if I do relate to Fiona? And what, other than affectation, can I now call our pose of being "Les Biches"?'

Cries of 'Darling', 'Angel-tits', and a general surge towards the door informed her that Toby had arrived. Lorraine downed her wine, poured another and forced herself to return to the drawing room. Saving face, she told herself, mattered much when you had little else to save.

Fiona, her mouth full of pins, deftly tucked the hairpiece into Georgiana's chignon and fastened it. Years of working with tiny objects in gold and silver had given Fiona great dexterity, and the touch of her fingers sent molten streams through Georgiana's body. 'That do you then, Georgie?'

'Doesn't feel very secure, darling.' Georgiana had not till then raised the subject of unanswered telephone messages, wanting to give Fiona the opportunity to raise it herself. But time was pressing. 'Don't want it to fall apart. Just as I don't want us to fall apart.'

'Oh that!' Fiona pushed a final pin into the chignon. 'I've been meaning to talk to you. But, blame yourself, dear heart. I've been taking your advice, and having fun. I knew you'd understand.'

Georgiana was not on Steven-John's telephone circuit, so was one of the few members of the crowd not to know of the about-turn in the Lucy affair. Toby, her usual confidant, had said nothing: he understood Georgiana's love for Fiona too well to treat it with levity. 'I'm pleased for you,' said Georgiana. 'Is it anyone I know?'

'Not your favourite person, I'm afraid. That's one big thing I regret about it.'

'Oh God! Chelsey?'

Fiona laughed. 'I'm not completely out of my mind. Almost, but not completely.'

'So you're very much taken with him? Her?'

Fiona sighed. 'Wish I knew. Only know I'm playing with fire, and right now that's very exciting.'

'You mean dangerous?'

Fiona nodded. 'I can't let it go on for long. I worry about Lorraine.'

'Pah! Lorraine had this coming to her, getting off with that common little tart.'

'Maybe.' Fiona looked thoughtful. 'But I'm hurting her; and I'm hurting you.'

'Me?' Georgiana raised her eyebrows: 'Darling! Don't worry yourself; you don't know how tough this old hide is.'

Fiona laughed. 'I've some idea.' Then, her face suddenly serious, she added, 'No, I don't. I dunno, Georgie. It sometimes seems as if I'm letting myself be made over by a Frankenstein.'

It was now Georgiana's turn to laugh. 'That explains the demonic vest.'

Fiona pulled the T-shirt over her head, and put it on again, inside out. Georgiana watched closely. Fiona had almost no breasts; her body seemed vulnerable as a child's. 'You look so gorgeous, darling, I could eat you.'

'You'd best do that now, Georgie, while you still want to.' Fiona put her arms on Georgiana's scrawny shoulders and whispered, 'And while you still want to hear it, let what remains of me say that you are the one thing on earth that I truly believe in.'

Even coming from Fiona, this was a lot of emotion for Georgiana to handle. 'You're talking riddles, child, while I have work to do.' She reached out for the hand mirror, one of her surviving treasures, a lovely object with mother-of-pearl inlaid back and handle. She wiped the condensation from its mottled face and examined her chignon. 'Almost as good a job as that Frankenstein's done on your hair. Now I'm ready for Toby. Let's away.'

Steven-John retreated towards the kitchen when Toby arrived. He met Lorraine en route and paused out of the need to say something consoling, but she, stony faced, pushed past him and marched over to the furthest window. Unlike himself, he did not pursue her. His thoughts were focused on Toby. Toby had turned icy since Steven-John had learned his HIV status. His telephone messages were now diverted to a service which required a password for access, and he had left a note reminding Steven-John that his duties concerned Jezebel and not Toby's mail. Steven-John did not resent Toby's rudeness. He felt horribly hurt, but loved Toby better for the insight he now had into Toby's courage, and his pain was mollified by his sense of the righteousness of his own case: out of loyalty to Ulric he would not tell Toby the truth about Ulric's staphylococcal infection.

He was tempted. If he told, Ulric's cruelty to Toby would be explained and become forgivable; the rift between Toby and Ulric could be healed, and Steven-John could play a part in helping Toby deal with his own terrible prospects. But Steven-John, the great gossip ready to make well-intentioned if clumsy charges into anybody's life, knew that this was a situation that did not belong to him, and on this matter he kept his knowledge and his pain to himself.

These now familiar options ran through his mind as he arranged the wine bottles into ever neater rows on the kitchen table and half listened to the chatter from the drawing room. Toby was telling a story about the secret life of a minister of state whose great passion was to have his feet tickled by his mistress. Toby's manner was as grandly camp as ever, without any hint of the horror of his own secret life, and his listeners giggled as if their own feet were being tickled. Steven-John felt a great warmth and pity for all these people, and wondered if this was how the gods felt when they saw humans sporting with such innocent temerity – children playing tag on the edge of a precipice. He heard Toby embrace Georgiana and Fiona with cries of delight and his characteristic phrases, which managed, somehow, to sound the more insouciant and elegant for being a little shop-soiled by their predictability.

Beyond the voices, sounded the clang of the lift gates. His heart leapt as he heard the steady tread he loved so well. He stood absolutely still, his ears sharp as a dog's. He heard Hugo's hellos and, in response, the great, deep, beautiful and yet prissy voice saying 'Steven-John not here tonight?' It took all Steven-John's strength not to explode.

Steven-John was still waiting when Ulric made his way into the kitchen. He listened to the scrape of a chair and the rustle as Ulric laid his coat and hat on it. Then more footsteps, then, what he had been waiting for, the hand on his shoulder. 'Do I get a glass of wine too, Mr Barman?'

With a sob, Steven-John swung around, and flung his arms around Ulric's chest.

Lorraine watched Toby's taxi disappear into Avenue Road, leaving the driveway of the block clear, bar a few recognisable cars: Sarah's Rover, Tim's now ageing Merc. The wet, cold night gave the tarred path a silvery sheen, a semicircle of brightness between the building and garden. Beyond the waving silhouettes of trees, car headlights traced dotted lines up and down the road. At her back, the party was livening up. Fiona and Georgiana had emerged from the bathroom and were now in a gaggle with Toby, mocking some foolish politician for sexual tastes rather less peculiar than their own. Lorraine wanted to go home, and she didn't want to go home.

Without much interest, she watched a small car halt in the middle of Avenue Road, the indicator light flicking its intention to make the right-hand turn. After missing two or three opportunities, the car surged forward, almost in the path of a bus, and screeched into the drive. It was a Mini. Laboriously, it lurched back and forward, fitting itself into a parking space of a size to take a ten-ton truck. It had to be Midge: how very unwise of her to drive.

The engine stalled and lights went out, and both doors opened. Lorraine's stomach tightened even before she recognised the cropped head and duffel coat emerging from the passenger side.

A muffled clang from the ground floor gave notice that the pair were now in the lift. Lorraine glanced over to Fiona: Fiona's neck arched as the lift whirred into action. Fiona was listening. Did she know that Lucy was coming? Was this a set up?

Very slowly, Lorraine moved towards the group still centred on Toby. Lorraine's control had once already almost slipped. That had been a trivial lapse over a tasteless T-shirt, but it had, she thought, driven Fiona into Georgiana's bathroom, and she didn't want to risk disgusting Fiona with another. But, if there was a plot, she was determined to sniff it out. She would not, yet again, be made to play the fool.

She was intercepted by Chelsey. 'I'm your good fairy tonight,' Chelsey said easily. 'Now you two can transfer your anger with each other to a third party – the great safety valve of what you call "marriage". You could say thanks.'

'Thanks,' said Lorraine (who hadn't the faintest idea what

Chelsey was talking about), without taking her eye off the door.

In bustled Midge, her arm firmly clasped about Lucy's waist. 'Good evening all,' Midge said determinedly. Lucy's face and ears were flooded by a furious red blush. As at Lucy's previous entry, conversation faded.

When the various groups had absorbed what there was to be had from the tableau at the door and turned back to their previous conversations, Lorraine found herself still facing Chelsey — who was now silent, though her eyes devoured every nuance. Lorraine was determined to keep her dignity — difficult, as the wine she'd drunk so quickly was buzzing in her veins. Stealthily, she watched. She saw Fiona take Midge's place at Lucy's side. Chelsey was watching too. Lorraine shifted her position to obscure Chelsey's view, but Chelsey openly peered past the bulk of Lorraine's body. Lorraine moved again, and saw that Fiona and Lucy were now talking to Toby. So Fiona's party-talk with Toby could include Lucy: it never included Lorraine! Then Lorraine saw Fiona head towards the kitchen. Meek as a lamb, Lucy followed. Yes. This was a set-up.

'Lucy's looking good, don't you think?' said Chelsey innocently. 'Fiona too: a remarkable recovery from her depression.'

Lorraine had already observed that Lucy was looking good; when her blush faded, her skin had the delicacy of a porcelain doll. Worse, this public exposure showed Lorraine what she had failed to see when Lucy was her secret lover: that Lucy had an elfin gracefulness — qualities to which big, burly Lorraine could never aspire.

'And I do declare,' said Chelsey brightly, 'that she's wearing one of your fancy T-shirts, or something very like.'

No longer caring to protect her dignity from Chelsey's grin, Lorraine roughly thrust her arms back into her jacket and zipped it up fast. It was a plot, and Midge was in it; Fiona and Lucy were in it, and so was Chelsey. No doubt everybody knew what was going on, except Lorraine. If so, what was?

'Excuse me, Chelsey.' Lorraine pushed her way past, and waited, hovering outside the closed kitchen door, to trap the two conspirators.

Fiona had frozen when Lucy appeared in the doorway. She didn't hear Midge's greeting. Open-mouthed, she stared at Lucy as Midge, with a deal of palaver, took her backpack, gloves, scarf and then struggled to ease off her coat. Blushing furiously, Lucy stared straight ahead, her hands so stiff at her sides they could have been chained. By degrees, the coat came off, and Lucy stood exposed in her Doc Martens, jeans and a sleeveless black T-shirt bearing the legend OUT & PROUD & . . .

Faintness struck Fiona. This was dirty tricks. This was assault. Only a few moments before, she had come close to telling Georgiana about her affair with Lucy, but now the certain prospect of its exposure appalled her. Fiona's body had, automatically, thrilled at the sight of Lucy, but consciousness converted that pleasure into shock. Fiona was still staring when Lucy's head turned. They faced each other, blankly, for a second. Fiona's lips tensed. 'Hello, Lucy,' she said, and turned back to Toby's conversation. Georgiana, standing at Toby's other side, ran Lucy through with looks like slivers of ice.

Midge rubbed her hands together as if all was for the good in the best of all possible worlds and said, with an avuncular chuckle, 'Right! We're here. Now we'll go to the kitchen, Lucy dear, and fix you a socking great drink.'

Fiona interrupted Toby's story to call out: 'I'll take her,' and then: 'Oh, Toby, this is Lucy. Georgiana: you two have met.'

Georgiana didn't answer, but Toby bowed very low: 'And so have we.' He took her hand and kissed it. 'An unforgettable experience.'

Lucy, fingers wriggling, quickly withdrew and moved to Midge's side. But Fiona reached out and pulled her back. 'To the kitchen,' she said. Lucy followed.

❖

Midge could have wrung her hands in despair. She had instantly lost control of the situation. Lucy had gone off with Fiona – the very thing the plan had been set up to prevent – and Midge was now pinned to the spot by Sophie. Midge found it particularly difficult to deal with Sophie: she still felt guilty that she may, on that occasion of some ten years back, have dropped her. She was obliged to an assiduous and time-consuming gallantry.

'What a lovely dress, Sophie dear,' she said unconvincingly.

Fiona shut the kitchen door, leaned against it, folded her arms. 'What are you doing here?'

'I had to come,' said Lucy, 'you know I have to make Georgiana take back the horrible things she said.'

'Georgiana is my best friend.'

'That's why it's so important —'

'— And why you will leave her to me.'

Lucy's blush coagulated in blotches on her cheeks and ears. 'It's that double standard again,' she said, knocking her fists against each other in frustration. 'Even in the way you look. We're all wearing our special T-shirts, but you've got yours on inside out; your shirt shouting for openness, and your face shut like a cage.' She paused. 'And it's cruel. When we bought those shirts, we were Out to each other and Proud of each other. I thought,' she added, her voice cracking, 'it was a breakthrough.'

'Sometimes,' said Fiona drably, 'I could take you for a moron.'

'I must be a moron. I love you.'

Fiona shook her head furiously. 'Don't say that. We have no right, either of us, to talk about love.'

'Talk about it or not,' said Lucy quietly, 'it's there, and you know it's there.'

Fiona made no reply.

'And I do have rights. I have the same rights as you do to be respected.'

'Then you could make a start,' said Fiona dryly, 'by respecting mine – for a start, my privacy.'

Lucy again banged her fists furiously against each other. 'The Scottish upper classes think privacy is their particular birthright,' she said angrily, 'along with ponies and castles and guns for shooting grouse.'

Fiona gave a short, scornful upper-class laugh. 'Privacy is boundaries. It's a necessity, so as much of a right as anything is.'

'Why should I respect yours?' Lucy snapped. 'You don't respect mine. Where are my boundaries? I'm supposed to appear whenever you feel like seeing me and disappear when you don't; I'm supposed to feel this or feel that – whatever fits in with your plan of the moment for me and Lorraine.'

'Leave Lorraine alone!' Fiona folded her arms.

'I haven't even spoken to Lorraine. You're the one dragging her into the argument!'

'You aren't going to speak to anyone. I'll get your coat and call you a taxi.'

Lucy stepped back. 'I'll talk to Lorraine whenever and if ever she wants to talk to me,' she whispered, 'and when Midge and I are ready, then I'll go home.'

Fiona nodded. 'Remember this,' she said, reaching for the door, 'because I am not going to forget it.'

The din of the party rushed at them. Lucy, with a sob, tried to hold Fiona back, but Fiona turned her about, and marched her into Georgiana's drawing room.

Out in Georgiana's drawing room, it was one of those moments when the party runs the people and not the other way round, thought Chelsey, standing alone by the windows: stereophonic outbursts of squeals and laughter unconnected with pleasure; bonhomie as false as the crystal of Georgiana's chandelier; voices with rather too much bark and bravado to delight the neighbours. Sarah-Sophie and Tim and Thelma, wine in their voice-boxes, were spluttering over some disaster. Martina and Steven-John were biffing each other like footballers, while Ulric egged them on by appealing for calm. Toby, in the centre of a crowd, was reporting further incidents of current Foreign Office gossip. Georgiana stood beside him. As soon as the kitchen door opened on Lucy, her smile shut down like a trap.

Chelsey too looked at the kitchen door, and at the prowling figure of Lorraine, bomber jacket zipped up to the gullet, beside it. She caught Lucy's eye and, with a flick of her head, signalled: 'Chin up'. Then she moved a little closer, to prevent Sophie's shrieks from drowning the conversation outside the kitchen.

Lorraine looked at Fiona and then Lucy. 'So?' she said. 'So!' Neither responded.

'So! It seems I've arrived too late to join the two lovebirds in a snog in the kitchen.'

'It seems you have,' said Fiona. Pushing her way past Lorraine, she went off to join Georgiana.

Lucy's face blanched as Lorraine bore down on her, put a hand on her shoulder, pushed her back against the doorway, and stared into her eyes, saying nothing. Just as abruptly, Lorraine then turned and marched over to Fiona. This time she grabbed at Fiona's shoulder and turned her round, roughly, pulling her away from Georgiana. Talk and laughter died in one group after another, until there was silence throughout the room. 'Why,' she hissed, 'did you do this?'

Fiona's face was as white as Lucy's had been. 'Let go of me,' she whispered.

But Lorraine didn't let go. 'Why, why, why?' she cried. Fiona's head jerked as Lorraine shook her.

But Midge, predictably, leapt in. 'Please. It's all my fault,' she said. 'It was my idea, entirely mine, to bring Lucy tonight. I wanted us all to have the chance to talk sensibly and –' her voice trailed away '– clear up misunderstandings.'

For a second, Lorraine looked irritated, or perhaps puzzled, and Chelsey moved in smartly. 'Don't take things so hard, Lorraine,' she called out, 'a woman in Fiona's medical condition needs a bit on the side.'

Fiona angrily brushed at the air beside her ear as if Chelsey's voice was the buzzing of some noxious insect, then turned to Midge and snapped: 'Haven't you done enough damage already?'

The crowd picked up the cue. Sarah muttered: 'Typical of old Midge to put her foot in it,' and Toby called out: 'Where's the wine got to?'; while Thelma, gushing with enthusiasm, added, 'I'm dying to hear how Lorraine managed to escape the dysentery plague in Malawi.'

Chelsey held her breath. Lorraine now had a clearly marked escape route. But she didn't take it; perhaps she didn't even see it. Without moving her glance from Fiona's face, she said: 'I've come home to a far more deadly plague.' Lorraine may have been drunk, but she'd never before reached such heights in Chelsey's estimation.

Nor had Lucy. Now standing midway between the kitchen and the group in the centre she cleared her throat and said, in a public voice: 'Fiona didn't know I was coming tonight. I came –' she pointed at Georgiana '– to talk to you. I'd rather have talked to you alone, but you can't always choose your moment.'

'No, you can't, can you?' said Toby. 'And the moment isn't now. Steven-John – take her to the tube station, will you?'

Chelsey reached out to detain Steven-John. 'Let her talk.'

Lucy thought for a few seconds, then said: 'I've come to claim my rights as Fiona and Lorraine's friend, and Fiona's lover.'

Lorraine, sweating profusely and breathing like an exhausted wrestler but till then silent, wailed, 'Oh Fiona, no!' The face she turned to Fiona was crumpled with grief. 'No, darling, no!'

Fiona took a step back and, with the briefest glance at Lorraine, muttered: 'Stop it. You are disgusting.'

There was an embarrassed silence. Georgiana stood stock still. Lorraine stumbled off towards the bathroom, and the room resounded with anxious exclamations about how late it was getting.

Lucy called out: 'Wait: I haven't finished yet.'

Chelsey knew the girl had guts, but this exceeded expectations. 'Talk, Lucy.'

Lucy did. In a small but firm voice, she said: 'You see how Fiona looks now? I did that. I brought her back to life. You were killing her.'

Lorraine, halfway to the bathroom, stopped but didn't turn. Fiona, Georgiana, Toby, all were stiff as pillars of salt.

'I have to tell the truth, Fiona.' Lucy was still standing apart. 'All of it. They were dragging you down into their dead world. Especially her, Georgiana, the Queen of the Dead.'

Fiona gave a horrible cry, and Georgiana stormed towards her. In a queer voice, cracked and shrill but still very county, she waved her arms and said: 'Out, out!' and hit Lucy, hard, across the face.

Lucy didn't flinch. She said: 'I had to do it, Fiona, even if I lose you for it.' Then she burst into tears.

17

At 12.30 most of the crowd left rather quickly. Chelsey had enjoyed this one more than any of Georgiana's parties in years, and was one of the few to linger. She helped Thelma shove Lorraine into a taxi, then hung about the kitchen, where Martina was doing the washing up. Fiona drove off in the van, without offering her a lift so, in the end, Chelsey hitched up her cloak, and walked home. Frognal was only a mile or so up the Finchley Road and there was always the chance that half an hour of fresh air would beat her insomnia problem. It didn't. Chelsey was so thrilled by Lucy's performance that she kept leaping out of bed, sometimes to make speeches to the kettle, sometimes to embrace the cushions of the settee, at others to curl up on the rug in frustration. She longed to call up her spirits – but knew they wouldn't come anywhere near someone so frenzied – to ask just one question: was there any faint chance that the seed winged like a sycamore, which would fly her to freedom, represented not, as she'd thought, the voice of Iolanthe, but of someone rather closer?

By morning, she did fade out into something like sleep, punctured every hour or so by church bells. When finally, around 3 p.m., the telephone rang, and she heard the voice she'd been dreaming of, she was almost too tired to care. It being Sunday, the at-home day, she casually asked Lucy over for tea.

When Lucy arrived, the dying day shadowed the Victorian gothic of Frognal in glamorous gloom, inviting long and intimate talk around the electric fire. Chelsey was washed and dressed and feeling somewhat revived, and long psychedelic drapes covered not only the mirrors but as many as possible of the cracks in the walls.

Chelsey had prepared herself to deal with tears, but Lucy came in bright-eyed as a sparrow, and said: 'I don't want to impose on you, but this is one day I'd rather not spend alone.'

Chelsey was impressed by this *sang froid*; she admired those who, like herself, could treat adversity with a shrug. Her respect for Lucy rose further when she found that, while Lucy wanted to talk, she evaded questions about herself. Chelsey learned only that Lucy did not regret one word of what she had said.

So talk, while necessary, was soon short of a subject. This was provided by Lucy. She encouraged Chelsey to speak frankly and at length about the hostility between herself and Fiona. Chelsey had devoted many hours of therapy to this painful subject, but the only real person who knew the depth of her pain had, till then, been Steven-John. As she relived incident after incident, Chelsey was aware that dear Lucy could be a dangerous choice of confidante; flickeringly, it occurred to her that perhaps all this ancient history was boring, but most of all, she was aware of an energy that flowed into her as the poisons flowed out. Lucy was a wonderful listener: Steven-John always interfered, trying to prove that everybody meant well at bottom; Lucy merely paid attention, asked sensible questions at decent intervals, and was unencumbered by illusions. Chelsey had, even if only for a short while, found a kindred spirit, and her whole body, down to her normally frozen fingertips and toes, was warmed. The monstrous image of Fiona paled – so much so that for whole stretches of minutes, Chelsey almost forgot that Lucy was in love with her.

They drank numerous cups of coffee, examined Chelsey's instruments and symbols to aid clairvoyance, admired the cuttings in her scrapbook of theatrical successes, gave each other a Tarot reading, and talked through to the small hours. Lucy was in no hurry to leave, and willingly agreed to sleep over on Chelsey's sofa. Lucy did not touch Chelsey, not even for the conventional good-night kiss, and Chelsey accepted this without grief. But when she lay in her bed listening to the breathing of another human body in the room beyond, Chelsey was aware of a sense of connection that she hadn't felt since the time of Midge's mother's funeral – when Raffles had briefly been boarded at the Frognal flat.

At moments, she slept, at others the spirits wove themselves around her consciousness, and touched on the possibility that this young woman might become important to her. Though Chelsey had been disappointed too often to take comfort from their sly hints, she did just once indulge herself by imagining Fiona and Georgiana's faces if she could take Lucy to the next party and say: 'Of course I don't need to introduce my new lover . . .'

In the morning, she rose at ten with a song in her heart, and her thoughts running with further tales to tell Lucy – about Fiona's crimes only, since Chelsey still couldn't bring herself to expose the duplicity of Georgiana.

But Lucy was gone. The quilts had been neatly folded and placed on the arm of the sofa, and on the table was a note. It read:

'Your kindness last night is one of the nicest things that has ever happened to me. I feel healed and able to do what I must do: go to Fiona to explain why I did what I did. I don't expect to get together with her again. I don't even know that I'd want to. But I do want to get things straight. I hope I may always call you my friend.'

It was not in Chelsey's nature to weep, but she folded and refolded Lucy's little note, walked to the window, and the

kitchen, and even within one pace of her telephone, and struggled to convince herself that this was a battle Lucy had to
fight alone. On a more local level, it did cross her mind to
wonder if she'd been wise to be quite so frank about herself.
However, it was life's habit to play ducks and drakes with
Chelsey, and the spirits certainly hadn't suggested that the
going would be smooth. She made coffee that was slightly
less potent than usual (even Chelsey was burdened with a
liver), and resigned herself to a long and possibly fruitless
wait by the telephone.

On Tuesday, the day predicted for the call of Chelsey's great
breakthrough, the phone rang.

Chelsey gave herself a second to haul in a breath then
drawled: 'Chel-sey Cham-ber-lain.'

But nothing remotely like a winged seed flew down the
line. She heard neither the touchingly swallowed consonants
of Lucy, nor the honeyed vowels of Iolanthe, but the familiar
military stutter snapping: 'Winters speaking.'

'Oh, blast you, Midge. I was expecting a call from my
agent.'

'I'll be brief. Have you heard from Lucy since that dreadful
scene at Georgiana's?'

'As it happens –' Chelsey prevaricated. She trusted Midge's
honour, of course, but she did not trust her wisdom. 'As it
happens, I've been rather preoccupied. They're about to start
auditions for the revival of *A Doll's House*. Nothing absolutely
positive on that front as yet, but –'

'Good luck,' said Midge briefly. 'Can you help me contact
Lucy?'

Chelsey tapped her fingers lightly against her chin. She
was back in the real world, the snake pit. 'Now, let me think.
You took her home after the party, as I recall?' she said
innocently.

'I didn't,' said Midge. 'I only drove her a few hundred
yards. She wanted to walk. It's three or four miles. She lives
in Dalston.'

'Dalston, my sainted aunt! I trust she got back still in possession of her bag and chastity.'

Midge didn't rise to this. 'I've been trying to phone her, on and off. Yesterday I caught her when she'd popped in to feed her cats.'

(Chelsey made a mental note: Lucy had cats. Chelsey respected cats, but was a little afraid of them.)

'We only spoke for a minute,' continued Midge. 'Lucy was in a great rush. She said things had come right for her.' Midge paused. 'She was off to an Ethiopian restaurant in Stratford. She was going with Fiona and Lorraine.'

Chelsey's heart plummeted like a shot bird.

Midge cleared her throat: 'It is my considered view, Chelsey, that those two are dangerous.'

Chelsey could not, would not, lash out at Midge for breaking her heart. 'Dangerous?' she said fiercely. 'They're two floundering middle-aged dykes, dangerous only to themselves.' Making a great effort to control herself, she said flippantly: 'Dangerous? Are you suggesting that, since famine has killed off Ethiopia's goats, the enterprising couple ate Lucy instead?'

Chelsey was only trying to deflect — Midge to some extent, herself in the main — but the exasperated sigh that escaped from the telephone line warned her that she was sliding towards bad taste. Chelsey, with the acquired watchfulness of a solitary, was careful, no matter how great her pain, to measure the rebound of the signals she gave out to a world that was not her natural element. And it irritated her that she so often got them wrong. She switched off the jocularity. 'Perhaps one should worry. Lucy has got herself into such a tangle that she's less able to assess risk than your Raffles.'

'Yes.' This time Chelsey had struck the right note. Midge spoke now with fervour. 'I don't like it, Chelsey. Lucy is someone who tries to *take on* the world; but she is hopelessly inexperienced. She's a post-institutional child. If she's confused, it's because she's grown up in a collapsing social order – modern Britain – like an animal pitched out of a cage into the bull-ring.'

Chelsey moved the receiver an inch further from the ear that Midge, in her most passionate pedagogic mode, was blasting.

'Do you know,' Midge spoke in escalating outrage, 'that when she was in her mid-teens, she was driven into the armed services by a harridan of a mother? Did she tell how she was abused there by men? She's never been allowed the tranquillity to sit back and think, to build, brick by brick. There's never been anyone she could trust. She hasn't learned how to give and take. She's vulnerable and, despite her manner, impressionable.' Lowering her tone, Midge added, 'I so hope that it will one day be possible to explain this to Georgiana.'

'Georgiana? You think Georgiana will ever in her life *understand* anything, *forgive* anything?' Chelsey laughed – loudly, though she was not in the least amused; she was absolutely furious. Midge had wrecked her hopes. A few words from Sergeant Peanut had turned the whole triumph of Sunday into illusion. If she and Lucy were so close, why did Midge know so much of Lucy's history and Chelsey nothing at all? If Chelsey, as she thought, so thoroughly understood Lucy's feelings about Fiona, why hadn't she foreseen that Lucy would go running back? Why hadn't her special insight into Fiona warned of the risk of some tearful, sexually charged reconciliation, driven by Fiona's *nostalgie de la boue*? Why, despite all her psychic gifts, could Chelsey envisage nothing of the inside of that probably disgusting restaurant, and why did that make her feel excluded and afraid? And how could Chelsey – the solitary, who knew that relationships are a great power – have been so naïve as to imagine that Lucy could ever be drawn away from the magnetism of Fiona and Lorraine?

But this she would not share with a duffer like Midge. 'Well, if they haven't eaten her, what do you think they are doing to her?' she said jovially. 'Something outside of the Queensberry rules?'

Midge gave another warning sigh. 'I think her outburst on Saturday was a sign of distress. I think she is becoming psychologically destabilised.'

'I don't know, my Midget. What big words you school-teachers use.' Chelsey groped for her mug of coffee. 'What do you propose to do about it?'

While Midge's uncertainty exposed itself in a dithering silence, Chelsey's rage cooled into her familiar bitter irony. She wondered how dangerous Midge would think her, if she knew that Lucy had spent the night at her flat. For one poor moment, Chelsey felt she'd got even with the world: how satisfying it was to embrace somebody someone else wanted to embrace. But Chelsey soon remembered that Fiona had that pleasure every time she hugged Georgiana in front of Chelsey. As the silence lengthened, Chelsey searched for something to grasp. Lucy, she thought: Lucy is the only uncorrupted thing in my life.

'I think,' said Midge eventually, 'that the hold those two have over her has to be broken. I don't think she can do it herself and, much as I would wish it, I don't believe she'd allow me do it.'

Chelsey would never – never – let herself become a weakling like Midge. 'Are you suggesting,' she said in a hard voice, 'that I do it?'

Another silence followed. This was probably the least word-driven phone call that Chelsey had ever had. 'It seems to me,' stuttered Midge, 'that you may be the only person who can.' (Another silence.) 'She's not at her flat or at work. Would you be willing to try Gospel Oak?'

Chelsey's heart leapt as if she'd just had a treble shot of coffee. 'What a bore!' she said in a cultivatedly bored voice. 'If I didn't get the answering machine knowing they were listening and choosing not to pick up, I'd get Fiona's hard lip. No, you do it.'

'I wish I could,' wailed Midge, 'but I'd embarrass Lucy horribly.'

'Let me see.' Chelsey tapped her chin. 'I really must keep

my line free for this agency call. I can't afford to keep missing parts this way. But later I could, I suppose, do something more positive than phoning. I could pop round to Gospel Oak. Will that do you?'

'That's more than I could have hoped. Thank you.'

Chelsey did not have much respect for qualms of any kind. So she did not pity Midge or, for that matter, herself. Chelsey knew that she faced a subtle and difficult fight that she would probably lose. But somehow, she was already triumphant. She was, at last, going to confront Fiona. She was going to do a job Midge would never be able to do. She would also have the satisfaction of phoning Iolanthe with the news that she'd be *hors de combat* that evening. In any case, Chelsey liked to observe the proprieties; it was no less than social duty to return Lucy's visit.

It was only when she calmed down after her call to the Hodgson-Brookes Agency, and had a couple of hours to kill, that Chelsey remembered that she'd forgotten to tell Midge the latest she'd had from Steven-John. She reflected a moment on this, and on Georgiana's till-now immortals.

So Toby was joining Ulric in the terminal ward, Toby with suicidal white blood cells and Ulric with their mirror image, cannibalistic ones. How ironic that Ulric should be the one whose system suffered an excess of virility. This was an idea she could explore with Steven-John, but only so far. Steven-John would all too soon get on to natural rhythms and yin-yang balancing. Chelsey was just as interested as he was in yin and yang, but she was stimulated by the polarities, while he was always searching for harmony. This softness in him dulled his vision. Chelsey could cite many instances. For example: how could someone so moved by Ulric's dance with death not see that Midge, too, was out on that dance-floor, and that hers was not a stately gavotte but a jig of exponentially increasing frenzy? When Midge was safely on the other side, she would tell him this. She would point out to him that he opened his heart to every creature in distress except

Midge. And she knew why: in the company of Midge, Steven-John lost the assurance of his manhood. Little Sergeant Peanut too much resembled his unreconstructed self. Chelsey seized her coffee in excitement at this new idea – Chelsey loved ideas. The coffee gave her another: she would tell Steven-John that one great disadvantage of the compulsion to do good was that where the do-gooder was unable to act he had to pretend there was no need to do so. Thus Midge's distress did not exist for Steven-John. Chelsey, entirely free of emotional chains, was the only individual in Georgiana's crowd who could be completely honest. Chelsey, and – if she could be freed from the devilish enchantment of Fiona – Lucy.

Lightheartedly, Chelsey called up her spirits for a survey of the immortals: Steven-John himself, come to think of it, was much too pale and far from healthy. If he didn't develop reactions against the pumping of his long-suffering XX-chromosomes with androgen, or get anaemia from his unspeakable diet of sawdust, he was bound to pick up something scaly from those birds. Steven-John would grow into a wizened little gnome with shrill voice and goatee beard; he would retire from the human race and spend his days in spiritual communication with a vast messy family of rescued animals.

And as for the others: Toby, Ulric and half the rest on the way out. Fiona and Lorraine playing Russian roulette. Sarah-Sophie believing their hospital would survive any crisis in the National Health Service; but their time would come. Then, they would take early retirement, and live vegetable lives at some country cottage until they were a hundred and ten. Tim viewed the decline of his management training firm with admirable stoicism, but he would pop off with a heart attack the day he found the postboy with his fingers in the petty-cash kitty. That would be when Thelma discovered the other side of her glorious offspring, finding herself dependent on them. The rest of the crowd didn't amount to anything, so could be left out of the count.

And the count would be: Georgiana, Chelsey, and of course the new player: Lucy.

Then Chelsey, after almost twenty years of cruel rejection by Georgiana, and through Georgiana by the entire world, would have the power. Hers would be the choice between them. If it pleased her, she could let the scales of love drop from her eyes and say: 'Well, Georgiana, darling, not much left now of our doll's house.' And, with the merest wink of one green eye, she could, if she chose, summon Lucy to her side. It looked so possible.

Chelsey, acclimatised to disappointment, struggled to control her exhilaration as she clambered down the sloping pavements of Frognal to the Finchley Road and, damning the cost, hailed a cab.

Twenty minutes later, in the closing dusk, Chelsey's head tilted and her eyes narrowed to peer through the vertical blinds of the white cottage at Gospel Oak.

The neighbourhood, she had already noted, was extremely respectable and, apart from the screeches of expensively uniformed schoolgirls at the bus stop, quiet. It was the sort of community where the women initiate each others' teenage sons in the delights of satin sheets. Fiona's house was in keeping. Wisteria gracefully followed the lines of the bay window and subtly embraced the burglar alarm, itself giving support to a now despairing clematis. The front garden was stocked with delphiniums, stocks, pinks and various other expressions of old-fashioned Englishness, all slaughtered by frost. The countrified laurel, beech and firethorn hedge blossomed with crisp bags and beer cans; lichens and moss invaded the flagstone path. An ancient and toothless 'Chien méchant' sign graced the garden gate. Chelsey priced the house at £205,000, enough to buy her one and a half Frognal flats.

She focused more closely. Inside the room, spaced like the three points of an equilateral triangle, stood Fiona, Lorraine and Lucy, erect, arms akimbo. The dog, tail trembling, crouched behind Fiona. Unfortunately, Chelsey's ears received nothing but the screeches at the bus stop. Curbing her desire to throttle at least one schoolgirl, she moved round to the porch and rang the bell.

After a minute or two, Lorraine's bushy head appeared at the door. 'Chelsey!' Lorraine's voice had the squeak of someone caught *in flagrante*. 'Chelsey, what a surprise.' Chelsey smiled. The door opened a very little wider. 'We were about to put out the sundowners. I, um, left work early today.'

Chelsey entered, almost stepping on to Lorraine's feet. Lorraine, bumblingly, led her towards the kitchen. They passed the open doorway of the room from which one of the angles of the triangle had been removed. Chelsey didn't turn to look, but caught the sound of hard breathing.

Lorraine clattered about the preparations. She ferreted under heaps in the sink and hauled out four glasses; she yanked a bottle of supermarket claret from a crammed wine-rack, hauled out a corkscrew, rammed it brutally through the foil and into the cork, and opened the bottle with the air of an executioner. Then, in a touchingly innocent gesture, she reached into the fridge for a small dish of olives.

Chelsey watched, and noted. She did not think more about her mission. She had already concluded that Lucy's determination to 'explain' things to Fiona was somewhat disingenuous, and that Lucy was playing a full part in some new and probably worse game. Chelsey aimed to cast a chill over this. The spirits would show her how. Lorraine slopped wine into the glasses; some spilled onto the olives. She pointed towards one of the three kitchen stools. Chelsey sat. So far so good. Chelsey was pleased that Lorraine, not Fiona, had answered the door. Lorraine lacked the moral courage to refuse entry and thus cause offence to someone who had not yet been rude to her.

After another half-minute of no conversation, Fiona, and then Lucy trailed into the kitchen. Call of wine? Or curiosity? The dog followed and paused in the doorway, his questioning eyes on Fiona. At her cursory nod he padded in, gave Lucy a wide berth and, tail now waving gently, laid his muzzle in Chelsey's lap.

With one hand, Chelsey raised her glass an inch. With the fingertips of the other, she stroked Bonzo's head. Strange, she thought; dogs are supposed to be afraid of witches, yet she could always count on their support – Raffles, Bonzo, Jezebel, any member of the canine tribe. Unlike cats, dogs were delightfully stupid. 'Gesundheit,' she said.

Fiona, with a brief snort in reply, seized a glass and drank. Lucy, though clearly discomforted, took the smaller of the remaining glasses and raised it, answering Chelsey's toast with a bronchial 'Skol'.

'Well,' said Fiona, flopping down onto the stool furthest from Chelsey's, 'to what do we owe this unexpected honour?'

Chelsey smiled. She was so used to being the butt of Fiona's naked arrogance that she felt not the slightest prick. She paused while Lorraine and Lucy gestured to each other to take the middle stool. It gave her satisfaction to note that Lucy was the one to sit. Lorraine began to prowl at Lucy's back.

'As a matter of fact,' Chelsey spoke in her Portia voice, 'I don't like the look of what's going on, and I'm here to take Lucy home.'

'Why don't you mind your own business?' muttered Lorraine.

This Chelsey ignored. 'Although I was answering Fiona's question, it is in fact Lucy I am addressing.'

'I'm all right, thank you, Chelsey.' Lucy's blush betrayed her. She swung around to Fiona and then Lorraine. 'Chelsey has been ever so good to me – I told you about it.'

Chelsey recalled Lucy's attention to the issue. 'You weren't all right a couple of days ago.'

'No. Things have changed.' Lucy avoided Chelsey's look. 'What happened between us at the party was all a misunderstanding. We've forgiven each other. And we're going to try again, Fiona, Lorraine and me together. We're going to be open and true; starting today.'

'All of you?' said Chelsey. 'In a threesome? Naughty girls.'

'Dirty-minded cow,' muttered Lorraine.

Fiona rose. 'You can bugger off, Chelsey.'

'As I said earlier,' said Chelsey coolly, astonished that things were so easily and quickly going her way, 'it's Lucy I'm addressing.'

Everybody looked at Lucy. Silence held them. Delicately, Bonzo licked Chelsey's hand.

Lorraine broke in. 'Cat got your tongue, Lucy?'

'Lucy?' Chelsey offered a warm and, she hoped, motherly smile.

'It's different.' Lucy's voice was pale. 'We have been each others' lovers, but separately, and it didn't work out. We were hurting each other. We're going to try doing sex together.'

'You've just decided this?' Chelsey raised her eyebrows. 'You poor dears; you didn't look too erotically engaged when I arrived.'

'That's right,' said Lucy. 'We think it's going to be quite difficult.'

'So it's not for pleasure, then. What is it: therapy? Is your task to perk up Fiona and Lorraine's flagging relationship?'

'This is impertinent!' Lorraine swung round. 'You really have no right to—'

'We've had enough about rights over the last couple of days,' drawled Fiona, 'let's stick to facts, like Lucy is.'

'All right,' said Lucy, now with a slight tremble. 'We're in love. With each other.'

'How charming,' said Chelsey, switching now to her Lady Bracknell mode. 'All of you? Like the angels, without individual possessiveness?'

'That's it. That's exactly what we want,' said Lucy.

'But not what you'll get.' Chelsey was conscious of the importance of maintaining her early advantage. 'There are always lovers and the beloveds; that's the way passion flows. So who is most in love with whom? For a start: which one is Lucy more in love with?'

'I don't know. Sometimes one, sometimes the other. It depends.'

Lucy had not once looked up at Chelsey. Right now, she was studying the bitten ends of her fingers. Chelsey helpfully spilled a little of her wine on the table and was gratified to see Lucy's finger reach out and begin to draw labrys symbols. 'Depends on what, my dear?'

'Um. Lately it's been Fiona, more often; Lorraine's been so difficult. But I sometimes think I'm really in love with what they are together – though I'm also jealous of it.'

Chelsey nodded. She had expected that, at the second stage, her main problem would be the victim herself. But, before Chelsey could change the subject, Lucy ran on: 'The way they stand together; the way they wear each other's clothes; the way they know when the other wants to say something.'

Neither Fiona nor Lorraine intervened, but both watched like hawks.

'I see,' said Chelsey, her glance raking the ceiling in something like embarrassment, 'which leads, sticking to facts, to the next question: where, around, amongst or between this beautiful couple does Lucy come in?' Chelsey circled round to catch Lucy's gaze. For a second, she caught it: Lucy's eyes, wide as a baby's, transparent as new honey, were brimming with emotion. Chelsey's heart sank. Without answering, Lucy returned to her doodles.

But the spirits were hissing like tinnitus in Chelsey's ear: 'Don't give up. Don't give up.' Chelsey drew on her last strength: 'Or, to put it another way,' she spread her legs as wide as the confined space would allow, 'what does Lucy want? Are you saying that what you really want is to *be* Fiona, or to be Lorraine, and *have* the other?'

'I hadn't thought of that. Perhaps that's it.'

'So which would you rather be?'

Lucy bunched her fist. 'I want to be inside Lorraine's head. The world must be so exciting from there. I desperately want to be Lorraine.'

Lorraine, coming up behind, touched Lucy's shoulder. 'I'm sure you wouldn't make such a hash of it as I do.'

Lucy shook her off. 'Because Lorraine doesn't know who she is. I'd know. Lorraine has so much power. She has the job. She has status. She has money. She has the car. When she talks, people listen. And she has Fiona. And she just throws them all about.'

'Well. That is interesting.' Chelsey's nostrils caught the scent of victory. 'So tell me, dear, how you can become Lorraine, without taking the money, status, car, job and Fiona off her?'

'Chelsey,' said Fiona, rising like a volcano. 'Enough. I'd like you to go now.'

'I'm not here for your pleasure, I'm afraid,' said Chelsey, 'but to help Lucy. I'm acting on the instructions of people who want to protect her.'

'You can act under instructions from me. Bonzo, come here. Lorraine, fetch Chelsey's coat.'

'Lucy and I have more to say to each other, I believe,' said Chelsey, making an effort to rise to a concerned Desdemona mode – not easy to do when Michelin Man is forcing your arms into woolly sleeves.

'I think you should leave now,' Lucy said softly. 'But thank you; thank you very much.'

'Let's meet, Lucy.' Lorraine was now thrusting Chelsey's bag into her hand. 'On –' she thought fast: soon, but not so soon as to seem anxious, '– on Friday.' Somewhere near Gospel Oak but not too near '– at Highgate Cemetery. Eleven o'clock.' She glanced briefly at the heap of photographic equipment on the dresser. 'Marx's grave is always mobbed by photographers, so meet me at George Eliot's.'

Chelsey's farewell to the dog was somewhat curtailed. She was frogmarched to the door.

But, as she waited at the bus stop, mercifully deprived of the company of schoolgirls, Chelsey's emotions were awash with something close to triumph. There would be little ease at the white cottage tonight. Chelsey had changed the balance of power. She had done a good job and one Midge would, most certainly, not have been able to do.

18

Tuesday, 21 November, Kilburn

Chelsey was right. Midge certainly wouldn't have been able to stir that hornet's nest, or do any job requiring dexterity in malice. Even in the classroom, she had never used guile. Teacher was raised so high above her charges that power came with the job, and Midge deployed it without questioning the source. Midge never doubted, and neither did her pupils, that she represented the *comme il faut*. And thus even when she was severe – most consciously when she was severe – she could act out of love. The planet inhabited by Midge was governed by a moral order. The deep chaos which, for Chelsey, could be held off only moment by moment, with slippery cunning and clinging to the hope that one day it would be possible to strike back was, to Midge, no more than that diminution of vision from which it was her function to save a child.

But Midge was no longer a schoolteacher. Now, her only charge was herself, and this pupil was deviant and sly. Midge's list of seven good intentions, now transcribed, in her neat schoolteacher hand, onto the chalkboard above the kitchen sink, received from Midge's sole pupil only ever more subtle ways to circumvent it. Midge, though strong in intention and desire, was weak in will. For this, she despised herself. But she could find no way to change her character, except by doing what she was already doing: through repeatedly trying to apply that feeble organ of will.

At about 4.30 p.m., well before the schoolgirls had abandoned the Gospel Oak bus-stop, even before one could positively affirm that the sun had dipped over the yard-arm, Midge marched into the kitchen at the prompting of the inner voice that told her that she had tried very hard to be good that day and was entitled to her first evening drink which, as properly prescribed by her list, would consist of a single whisky and one Red Stripe. She sipped the whisky out of the bottle, and her virtue was rewarded. It flowed sweetly into her fingers and toes; the jagged ends of her nerves lay down like lambs.

Then, forewarned by experience, she took the next stage more carefully. She fetched a glass and seated herself before she opened the can of beer which, to reduce its moreishness, had been kept in the refrigerator. She scooped Raffles onto her lap. Perhaps if she had something to eat she could delay this next stage? Midge hadn't as yet had a meal, though through the day she had nibbled at this and that at promptings which she could not have named hunger. Eat or drink? Midge sank her face, questioningly, into Raffles's fur. Raffles was a bit smelly. Midge felt cautiously around the collar, the rattier tangles of fur and other suspicious places but, no, Raffles hadn't rolled in anything nasty; Raffles smelled of the functions of her own middle-aged body. It was bath and anal-glands squeezing time. To neither of these processes would Raffles submit without a struggle. Midge stroked the little dog tenderly. Raffles, like Midge, like this abused planet, was subject to decay.

Yet the day had had its achievements and, if her consciousness were not awash with doubt about the wisdom of putting Chelsey on Lucy's trail, she would have been pleased by them. Phone calls to Lucy, an even more fruitless drive round to Dalston, and the arrangement with Chelsey, had not been her only activities. Midge had taken a full half of her scheduled

two-mile walk, and to the Kurdish Refugee Centre. To slow
the demolition of the beer while she awaited Chelsey's report,
Midge distracted herself with assessing these small successes.

She and Raffles had taken the route past the Irish church,
where they paused to sniff the incense and Midge to wonder,
for the umpteenth time, if she might be able to become a
Catholic. Then, noting a heaped skip, she and Raffles had
crossed the road. Skips aroused the scavenger in Midge. She
enjoyed them more than shop windows (toyshops and gentle-
men's outfitters apart) and soon she was rooting around. Piled
and broken furniture, pots and pans, an ancient kettle thick
with limescale, old and rather smelly clothes. She spotted a
leather music case, with 'M. A. Davis' still legible in worn
gold-blocking. Inside was the score for 'In a Convent Garden'.
Midge was excited. Would this, cleaned and polished, be of
use to Ulric? But, as she brushed it down and straightened the
corners, the leather cracked and then split like dry bark. She
replaced it in the skip and moved on.

A few yards down the road, Midge's hand flew to her
mouth. That was the skip of a house clearance. But that house
was inhabited. An old woman with a bent spine lived there.
Midge rushed back. The lace curtains which had, for as long
as Midge could remember, kept the house decently obscured
from the neighbourhood had been ripped away. A 'For Sale'
sign swung on the gatepost. Midge doffed her woolly hat and
stood silently to attention before the empty house.

Why were this woman's things flung out and exposed to the
street when the woman herself had been so private? Why
had Midge made not a single move, over half a century, to
befriend her, help her, even to praise the daffodils which
appeared every spring in her garden? Why, when all Midge
wanted from life was to be allowed to do some good, had she
not seen that somebody right here, in her own neighbourhood, needed protection?

Midge reached into the muddle of the skip. She gathered
together cardigans, crooked shoes and tea-rose-pink under-
clothes, and covered them with a scrap of carpet. Her lips

ached to utter the last hopes of the funeral Mass, but she dared not: M. A. Davis might have been a Protestant. Yet she wanted to do something. After a minute's thought, she took out the music case. Perhaps, with a good soaking in oil and careful stitching, some small thing of M. A. Davis might be preserved, at least a little longer? She walked on, her step slightly shaky, as of someone who had for a second made contact with something scary and very large. Raffles, also subdued, walked soberly beside her.

Ten minutes later, she approached the vestibule of the former Presbyterian chapel which now housed the Kurdish Centre. With Raffles clamped under one arm and the music bag under the other, she entered it, as far as the peg-board in the hall.

(Next, came the embarrassing part, and Midge briefly broke off her recollections as she wondered if a second Red Stripe might help her to evaluate things objectively. After all, the needs of the soul and those of the liver were not necessarily compatible, and who would be so coarse as to give precedence to a blood-filled sponge-bag? Sighing, Midge took a round journey which included the fridge, and stood the unopened can on the table before her.)

Few of the notices on that board had been written in English, and none of those which were invited unemployed schoolmistresses to teach English language classes. At the reception desk, sat a woman. A quick glance caught horn-rimmed spectacles, a blackened untidy bun, furrowed brow, a spine-damaged paperback between inky fingers, and very short patience. Probably not the sort to keep an AK-47 under the counter, but most definitely one that would be impervious to Midge's charms. Raffles's perhaps? Midge clamped the music case between her knees and shifted Raffles to her other arm, so that the dog's bottom and stringy tail were in view of the desk. But no voice called: 'What a sweet little dog', or even 'Get that animal out of here' – either of which would have given Midge some opportunity to respond.

Midge peered at the remaining notices, in an incomprehensible script in an unknown language. As she hovered, a door burst open. The air pressure shot up as the corridor swarmed with bodies, movement and noise, then as abruptly fell as all these energies were funnelled into the cafeteria. The smell of local-authority cooking seeped into the vacuum. For the second time within an hour, Midge was shaken. Were these the refugees, these bulging young men? They were so many, so physically present with their shoving and joking, their jeans, earrings and boots, so much more adult and assured than Little Miss Margaret Winters. Midge quailed. She thrust a few coins into the collecting box and fled.

Was this an achievement? Certainly it was. Tomorrow, she would telephone and offer her services. If not tomorrow, the first day that she felt strong. If not the Kurdish Centre, then the nearest old people's home.

Perhaps that was sufficient for a day which could not be judged until she heard Chelsey's dry voice on the telephone. Very thoughtfully, Midge opened the second can, and took a small dose of her aid to clear thinking. The treatment worked. Midge was now bold enough to consider not only the fates of M. A. Davis, refugees or Raffles's glands, but of little Lucy.

While Midge was at the Refugee Centre, Chelsey had been, at Midge's behest, at Gospel Oak, finding out what exactly was going on there, and bringing a draught of the cool air of the ordinary sensible world into that hothouse. Chelsey, Midge knew, would perform well. Yet she also knew that Chelsey was a dangerous woman to send on an errand of mercy. If Midge had not been a character of monumental feebleness she would have done it herself.

Yet she had done what she could. She had been in regular communication with Lucy's telephone answering machine and once with Lucy herself, but made no progress. She had, in preparation for asking Lucy round to Kilburn for supper, made a start on tidying up the kitchen. Evidence of this was clear: in the hall, bundled in threes in shopping bags, were the empty bottles which had previously stood beside the waste bin. These she would dispose of nightly, bag at a time, in other people's rubbish. (Midge suspected the binmen of counting the bottles in her own.)

Midge had also thought long and hard about Lucy's outburst at the party. She was much distressed by it. Midge hated to see any humans hurt each other. But an attack on Georgiana was something very much worse; it was blasphemy. Enclosed within her shapeless fear of danger to Lucy was a sense of threat to Georgiana. Georgiana would be driven mad by a serious liaison between Fiona and Lucy: jealousy and moral outrage would tear her to pieces. Midge loved and admired Georgiana, and now she feared for her. She also feared for herself. Some part of her knew that if Georgiana's crowd broke up, Midge, as well as Georgiana, would break with it.

But most immediately, she feared for Lucy. Those dreadful words ('Georgiana, the Queen of the D—') had cut Lucy off from the entire planetary order. Lucy now had no protection against the most malign influences.

As she sat now, her oesophagus numbed by the coldness of the beer and waiting for Chelsey to telephone, she bitterly regretted that she had made such a mess of befriending Lucy. Why, when she meant well, had she persecuted the poor girl? 'Sexual harassment' Lucy called it. Seeking to charm, Midge had bullied Lucy. Midge beat her fist against her forehead. But, even as she punished herself by forcing her imagination to re-create Lucy's look of absolute disgust, Midge's loneliness welled up in a wave of sexual longing. 'Oh Lucy,' she whispered, squeezing the beer-can in her hand. If only Lucy could allow Midge just a little trust. Raffles, aware of the softening in her mistress, raised her muzzle for a kiss. Midge patted her vaguely. 'First, my Riffraff, we shall have to sanitise your person.' Then Midge kissed the dog anyway.

Five minutes later, Midge rose, not yet to bathe Raffles, but to try Chelsey's number. The phone rang and rang. Lucy's number gave her, as usual, the answering machine. Midge returned to the kitchen. The second can was now empty. The whisky bottle smirked at her. She rose to her feet, tightened its cap, put it in the refrigerator, and made herself a cup of tea. It was not yet 5.30 p.m. She would wait on Chelsey's call.

Five more minutes, and Midge's need for distraction was nearing desperation. She carried the little dog upstairs, found her father's best magnifying lens, her mother's best nail scissors and the dog's most disinfectant shampoo and subjected Raffles to the demands of hygiene. Instinctively, she used the war cries by which she'd driven her pupils through delousings and the like – 'You'll be so much happier after this'; 'You'll feel so good'.

And Raffles did. Smelling clean as a newly mopped school lavatory and showering water over everything, she leapt and danced and most of all wanted Midge to seize her in her arms and tell her she was such a gorgeous girl.

The phone rang. Midge dropped the dog and ran to it.

'Bad news, Midget.' It was Chelsey in her funerary mode. 'There's no hope, none at all.'

Midge, after two Red Stripes and a smidgen of whisky, had enough spunk to want evidence before yielding to poetic despair. 'What do you mean? You did, I hope, show Lucy the danger of strong influences? You did make it clear to her that she has friends?'

'Well,' Chelsey drawled, 'I presented myself as a friend and counter-influence, but what do I have to offer? I can't compete with those two in glamour, money, the good time.'

Midge was too wise to agree. 'You could give her the warning that comes from one who has her true interests at heart.'

'Oh, it fell on deaf ears,' drawled Chelsey. 'They're deep in it, three deep, you could say.'

'Lorraine too?'

'Very much so. No more gruesome twosomes for those girls. They're planning, my dear, a gleesome threesome; unless the dog makes it a moresome foursome.'

Midge let out her schoolmistress's warning sigh, and Chelsey steered her talk back into a socially acceptable mode. 'Yes, Lorraine too, but Fiona is running the show. Unless –'

Chelsey paused, and then, in a low, questioning tone, added: '– unless the little waif is running it herself.'

Midge scoffed. 'The poor child doesn't know what she's doing.'

'Doing to whom?'

This wasn't what Midge meant. 'She cannot measure risk.'

'Risk to whom?'

'To herself, of course. And to them. She doesn't understand relationships. She's never had the chance to acquire skills of friendship or even of ordinary conduct.' Midge was irritated by Chelsey's teasing, but her only defence against it was a schoolteacher manner even she found pompous.

'What risk to them?' Chelsey was enjoying herself.

'To their relationship.'

Chelsey sniffed. 'Given a choice between a silly girl and a relationship that secures them that house, any sensible pair would go for the house. When the going gets rough, they'll throw her out.'

'Fine,' replied Midge coolly, 'then there's no risk to them.'

'Oh, but there is.' Chelsey paused significantly.

'What risk, and to whom?' she said wearily.

Chelsey answered immediately: 'Looks like our big loser could be Lorraine.'

'Come now!' Lorraine was a decent enough sort, but nobody could call her thin-skinned or innocent.

Chelsey elaborated. 'Young Lorraine,' she said, 'may bring this whole thing crashing down. She isn't playing it right. She's getting into the heavy breathing. She's looking, as sports commentators say, vulnerable.'

19

Wednesday, 22 November, Marylebone

How the change had come about was unclear to Ulric, but it had happened. On this day, only four days after he had read-mitted the foolish boy into his life, Ulric was to have chemotherapy treatment.

On Saturday night, they'd sat up long, talking, first about the party, then about blackbirds and much later, when Ulric was too tired to pay much attention, about cancer. Ulric had, he thought, finally convinced Steven-John and, through this ultimate collapse of Steven-John's resistance, himself, that any further engagement with the loathsome National Health Service would be demeaning, exhausting, infuriating and medically futile. So how had it come about that there was an appointment card pinned by a glass of water to his bedside cabinet, instructing him to report to the Oncology Department at University College Hospital in Gower Street, Bloomsbury, at 1030 hours that very day? Ulric, lying on his back, his hands laced over his diaphragm, glanced briefly at the cunning, unevenly folded white object in which his arrangements were inscribed with globby ballpen in a semi-literate hand, and allowed himself a sceptical 'humph'.

There were still several hours to go for, even in November,

day comes early to Marylebone. From 6 a.m. the yellow stares
of car headlights began splaying the curtained tails of the
birds of paradise, though the starlings, indifferent to the false
sunlight of human engineering, remained as yet morosely
silent.

Ulric's head and his more speaking hands poked stiffly out
of the covers of his vast bed. His eyes were wide open, but
despite his outrage at the trick played on him by unknown
forces, they were unusually moist and tender. Out of the
bottom of the covers protruded a tangle of curls, bedraggled
as the petals of an aged chrysanthemum.

Ulric nudged this with a toe. 'Since sharing my bed is
becoming a habit with you, Steven-John, house-training
begins now. Lesson One: we are up by seven.'

'Oh. I was awake and ready.' The startled note in Steven-
John's voice suggested that his famed reputation for honesty
might be founded on incomplete knowledge of his habits. 'I
was thinking about Rufus.'

'The bird? That wasn't thinking; that was dreaming. You
were chirruping in your sleep.'

Steven-John rubbed his eyes. 'I was wondering, well, if it
wouldn't be an imposition, if I could build a nesting box on
your window ledge for him and Aurora. I wouldn't let them
into the flat.'

'You'll do no such thing. The starlings would have them for
breakfast.'

'Yes.' Steven-John accepted this with a sigh. 'I don't know
what to do. Of course I'll go over daily to feed them, but
they'll be lonely. Damien does his best, of course, but I can't
help feeling disloyal.'

The blackbirds, the homeless youth. Where Steven-John
was, was a gathering point, was what became a home.
Furthermore, where Steven-John was, occurred a significant
amount of power-play. Steven-John's title of the world's
biggest fixer was honestly come by. Ulric again reminded
himself to keep up his guard. 'Enjoy that feeling, dear boy,
while it lasts. We don't all have the power to betray.'

'Yes.' Another sigh, then Steven-John rolled out of bed and padded towards the bathroom. 'I'll go over and check things out soon as we're through with the hospital. I wish I'd made sure that Damien won't feed Rufus bits of hash. Oh dear.' Steven-John was the sort of person who was wobbly in the mornings. 'Will you shave first today,' he said, holding wobblily to the frame of the bathroom door, 'or shall I?'

'You go ahead. But don't be too long. I'd like some tea while I do my voice exercises.'

Steven-John accepted this, too, with philosophy. There were limits to human relationships, even the one he sought with Ulric. He wanted to work towards what he called marriage, a Boston marriage. He had not yet dared to utter the word in Ulric's hearing, but hoped to do so when he could get him into a suitably accommodating mood. He would do his best to acclimatise Ulric to the word 'marriage' just as Ulric's persistence had now made it possible for him to utter without horror the word 'cancer'. It did not in the least bother Steven-John that Chelsey would call such activity manipulation. The arrangement between him and Ulric was a serious one with many consequences, some of which could not be foreseen; it required a long and delicate process of negotiation.

Much had passed between the two men since their reconciliation four days earlier. They had since been almost continuously in each other's company. Steven-John had been absent for an hour each afternoon, when he'd rushed off to Kentish Town. For similar stretches of time, he'd been on the telephone. Twice he'd rung Toby to explain that Jezebel's walkies would be somewhat delayed on Wednesday and any other days Ulric was to have staphylococci treatment. Rather more than twice, there'd been whispering calls to Chelsey.

Ulric, too, had attended to external matters: Steven-John's passion for the telephone was contagious. When he was, for a few minutes, off the line, Ulric had once taken it himself. On Sunday, he'd interrupted a birthday party at the home of the Principal of the Guildhall School of Music to say, with apologies for the inconvenience, that he had a terminal illness. Immediately afterwards, he'd rung his agent at her home, asking her to book him a studio to make an unaccompanied recording of '*In questa tomba oscura*'. She'd been rather surprised: what did he hope to do with this 3-minute thing, barely long enough for the hit parade? Was he sure he didn't want an accompanist, or a deal with Virgin Records? Ulric didn't mind; he didn't so much want it to be published, as to exist outside of his own mind. Since he was so interested in this curious piece, she then suggested working it into a live performance, with a few other artists, say this time next year? But when Ulric began to make inarticulate sounds of distress she agreed to everything he demanded. Ulric proposed a date – ten days hence – and clicked off the call; he could ask what he liked; surely he amounted to more than a few per cent of her income? And then, smiling feebly, he'd handed the phone back to Steven-John, whose brow was rucked with curiosity.

These diversions aside, the two men had been constantly engaged with each other. Ulric had never, since the loss of Peter, been so long closeted with another human being. The experience left him exhausted – his facial muscles, in particular, felt strained and now stiff – and emptied. But another feeling skipped along his veins in tandem with fatigue. He couldn't at first place it. He noticed its existence when the image came to him of the Roman crowds throwing their sweaty caps into the air at the latest triumph of Caesar: it came in a sudden wish that he had the cap of such a mechanical and could launch it, calling out 'Whee!'.

And then he looked at Steven-John and thought: what's going on? What is it between me and this person, this boy who is not a boy, nor a girl neither? This gossip; this not particularly amusing clown at Georgiana's parties; this fellow I have indulged because he was more than ready to indulge me; because he regards me as a significant artist; because, despite his ramshackle mental discipline, he believes in something? Or am I merely relieved that there exists some

simpleton willing to stay by me while my body is eaten up by
its own madness? What is it about this person that his mere
presence should fill me with something like – even in his
thoughts, Ulric hesitated to give form to words so like Steven-
John's own soft utterances – something like joy?

While he debated with himself over these thorny matters,
Ulric, who was a most practical person, also considered the
implications. On Sunday morning, Ulric had offered Steven-
John a low-grade, low-paid and impermanent job.
Steven-John had accepted. They had discussed the duties of
the assignment. During that process, the list had grown worryingly large and vague, and the commitment which underlay
it (which Ulric doggedly insisted on calling their 'contract')
developed into a stuttering offer of lifelong loyalty and devo-
tion from Steven-John.

Fair was fair. If Steven-John was willing to nurse Ulric
until his dying day, then Steven-John was Ulric's responsibility. Ulric had some money; not much, the best of it the relic
of the shares in Malaysian palm oil his mother had forgotten
she possessed. But this, to Steven-John, would be a fortune.
Ulric would call in the family lawyer and make a will. When
he became too ill to keep himself clean, he would hire a nurse.
But before that time, from this moment, he would encourage
Steven-John to keep his other friendships in good order; even
the unspeakable Chelsey would be allowed into the
Marylebone flat, the home that he would from now be sharing
with his friend, and which would in due course be Steven-
John's own, to create in it whatever sanctuary he could for
appalling unhousetrained boys and blackbirds. Taking these
things into account, Ulric decided that the deal he was agreeing with Steven-John was as fair as he could make it.

That settled, Ulric would have peace to think about his
'*tomba oscura*'. He avoided discussion of the subject with
Steven-John, and Steven-John showed no curiosity. Ulric
found this disconcerting. Why didn't Steven-John think it
significant that Ulric was working so hard at voice exercises
for the prolonged, understated note that was so difficult to

hold, that was like yoga, like the low moan of a cello? Occasionally, while cooking, pottering about or even ineptly cleaning, Steven-John sang along, in a queer little metallic light-baritone, the voice of a tin soldier. Ulric switched off his aesthetic sensibilities and enjoyed these duets. But he was perhaps disappointed that Steven-John seemed to give as little conscious thought to Ulric's exertions as to the songs of his blackbirds. Ulric was occasionally beset by a fear that he was not the whole centre of Steven-John's life.

Even while these thoughts came to him, Ulric was aware that he was in part using them to keep at a comfortable distance a more immediate nuisance: this hospital business now due to begin in a mere two-and-a-half hours. It irritated him that he allowed himself be so distracted. But Ulric had knowledge of chemotherapy. His mother had been subjected to it until her blood was so poisoned, her energy so depleted and her beauty so ravaged that she thought, of the two evils before her, she would rather have the cancer.

So Ulric waited in some impatience for Steven-John to emerge from the shower. Even though he did not wish to talk to him about voice exercises or chemotherapy at that moment, Steven-John's presence gave his thoughts on any subject a certain orderliness, and ordinariness. More than this, Ulric wanted to see the lad with water dripping from his hair. He also wanted Steven-John to get this Bloomsbury business up and running, and have the damn thing over.

Ulric was relieved that Steven-John would be accompanying him. Ulric wanted Steven-John to be in control, so that Ulric would not need to be. He didn't trust the bumbling medics with chipped finger nails; he didn't trust the chemicals they would infuse into his veins. But, for some reason he could not explain to himself, he did trust Steven-John.

'I say, Ulric,' said Steven-John, emerging from the shower with one towel looped about his hips and another, sadly, over his curly topknot, 'it's going to be really important for you to get plenty of exercise, keep yourself healthy. Lots of long walks would be the answer.'

'Yes?' There was a faint note of suspicion in Ulric's voice.

'It's so very much more satisfying to walk with a – well, people smile and talk to you if you walk with a – well, as a matter of fact – if you walk with a dog.'

'Absolutely not.' Thoughts of great art and even minor medicine paled into insignificance as Ulric shrank at a vision of horror: one of those beasts in his flat – spreading its muddy paws on his bed, leaking at lips, nose and every other exaggerated orifice; smell of dog, breath of dog, fleas of dog, bark of dog, sloppy tongue of dog, repulsiveness of dog. 'Never. Not while I'm here, anyway.'

'Oh, all right. We can still have nice walks.' Briskly, Steven-John towelled his hair. 'And dogs, even well-trained ones, do tend to scare off the birds.' Steven-John teased up the wet curls with his fingers.

Ulric sighed wearily. 'Oh, I don't know, Steven-John. I don't know. If it was, say, half the size of Midge's little thing, and didn't scratch itself or pant in your face, and if it could be persuaded either to wear knickers or at least refrain from gnawing its testicles in company – it's a thoroughly rotten idea, but, I don't know . . .'

'Let's leave it for now. Shower's free.'

Ulric, majestic as a high-priest in his robe, made his way towards the bathroom and his ablutions. It was perfectly clear to both men that they'd be off to Wood Green Animal Shelter within a week. Ulric told himself that he was going to have to be much firmer about things in general. He decided that he would, this time, firmly demand a saucer.

As Steven-John made the tea, the tinkling of porcelain cups was drowned by rather less musical sounds emerging from the bathroom – of a singer gargling, swilling, hawking, snorting and spitting in the morning ritual of cleansing his vocal chords of the night's accumulation of phlegm. Then followed a shockingly powerful outburst of scales and arpeggios, without a pause, without a breath. Steven-John, muttering a prayer for divine intercession on behalf of any neighbour who'd hoped to sleep till eight, tightened the clasp of the kitchen window. Ulric, merrily but still very loudly, began to sing 'Die beiden Grenadiere'.

The hospital visit began quite well. They found their way to the Oncology Department without difficulty, since Steven-John had checked the route when he called on Monday to fix the appointment.

After that, their troubles began. They entered a place of silence heavy with uneven laboured breathing. It was crammed with patients, patiently waiting: pale faces, baldness, wheelchairs, the terribly ill sloping against their neighbours or holding themselves rigidly upright. Ulric quailed. A young woman got unsteadily to her feet and offered him her chair. Steven-John pushed him down into it and went to the reception desk to book him in.

Ulric could not sit near those poor people. Weak though his knees felt, even greater was his weak fear that he might catch something. He moved over to the posters – Kew Gardens, Kathleen Ferrier and the like – which took the place of windows. There was a powerful sweet and bilious smell, as of regurgitated candyfloss.

When Steven-John returned, he was convinced that they had lost his records. He was wrong, but it was worse. His records were not lost (though at another department) but his schedule would be to see the consultant (who had not yet arrived, and had several people to see before Ulric); then to have a blood test, then to collect the results of the blood test, then to see a specialist who would analyse the blood test and prescribe the drugs, then to have the drugs made up, then to have them delivered to the Oncology Department, and finally, if all these things were achieved, to have the infusion. The receptionist, in response to Steven-John's insistent questioning, had admitted that this process might take a bit of time. Taking account of delays inevitable in a headless bureaucracy like a hospital, he should allow about five hours, four hours of waiting and a total of about one hour in having things done to him.

'These people –' Ulric gestured about him '– these terribly ill people; they have to wait five hours in this, this police cell?'

Steven-John nodded. 'The new ones, yes.'

At 10.30 or thereabouts, a tall, tanned figure with a seven-league stride bounded in like someone emerging from the gym. 'Morning, everyone,' he called out, in a basso profundo Ulric might have envied. 'Isn't it a perfect day for the seaside?'

'Perfect, Doctor,' responded a feeble chorus, in trembling treble voices.

'I'm getting out of here.' Ulric was in motion.

Steven-John grasped his wrist.

'Your friend all right, dear?' called the reception nurse.

Steven-John let go of Ulric's hand and rushed up to the desk for a whispered consultation. They had an hour to wait before the first move. They spent part of it at the coffee vending machine.

'Why am I here, Stevie? We don't either of us believe that this treatment is going to work.'

'Because we're going to give it a try.'

Much against his inclinations, Ulric did.

The Haematology Department (housed in another building in another street) was worse than the Oncology Department. The hospital, like so many hospitals in 1989, was then billed for closure. But the maintenance people seemed rather ahead of the game, as they were busy with pneumatic drills pulling down the wall behind the row of broken plastic seats on which Ulric and Steven-John waited for yet another slot to fall vacant.

They sat in a fine rain of plaster dust. Steven-John, as ever, filled the unforgiving minute. Beside them was a woman with a Carmen Miranda wrap over her head, her nicotine-stained fingers anxiously plucking at this headgear.

'Does this pre-chemo blood test thing hurt?' he asked her in a subtle whisper. Within seconds, they were friends; in minutes, she had confided to him her life story and, before Ulric was called to have an eggcup of blood extracted for testing, they were exchanging addresses and Steven-John had promised that, when she could no longer refuse hospitalisation, he would take care of Thermopylae, her budgerigar.

'She's so plucky,' said Steven-John, as the woman preceded them into the vampire room.

Ulric could barely look at her; what he saw, he found utterly repulsive.

Blood test results are relayed from Haematology to Oncology Departments on networked computers, but this hospital didn't then trust technology: Ulric was to wait yet another hour until a sufficient number of reports had been produced to make it worthwhile to call a porter. So Steven-John slipped away on another of his mysterious consultations with staff of the lower orders. His offer to carry the papers himself was refused (despite his winsomely embracing the grinning Garfield toy on the reception desk); his attempt to bribe the nearest porter too failed, as a policeman walked by. Finally, Steven-John, doing stage tiptoe, burgled the out-tray, taking two reports: on Ulric and the woman with the Carmen Miranda head-dress. He ran these over the road to the Oncology Department, then returned and, with dignity, walked Ulric back. He used similar wiles to speed up each stage, hauling messengers away from card games, luring nurses out of long consultations with each other, tidying away the clutter of abandoned wheelchairs to facilitate movement, himself putting Ulric on the weight scales. He even beat the pharmacy (where strict security governed the transport of dangerous drugs) with methods it would not be wise to make public.

During Steven-John's absences, Ulric's confidence declined. At these times, he could not understand how he had come to agree to this thing. 'What is chemotherapy?' Steven-John, in his blunt way, had said to the first consultant. It is blasting the body's cells with poison because more rogue cells than healthy cells will die. Consequently, though all the cells will reproduce to make up their losses, so long as the patient is reasonably strong, the proportion of rogue cells to healthy cells will steadily decline. 'It's a bit like,' said the pretty fellow

Ulric had rather fancied and Steven-John hated, 'firing a handful of pellets into a henhouse to knock out a fox; you can't avoid killing hens in the process.'

Very funny. An allegory of Ulric's understanding of chemotherapy would more likely have been of firing a handful of foxes into the henhouse and shutting the gate on what followed. This 'therapy', which was supposed to make the patient less ill, had caused his mother's hair to fall out, turned her face grey, given her, after each treatment, days of horrible dry nausea, and left her weak, exhausted and dreadfully depressed. The pretty fellow had assured Ulric that the treatment had become more sophisticated in the 35 years since. But he admitted that it still worked on the same basic principle. Waiting in one plastic chair after another, or leaning against walls when no chairs were free, Ulric's need for the reassuring sight of that chrysanthemum mop grew with each absence.

Though Steven-John had halved the waiting period, by the time Ulric was installed in the dentist chair in the chemotherapy cubicle, he was tired and fractious. The nurse entered, wheeling a stand (known as a 'dog', because patients attached to drips must trail it about after them, although it better resembles the skeleton of a Christmas tree). On this hung transparent bags of chemicals in the bright colours of poisonous insects. Ulric looked away from the dog and examined the nurse's down-at-heel shoes.

With a shy grin at Steven-John (few medics dared to smile at Ulric), she said: 'This big bag at the top looks fierce, but it's only saline, to dilute the mix and ease things for your friend's kidneys. These two here are different types of anti-nausea medication, and this nice little one has something to cheer him up. So it's not all bad.' Ulric looked away hastily as she unwrapped a needle big enough to inseminate a horse. 'You'll be surprised by how little this needle hurts.' Gently, she extended Ulric's long, bony arm and wrapped a pressure bandage just below the armpit. Then she folded his fingers into a fist, relaxed his arm with a few up-and-down movements and tapped at a vein in the crook. The vein swelled, eager as a nipple in a baby's mouth. Ulric didn't see any of this; his eyes were still averted. He did not seem even to be aware when the nurse inserted the enormous needle into his vein. 'The infusion is slow, to minimise shock, and takes about half an hour. Would you like the radio?' She reached up to the shelf behind Ulric's head and switched it on. The voice of Tracy Chapman whirred through the air.

'Or,' she continued, observing the grimace of distaste on Ulric's face, 'you could have Radio Three.' She switched over. By an unfortunate coincidence, they were discussing '*In questa tomba oscura*'. 'A very minor work,' said the critic, 'not even worth an opus number.'

'No!' howled Ulric.

Hastily, she retuned and they got the cricket test in Barbados.

At Ulric's wish, she then left the two men alone, but they could hear her moving about cautiously in some cubbyhole or spyhole next door. Every few minutes, she returned to adjust the taps of the drips, and check up on Ulric's arm. She seemed satisfied to know that it felt weird and numb, and then developed pins and needles. Ulric was somewhat consoled. Whatever he thought of the hospital, he believed that this nurse knew what she was doing.

After she had unleashed Ulric from the dog, and given Steven-John a stock of additional anti-nausea pills in case of need, Ulric rose on a pair of very unsteady legs.

'You'll be seeing the oncologist again in a week,' the nurse said, 'so that we can, if necessary adjust the treatment or – if it isn't suitable for you – use a different therapy.'

Ulric waved away the appointment card in her hand. 'Thank you,' he said, 'but I prefer not to commit myself to another appointment as yet.'

All that Wednesday night the pellets of the chemotherapy drugs flew about Ulric's veins, slaughtering hens and foxes.

Despite this frenzied activity within, his limbs were pinned to the bed. Eyes soft-focus with fear, he gazed into Steven-John's face.

Steven-John was seated on the petit-point footstool with his knees tucked up under his chin, but his usual calm was lacking. He scratched at his head, winding the curls into greasy corkscrews; he tugged at his moustache in a manner that seemed to Ulric distinctly shifty. From time to time he rose to deliver an indecisive laying on of hands. He made several mugs of camomile tea which Ulric, afflicted with nausea, was unable to drink.

At last Steven-John spoke. 'I can sense what you want,' he muttered, 'you want somebody to say what's going on.'

With an eyeblink, Ulric indicated that he did.

'Well, I guess it's going pretty much the way the nurse told us it would, so I guess it's okay.' Steven-John drew in his breath. 'I guess it'll pass.'

Ulric's expression did not change.

Steven-John sniffed the air like a horse seeking water or a poet seeking inspiration. 'It's what they said, Ulric. It's war.' Steven-John struggled to his feet. 'It's zapping those rogue cells,' he cried, with a very unconvincing show of enthusiasm.

Ulric responded with a droll droop of an eyelid.

Abruptly, Steven-John sat down. 'Perhaps,' he said in a different, flat, tone, 'I should call the emergency number?'

Ulric's eyes wandered over the face and figure of his friend, distant as a view through the wrong end of a telescope. 'No, that hospital has done enough damage. Stevie –' his adam's apple moved jerkily, a disturbing contrast to the utter flaccidity of the rest of his body, '– don't trot out that zappy doctor talk. Just try to tell me why I feel so awful.'

'Well,' said Steven-John almost aggressively, 'your ear seems better.'

Ulric nodded.

'And those ultrasound and biopsy things didn't show any spread of the cancer.'

'Not as far as their myopic instruments could see.'

'It's such a bugger, this cancer thing. Even the experts only try this and that and then cross fingers.' Steven-John scratched viciously at his skull. 'God, Ulric, if I could heal you by giving my life, I'd do it gladly.'

'Don't say that,' said Ulric dryly; 'I might accept. Try another line.'

'Okay.' Steven-John thought. 'Well, maybe we could just think of this as a bad trip.'

'Trip?' Ulric's eyebrows rose. 'Where to?'

'To another place. Ever taken LSD?'

'No,' replied Ulric, sounding almost interested. 'LSD makes you feel like *this*? And people do it for *pleasure*?'

'Yes!' Steven-John seized his opportunity. 'They do it for kicks. That's what you're getting – kicked. You're having an out-of-the-body experience.'

Ulric gurgled in a sound that approximated to a laugh. It was almost a relief to think that whatever was happening, however dreadful, had a name, had been experienced by people before, and maybe even meant something. 'Well,' he said eventually, 'do you think one day I might get what you call "psyched up" enough to like it?' –

Steven-John, with a neatness any used-car salesman might envy, closed the deal: 'By the third dose, those rogue cells will be screaming for mercy, and you'll get a trip round the moon and the stars.'

'Make it Hungary, dear boy. I always wanted to see those wild horses.'

20

When Chelsey, pleased with the chill she'd cast over the Gospel Oak ménage, clipped briskly down the garden path, she had probably allowed for, and discounted, the likelihood that the first response would be mockery. It was. The three women held their breath till they heard the squeal of the garden gate. Then they burst into laughter. 'Are you saying,' intoned Fiona in a sepulchral impersonation of Chelsey's Lady Bracknell, 'that you really want to *be* Lorraine, and *have* the other – in a *handbag*?' And they laughed all over again. But the game ran out of steam even before Chelsey's bus had arrived. Nobody seemed quite to know how to begin the only other game on the programme.

After a few dithering moments, Fiona moved over to her workbench and picked up the half-finished image, in silver, of a heron. 'You two make a start,' she said, 'I need a little while with this thing.'

Lucy, who had gone rather quiet, looked at her, disappointed.

'Go on,' she said, 'go upstairs if that makes you feel better.

I'll be along. Take a bath if you can't think of anything better
to do.'

Fiona lingered at the bench for a few minutes, then drifted
into the kitchen. Bonzo followed her. Fiona took hold of his
muzzle and stared into his eyes. 'You, my boy, made a
schmuck of yourself fawning over Chelsey Chamberlain.' He
avoided her glance and tried to lick her hands. 'Who feeds
you, Bonzo? Who walks you, Bonzo? Who, by the law of
England, *owns* you, Bonzo?'

Bonzo, beginning to be distressed, drew away and began to
gnaw at the laces of Fiona's shoes, a regression to his post-
dogs'-home days, when he had been fatal to footwear.

Fiona did not restrain him. This poor confused being had
turned to Chelsey because he needed someone to trust.
Chelsey was the one person in the room who had not abused
him. Bonzo's loyalty was his own to give, and he did not have
to give it, or his love, to the woman who fed him. 'You've
shown me up, my Bonze,' she said. 'But I wish you hadn't
done it in front of Chelsey.' Fiona was, for reasons that were
obscure to her, somewhat afraid of Chelsey.

Bonzo now seemed as contrite as Fiona herself. He slouched
off to his bowl and returned with a glob of something brown
and greasy, which he deposited at Fiona's feet. She scooped it
up. 'Thank you, Bonzo,' she said, 'but your need is greater
than mine.' Snorting, he licked the meat from her fingers; then
he stood, nose at the level of her knees, waiting for the rest of
his supper, morsel by morsel, to be fed to him. Bonzo made no
secret of his dislike of the situation. Fiona wanted to make it up
to him. But she was inarticulate in tenderness, and even if she
could show him how sorry she was, would they ever be as
they had been? Between them was broken trust.

And this worried her. Though she told herself that all living
tissues, including the tissues of the mind, can heal, she wasn't
sure that this principle held solid for trust. Trust wasn't like
other things. Trust came quietly. It grew secretly under cover
of regular meals, fondling, the habit of gentleness, the scorecard

of occasions when you had protected him and when he had protected you from an enemy, until it broke cover and you recognised that the padding of four particular paws across the floor of your studio was a sound of very particular sweetness. Nowdays, the paws were ever so slightly out of rhythm, and in Fiona they aroused not sweetness, but grief for what she had done.

If Bonzo recognised his part in Fiona's inner conflict, he made no effort to help her resolve it. After swallowing a few mouthfuls, he turned away and lay down to wipe his chops with his forepaws, in slow, deliberate, depressed absorption in himself. Fiona watched, her face grave. Had he, in the days of his innocence, had quite so many ribs?

It was not only on Bonzo's account that Fiona lingered. It was also for Lorraine. Chelsey, with the awful sharpness of her cynicism, had exposed the contradiction at the heart of the situation. Lucy called it 'sharing'. But in this unequal world, how can there be sharing unless she who has much is diminished? How long could the fun last before Lorraine cried 'thief!'? Fiona heard the boiler roar; hot water was pouring into the bath.

Should they be doing this thing? Fiona was not in doubt: they ought not to do it, but had to: it was the only thing left. Between herself and Lorraine – as between herself and Bonzo – was a broken trust. They could not go back to what they had been. Chelsey was right.

After the party, Fiona and Lorraine had slunk about the house, as conscious of and uncomfortable with each other as enemies during a wartime truce. They'd offered each other cups of tea, stepped out of each other's way in the passages, and taken refuge in different rooms. Every time Fiona caught Lorraine's glance, she read the same statement: 'You find me disgusting.' Fiona could not unsay what she'd said: one cannot retract what is true, and expect to be believed. Fiona also knew that Lorraine's grovelling shame, if they opened the subject, would re-awaken and increase her disgust.

Then, soon after Lorraine returned from work on Monday evening, Lucy arrived, fierce, uninvited, and demanding – out of right, not pity – to be heard. The dead air in the house was instantly sparkling with electricity. The ardent little hothead, her ears bright red but her voice controlled, filled Fiona's being with a flood of love. Unsheddable tears roared in her ears. But Fiona could not, would not, lower her defences against this force, wild and terrible as a hurricane. Lucy's love would destroy everything else in Fiona's life – and how could she, at 50, sacrifice Lorraine, Georgiana, all her safety?

Lorraine – it had to be Lorraine – had suggested a safe way out, a threesome. Lucy leapt at it. Fiona too was excited: if it could work, they would have the gift of both Lucy and each other. But she demurred; there wasn't enough in the deal for Lorraine, and Lorraine was not someone who could just tag along. Later, she realised that, for Lorraine too, this was the last throw. Like Fiona, Lorraine could not face the wreckage of their world after Lucy. Lorraine wanted to regain her self-respect by showing that she too could play the game; and Fiona wanted Lorraine to succeed in this. How very ironic that an arrangement considered so naughty should have so little erotic drive behind it, and so great a wish to do the least-worst thing.

Lorraine had proposed it, yet Lorraine was the one who was making it difficult to do. Lorraine could be a lot of fun. But right now she was inconsistent, sulky and suspicious. She was losing control. If her intention was to reassert her power over Lucy, or over Fiona, she was driving herself to failure.

Fiona did not want Lorraine to fail. Nor did she want her to win. She wanted them all to keep the game going, vertiginous but in balance, the play of trapeze artists. Because, while the game lasted, Fiona's psyche was carried up and out of the reach of the wasting disease of age. But what was happening to Lorraine not only threatened the game. It put at risk also the status to which they would return when it was – as it must before very long be – over. If Lorraine's nerve failed, the world would be a dangerous place, too dangerous.

Third, Fiona lingered on her own account. Fiona knew where she was going: into the dark. Until that weird afternoon when Lucy's dolls and pandas and long-eared grasses summoned her, she could smell it on her person, the smell of an old woman's wardrobe. Then Lucy, with a kiss, had sent her tumbling down the rabbit hole. There was light now, the glow of an underworld of mushrooms and bottles labelled 'Drink Me'.

What was happening to her? Had she gone mad? All her life Fiona had been shadowed by a horror of madness. Perhaps this was what madness was. If it was, who could have guessed that madness would be so pleasant, such a tingling in the nerves?

Or was something quite different happening; was Fiona sanely, coldly and cunningly playing a dangerous game because she did not believe she could lose? Fiona had only to gaze and Lucy's soul fell open to her. Fiona had power over Lucy. But Lucy – although she loved power – did not have power over Fiona, because Fiona was shielded by Lorraine. And Lorraine did not have power over anyone, not even herself, because Lorraine could not believe that she was loveable.

Fiona's spouse and her new lover were upstairs in the bath. Perhaps Lorraine was making advances to Lucy; perhaps she was trying to drown her. Shivers ran down Fiona's spine. Ought she to stop this thing, right now before it started? Or ought she to let it run, at least until they knew what they were doing? She decided to try to think.

'C'mon, Bonski.' Hampstead Heath would be magical on this chill, misty night. Fiona formed with her lips, but did not utter, the word 'walkies'; a dog could take only so much excitement. Bonzo, instantly metamorphosed from cur into dervish, spun himself out of the kitchen and at the heaps of coats in the hall, nosing among them for his lead. Fiona unhooked it, gave it to him – by the metal end to reduce his chances of braining himself as he swung the thing about. Then she reached for her own camel-hair, but, after an unthinking pause, put on Lorraine's ski-jacket. They went out onto the Heath, shrouded in night but safe enough with Bonzo's protection. Fiona planned a long walk, a long think.

Even as an adolescent girl, Fiona had been unsatisfied with life, the life that offered itself to her, the cheapness of it. Perhaps, she thought grimly, this discontent arose from her own conceit. But, from wherever it came, she was driven by longing to find something more meaningful, more beautiful, more true. Fiona could not give herself up, as her classmates did, to playing netball or joining the Young Socialists or messing about with boys in the back of a car. Instead, she veered between two contradictory courses.

On one, she had explored sex, first with a sculptor, a man with daughters older than she was, and a cultivated sense of the peaks of the exquisite. He had been followed, at intervals, by others, men and women, aesthetes and brutes, different excitements, some of which failed, some, for a time, held her.

The other course represented a different kind of apotheosis. Fiona also longed for the religious life. She tried Buddhism, but its symbols were too foreign to her; she could not instil the faith in the gut. Later, after the failure of another love affair, she took instruction to enter the Catholic church, and dreamed of becoming a Cistercian nun. She struggled, through prayer, meditation and study, to surrender her consciousness to an extreme, bare discipline. But she could never make her mind simple enough, never believe wholly enough, never work hard enough, never achieve complete sincerity. Her mind wandered when she said the Rosary; the tobacco smell of the priest's hand distracted her when she took Communion; at the Confessional, she avoided the kiosks of the dullest priests. After a year, she fled from religion into yet another blind rush into love.

After that, she made a new resolution: to go out alone, with no words in her head or dreams in her heart, and wait for truth to come to her. But she was weak in resolution, patience and courage. And long waits bring doubt. She yielded to and for two-and-a-quarter years took comfort from the man who paid more than half of the mortgage and financed the launch of Fiona Douglas Jeweller-Artiste. He was the only one of Fiona's various partners to win Georgiana's approval.

When Fiona, seeking nothing, found love in the earthy dynamo striding beside Midge on that day on Hampstead Heath, it seemed, as it seemed every time love came to her, that she had found a short-cut to God. She was not blinded by Lorraine's charms. She saw through Lorraine even while the fireworks were exploding around and within her. She saw the grandiosity and the commonplaceness of her. But she also saw the optimism and energy. Lorraine was, at bottom, sound. Lorraine was what she lacked. Fiona let herself be taken by Lorraine's frantic, extravagant courtship. She knew, even then, that she was sliding back to love, the rat-run. Yet, she reminded herself, she had never in all her explorations, found anything to equal love, anything that could, while it lasted, so powerfully deliver faith.

And it had delivered. From the day she met Lorraine, Fiona had been given many blessings. She had love; the love lasted, she had success in her art; she had, all through her forties, been the most beautiful woman in the room. She had not felt, till her fiftieth birthday, the slowly rising tide of the waste that remains, the gathering poisons.

Perhaps if marriage was something of a disappointment, it was because its promise was fulfilled. It had delivered too many things, too many material things, and material things are burdens if you cannot take them into something beyond. Fiona hated her possessions, yet clung to them. They did not satisfy. They left her envying the simple hungers of the bag lady. Yet she breathed and lived on these things – these Chinese vases, these small oak escritoires, these rugs with fading images of the Tree of Life, these job-lots of silver and copper. She coveted and then loved them, but they stank of decay.

Fiona had long dreamed of making, in silver (her favourite medium), something utterly simple, utterly perfect. One unbroken thread that would rise from the form into the essence. But latterly she had struggled even for the beginnings of form. She looked at the world's masterpieces of simplicity — Picasso's nervy line or Degas's soft curve, a Japanese garden, Blake's songs of innocence, Rothko's meditations, the detail that revealed itself when the breeze shifted the leaves of a tree, and suddenly you had glimpsed what you didn't know till then you were seeking. These things, that had once so delighted her, had become empty, false. There was too much style in them, too much consciousness; they were self-gratifying, sentimental. Their only innocence was their vanity.

Nor could Fiona, in those limbo times, find again the lure of sex. When Lorraine was off on assignments to photograph a handshake or the christening of an Honourable, Fiona had sometimes dropped in at the darker gay places, where the bouncers had pitbull terriers and kept an eye out for police. There, she watched thighs straining against black leather, and dykes spinning the hormones through their veins — pool, booze, dance, drugs, sex, then more pool. Fiona did not find these places arousing. Though occasionally she noticed someone she might have fancied if they'd exchanged glances in a crowded tube train, at the clubs none aroused her desire. Yet, she had returned, not to cruise but to lose herself in the crush, the closed faces, the numbing brutality of disco — anonymity among her own kind. The women who interested her were not the young and beautiful centres of attention but those who stood alone at the fringes, looking down into their glasses. She did not speak, or wish to speak, to any of them, but saw in them what she saw in herself: fear of time, the suffocation of dreams in a pill bottle, the futility of praise for works in silver you can no longer love, the feeble grip of the dead spider.

Was this the menopause? As she tracked down the tree-lined walks towards the Lido, watching out now for night prowlers, it seemed to her that the poisons that erupted with that last gushing menstrual bleeding had been in her from birth, and slowly filling. Fiona did not, in general, suffer from female complaints, so why should she have such a dreadful menopause? She had not had painful periods. She did not giggle or blush. She had never had difficulty in expressing herself in sex. She had no great craving for penetration. She had never wanted to give birth or kidnap a baby. She was not ashamed of her body. She wasn't excited by movie weepies. She never had to fight the temptation to gorge; she had no interest in chocolates.

It had always been there, waiting for her, this malaise. The menopause had merely forced her to pause, and see. She saw her beauty filched from her, a little each night, and in its place came a whining grief, accompanied by hot flushes, uncertain temper, inexplicable rage, and exhaustion. She saw that the great future which she and Lorraine dreamed of had – perhaps when they were making love, perhaps when they were quarrelling, perhaps when they were just melting down in Georgiana's undemanding circle, certainly when they weren't looking – become the past. They still presented themselves on the gaming board but were no longer the pieces on which the gods placed their bets. They didn't matter any more.

While Fiona was dimly becoming aware of this, Lorraine, with increasing vehemence, would shout her praise of Fiona's beauty. Fiona only wished she wouldn't make so much noise or go on so long. Lorraine was trying to drag her back into the vortex of a battle of which she had grown weary. She didn't know that Lorraine's excitement came out of the frisson of loving another woman. Fiona had then, unexcited by jealousy, merely longed for Lorraine, one day, to give her the lash of pure truth, to say: 'You've become ugly, Fiona. Your face has collapsed into the mask of a troll.'

Even then, even before the menopause had handed her the gift of terrible truth, Fiona knew that what she had been doing with Lorraine was defying the natural order. They had had something approaching contentment. Such complacency must surely have been an irresistible challenge to the gods.

And now? What was she doing now with this girl, Lorraine's toy, this poor abused thing who was trying to build some little power for herself out of the waste of theirs? Was she harming Lucy as Chelsey chose to think? How could she be doing harm, when all she sought was to keep alive the good magic that had filled her distressed mind with delight? Even the thought of Lucy's touch, out here on the chilly Heath, sent desire thrilling down her nerves, into her lips, breasts, the crook of her elbow. This was pleasure? It felt more like electric shock treatment.

But if it was, like that controlled medical violence, it had aroused her, as the slaughter of Patroclus had aroused Achilles. Surely there was virtue in a force that infused her body, and even her art, with the return of her old powers? How could she resist the sweetness that leached out of her membranes at the thought of surrender to the blank-faced, curdling smile of the young woman who wanted her, even if she only wanted her for the punishment of Lorraine?

Was it to escape facing the blunt fact that she was doing what she felt to be sinful, that she told herself that this was the gathering up of her strength in one last big throw? That she knew she would have to pay, and the price could be everything she had had before? Could she justify the risk to herself and Lorraine? And, if she said yes to that, could she justify the sacrifice of Bonzo?

Bonzo, who till then had padded beside her, diverting only to mark a tree or investigate a rustle in the grass, made a rush at a shape emerging from the darkness. Another dog. A friend. Jezebel. The usual dog ritual proceeded.

'Oh, it's you, Fiona. Lovely evening.' Flicking a finger at his cap, Toby passed on.

Fiona was pleased. Toby was one of the good things about the world to which she would soon have to return. But the shock of encountering a human in this empty landscape recalled her to the sense of time. Lorraine and Lucy would now either be concerned about her, or so wrapped in each other that they hadn't noticed her absence. In either case, she ought to worry. She didn't. But she ought to turn back. She was somewhere near the north end of the Heath, the broad sloping meadows, woodlands and thickets of brambles. She called Bonzo and began to head towards the misty haze over the ponds and, beyond that, Gospel Oak and the sleeping city.

Back at the cottage, Lorraine and Lucy hadn't, as Fiona feared they mightn't, been able to think of anything better to do. So they followed instructions and traipsed into the bathroom. Lucy turned on the taps and Lorraine undid a shoelace. The room filled with steam.

'Well,' said Lorraine, 'I don't feel quite so bullish as I did – when was it? – a month back, when we were – what – lovers, I suppose. But, then, we never had a bath together, so I suppose . . .'

Lucy tossed off her clothes. She tested the water with her toe, then slid into it. 'I suppose,' she said, with a smile.

'You look so sweet.' Lorraine hovered. 'Like a little pink gecko.'

'And you look like you've been digging at the coal-face.' Lucy tossed a handful of bath-bubbles, little coloured marbles, under the taps. 'Jump in and I'll scrub your back.' Lucy sank into the foam. Her toes emerged and expertly adjusted the taps.

Lorraine watched, suddenly shocked. How very familiar Lucy was with this bathroom. She'd reached up, unerring, for the bag of Body Shop bath-bubbles on the shelf. (And this bag, a stocking filler from somebody or other which had lain gathering dust for months, was now almost empty.) How many scented baths had Fiona and Lucy taken together? Lorraine slowly pulled the sock she'd just plucked off back over her foot. 'Actually, I was thinking of taking a shower.'

'Oh Lorraine,' Lucy said with a sad little smile, 'you aren't going to have one of your turns? No, not tonight. Come on, the water's lovely.'

The blood rushed to Lorraine's head. 'What do you mean "one of my turns"?'

Lucy captured islands of foam and spread them over her arms. 'Lorraine, don't. Please don't be like this.' She reached out a soapy arm. 'Please try. I'm trying.'

'Trying what?' Lorraine stepped back from Lucy's extended hand. 'Trying to put up with me?' The blood in her head came to the boil.

'I wish you wouldn't do this. I'm trying, Fiona's trying, to make it work.'

Lorraine snorted. 'So you sorted it all out, did you, you and Fiona?'

'Lorraine, the threesome is *your* idea. We're doing what *you* want.'

The slow patience in Lucy's voice further enraged Lorraine. 'Answer my question: did you set this up, you and Fiona? Did you plan how to handle me? Did you decide, the two of you, that Fiona would go out with the dog and you would soften me up? Was that the idea?'

Lucy sat up. 'Lorraine, you're trying to drag me into a fight. I don't want to fight. I want – or, until a minute ago, I wanted – to hold you.'

'You still haven't answered my question. Did you plan this?' Suddenly, it was all horribly clear. The boiling confusion in Lorraine's mind cooled instantly. 'I know what happened. You set it up yesterday while I was at work; you planted the threesome idea in my head; you two have been in the bath today.'

Lucy's face, already red from the hot water, was now set tight. 'This is paranoia. I won't be drawn into it. But I did answer your question. *You* planned the threesome. We fell in with you.'

'So! You don't deny that you had sex in the bath with Fiona today?'

'Jesus Christ!' Lucy reached for a towel. 'You're busting for trouble. You're distorting everything, absolutely everything.'

'Come on,' hissed Lorraine. 'Tell me. I know you're in love with Fiona.'

Lucy nodded. 'Of course I am. But I love you too.'

'Do you?' Despite the heat of the room, Lorraine was beginning to shiver.

'Yes, I do. Whenever you'll let me. But I'm not at all sure that you love me.'

Lorraine raised her eyebrows. 'Maybe you're right to have doubts about that.'

'That's okay, I can love you anyway. In time, you'll come to trust me. I know you will.' Lucy reached out and this time caught hold of Lorraine's hand. 'You're trembling.' Lucy drew Lorraine's hand to her lips.

'Oh God, Lucy,' said Lorraine tremblingly enough. 'I don't know what's happening to me. I'm turning into a horrible person.'

'It's all right, baby. Come, put your arms round me.'

'Hi, girls.' Fiona, followed by Bonzo, trotted into the bedroom.

Lorraine, suddenly guilty, sprang away from Lucy's arms and beckoned to the dog. He came over and laid his muzzle in her hand. He smelled of mist and grass.

'We had a nice walk.' Fiona was hauling on her ancient pyjamas. 'We met Toby and Jezebel. Fancy some tea?'

'I'll make it.' Lucy sat up and reached for Fiona's white satin robe. 'Camomile, Earl Grey or Indian brown?'

As Fiona, absently, said: 'Brown for me,' Lorraine leapt out of the bed.

'Indian brown' was Lorraine's own invented term for supermarket teabags; it was a private expression, for her and Fiona. '*I'm* making the tea,' she snorted.

'Okay, Lorraine,' said Fiona with a wry grin, 'but don't forget to use filtered water.'

'I'll use bloody lavatory water if I want.'

Lorraine paced up and down, trying to hear whatever was going on in the bedroom – the kettle was taking a long time to the boil. Lorraine, unlike her usual mono-orgasmic self, was still awash with lust. Her body from womb to knees felt as if she'd not long eaten a tigerish vindaloo.

Could this be love, this frenzied grabbing, this grovelling, this brutality? Was she in love with Lucy? She didn't even *like* Lucy, so why was her sexual reaction so charged? Was she in love with Fiona? She could hardly bear to look at Fiona. When she caught a glimpse of Fiona's eyes; her long pale limbs that, no matter how casually flung, were always full of grace, she felt a pang, a searing injury, that made her want to fling these visions from her.

The kettle began to splutter. Lorraine, abruptly recalled, reached for the overflowing cupboard, and found the Indian brown. What on earth had Lucy ordered? Whatever it was, what she got was Waitrose's unpleasantly medicinal lemon zinger. Lorraine sloshed rum into her own mug.

As Lorraine was hooking the three mugs onto her fingers, Bonzo padded into the kitchen.

'Hello, old chap.' Lorraine, out of some obscure impulse, unlatched the mugs and went over to stroke his ears. 'Didn't you get enough supper?'

Bonzo sat. He gave her a serious look, then glanced pathetically at his dinner bowl, which had been carefully sculpted – one quarter of the bowl carved out by Fiona's fingers, the rest untouched, its jelly-coated meat and meal now set in a solid clot.

'I see.' Lorraine came closer. 'You're a bit off your food, mate. I wouldn't yield to that if I was you. With only so many shopping days to Christmas, I wouldn't want them mistaking my ribs for reindeer antlers.'

Dragging his bottom over the quarry tiles, Bonzo slid closer to Lorraine and offered her a dry paw.

'Well, I don't know, Bonze. No point in flannelling me. You're Fiona's boy, not mine. I'm just a lodger in this house these days.'

Bonzo began to paw at Lorraine's legs. She studied him: he wanted the world to be at peace and, for him, that meant her and Fiona being at peace. But he could do nothing to bring it about. He was only a dog. He had no power. 'Oh, poor Bonzo. It's such a complicated world.' Lorraine sank to her knees and wrapped the dog in an embrace Chelsey would surely have found clumsy, since it certainly was.

Giggles erupted from under the bedclothes as Lorraine came in. Without a sound, she laid the tea and lemon zinger down on Fiona's side of the bed and watched the covers heave in the scuffle going on under them. Her dangling hand encountered Bonzo's ear, which she stroked absently. After a minute, she made to leave the room. Bonzo, seeming unsure whether to stay or follow, whined. 'Quiet, Bonzo,' she whispered.

But Fiona was up like a shot. 'Lorraine! Thank God you're here. You've got to save me! This woman's tickling me to death –' Fiona's protest ended in squeals as Lucy assaulted the soles of her feet.

Lorraine stood immobile, her hand again on the dog's head.

'Lorraine?' Fiona sat up, pulling the covers up to her breasts, and looked at Lorraine with hurt in her eyes. 'Lorraine, what's wrong?'

'Oh, I don't know,' replied Lorraine vaguely. 'Suddenly I'm sick of sex. All I want right now is a digestive system that knows what to do with food.'

'We're only playing. Come on, Lorraine; you like to play.'

'Yeah, sure I do. But tonight, I'd prefer sleep. I'll take the spare room.'

Lucy too sat up. 'That's not fair. You set up this threesome thing. And you've just done sex with me.'

'Well, dear hearts,' said Lorraine, 'this is your chance to catch up.'

Bonzo, glancing one way and then the other, eventually chose to bed down on the landing rug, midway between the two almost-shut bedroom doors.

21

Friday, 24 November, Highgate Cemetery

On the foggy Friday that followed, a full half-hour before
Lucy was due to arrive, Chelsey paced the pathways in
Highgate Cemetery's East Wing. Chelsey liked cemeteries.

She found George Eliot, then paused at the grave beside it,
of the woman whose stone proclaimed her love for Eliot, and
whom Eliot had called 'daughter'. 'Yuk!' said Chelsey and
turned her attention to the obelisk rising out of Eliot's grave.
Who, she wondered, had chosen this phallic and pseudo-
Egyptian monument for England's most woman-proud,
England-proud and socially intelligent novelist? And who had
decided that she was to be buried in this bourgeois cemetery
and not in Westminster Abbey? But then, she'd had a child
before marriage, so her body was too soiled to lie near such
models of propriety as the syphilitic English kings. Chelsey
chuckled in anticipation of sharing these reflections with
Lucy.

Gaily, she took off along the overgrown tracks beyond,
keeping the obelisk in view. She pushed her way through
hanging boughs, thorny arches of roses gone native, ivy and
brambles enclosing alleys of forgotten graves: John (Jackie)
Andrews, age 8, mourned by an armless cherub, Marthe

Besson, whose great gifts had astonished the masters of the musical world; Frances and Ottiley Reissman, sisters of 16 and 14, their grave guarded by a formidable angel. Overhead, crows cawed and magpies scavenged. This was the perfect place to meet; here, the magic which had for so many years bound Chelsey to Georgiana lay thick as mist.

There was light traffic over at the obelisk: couples photographing each other in front of it, earnest young women reading out the inscriptions in the tones of East Coast assistant professors. Chelsey willed each party to move on: there must be no stranger present when Lucy arrived.

Bells from somewhere beyond the crest of Highgate chimed eleven o'clock but brought no sign of the girl. Chelsey struck out towards the grassy spur above Karl Marx's tomb. By ten minutes past eleven, a slight frown was beginning to appear between her brows.

It had by then occurred to Chelsey that it would be characteristic of Fiona to sabotage this meeting. To leave Chelsey dangling and humiliated would be something Fiona might do for the sheer pleasure of it. She had done it many times before. This brought on a familiar sequence of different thoughts, the old injuries that kept her awake through the night. With a sigh, she reached into her Pandora's box of memories:

It was one of Georgiana's parties, quite recently – some ten or eleven years back. It was near the end of Fiona's time with the cheque-book man – though he was usually too snotty to show up at Georgiana's parties. Winter night pressed against Georgiana's long windows. Chelsey's memory had failed to record what Georgiana was wearing that evening, so fantasy filled the gap, putting her into the long black silk robe Georgiana had worn as an undergarment when playing the Dowager Empress Tz'u-hsi. Ulric was there, embarrassing everybody by girlishly fawning over his Tarzan in a dog collar. Standing apart, in one of the long windows, were Fiona and Sarah. Sarah (then two stone lighter and devoted to tight suede waistcoats and onyx rings) was a dashing figure. The two women were looking out at nothing and talking in low tones. Chelsey watched them. They did not touch but, from an edging movement of Sarah's shoulder, Chelsey picked it up: those two bodies knew each other. Chelsey was instantly excited. She sidled closer till she could feel the frisson between them. She wanted to share; she wanted to have a bit of innocent fun; she wanted to tease. She came up behind and spread her arms in a wide pincer. She could see her advance reflected in the window-panes and knew they saw it too. With a gorilla growl, she fastened her hands around Sarah's neck: 'Gotcha!'

Sarah's face reddened, but she laughed. Fiona moved away; she did not laugh; her face had the expression of someone who had found a slug in her salad.

Chelsey's hands, long and strong, gripped fast. Sarah choked as she laughed. 'What you going to do with me then?'

Chelsey looked straight at Fiona: 'I'm going to sell this gorgeous doll into slavery.'

This statement, the end of the game as far as Chelsey had planned it, coincided with one of those moments when angels were passing over. Everyone heard, and stood waiting for more.

'Hey,' cried Sophie, 'Take your hands off my Sarah.' Her voice was jovial, but as it spread through the silence, a bristling in its undertone ran like a shiver up Chelsey's arms.

The person who was now Steven-John but was then Sheila-Jayne and Chelsey's lover came to Chelsey's rescue. 'Grab Ulric instead, Chelsey,' she (he) called out, 'if we wrap him in silks and jewels, he'll go for a fortune.'

'So long as you sell me to a desert sheikh with eyes black as sloes, and promise not to tell Peter,' chimed Ulric.

'Done! Get him, Chelsey.' Sheila-Jayne already had hold of Ulric's trailing Indian scarf. 'We'll trade him for a thousand horses.'

Sarah emitted a semi-throttled but genuine laugh. Chelsey was saved.

All she had to do was release her hands and move two

yards across the room. She could even cover her retreat with a quip about giving up her prize for a greater one. But Fiona's gorgon stare had transfixed her. She couldn't let go. She couldn't let them get away with it. She couldn't leave Georgiana in ignorance that her precious Fiona was once again wallowing in sleaze with another woman's property.

'I'll stick with this one,' she heard herself say. 'She'll fetch up *somebody's* bottom dollar.'

But Chelsey was losing her audience. Georgiana had already turned away. Chelsey raised her voice. 'This time, everybody,' she called out, 'this time Fiona isn't going to get it for free.'

Sarah wrenched herself away. Chelsey's wrists stung from the rasp of her hands, as if they'd been struck by a whip. Sarah swung round to face her. Chelsey raised one burning wrist to her mouth and touched the skin to her lips, hot, but not as hot as Sarah's furious eyes.

'You envious snake,' Sarah spat.

A sound between a laugh and a squeak came out of Chelsey.

Then, pushing Chelsey aside, Sarah marched into the bathroom, slamming the door. Seconds later, Sophie was in the bathroom too. Voices filtered out into the drawing room. Though hushed, they were angry, very.

'Women, women,' Sheila-Jayne noted wryly, but did not move over to Chelsey's side. And Fiona had somehow been transported across the room. She was now beside Georgiana, whose hand tenderly stroked her shoulder.

Chelsey was alone in front of the windows, deserted. Chelsey had done no wrong. Chelsey made no secret liaisons; she lured nobody into unfaithfulness. But there she was, as usual, condemned, the rest of them lined up like a firing squad against her. Breathing deeply, she stood tall and stared grandly over each cruel head. Then with dignity, she turned to the window-panes. By degrees, conversation resumed, until it was as if nothing had happened. Chelsey took no part. She stared at the fragmented reflections of so much of her broken life. Recorded there for ever was one more crime for which Fiona must be made to pay.

By now Chelsey was trembling, a danger sign. She pushed the memory away, forcing her eyes to see not the windows inscribed with her sufferings, but a cemetery, a calm, wintry, final refuge. Chelsey told herself for the umpteenth time that she had to protect herself against her memories; they had too much power; they would lead her to do to herself what the world was trying to do to her; they would destroy her with madness. So she looked at the battered grasses at her feet, the distant obelisk and then her watch. It was a full twenty-five minutes past eleven. There could now be little doubt that Fiona was detaining Lucy, deliberately, out of spite. Chelsey marched back towards the Eliot tomb, kicking at whatever was still alive of the frost-ravaged plantings.

At twenty-two minutes to twelve, a small duffel-coated figure shambled up the path, pausing to examine at leisure every seraph, Celtic cross, draped urn and the rest. Chelsey perched on the flat slab beside the Eliot grave, folded her arms and observed the approach.

'Oh, hello,' said Lucy, at last catching sight of Chelsey. 'Spooky place, isn't it?'

Chelsey rose to her feet. She uttered no word about almost one-and-a-quarter hours' wait in near-zero temperatures, but the joke about the obelisk had rather lost its point. 'Come,' she said, 'we'll warm up with a brisk walk.' They struck out along the gravelled path, the public area with the big family vaults and nobody of any interest in them. When the silence was beginning to turn to dullness, she ended it: 'How is Fiona?'

Lucy sighed. 'I wish I knew.'

Chelsey wasn't impressed by this. 'Why don't you know? Has she walked out on you?'

'Oh no.' Lucy's backpack seemed to weigh half a ton. She paused to shift it to the other shoulder. 'She's in her studio, making a brooch thing.'

'And you? Did you spend the morning doing the washing-up?'

'Washing-up? No way. Lorraine gets peculiar if I touch anything in the house.'

'So what did Fiona do to hold you up?' Chelsey was careful to keep the sniffy tone out of her voice.

'Fiona? Nothing. She's been in her studio since about seven o'clock and Lorraine left for work not long after. I had a bath, and ferreted about for some breakfast, and then I came on to meet you.'

So the story was that nobody but Lucy had held Lucy up. And nobody at all had to apologise for Chelsey's inconvenience. 'Sounds like your threesome is a bundle of fun.'

Lucy heaved up her backpack. 'It's not working out.'

Chelsey's irritation faded: she slowed her pace. 'What is it, Lucy? You lot been quarrelling?'

'It never stops. Lorraine stomps off to the spare room every night, and now Fiona's gone cold on me.'

'I hope this drama didn't have anything to do with my visit,' said Chelsey, hoping that it did.

'Nothing to do with you,' said Lucy innocently, 'or anyone. I don't know what's going on. Lorraine keeps saying we should do things, and then she gets into a rage and won't do them herself. I can't get anywhere near her, and now I don't seem able to reach Fiona either.'

With a rustle like a breeze, the life-force woke in Chelsey's breast. Firmly, she led them off the gravelled road and down an overhung alley, where they walked between dim headstones into the quietness of leaves slowly falling and somewhere the gurgle of water in a drain.

'She's hard to read,' said Lucy. 'She's mysterious like these statues.' Lucy pointed vaguely at various weathered, algae-striped angels. Some had soppy faces most unlike Fiona's, and several had no heads at all, but one or two had a far-away severe look which Chelsey recognised with a tightening in the gut.

'I can never quite get hold of it, that she should fancy me. You know: me; nothing much.'

Chelsey snorted. 'Come on. You're a cute thing with a neat little body, and you've got a brain, and, even more important, you're young enough to have a future.'

Lucy made no reply. Perhaps she expected more. Chelsey took a quick sideways glance. Lucy's hood had slipped, revealing cropped but fluffy mousy blondish hair, bright pink ears, and cheeks apple-red in her otherwise pale face. Beautiful? No. Real beauty resided in the bones, and this child, like a cloth doll, seemed not to have any. But, wherever it came from, there was something about Lucy that made Chelsey's heart beat in a disturbingly uneven fashion. 'And you have a very pretty mouth.'

'Oh thank you. Fiona says that too.'

The tenderness flowing through Chelsey stopped dead in her veins. Fiona had said it: therefore it was true. Chelsey bit her own thinner, but better-shaped lip.

'I just wish I felt secure.'

'You will, my dear,' Chelsey said bitterly, 'when you get Lorraine out of the way.'

'Oh no.' Lucy spoke in alarm. 'I wouldn't do anything like that. Anyway, I love Lorraine too. I wish I could find a way for us all to have togetherness.'

Chelsey found 'togetherness', like any biological merging, fundamentally repulsive. Emotional closeness, she believed, occurred only when one psyche invaded and possessed another; 'togetherness', in Lucy's sense, was a delusion, because human beings simply can't bear each other at close quarters. They exude irritants like the skins of toads. The secretions of sex mask natural aversion, temporarily. 'You could only have "togetherness" with them,' Chelsey said carefully, 'if you were willing to be swallowed up.'

Lucy slowed to a halt. 'I do worry about that.'

Chelsey moved to sit on the plinth of a relatively clean and dry grave. On its headstone was carved a lyre and the name 'Lloyd Horowitz' encircled, in a flowing script with the words: 'What poise, what grace, what style, what charm'.

Lucy sat beside her. 'It's good to talk to you, Chelsey,' she said. 'You see things clearly. I feel I can trust you.'

'Only me? Not Midge?'

'Midge? Midge is kind. But she always seems to want to make me into something I'm not. She reminds me of my grandma.'

Poor Midge. If Chelsey felt an equivalent kindness, she would pass on this remark. 'Not Fiona, you don't trust Fiona?'

'Fiona?'

Lucy had an odd way of repeating the other person's words. This would be irritating if one lived with her. Right now, Chelsey saw in it a pleasing reflection of her power.

Lucy thought for a moment. 'I don't trust Fiona.'

'Perhaps, dear child, you should get out of this thing.'

'Oh no,' Lucy was startled. 'I can't say I'm happy, but I'm alive. Every single bit of me is alive. I've never had this before.'

'Then you do need to look into getting rid of Lorraine.'

'Never.'

'Or letting Lorraine get rid of herself.'

'Absolutely not.'

'Even that too much for your high principles?'

'Yes, but it's not that.' Lucy drew back. 'Fiona wouldn't want me if Lorraine didn't.'

'Lucy, my dear.' Chelsey grasped her hand firmly. '*Now* you're getting the measure!' Lucy's hand was frozen, colder by several degrees even than Chelsey's. Chelsey clasped it tight, then felt for the other and bound them in her own till the blood ran warmly between them. Lucy did not pull away. Chelsey felt sufficiently in control to dare a move that might offer Lucy an escape if she wanted it. 'Let's get out of this morgue,' she said, 'and go somewhere cosy. My place? I'll pick up a bottle of something fancy. Tequila?'

'Vodka for me please, and a packet of cheese and onion crisps.'

'Want to phone Fiona to say you'll be late?'

Again Lucy shook her head.

Better and better. This time Fiona would be the one kicking her heels. 'I'll call a cab.'

❋

Chelsey feared that things would go flat until the second drink
and they were easy with the changed environment, but Lucy
was so much impressed by the grandeur of the view from
Chelsey's apartment in daylight that there was little fall-off. It
was lunch-time, but Lucy had no interest in cottage cheese on
crispbread or whatever in the pasta line was available in
Chelsey's bare kitchen. Chelsey was too excited to be hungry.
So they drank vodka and ate crisps. Chelsey was careful not
to try to force their talk back to the high point they had
reached in the cemetery, and let Lucy lead the conversation.
Lucy, as before, asked about Chelsey, and she admired the
flat. Chelsey saw no particular reason to go into the tedious
detail of her brother's connection with it, but she did talk
about decorating the place, and her plans for black and green.
Lucy suggested long tapestries hanging from the ceiling,
depicting moons and stars. She thought there should be
incense burners in the vestigial candle-stick holders beside
the fireplace, and, of course, great log fires of cherry and
apple wood. She seemed unaware of the cracks and the peel-
ing paint and the dreadful draughts. Chelsey, normally so
possessive about her space, saw it through Lucy's eyes and felt
a surge of joy at its potential.

Then Lucy asked: 'What did you mean, about Fiona not
wanting me unless Lorraine did too?'

'Darling,' said Chelsey (after a few drinks, 'darling' was
an easy address), 'I didn't say it. You did. What did you
mean?'

Lucy tugged at her Tintin forelock. 'I don't know what I
meant. You tell me.'

'I think you meant,' said Chelsey with a smile, 'that whatever is going on at Gospel Oak is some long-running battle
between those two and Old Father Time. And that you, my
dear, are their ammunition against him – one small, soft
cannonball.'

Lucy laughed. 'God's sake, you are clever. But in this case,
you might be wrong. There are other funny things going on.
Lorraine gets crazy with jealousy for no reason at all. But,

worse than that, there's something horrible happening between the two of them, and they had something wonderful before.'

'You think they're going to kill each other?'

Lucy was silent for a while. 'I don't know.'

'Sounds ugly, darling. You should get out. You have to put Lucy first.'

'I know. I owe that to myself.'

'You are in love?'

Lucy nodded.

'With an idea – of freedom, sharing.'

Lucy shuffled. 'No, not really. I'm not trying to prove anything.'

'What, then, my dear soul, are you trying to do?'

'I want to make Fiona happy. I want Lorraine to be happy too. I want to be allowed to use the washing machine and the studio and the van. I want to be allowed to pay for dinner sometimes. I don't want anything to be fenced off. I want us to be sisters. I want to live in a world where nobody has to own anything, because everybody owns everything.'

'So, you wouldn't mind then,' said Chelsey, 'if one night Fiona went to bed, say, with Sarah?'

'Sarah?' said Lucy, with the vagueness of someone who couldn't imagine that anyone could want to go to bed with Sarah. 'I wouldn't mind who she went to bed with, so long as she didn't make it secret. I don't, actually, think sex is all that important; and you don't have to lock it up.'

'Not even if, say, Fiona sent you to the spare room and went to bed with Lorraine?'

Lucy started with shock. 'I'd hate that.'

'Why?'

Lucy looked uncomfortable. 'I oughtn't to feel this way, but when they do get close, they exclude me. I don't exist.'

'So, my dear, they need you to turn them on, and then they don't need you any more?'

'No.' Lucy looked away. 'Well, I don't know what they need me for. I only know that I want to make her happy, and Lorraine can't be bothered.'

'Her?' said Chelsey. 'Is making *her* happy what it's all about?'

Lucy laid down her glass. 'Oh God. I wish I knew. When I think about her, half the time I see something outside of this world, and the rest of the time I'm not sure if she exists at all.'

'She doesn't, my sweetheart.' Chelsey moved closer. 'It is your own loneliness that you project onto her. She is an empty vessel. You should try to love what has love to give. She has only her hungers to offer.'

'You mean I should love Lorraine? I do. And I hugely admire her, truly, I do.'

'Lorraine, or anyone.' Chelsey leaned forward and laid her hand on the tender little bones of Lucy's now so vulnerable shoulder.

'Chelsey,' said Lucy, looking into her glass. 'You look like a film star, and I like you very much, really a lot, you've been so good. But I don't actually fancy you. I'm sorry. God, I feel weird after all this booze in the morning.'

It was actually getting on for 4 p.m. and the light was fading fast. A seduction had not been on Chelsey's agenda. She had intended only to show that Fiona's desire for Lucy was no more than a new fetish in the long erotic fantasy of her so-called marriage with Lorraine. But Lucy's denial put new thoughts into her head. 'Weird, dear girl, is a way of letting go. Just let go.'

'I wish I knew what was going on,' said Lucy thickly. 'If I think about it, they're using me, aren't they? I'm sort of what Fiona calls a flux, what she uses to soften metals and make them bond.'

Chelsey was silent, but smiling.

'Fiona's so up in the clouds half the time, I can't tell what's going on with her. Sometimes I wonder if she'd know me if we met in the street.'

Chelsey ran delicate fingers through Lucy's short fur. 'Put her out of your mind for a moment. Think about you. Don't forget that you also have value.'

'I do try to do that.' Lucy drew an inch closer. 'Your scent is nice. What's it called?'

Chelsey was wearing the decade-old Givenchy III Steven-John had given her as a peace offering on his day of departure. There wasn't much left of it, and it reminded her of endings. 'You like it? It's yours.'

'You are kind. Fiona never gives me presents. Lorraine does. It feels like she's trying to buy me.'

'Don't make comparisons. Don't let yourself be hurt. Just – Chelsey took the step from which there was no polite way out. She drew Lucy towards her, and stared close into her face. But she didn't kiss her, or hold the look. After a few seconds, she sighed and, loosening her grasp, lay back against the cushions.

Lucy's body followed Chelsey's movements in a perfect parallel, as if the two were attached by a 12-inch strap. 'Chelsey?' she said questioningly.

Again Chelsey sighed, her eyes vaguely roaming over the cracks in the walls.

'Chelsey?'

'You're in control now,' said Chelsey in a tone almost of weariness.

'Oh God.' Lucy's slight weight descended on Chelsey's spread-eagled and sharp-boned frame. Timidly, Lucy threaded her fingers into Chelsey's fire-red bush of hair. 'I don't know what I want.'

'Nor me. This is unplanned.' With a minimal rolling movement, Chelsey's pelvis made light and slippery contact with Lucy's prominent little pubic mount. This was facilitated by Chelsey having that morning donned, doubtless directed by the spirits, her only pair of silk knickers, which were not a present from Steven-John but associated with him since Chelsey had bought them for his (then her) excitement. Lucy, suddenly agitated, pressed down tight. Their mouths joined in a deliciously clumsy kiss. Chelsey locked her hands around Lucy's bottom.

Delighted as she was with this unexpected development, another sensation came linearly to her. In the back pocket of

Lucy's jeans was a small object of a soft metallic fabric, which slid out at the merest nudge of Chelsey's finger. It wrapped itself, loose as a new-born snake, over her fingers. Whatever it was, the spirits clearly meant it as a souvenir of a pleasant experience. As Lucy responded to the touch of Chelsey's hand on her bottom by flattening Chelsey's nose with another kiss, Chelsey allowed the object to slither under the cushions of the sofa. It might not be as fine a trophy as the handkerchief which had played such a stylish part in Desdemona's story, but could be useful if Lucy ever chose to deny that she had, at least once, preferred Chelsey's favours to Fiona's.

Chelsey, who always tried to be honest with herself, also admitted the possibility that she might be falling in love. Chelsey felt no scruples about robbing the person she was falling in love with: Love was itself a most brutish act of theft, and the moment of falling was when she needed her strongest defences. Discreetly, Chelsey loosened the fastenings of her skirt.

22

Midge woke, and moved her head a millimetre. Not a bang, not a thump. Her cranium had the density of a block of granite but was without pain. Gingerly, she shifted Raffles to the other side and edged one bedsocked foot towards the floor. 'Tea?'

Raffles was instantly on her feet, frisking, grabbing at loose corners of Midge's none too sanitary blankets and shaking them into wakefulness. She then bounded off the bed and gave a similar rattling to the crumpled bottoms of Midge's pyjamas, before tugging them, and the stumbling form inside, down two flights of stairs to the kitchen.

Midge, absent-mindedly, submitted to the bullying. Her thoughts were elsewhere. She knew, of course, that the pleasing, vacant painlessness of her head was not the result of virtue. Quite the opposite. Midge was proving that the only sure cure for hangover is never to let sobriety catch up with you. She added a dollop of whisky to her tea, and drank it straight off.

But the hangover cure was not, alas, a cure for remorse. Miserably, Midge considered her list of noble intentions. She had not been back to the Kurdish Centre and, in her present gloom, she doubted that she'd ever return there. She had not been swimming. The bags of empty bottles by the door had not diminished in number. As fast as Midge disposed of them, more arrived from the kitchen. Only the resolution to take longer walks had been fulfilled, and even that only because Midge was ashamed of showing her face at the same off-licence twice in the same week.

Midge sat herself down while Raffles breakfasted. Raffles was slurping greedily. For this, too, Midge blamed herself. As Midge's life had shrunk, so had Raffles's, till the innocent creature's pleasures had diminished to this one satisfaction. Midge believed that Raffles loved her, but she could not see how the relationship could have value, since the object of it was unworthy of a dog's love.

She finished the tea, and suppressed the little flicker that aroused her sluggish body when it entered her mind that she might treat herself to another with a larger dollop. She poured her second cup and this time firmly got out the milk to pollute it before her hand could disobey her and reach for the more attractive bottle. The milk was slightly sour. She would drink the stuff none the less. One sip, her face turned lemony, and she pitched the tea into the sink. Start again. This time a small dollop? She added a very small one, and walked back, deep in thought, to her seat at the table.

Perhaps, Midge forced herself to say to herself, we ought to think about this? Perhaps we might just have a drinking problem?

Absolute nonsense, herself replied. We have a will-power problem. And the cure for that was no secret from either of her selves. But could herself, just fleetingly, entertain the thought that we might have something touching on the verges of a drinking problem, a slight thing in itself, but something that had got a bit out of control and might respond to a new and firmer hand on the tiller? Every atom of both her selves shrank in the firmest of negations. Midge would rather be dead than face the ultimate humiliation – of presenting herself at the door of the local Alcoholics Anonymous.

Herself told herself with the total and absolute certainty of a born-again that her drinking would cease to be a problem as soon as her life ceased to be one. The problem with her life was that she didn't have one. And she didn't have one because she was guilty of pride, sloth, lust, and all the rest of the seven deadly sins right down to despair. For these crimes she was culpable. She deserved the prison cell, not the charity of the redeemed at the AA. Indeed, this was what she had: Midge believed that the true punishment for doing wrong was the kind of person you became – and her person was her prison.

Softly through the wintry air came a rich sound that filled Midge's breast before it reached her brain: the organ of the church at the corner was playing the opening voluntary for 11 o'clock High Mass. She listened. The buzz of the assembling congregation was broken by a few urgent calls to children, and then the clipping of Sunday heels into the vestibule. Soon the flotilla of priest and acolytes would be sailing up the central aisle sprinkling the benches to right and left with holy water, while the families shuffled into their places with genuflections, whispers, much coughing and a few hasty signs of the cross.

Midge knew exactly what went on at that church though, in her half-century in Kilburn, she'd never been inside it. Of course, while Papa was alive, it wouldn't have been appropriate. Pa had not been at all happy to find that, year by year, his genteel suburb of Kilburn was turning into a Catholic ghetto. Though (allowing of course for the Remembrance Day service) he'd not entered a church in the years between Midge's baptism and Mother's funeral, Pa was a proud Anglican who held the view that Catholics were heathens. They worshipped the Virgin Mary (who was, after all, a woman), chanted in dog Latin, believed the Pope was infallible and bred like rabbits.

But Midge knew more about the church than he did and considerably more than she knew about, say, M. A. Davis, whose music satchel, as yet unrepaired, still lay before her on the kitchen table. As a girl, Midge had been fascinated by the forbidden rituals across the road, and had observed them often, from within the branches of the oak tree in the churchyard. She had absorbed the words of the Order of the Mass and, when Latin was added to her school curriculum, found out what they meant.

Now, she listened closely as the choir swelled into the antiphon, and the words came back to her – though they must have come out of her mind rather than through the air since she heard them in Latin while the choir was obliged to deliver them in the Sassenach tongue. '*Aspérges me, Domine, hysopo et mundabor*' – 'thou, Lord, wilt sprinkle me with hyssop, and I shall be clean; washed by thee, I shall be whiter than snow. Have mercy on me, O God, as thou art ever rich in mercy.'

Midge felt the music in her blood and her mouth moved with it, but no sound came out. Then suddenly, sound did come: judderingly and harshly out of tune she blurted: 'I shall be clean,' and then her voice broke with the first hard sobs of grief. Raffles looked up from her breakfast, her ears perked in surprise.

Midge beat her fist against her brow to calm herself. If this was a message, she should reply. She should rush upstairs, throw on some clothes, and join those blessed people at the Mass. Their God, rich in mercy, would make her clean. The people would receive her: of all the souls on this Planet, the Kilburn Irish community would understand Midge's weakness. But Midge did not move. Something told her that one sinner was so fundamentally disgusting that no amount of hyssop could disguise the charnel odour of her soul.

Midge stood up straight and cried out in a clear voice which echoed through the kitchen: 'What, dear God, is happening to me?'

At that moment, the telephone rang. With the spastic action of a mechanical toy, Midge directed herself towards it.

But she was more cautious, even cunning, in very quietly picking up the receiver. She hoped that, if the voice that came to her was Chelsey's, she would have the courage to put the phone down again. But she doubted it. Midge had never in her life forcibly terminated a conversation with anyone; she was, in consequence, a favourite target of Jehovah's Witnesses and double-glazing salesmen.

'Midge?' The slight tremble in the note at first disguised the speaker. 'Are you there?'

Midge, suddenly faint, fell onto the chair beside the telephone. 'Lucy.'

Lucy drew a thoughtful breath, then said, warily: 'I hope it's all right to call you. I feel odd. I think I may be frightened.'

'Lucy!' Midge could add nothing to these two foolish syllables. She was overwhelmed by a wave of emotion which, for its sheer power, could have drowned the church and its entire congregation.

'I don't know for sure,' continued Lucy, 'but I feel something bad is going on.'

'You've come to me! Oh Lucy!'

There was a short silence. In a lower voice, Lucy said: 'Midge, are you drunk or something?'

'No, no.' The powers of thought were at last returning to Midge. 'I'm deeply shocked. What's happened?'

'I don't want to talk over the phone. Could I come to see you?'

'Of course. But why don't I motor over to pick you up?' As these words came out of her mouth, Midge felt the pounce of the Mini's clutch, and was taken by a lurch of travel sickness.

'No need. I'll take the North London Line, Dalston to Kilburn in fifteen minutes.'

How very sensitive and considerate the child was. How desperately Midge hoped that this generosity did not arise from awareness of Midge's semi-inebriated state.

Midge put down the phone, and panic set in: 15 minutes! She pounded up the stairs and flung herself into the bath. Furiously she soaped all her hairy parts (head and upper lip included) and as furiously scoured at them with her inefficient because rather slimy flannel. Then she struggled into smart clothes – not an easy job as, in her hurry, she'd bypassed the

stage of towelling herself dry. The minutes increased to 45,
but even this was barely enough as Midge put on and threw
off every passably decent garment in her wardrobe. Raffles
watched, cocking her head first to one side and then the other.
Midge didn't feel strong enough to endure being mocked by a
dog, so wrenched the blue silk shirt over her head and tossed
it in Raffles's direction. Raffles settled down to gnawing off
the buttons. When, finally, the doorbell rang, Midge was
dressed in a pullover knitted in an Argyll pattern by Mama
(for Papa) over a tartan wool shirt (no time to iron crisp cottons), with cowboy neckerchief, Rupert Bear trousers, socks
with a strawberry pattern up the ankle and brogues, but she
was still rather shaky about the knees. In a cloud of Old
Spice, she made her way with dignity down the stairs.

She opened the door. Lucy stepped in. From far beyond the
small form came the distant tinkle of a bell, piping child voices
and then the soaring of the choir breaking out in 'Behold the
Lamb of God, behold him who taketh away the sins of the
world.' Lucy peered suspiciously down the street and then
firmly pushed the door to. Midge was still listening: '*Ecce qui
tollit peccata mundi*,' she heard, and the beauty of it swept her in
another emotional tide, which sent her staggering. Lucy
looked at her with the head-cocked slightly puzzled expression normally associated with Raffles. Midge was quite unable
to prevent what followed. She engulfed Lucy in a fulsome
embrace.

'Thank you for seeing me at short notice,' said Lucy edging
out of Midge's arms.

Midge was standing in Lucy's way. She took a step back.

'I do hope, Midge, that you appreciate that I come to see
you out of need and hope I won't have to take a stand on
issues of harass—'

Midge came to her senses. 'Of course not.' She busied herself taking up Lucy's backpack and ushered her towards the
kitchen. 'I wouldn't dream of . . . No question of . . . Will you
take tea? Or as you're stressed perhaps something a little—?'

'Have you got vodka?'

Midge spread her hands. 'I'm so sorry.'

'Tea will be fine, thank you.'

'I may have a drop of whisky somewhere,' said Midge hopefully.

'Okay, that'll do.'

Midge seized the keys and charged off to her father's cabinet. En route she remembered that Lucy hadn't thought much of Papa's best single malt and might less dislike the Safeways Blended in the refrigerator. It had to be Pa's best, for Lucy's sake mixed with lemonade.

The conversation got off to an awkward start, since Midge could find nothing to say and Lucy's first utterance was: 'What's that thing on the table?' Then, in a brave attempt at a joke: 'It looks like the dried foetus of a hippopotamus.'

'Oh that,' said Midge, seizing M. A. Davis's music satchel and protectively hiding it under her chair. 'It's an antique. I'm restoring it.'

'Is it valuable?'

Midge thought for a moment. 'Yes.'

'Really? Can I see?'

It wasn't the alcohol in her blood; it was definitely something else, something harder, that caused Midge, after a few seconds' uncertainty, to shift the satchel more firmly under her chair and say: 'It's rather fragile. I'll show it to you when it's done.'

Lucy shrugged. 'Okay. I wasn't desperate to know, just starting the conversation.' She took a sip of her whisky with lemonade and coughed.

Midge took the cue. 'You're worried about something, my dear?'

'Frightened.'

'Is somebody harass— somebody troubling you?'

'Not exactly. It's a feeling I have, that there's a plot, and I'm in it. It's weird.'

'Is this to do with Lorraine and Fiona?'

'Them, and Chelsey.'

Guilt struck Midge with its familiar flat-fish slap against the cheek. 'I'm sorry to have to tell you that there has been a plot,' she said solemnly. 'I put Chelsey up to visiting you – and them – at Gospel Oak. Truly, dear, the fault for that intervention is mine.'

Lucy shifted in her seat. 'I don't understand. There are thousands of dykes out there who go nuts about older women. What I can't figure is why you lot are all so interested in *me*?'

'Well,' Midge struggled with what was a large question. 'Lorraine, I suppose, took a fancy to you, in the way that married people occasionally do; and she and Fiona share everything, so Fiona was drawn in. But Chelsey and I rather feel, my dear, that it isn't good for you to get involved with such a strong couple. At least not without knowing the rules they live by, and not, um, with you so alone and exposed.'

'That doesn't answer my question,' said Lucy patiently. 'Why does it have to be *me*?'

'Well,' Midge, without looking at Lucy, allowed a little smile to creep into the corners of her mouth: 'There are penalties to being a pretty girl.'

'I'm not.'

'Oh, but you are.' Midge's hand inched towards Lucy's.

'I'm not,' said Lucy, firmly moving out of range. 'I'm not a girl. In four years I'll be thirty.'

Midge collected herself. 'Sorry, dear. Old-fashioned language. I meant it kindly.'

'You did not. You treat me – you all treat me – like some kind of doll.'

Midge had nothing to say.

'Lorraine pulls me apart, like a dog does a rag doll; and Fiona – God knows what goes on in Fiona's mind.' Lucy rose to her feet and sloshed more of Pa's best into her glass. 'Well, God knows and I know: Fiona plays with me when she finds it amusing.' Lucy then sat down abruptly.

'I'm so sorry,' said Midge. 'I've been so afraid harm would come to you from that connection.'

'It's not only *that* connection that bothers me. It's how you're all in it; how this thing is incestuous; you all seem to want to win points off each other through me.' Lucy thought for a moment. 'You see, I do want to be in your world. It's the only thing I want. But not this way. I want all of you – especially Georgiana – to see me as a real person.'

Midge understood. But she couldn't help. 'We mean well, most of the time,' she said lamely.

'You don't. Certainly *you* don't. You keep coming on to me. I've never asked for it.'

'I apologise. I won't do it again.'

Lucy paused, but did not seem mollified. 'And what about Chelsey. What does she mean?'

Midge frowned. 'Mean by what?'

'By nothing,' said Lucy, pulling back.

'Tell me?' Midge's concentration now had a sharp edge.

'Well, on Friday she took me to her place. We drank a lot of vodka, and.'

'And what?' Midge could feel her blood pressure rising.

'And she, we; we talked a lot, and.'

Midge was on her feet. 'She seduced you?' Midge's voice came out in a roar.

Lucy, looking down into her lemonade cocktail, shook her head. 'I can't say it was her that did the seducing.'

'The cad!' Midge, enraged, swept back her chair, crumpling the valuable antique under it, and made as if to sweep all the paraphernalia off the kitchen table. 'That was *absolutely* out of order.'

'But,' interposed Lucy quietly, 'I thought you were trying to do much the same thing.'

'But I, but I,' Midge, defeated, sat down again, subjecting M. A. Davis's music satchel to a second battering. 'I only want to help you get out of a dangerous situation.'

'Yes,' said Lucy, mollified at last. 'It seems you all do. And I don't know who to trust. Unless it's Chelsey. Everybody says she's a snake, but she's the one who sees things from my point of view.'

Midge grasped Lucy angrily by the wrist. 'Think how Chelsey took advantage of you –' Midge stopped herself: one did not slander one's friends.

'Midge,' said Lucy. 'Please pay attention. It's not important that I did sex with Chelsey. It was nice, but so are lots of things. There's something much more important: I can't tell Fiona I did it.'

'Of course not,' said Midge hastily, 'There is an ancient enmity between those two. It would do terrible damage.'

'But I have to be honest. It's the only thing I am.'

'You must, must, get out of this mess,' Midge cried out loud. 'Lucy, why? Are you so besotted with these people that you can't see them – us – for what we are?'

'Oh, yes I can,' said Lucy earnestly. 'Fiona is the most beautiful person I have ever known. Lorraine has so much power. I've never before encountered anyone with Chelsey's insight. Nor anyone as kind as you. You all seem huge to me. You live out of your own centres in a way nobody else does. I want to be like that. I just don't want you to abuse me.'

'Oh Lucy, you poor girl.' It being utterly impossible to embrace Lucy, Midge could not prevent her emotions from flowing into another channel. She was, all at once, awash with tears. 'You should run, my dear, run for your life; you should be with young people. You should be playing tennis, getting to know the Youth Hostels in the Lake District. You must work to save your job – or get a new one.' Midge scooped Raffles onto her lap and wiped her eyes and face on the little dog's fur. 'You should not be sitting here drinking whisky.' Midge, who had not touched a drop since Lucy's arrival, grabbed at the bottle and shook it angrily. 'Lucy, open your eyes. You think we are sophisticated or influential or something of the like. We are not. We are old. We haven't even procreated. We are nothing.'

Lucy watched for a second, then said, quietly, 'I think, Midge, that you may be a bit drunk. Perhaps I should go.'

'Yes, you should. No, don't. Please, stay a little while.'

'I think I want to go.'

Midge reached out her arm to detain Lucy. Lucy seemed to be fleeing. Unexpectedly, Midge found that she was sitting on the floor. Had she slipped? Had Lucy pushed her? 'Lucy, please –' Midge lifted up her arms like a child. 'Oh, lamb of God, I desperately need to love someone who needs to be loved.'

Midge was talking to herself. Lucy had already left. Raffles, with a tender muzzle, licked the tears from her face.

That afternoon, Midge demolished the rest of the bottle of her father's best single malt. But the remaining dozen or more bottles remained untouched. Midge had passed out on the kitchen floor.

23

Tuesday, 5 December, Frognal

In the days that followed, Midge struggled to remember what
had happened that Sunday: the only things that were clear
were that Lucy was in some terrible danger, and that she,
Midge, had behaved abominably. She didn't dare call Lucy, so
rang Chelsey. Chelsey – who was also in the dark – told
Midge to button up. But both women waited by their phones.

On Tuesday, the spirits' day, Chelsey's rang. She pounced
on the receiver. But at the first crackle of the familiar fractional laugh, she snapped: 'Steven-John: how often must I tell
you not to phone on a Tuesday morning.'

In a suspiciously unchastised and jolly voice, Steven-John
replied: 'I waited, dear Chelsey, until Toby's grandfather clock
made it five past twelve.'

Chelsey's hackles rose. 'Steven-John: you know that the
spirits think in millennia, not in minutes.' Chelsey reached
for her mug of coffee as her emotions descended from high
dudgeon to the less elevated state of feeling misunderstood.
'And surely you of all people appreciate that at this hour,
when matinee stars are waking to find themselves blinded
with hangover, it *is* Tuesday morning.'

'Sorry, old bean. I forgot. I've got a riddle for you.'

Chelsey, despite herself, was intrigued: 'What, pray?'

'When I walked into Toby's flat, I smelled men's hair oil.'

'Oh that!' Chelsey's interest folded. 'Toby doesn't take his trade home. You'll find he's changed his styling mousse.'

Steven-John laughed again. 'But you should smell this,' he said playfully: 'coconut oil plus something piney. Deeply butch.'

'And?'

'And there were smears of it on the pillows and the hearth-rug.'

'Well, well!' Chelsey turned her mind, still in its twitchy Tuesday-morning state, towards the spirits. 'I hope our Toby isn't going to get his pretty face queerbashed.'

Steven-John, as was his way, considered this. 'No danger of that, I would say. It's a policeman.'

'They're the worst.'

'Not this one. He's an expert in international jewellery fraud, from Hong Kong. Here on top secret business, for sure.'

'Twaddle,' Chelsey said. 'He's taking a cheap holiday.'

Steven-John, his pleasure undimmed, unveiled the rest of the story. First, he'd smelled the hair oil, then noticed the pillows. Next, he checked the spare drawers of the dresser. He'd found a neat pile of poplin shirts and the most beautiful underwear he had ever touched. In the big cupboard he'd found a suede suitcase, labelled as belonging to Chief Inspector Tong Wi Li. And in the bathroom, the usual supplies had been augmented by several packs of condoms. He'd reported this to Ulric, who advised him to mind his own business. Then, driven by curiosity to risk a reprimand, he called Toby. Toby, to Steven-John's delight, seemed to have forgotten his quarrel with Steven-John. Brisk and friendly as in the old days, he said 'Tommy Tong' was staying for a while, and would Steven-John mind awfully putting Tommy's socks in the washing machine.

Chelsey laughed out loud. 'I bet that had the entire Foreign Office agog.'

❉

After she'd put the phone down, Chelsey paced up and down. The spirits presented her with a clear picture of this Tommy: he was in his late-twenties, the beautiful, laughing, only son of adoring aged parents, sleek as a pitbull terrier, and exactly what Toby had been waiting for. She saw them in Toby's drawing room. Toby, in Aran sweater and loafers, was sprawled on a white leather sofa. Before him stood a handsome Chinese man, talking with wide gesticulations, about Emperor Bokassa's diamonds. She saw Toby deftly set down his long-stemmed wineglass and pat the slithery cushions beside him. She saw a wide smile crease Tommy's berry-bright eyes as he sank into white leather. She could feel what Toby's hand felt as it reached up to stroke the cutting edge of the jaw. She saw the slide towards the hearthrug, sensed the entwining of limb with limb in the perfect control of gymnasts; she felt the gliding of fingertips over taut and glossy hide in the first caress. How elegant they would be together. Toby had such style; so much power, strength, confidence, freedom; so much life-giving money. Chelsey had none of these things. All she had in common with him was their incipient doom: but while he kept death at bay with his zest for life, despair stared at her out of every shadowed corner.

At the end, everything came to this: for Chelsey, Toby's joy could be nothing but a cruel new light on her own deprivation. Steven-John had intended only to amuse; instead he had awakened her torturers. Chelsey made a grab at her coffee, and her mind threshed about for something to distract her. She dared not think of Lucy – the stretch of time since Lucy had last made contact was getting dangerously long. Instead she chose to blame the messenger for the message and her anger fastened on Steven-John.

She saw him as Peter Pan, the boy who refused to grow up. But she knew that, for as long as Ulric lived, Steven-John's infancy would be embalmed in loving indulgence, while she grew withered and cranky. The man who had once been Sheila-Jayne was putatively Chelsey's friend. He would grovel at Toby's feet, but had no more concern for Chelsey's sufferings than he had for Midge's, or for any woman's. Steven-John, she decided, was at heart a misogynist. Why otherwise would he have mutilated his breasts and excised his womb? How otherwise could he have cut off his body in a sexless marriage? Chelsey's fingers itched to call Steven-John back, and tell him that he had turned himself not into a man but a eunuch.

Recollection of the telephone brought another anxiety to Chelsey: Steven-John's call could have blocked one of the two that mattered: from Lucy or the agency. After bracing herself with a gulp of coffee, she picked up the phone and dialled the agency. Iolanthe had nothing on deck for her that day. Tommy might bring good luck to Toby but, like everybody else, he had none for Chelsey.

Nobody had anything for Chelsey. Steven-John neglected her shamefully now that he was so wrapped up in that ridiculous liaison with Ulric and death. Midge was furious with Chelsey for getting it off with Lucy: Chelsey dismissed this as envy, but still suspected that somewhere in the muddy depths of Midge's value system lay doubts about Chelsey's honour. Georgiana treated her as a nonentity. Now even Toby was pairing off – not that she'd ever had hopes of a friendship with someone as snobby as Toby. And, every minute of every day, at the corner of her vision, lounged the figure of Fiona, holding, in haughty possession, the only person in this world who could free Chelsey from the chains of despair.

Chelsey prowled, and wondered if even Lucy could save her. Sometimes it seemed that her only defence against her demons was her great fear of them.

When Steven-John and Jezebel returned from their trot round Regent's Park, the day had turned gloomy. Yet Steven-John was still in a mood of high excitement. His innocent pleasure in finding that Toby had a serious lover was only part of the cause. Steven-John hadn't yet told Chelsey the half of it. Chelsey was always prepared for bad news or – as in this case – gossip. For a miracle, on the other hand, Chelsey needed to be prepared with gentleness. And what Steven-John would in due course report was no less than a miracle: Ulric's chemotherapy treatment *was starting to work*. Ulric was getting stronger every day.

They both knew that adult leukaemia could not be cured; but, this morning, when Ulric, buzzing with ozone after a deeply physical encounter with his voice exercises, had run his long fingers through Steven-John's topknot, the word 'remission' was vibrating in both their hearts. 'Remission; please, Mother Earth, give us years and years of remission,' muttered Steven-John as he rubbed the dog's muddy extremities. And Jezebel, who was perhaps more docile with a policeman about the flat these days, had yielded each paw without complaint.

After putting out Jezebel's lunch of free-range chicken livers, black rye and a Vitamin E capsule moistened with Scottish spring water, Steven-John went off to wash his hands, out of respect for the birds who'd provided the livers. On Toby's spanking neat bathroom shelf squatted a dark-brown cut-glass bottle, the hair-oil. Steven-John sniffed it. Perhaps a little gross for Ulric's taste? Life would be perfect bliss if Ulric was everything that Ulric was, with just one small addition: a touch of something sensual. Try the oil? Steven-John tapped out a sample and rubbed it into his wiry curls. 'Please, Mother Earth,' he called to the ceiling, 'since you feel kindly towards us, do another favour: just once let me hold Ulric, tight round his body, when he isn't wearing his dressing gown.'

Then he went off to check the phone messages. This was once again possible, as Toby had relented about the agency service. He pressed the button:

'Toby: Georgiana here. I'm calling you at home, not the office, as this is apropos of our worst fears. Fiona is, alas, once again entrapped by the ferret; indeed, appears besotted. This I ascertained in a thirty-second phone call, although Fiona regarded my questions as impertinent and her answers were monosyllabic at best. We

have to *do* something: the creature reeks of depravity.
Call me the minute you get home. And convey my best to
Tommy, and my thanks to him for a delightful meal. He
is a charming boy.'

Steven-John stopped the machine. He played the message
again. His brow was furrowed. Steven-John had, of course,
been kept up to date on the threesome by Chelsey. The situation made him uneasy. Steven-John regarded three as a
magical and dangerous number. Only the gods could play in
threes. Threeness was constant movement, restlessness,
unharnessed energy. It was the dangerous unstable ozone
molecule; it was the mother of the free radical, the juggler,
musical chairs, the two masters, the message that returned in
a double echo, the impossibility of anything being simple and
at rest.

Yet this thing existed and would, he believed, do harm
whether it continued or came to an end. But how could it
come to an end? Neither Fiona nor Lorraine could end it
without offending the other, and Lucy would not end it, since
it gave her power without responsibility. It could never be
ended by mutual agreement, since its whole energy came out
of the shifting alliances of two against one, and every new
alliance renewed the divisions and the passion at the heart of
it. It had no internal dynamic to bring itself peacefully to a
conclusion; it escaped process. Steven-John believed that the
threesome ought not to be, and accepted that it could only end
through a blow from the outside. This was what Georgiana
appeared to have in mind. Steven-John ought to have been
pleased. But Georgiana's message left him disturbed and
unhappy. He found it infinitely depressing that people, even
nice people, had to be so horrible to each other. With a sigh,
he ran the second message:

'Toby. Georgiana again. Five past two. Fiona called me
back, in distress. That girl is up to something peculiar
with Chelsey and, it would seem, with Midge. Midge

doesn't matter, but nobody plays with Chelsey. Lorraine has taken to ranting and raving, but I don't doubt she is putty in the girl's hands. Put this together, and you'll see the incubus has Fiona surrounded. No more fine manners. Get Tommy to throw her into a Hong Kong prison or something. Smash her!'

Steven-John went cold all over. It wasn't exactly fear for Fiona, or for any of them, though he was afraid; it was the weight of brooding violence. He had to stop it. His hands were agitated as he rinsed his own and Jezebel's plates. Steven-John reminded himself that Georgiana didn't want to smash Lucy out of any abiding hatred of Lucy, but because she was afraid for Fiona. Though Steven-John shared her fear, he was absolutely sure that whatever process would free those three women from their demonic enchantment ought not to include injuring Lucy, or anybody.

His hands were still trembly when he phoned Toby to beg him to play the peace-maker. Toby's response was brief. 'Since you can't leave my telephone alone, you oblige me to restore the password system. Put Tommy's socks in the machine, and then bugger off.'

On this wonderful day when all of Marylebone had vibrated to Ulric's voice exercises, Steven-John had won back, and then recklessly thrown away, his friendship with Toby. Steven-John put on his coat. He took an emotional farewell of Jezebel, fearing that it might be his last. The world was a dangerous place, and Steven-John desperately wanted humans to be good to each other, but he didn't know how to make that happen.

Ulric, as one might have expected, was useless. 'People who choose to live in sewers will keep company with rats,' he said. 'So, leave their business to them and pay attention to your own. Camomile tea, with saucer, if you please.'

Steven-John served the tea. But his distressed state took its toll on the lunch which followed: two lightly boiled free-range eggs (hopefully from hens with livers intact), accompanied by a salad of beansprouts and radishes in peanut butter. Ulric turned up his nose and Steven-John retreated to the kitchen.

Since Ulric would not help him, Steven-John had no choice but to make Chelsey his ally. Some part of himself balked at it. He would have to conceal Georgiana's remarks about Chelsey, and he felt uncomfortable about that. More disturbing was the knowledge that Chelsey could not be relied on to be charitable about anything to do with Fiona. But he had nobody else to turn to. While Ulric, having laid aside his lunch but warmed his larynx with tea, ran through a few dazzling arpeggios, Steven-John slipped into the music room to phone.

When Chelsey replaced the receiver, she too was quaking. She too could smell the violence. The cracks in her walls seemed to vibrate. She paced the room to calm herself.

So, the 'incubus' had Fiona surrounded. Equally important, the dear incubus had Georgiana surrounded. Chelsey could feel Georgiana's fingers itch with desire to throttle the little brat. But a general does not do his own dirty work. Georgiana needed a hired assassin. Well, Chelsey had waited many years to meet Georgiana's need. She flipped open the secret drawer at the back of her escritoire and pulled out the little object which had slid from the back pocket of Lucy's jeans, sweetly yielding itself to her.

She held in the palm of her hand a small change-purse of very fine, soft silver mesh, cool and supple as the skin of a snake. It was old, and beautifully made. Chelsey knew it well; she knew its lining of black velvet, rubbed hard by old copper pennies. She knew the engraving on the inside of its lip, and closed it quickly. The soft click of its slightly loose clasp carried her away, back to the tour with *A Doll's House*.

Stars, even in repertory, don't carry money, not serious money, but Georgiana didn't smoke at the time everyone had cigarette cases and lighters to fiddle with, and this little purse was often in her hand. Chelsey's eye would follow the slither of its fine mesh as it was played between Georgiana's beautiful fingers, and she longed for it. Was it a family heirloom, she asked? No, it was just a bit of nonsense Georgiana had picked up at Grays Antique Market in Bond Street, but something Georgiana was fond of. Chelsey wasn't convinced; she knew it was valuable. Perhaps, at that wonderful time, Georgiana might have given it to her, but Chelsey didn't ask. A great mistake, for only a few weeks after the tour had ended, the little purse was in Fiona's hands, and Fiona, herself a silversmith, was delighted to own something of Georgiana's which so beautifully expressed the silversmith's craft. Within days, Fiona had put her mark on it, by engraving, in minute script, the letters 'g' and 'f', with the descenders intertwined. This graffiti was the signature of Fiona's possession of Georgiana.

And now, somehow, it was in Lucy's pocket. How had Lucy come by it? Chelsey's spirits claimed that she'd stolen it. Chelsey chose to disbelieve them. Fiona – Fiona the betrayer – had freely given it – this token of Georgiana's love – to her new lover.

Thoughtful now, Chelsey made her way back to her escritoire, put the telephone out of view on the window sill, and set the chair straight as she seated herself. Out of the top left-hand drawer, she took one of her best parchment envelopes. From her pen-tray, she took two first-class stamps (pretty ones, picturing Sissinghurst gardens) and her Watermans fountain pen. She checked the nib and ink flow on her blotter, a good, strong but shaded italic line in her favourite viridian ink. She addressed the envelope. With a bubble of spit on her fingertip, she moistened the stamps and applied them. She turned over the envelope, and lifted its fold. Then, casually, she laid the little purse on top.

After a moment's finger-tapping, she drew out a sheet of her headed paper and, making no attempt to subdue the flourishes of her hand, wrote: 'Georgiana: I have this from Lucy, but believe it to be yours.' She wrapped the note around the purse, thrust it into the envelope, and sealed it.

Humming a little tune, she put on her coat and popped out to the posting box.

24

Sunday to Wednesday, 6 December, Gospel Oak

While Georgiana and Chelsey were working to stop the three-some, the women in it were still struggling to get it to start. But luck was not on their side.

On the Sunday after her cemetery walk, Lucy came down with a cold. The threesome was put on ice; Lorraine gave her attention to vegetable soups, and Fiona drove each evening to Dalston to feed the cats. Within a week, Lucy was well enough to go out, though still coughing. Lorraine took them to an exhibition of World War II photojournalism and Fiona to one of German post-expressionism at the Saatchi Gallery. Lucy wanted to see *Batman*, but didn't press the point. In between, they drank a great deal, and talked about sex. Lucy was keen to translate talk into action, but the cough was a dampener; Fiona and Lorraine circled each other uneasily, and Fiona fretted over having mislaid her little silver change-purse. Though things sometimes started to go with a swing, quarrels hovered over every decision and the unmerry merry-go-round quickly brought them back to the starting point.

Lorraine, back at work on the Monday after Lucy's recovery, could not rid herself of images of what the other two might be doing in her absence. She came home early, sharp-nosed with suspicion. She found Fiona engrossed in her studio and Lucy in the bathroom with her head over a basin of Friar's Balsam; Lorraine took this for clear evidence that something was being covered up. Within an hour, they were quarrelling; within two, Lorraine had slapped Lucy's cheek, then crashed off to bed. Something of the like happened each day.

Over and over, Lorraine resolved to take herself in hand. She had discovered that the self is a breakable thing. And she believed that she was breaking hers. Something was going horribly wrong in her life. But she didn't know what; she didn't know what she or anybody else could do about it. She knew she was jealous and unhappy, and some gritty part of her mind would not let go of a conviction that there was a plot to drive her into the wilderness. She didn't know who was plotting or what the plot was, and she feared that her fears were paranoid, but went about like a cat sniffing at corners, and every one reeked of plot.

Perhaps most unsettling of all, she didn't know what she wanted. If she asked herself if she wanted to return to the *status quo ante*, the dreariness of the life she and Fiona had led before Lucy came into it, the answer was no. If she asked if she desired Lucy, the answer, likewise, was no, not any longer. Too many fights had dimmed Lucy's capacity to lift her spirits. Yet, nor did she desire Fiona. She didn't want Lucy in the house (Lucy appeared to be living there now), and she didn't want her out of it. She didn't want to be with Fiona, and she couldn't bear the thought of being separated from her. The only thing that roused her – and it roused her till her blood thumped hard enough to burst its vessels – was the image of the two of them exchanging glances. Jealousy was not a passion Lorraine had considered inherent in her nature. Yet it rose up in her so fully formed, fascinated with itself and powerful that she could have been rearing this monster from the day of her birth. This jealousy was fiercer than sex, more scary than fear. It was possession by unreason and violence, a mad force which presented itself to her as a quest for truth. Lorraine didn't want to feel what she was feeling. Yet,

apart from this one ferocious passion, all her feelings were
confused. And the one passion was impossible to satisfy. She
wanted Fiona and Lucy to be deprived of each other, but not
to have either of them delivered to her. She wanted, she
thought, justice; she wanted revenge. But even her fantasies
gave neither. There was no restitution to be had. This was not
crime; it was a game. And she was playing badly.

And she had started the threesome game. Why? Her fears
told her that she had been manipulated into starting it, but her
whole mind said otherwise. She had started this game, deliberately, to win. She'd wanted to win Lucy – so that she could
throw her aside. She'd wanted to beat Fiona – to show that,
despite Fiona's natural advantages, she was Fiona's equal.
She had played dirty from the start. If she lost, she would
have got what she deserved.

But, as soon as her thoughts reached this point, they circled
round to the beginning: she had been manipulated; they were
cheating on her.

And then she thought that all she sought was to force them
to admit out loud that they were cheating. Only then, it
seemed, would she have her self and her freedom again. But
what if they were not cheating on her? And what was cheating, anyway, where there were no rules? Lorraine's thoughts
got nowhere.

But on Wednesday, something changed. It happened in
Deptford, where she was photographing the official opening
of a Commonwealth garden inspired by the President of
Malawi. But she didn't at the time recognise it.

She drove from Deptford directly to her laboratory, and got
to work on developing the pictures. Lorraine knew the photographs would be bad and, as she lifted the first strip out of
the tank, this was confirmed. Preparation of the site, a triangle of waste-land surrounded by post-industrial dereliction,
had fallen behind schedule, so council workers had shrouded
the unsightliest heaps with plastic sheeting. The event had
been poorly attended. Several of the dignitaries, wearing the

wrong kind of shoes, were glued to the mud; on account of the drizzle, they wouldn't take their hats off, and so were faceless in the photographs. The grainy pictures were suggestive, not of a tropical oasis in the middle of London, but a shivering straggle of refugees at a bomb-site. The camera had caught all the lumpen gloom of the occasion and nothing of the dream of a new President to bring the gift of the bright and beautiful tropics to people who were rapidly forgetting them.

This was a small job, not worth hours of sweat. But Lorraine had seen Malawi, and understood the President's dream, and now she wanted to make it come true. All afternoon, she pored over her work, giving the whole of her concentration to something specific, wholesome and only vaguely improper.

Lorraine was discounting the Luddite views of the newspaper industry about tampering with facts. She scanned the only passable picture into her computer and selected a filter. She dimmed the outer circle of dignitaries, bringing into prominence a young tree, held upright over a hole in the muddy earth by an African girl and a thick-set Asian man in mayoral robes. Over their heads loomed tower-blocks; around them, high chain fencing. By degrees, Lorraine increased the light on the tree, brightening the little globes of its cherry-sized fruit, known in Malawi as Chinese guavas. Though frost-pinched and shrunken (the tree having been subjected to disinfection and acclimatisation since embarkation) these vulnerable, plucky-looking little fruits seemed still to hold some of the warmth of Malawi. The girl, staring at the camera, gripped the tree's slender trunk as if to save it from being swallowed by a swamp. The lightest swirl of the air-brush tool gave the hint of a vortex to the mud pool. The mayor smiled benignly, representing all the good citizens who would, in due course, wander among the splendour of a tropical garden. Lorraine resisted the temptation to give just a degree or two of enlargement to the fob-watch nestling comfortably over his appendix. Instead, she carefully diffused the points of light on the mayoral chain until it, too, suggested something organic. She deepened the mass of the tower-blocks, increased contrast around the fencing, then, with a nervously excited keytouch, saved the file, and sent it to print.

Five minutes later, she was examining the proof-copy of a drama of light and dark. She had interfered with the camera's vision, but only as an artist might, to show more clearly what was there. This picture would only make the Deptford locals and the *Times of Malawi*, but it was a far better thing than those AIDS hospital shots beamed round the world on the Press Association satellite.

For the first time since her return from Malawi, Lorraine failed to hear the bell of the afternoon tea trolley. The shuffling exit, as Big Ben clanged out the hour of five, of middle-ranking officials passed over at the last annual review, reminded her only to hurry: there was always a chance one of the dailies might use the picture to plug a gap on an inside page. She didn't even want to join the hordes charging along the corridors at 20 seconds before 5.30. Instead, she made a brisk telephone call to the press officer, asking him please to hold the release just for another fifteen minutes, as her pictures were almost ready.

It was nearer six when she charged upstairs with a stack of fine-screen enlargements. One copy she withheld from the distribution. She wanted to leave this on Toby's desk – a token, perhaps, of her intention to improve her performance. But, as she approached the Head's office, she heard the low drone of his voice, seemingly on the telephone. Lorraine wanted Toby to see the picture, but she didn't want Toby to see her. Not because she was ashamed, or not for that reason only: her new mood was too fragile to risk in an encounter with another person, particularly this ironic person who knew far too much. She slipped the print into her satchel and stole away. Perhaps Fiona might like to see it. She would have to explain to Fiona, as she would not have had to explain to Toby, why it was an interesting picture. But even so. She tidied the laboratory, collected her ski-jacket, indulged herself with another look at the photograph, put it back into her bag, and then ambled off to the van. She did not even think to congratulate herself for not thinking about Fiona and Lucy for a whole afternoon.

In the car park, again, she lingered. There was an orange glow in the night sky which reflected itself in the upper windows of King Charles's Street. From the vestibule of the Foreign Office building came spills of yellow light; one window was in part obscured by the immobile outline of a security guard, lengthened in its replication on the paving flags. The stillness of the scene seemed to belong to the beginning and the end of time. As she switched on the engine of the van, she was momentarily shocked by its roar, shattering what had been a powerful silence.

On the drive home, she stopped at a petrol station to get some flowers, then, as an afterthought, threw in a bag of liquorice allsorts for Lucy. Lucy seldom bought herself treats these days: her job was dying on her, and most of the redundancy package would be claimed by Barclaycard. Lorraine tossed the sweets onto the dashboard lip: if Lucy didn't want them, Bonzo would eat the pink ones with coconut. Then she combed her hair and wiped the shine off her nose. Even without reading glasses, the rear-view mirror showed puckered and swollen skin around her eyes; and she needed a haircut. Well, she was what she was. She touched the pedals gently as she took the final half-mile, and parked under a large plane tree.

The house was quiet. This pleased her, then gave a sudden shock. They were in bed. The Commonwealth garden, which had for eight hours screened her from fear and shame, lost its power, and the key shook in her hand as she fumbled for the lock.

Bonzo was just inside the door, his muzzle raised to be stroked. She stroked it. He licked her hand. The quiet of their greeting cleared her ears to hear something unconnected with the bedroom; it was the hiss of the propane torch. Fiona was not upstairs with Lucy. She was in her studio. Lorraine made her way to it. She saw Fiona bent close over a silver thread which arced softly under the flame. Lorraine warned herself to be careful.

'For you, Fifi.' She kissed the back of Fiona's neck, and laid the flowers on the workbench.

Fiona glanced up briefly. 'Move them, quick; they'll get scorched.'

Lorraine picked up the flowers. 'I'll put them in water.'

'Yes, put them somewhere.' Then, after a pause, Fiona added in the same toneless voice, 'Fancy finding delphiniums in December.'

'A miracle,' said Lorraine, with equal indifference. At the filling station, she'd imagined they'd come from Malawi. But still she lingered behind Fiona's stool.

'Look, I can't break off now,' muttered Fiona, who hated to work with someone peering over her shoulder. 'Got to get on with this job. Got to earn some money.'

Lorraine took the flowers into the kitchen. The skin of her face felt tight and tender as if it, rather than the flowers, had been exposed to scorching. Fiona wouldn't speak to her. Lucy was hiding somewhere.

Lorraine thrust the flowers into one of the pans awaiting washing in the sink and set out to search for Lucy. Not in the bedroom: not anywhere. Thoughtfully, she returned to the kitchen. There were no visible preparations for supper: nothing defrosting in a bowl covered by a plate in Fiona's neat way; no brown pulses bubbling on the cooker in Lucy's. She went back into the studio. 'Where's Lucy?'

'Gone off to consult the local witchdoctor.'

Lorraine hovered, her hand on the door. 'Chelsey, again? Is she upset?'

Fiona gave a sigh. 'Can't stop to gossip. I'm late with this commission.'

'Tell me in a word.'

'A word? You do anything in just one word?'

Lorraine made no reply for a few seconds then, quietly, said, 'Would you like a drink?'

'Whisky,' replied Fiona, without looking up.

For the third time, Lorraine made her way to the kitchen. Bonzo padded in from the rug in the hall and whined softly.

Well, Bonzo was still speaking to her. She touched his ear. 'I don't know what you want, boy. I can see from your bowl that Fiona's put out your supper.' Lorraine poured Fiona a whisky and herself a glass of wine. It felt peculiar to fill just two glasses. She took the drinks into the studio. With an instinctive appreciation of the Pavlov principle she put Fiona's drink not on the workbench, but on top of the 'Unpaid Invoices' tray on the desk at the other end of the room. She took the typing chair beside this desk, and pulled up another.

Fiona turned down the flame on the torch and, straightening her back, came across to take the proffered chair and the drink. 'I really haven't time, you know,' she began.

'Fifi,' Lorraine touched the hand that lay limply on Fiona's lap, 'I'm sorry about last night.'

'I don't want to talk about it. If one of us doesn't get back to the real world, we'll be facing bankruptcy.'

Lorraine noted Fiona's leg, stretched out long as a colt's and as far away as possible from Lorraine's. How, in her anger, had Lorraine forgotten how beautiful and how utterly untouchable Fiona was? Lorraine swallowed against the swelling threat of tears. 'Fifi, if I've driven Lucy away, I'm sorry, but not half as sorry as I am if what I did last night has left you with me, but deprived of her, and so hating me.'

'Last night! You're sorry about one night! You've been torturing yourself, and everybody else, for weeks.' Fiona scraped back her chair, making to rise. 'Anyway, I don't want to talk about it. We all need space. I need space to work.'

'Please.' Lorraine leaned closer, then drew back. 'I want you to have space.'

'Last night,' said Fiona grimly, 'you were hysterical about Lucy's relationship with me. But the only relationship you want with her is to batter her. You won't let her go; you won't let her stay. You don't want me; you won't leave me alone. I don't know what's going on with you, and I'm not sure I want to know any more.'

Nerve ends in Lorraine's neck tingled. She could so easily break out into another rage. 'I'm sorry,' she whispered. 'I

wasn't myself. I'm going to be very civilised from now on. I
want us to get close again.'

Fiona cut across. 'Get close to you! I don't want to be anywhere near you.'

'Oh God!' Lorraine covered her face with her hand. 'I disgust you.'

'You. You. You. Nothing in the world is so fascinating as
Lorraine and her delicious angst.'

'There's something outside of me that gives me angst. I'm
afraid of losing you.'

Fiona slammed down her glass. 'You aren't going to lose
me, despite your best efforts.'

'I'm talking about losing you to Lucy.'

'God's sake, that's not in question. But can't you see how
you drive me to her when you're so cruel to her?'

'Why? Are you in love with her?'

'I might ask why,' said Fiona with a sigh, 'you're trying to
push me into being in love with her. If you could spare one
moment to think of me, you'd understand how little I want to
be in love with anything. All I need is something to help me
forget.'

'Is my life with you so horrible that you have to forget it?'

'It's you, you again. What about me? Why can't you listen?
It's me; it's fifty-year-old me. It's me trying to deal with age,
with death. It's *me* I'm trying to forget.'

'How does Lucy help you do that if it's not by being in love
with her?'

'Lorraine,' Fiona said grimly, 'be careful. I *can't* talk to you.
I know you too well. You won't listen; you won't try to understand. You'll save up anything I say, and the next time we
quarrel, you'll use those words as a weapon against me.'

Lorraine took a deep breath. 'I am being careful.' Her voice
was low. 'I am trying to understand. But to understand, I
need to know. Tell me.'

Fiona sighed. 'It's not just Lucy. It's all three of us, it's
having something that makes me feel alive.'

'And Lucy, especially, makes you feel alive?'

Anger flashed across Fiona's face. 'Yes she does. Satisfied?'

Lorraine looked away. 'Almost. Just one more question. What is it about her that makes you feel alive?'

Fiona was silent.

Lorraine soundlessly mouthed: 'please'.

'All right.' Fiona stood up, her knuckles in the small of her back.

Before she could speak, Lorraine said: 'No, don't tell me. I know. She's young and pretty and she adores you, and that makes you feel powerful.' Lorraine turned towards Fiona and, as she said the last words, glanced quickly at her face.

Fiona's eyes were cold. 'She's not particularly pretty. And she's too hard-nosed to have charm.'

Lorraine held her breath.

'But I feel touched by her. Every time you go into one of your rages, like a mad drunk outside a pub, I want to protect her. Every time you shout at her, I see how hurt, and how brave, she is.'

'I get it,' said Lorraine, whose voice seemed a whisper from the far end of the room. 'She is my gift to you.'

'She reminds me,' said Fiona, now half turned to the uncovered night window, 'of a song.' Absently, Fiona intoned: '"Yes, they call me Mimi, but my name is Lucia. My story is brief. I embroider linen" –'

'– Okay, got it. Puccini. *La Bohème*. Thank you.'

Silence fell. Lorraine knew that something important had happened which she did not as yet understand. What she did understand was that her life had collapsed. After another silence, she rose heavily to her feet. 'Well, maybe it's not the night for this and that. Perhaps I'll just go up to bed.'

'That's fine,' replied Fiona, 'I'll walk the dog.'

'Don't trouble yourself, I'll walk him.'

'I'd prefer to do it myself, thank you.'

Their voices were low, but they were once again quarrelling. Even if neither of them knew why, they both knew that it would now be impossible for them to reach each other. Lorraine, with a sigh, recalled her resolution: to be civilised.

'Would you like to go somewhere really alive, to eat?' With a heavy stab at wit, she added, 'Perhaps we could compensate for the absence of Lucy by consuming something not quite dead yet, like oysters.'

'Tonight,' replied Fiona, still upright and fisting the small of her back, 'you want to eat oysters. Last night you drank our best wine while you wept about your debts. You wanted Lucy to pay back money you had, I now discover, spent on taking her to various hotels. Hotels! So that's what you were doing in the weeks you found work so very enthralling. Well, that's just one of those things, though I find it ironic that you took her to the same hotels you took me to ten years ago.'

'Fiona. I am very, very sorry.'

'For heaven's sake.' Fiona brushed this away. 'I'm glad you had a good time. I was giving you a bad enough one. But the fact is that performances like yours leave me with no concern beyond solvency.'

For a full minute, they stared at each other like strangers. The painful love for Fiona that had risen up in Lorraine died away into a numb aversion. She was equally conscious that Fiona felt no more for her.

Lorraine broke the silence. 'I had too much to drink last night.'

'That goes for us all.' Fiona's face, paler than usual – perhaps the result of a day of poring over metal – was set, unsmiling, unfrowning, remote. 'But you're a charming drunk, when you're just a drunk. These days you use drink to let out something else.'

A bubble of something that wanted to stop being civilised rose in Lorraine's breast. 'You'd be more than happy to go out to eat some vegetable still screaming from the knife, if Lucy had suggested it.'

'Right. If that's your angle.' Fiona picked up her glass. 'This is mine.' She marched across to her workbench and turned the propane torch up high. The silver wire rolled itself into a ball, and she cursed it.

Lorraine sat very still for perhaps five minutes, but Fiona did not turn back. Lorraine slouched out to the kitchen. Bonzo was standing guard over his supper, but had still not eaten. She reached down to stroke his ears. More she could not offer. She poured herself another glass of wine. Out of the need to do something, she opened the fridge. It contained nothing to change her attitude to food. She topped up her wine and sat down at the table. Her eyes wandered round the neglected room, then settled on Bonzo, a perfect example of hunger-strike. If only she could care enough about anything to want to encourage him to eat.

The phone rang. Lorraine put down her glass and lumbered towards the hall. But Fiona had already picked up the extension at her workbench.

Lorraine pressed her ear to the studio door. 'Oh, it's you,' she heard Fiona say vaguely, too vaguely. 'Well, maybe not. It's best we don't see each other for a while.' Then a silence, before Fiona's voice sounded again. 'All right then, if it's that bad.' A longer silence, then: 'Me too – Lucia.' The instrument in the hall, at Lorraine's back, gave a crisp click.

Lorraine crept away from the studio door and returned to her post in the kitchen.

Forty minutes later, Bonzo pricked up his ears. There was a mousy scratching at the lock; the door squeaked open, clonked softly to; an umbrella folded with a wet flip and the coats in the hall rustled as another was heaped onto them. Lorraine, pouring her umpteenth glass of wine, did not move from her stool. There were indistinct words, of greeting or warning, as the Doc Martens side-stepped Bonzo and squealed across the floorboards towards the studio. Bonzo ambled back into the kitchen. Lorraine stilled him with a hand. Nothing audible emerged from the studio. Before Lorraine could nerve herself to sneak out to listen at the keyhole, the Doc Martens sounded at her back.

'Hi.' Lucy's voice, though low and cautious, made Lorraine start. 'Did you have a good day?'

Did she? Lorraine recalled the photograph in her satchel. No, she did not want Lucy to see it. 'Yeah,' she replied without looking up, 'fine.'

Lucy sat beside her and touched Lorraine's wrist with an ice-cold hand. 'Don't you want to ask me about my day?'

Lorraine glanced up, and caught the quick fading of a challenging smile. Lucy's cheeks, chin and the perky points of the ears were rosy from cold. There were spots of rain on her hair. Her breath was cool and fresh as if she'd been swimming in the lake. This little nymph wanted to play. 'Not particularly,' replied Lorraine, turning away.

'I've been with Chelsey. Don't you want to know how I got on?'

'That least of all.'

'Well, I'll tell you anyway.' Lucy filled Lorraine's glass and drank from it. 'I told her all about us. I didn't keep anything back. Not even that Fiona has announced a sex ban.'

Lorraine's mind was slow. 'Sex ban? What sex ban?' Lorraine had thought they already had one, more or less. She stared at Lucy's hand around the stem of her glass for several seconds before sense dawned. 'Good,' she said. 'I hope you both enjoy it.'

Lucy reached into the sink for another glass, filled it, and pushed it towards Lorraine. 'Not just her and me. It must apply to us all, including you and me, and you with Fiona. It's not fair otherwise.'

'Fair?' Lorraine shook her head in an attempt to clear the fumes of wine and the gathering of inchoate fury.

'Yes. And I have to trust you not to do anything dishonourable behind my back.'

Lorraine stared at Lucy as her chest tightened, squeezing her breath.

Lucy was still closely surveying Lorraine. 'The ban is to run until you've got yourself sorted out, and afterwards Fiona won't do anything that doesn't include you. That's the programme – hers, not mine.'

'Oh.' Lorraine stroked Bonzo's muzzle, which by some

dog-magic had materialised at the ends of her trailing fingers. 'And what would yours have been?'

Lucy laughed. 'What does that matter? I have to take what you two fling at me. Unless, of course, I decide to go. But if I did have power, I'd want us all to be together, all equal and sharing. Why can't we be? Even the heteropatriarchy allows for relationships that have more than two, that include children.'

'You want to be the child?'

'No,' said Lucy, speaking carefully, 'you do.'

Lorraine forced her constricted lungs to open with a magisterial: 'Then that's what I'll be. And if I'm too infantile to observe the sex ban, I can shop you for child abuse.'

Lucy pulled back an inch, then grinned. 'Guess I'll have to keep things under control.'

'What makes you think you'd be able to control me?'

'I think I know what you need,' said Lucy carefully. 'You need to be alone for a while. But Fiona doesn't know that and, more important, you don't yourself.'

Lorraine guffawed crudely. 'You talk enough psychotrash to pass for an expert on child abuse.'

'I know something about child abuse.' Lucy's tone was now serious. 'I've experienced it.'

Like Fiona, Lorraine had paid little attention to Lucy's theories about unremembered mental damage inflicted on her infant self, but now, looking now into the bright, defiant, yet pathetically vulnerable face, she could envisage it, and the horror of it came to her with a desire to crush the little brat. Rising like a fountain, she gripped Lucy by the shoulder, shook her, and said: 'Okay, if you want to control me, come upstairs – Lucia.'

'No,' said Lucy, turning pale. 'We've got a sex ban.'

'I haven't agreed to any sex ban.' Lorraine's voice came out in a roar.

'Don't.' Lucy wriggled free. 'I won't be bullied.' She slid off her stool and backed away. Lorraine, lumbering after her, trapped her against the fridge. 'No, please.' Lucy's face was white. 'This is how you were last night. I don't like it. Truly.'

'You'll get used to it.' As she kissed Lucy, Lorraine could feel her dragon-breath burning Lucy's cheeks, still chill though she'd been indoors for a quarter of an hour.

Half an hour later, Fiona came upstairs, accompanied by Bonzo. Lorraine burrowed under the pillows. Lucy, flat on her back beside her, lay still. Lorraine could feel Fiona's hand lift a corner of the pillow. Astringent scents of flame and alum mixed with the animal smells of the bed. Lorraine sensed air and coolness. 'You didn't tell me about the Commonwealth garden,' said Fiona.

Lorraine sighed. What Commonwealth garden? The Commonwealth garden was a wraith.

'Was it a riot of those flowers that made a comet's tail on the road from the airport?'

Lorraine sat up. She had forgotten the cosmos flowers lining every road in Malawi even though, at the time she had seen them, their beauty had seemed to enter and transform her very soul. This – everything of value – was gone from her life. 'No flowers,' she said sourly, 'only one guava sapling flown in from Malawi to die of frost, fog and carbon monoxide.'

Lucy, who had been ignored through this exchange, leapt up from under the covers. 'Sex ban's bitten the dust,' she said. 'Lorraine and I did it.'

'Rules, my darling,' replied Fiona gently, 'are made to be broken. So why don't we break another, and watch a video tonight? They've got *Dangerous Liaisons* at the local shop.'

Lorraine hated videos, though not half so much as she hated being patronised, and losing the initiative. 'If that's what you want; it's what you'll get.' She leapt out of bed and, in a single movement, hauled on trousers and shoes, and bounded, followed by a revivified Bonzo, towards the hall.

Despite Bonzo's longing glances in the direction of the misty Heath, she rushed back in minutes, the video clutched under her ski-jacket. In that short period, she had already decided that she would see a different film; it was about cosmos flowers and Chinese guavas and maize sprouting in wobbly contoured lines on the hills of Malawi.

Fiona and Lucy were already downstairs and seated before the television set, placed demurely at opposite ends of the sofa, with space in the middle for Lorraine. Lorraine pushed in the cassette, started it running and, before the credits were halfway through, said, suppressing as well as she could the surge of power that came with the prepared statement: 'I'm going to bed.'

Fiona half rose.

'No,' said Lorraine, gesturing her to stay, 'excite your young blood with duelling and death, if you like. I've got a date with a Commonwealth garden.'

Lorraine could hear the unspoken words in Fiona's heavy sigh.

'No worry,' she added, 'I'm not having a turn, not tonight. I've taken the best picture of my life today. I want to think about that, not –' she pointed to the flickering screen '– this.'

Bonzo, waiting in the hall, whimpered as Lorraine made her way up the stairs. She shut out the sound by slamming the door of the little room and, stripping off her outer layers of clothing, tumbled into the fold-up bed.

Fiona and Lucy would watch maybe half of the film. Then they would go up to bed. They would reconsider the sex ban in the light of Lorraine's having violently broken it. They would cuddle up together telling each other that there would be nothing more and then, excited by that nothing, there would be more. Lorraine reached for her satchel. But, remembering that the print showed only a girl and a man and a tree over a muddy hole, decided to view the photograph in her mind's eye instead. She thought of the tower-blocks behind the figures and tilted them forward by 15 degrees. Then a little more, till the crest of the spindly tree was holding up their crushing weight. Trees: they were the life-givers of the earth. In Malawi, at the high edge of the Rift Valley, they reached, cathedral-like, to the sky. Steven-John claimed that he wished, in his next life, to be born a tree. What would he be? A neat privet, perhaps, surrounding a suburban house with its protection and its watchful eye. What would Ulric be? A lonely pine, leaning in the wind. Toby the Chief? A flowering cherry in the gardens of Buckingham Palace. None of her friends was fine enough to be a great forest tree screening from the eyes of lions the Thomson's gazelles trotting down to drink at the shores of the great Lake Malawi. Pleased with these thoughts, Lorraine switched off the light to concentrate on trees.

She heard the soft padding as Fiona, Lucy and then Bonzo, made their way upstairs.

Fiona came into the room and gently shook Lorraine's shoulder. 'Come to bed.'

'I am in bed.'

'Okay.' Fiona turned away. 'If it's what you want. God bless.' She closed the door.

It was all right. They weren't going to have sex. Fiona had imposed a ban. Fiona was tired after slaving all day to recoup damage done by Lorraine to their finances. She listened to the soft scratching of Bonzo's claws as he made himself a bed on the landing. Lorraine returned to the winding road lined with cosmos flowers which in her dream led, not to the mediocre capital of Lilongwe, but to a great forest of tropical trees, a gene pool deep as Lake Malawi itself, where crocodiles lay with their great log-jaws sodden and, from the fever trees, little creatures croaked in hope of booty when the great jaws snapped.

'Are you awake?' There was a hand on Lorraine's shoulder.

'What? Yes, awake.' A red-eyed tree frog vanished into the groin of a creeper-encrusted ebony oak, and a pale, serious face materialised out of the darkness – Lucy.

'Lorraine. You didn't say goodnight. Aren't you going to give me a kiss?'

Lorraine shook her head.

'Okay. We can't sleep, Fiona and me,' said Lucy, her hand stroking at Lorraine's rough hair. 'We need to do sex.'

'You do?' Lorraine brushed off the touch at her hair, which felt like pulling. 'Then go ahead.'

'Don't you want it too?'

'With you? I've just had it. I don't think you cared for it. For myself, I reserve judgement.'

'I mean, with Fiona, with all of us together like we always wanted to?'

'Not just now. I'm tired. I'm taken up with crocodiles, and . . .'

'C'mon, wake up. You want her, you want me. *Why* are you making it all so difficult?'

Lorraine pressed hard against the thin, unstable mattress under her. 'I don't want anyone. You two go ahead.'

Lucy withdrew her hand. 'You'll make trouble if we do.'

'I won't. Believe me.' Lorraine turned onto her stomach and pulled the covers up tight.

'You know, don't you, that I need to strengthen my relationship with Fiona? You accept that you and I had almost a month, just the two of us, when things were very romantic, while with her it's always been fraught. You do agree that that isn't fair?'

'Nothing's fair.' Lorraine spoke into the pillow.

'Lorraine. I wish you could be happy.'

Lorraine sat up sharply. 'I'm not *un*happy. I'm just involved with other things.'

Lucy was now standing upright, her arms folded over her breasts. 'You're sure, you're absolutely sure you want to be left alone?'

Lorraine flung the pillow from her and sat up. 'Yes, for Christ's sake.'

'And you'll do it with me in the morning?'

'Oh, I don't know. You sound like a tart. Please go away.'

Lucy sighed. 'I'm trying so hard to hold this thing together. Nobody but me is prepared to do any real work to keep us all united.'

'Everything will hold together brilliantly if you'll just let me get some sleep.'

Lucy padded out softly, leaving the door half open behind her. Within seconds, the absence she left was filled by Bonzo, his moist nose prodding the covers for contact with Lorraine's shoulder. 'And you go away too, Bonzo.' Bonzo returned quietly to the rug on the landing.

Lorraine rolled back onto her stomach, allowing to trickle up into consciousness the pain in her left shoulder associated with hours hunched over the computer. It was a companionable presence, the signal of wholesome labour, of digging potatoes, midwifing a photograph, holding still and tight to a tree so as not to be thrown into the jaws of the hungry lake.

Lorraine tried to recapture the lake of her dream: she was methodical. She re-invented the wavelets, the thin sandy shore, the timid gazelles darting down to drink, the red-eyed frog. She got out her cutting tool and excised the crocodile. There were noises from the bedroom, movements in the bed. Bonzo whimpered. No matter. These sounds were London, and she was a frog hidden among the globes of the Chinese guavas, warmer to the touch than the duvet over her face. Giggles came from the bedroom. She didn't mind. It was only sex, only a spasm, only what she had, mindless numbers of times, done with each of them. Lucy knew what sex was: nothing! She must not mind.

Lorraine rolled over onto her side and began another game: naming waters by the letters of the alphabet, where Lake Malawi would, appropriately, fall in the centre of things, between the Laptev and the North Seas. 'Atlantic, Lake Baikal, China Sea, D —' Lorraine was felled by 'D'. All right, try countries, where Lorraine, with her Foreign Office job, was well equipped: 'Argentina, Bangladesh, Cyprus, Dubai [good, beat the D], Egypt, France,' and so on to Qatar, Rumania, Spain, Turkey, Uruguay, Vietnam, Western Samoa.' But 'X' was impossible. Perhaps some other geographical phenomenon could be allowed to stand for 'X'. There was Xai-Xai (a true 'X' although pronounced 'Shai-Shai') in Mozambique, a seaport horribly wrecked in the civil war but where, please God, defoliants had not been used and tree frogs would survive.

Out of the vacuum of the difficulty of 'X' came, from the

bedroom next door, in tones precise as a metronome, and in Lucy's guttural expectoration, the cries: 'Ugh-ugh, ai-ai, Xai-Xai' and on and on and on. Lorraine covered her head with the pillow.

All was quiet again, cloaked by the soft snoring of Bonzo on the rug. The frog was gone. The lake, Chinese guavas, all gone. Just dark night, every now and then an owl, and long fretful sleeplessness. Lorraine reviewed everything, calmly, point by point. Then she went over the same arguments in a fury. Why was this December dawn so much more delayed than any other? She reached over for her watch. It was only 2.30. Five hours to go. There was still time to take a sleeping pill. The pills (Fiona's menopausal temazepam) were in the cabinet beside the bed in the next room that would smell of sex. Lorraine pulled on the outer layers of the garments on the rug and ventured out. Bonzo was just outside the door. He, firmly, dragged her down to the kitchen instead.

Bonzo's supper, untasted, was drying in the bowl. She boiled a kettle to freshen it up. Morsel by morsel, he yielded to hunger, but would only eat while she stayed by him. When his bowl was near empty, she slipped into the living room and dropped the needle onto the seventh track of *La Bohème*:

> *Yes, they call me Mimi,*
> *but my name is Lucia.*
> *I don't know why . . .*
> *I live alone, quite alone,*
> *in a little white room.*
> *But when the thaw comes,*
> *the sunshine is mine.*

Lorraine leaned her head against the chimney breast, and the tears flowed onto it. She was unaware of Bonzo mouthing the tails of her shirt, or of his trying to drag her back to the kitchen, but her fingers, automatically, curled around his life-eroded whiskers.

25

Wednesday, 6 December, Frognal

When Chelsey's door-bell rang at 11 a.m. on Wednesday, the only pleasure Chelsey allowed herself was to congratulate the Royal Mail on, for once, living up to its promise of next day delivery. Without changing out of her socks and old man's cardigan, she made her way up the half-flight of stairs to the hall and dimmed the light (which cast a funereal tungsten pall, especially in the mornings). Through the stained-glass panes in the door, she saw what she wanted to see, and opened the door wide. 'Georgiana! What a surprise,' she said.

Georgiana – head erect and chin up, though she leaned a little on her old-fashioned gentleman's umbrella, giving her body an elegant 1920s torque – said, in a voice as false as Chelsey's: 'I happened to be passing.'

'Do come in.' Chelsey held the door open, but did not embrace Georgiana.

Nor did Georgiana embrace her. She stepped into the dim hall and looked about, uncertain of the direction.

'Down the stairs and turn right,' said Chelsey. Noting Georgiana's slightly hesitant movements on the worn, unlit stone steps, Chelsey followed her into the living room.

The room, facing west, was gloomy in the mornings,

though the windows glittered with light reflected from the wet foliage of the wilderness below. Yet Chelsey's room was the near equal of Georgiana's in its ambience of decayed grandeur, and Chelsey was not disappointed with the scene it presented. She had no need to voice the words 'to what do I owe this unexpected honour?' since the question hung heavy in the air.

Georgiana, still wearing her coat and fox fur, lowered herself, uninvited, onto the centre cushions of the settee. 'Thank you for returning the purse,' she said.

Chelsey didn't sit, but leaned against the back of the armchair opposite. 'Oh good, I did seem to recall that it was yours.'

'As a matter of fact,' Georgiana extracted the envelope from her bag, 'it isn't. It had long passed out of my hands. If you don't want it, you had best return it to the person you got it from.'

The so-familiar, almost comforting, thud of disappointment hit Chelsey in the breast. 'I'm rather busy at present,' she said, on reflex, 'I'm due to be called for an audition probably this afternoon.'

'Splendid,' replied Georgiana. 'Then you have the rest of this morning to return it.'

Chelsey was defeated. 'I suppose I do.' She took the package from Georgiana. It was not possible, under Georgiana's stare, to open it and stiffen herself with sight of the entwined 'g' and 'f', powerful and terrible as a spell. She dropped the envelope into the sagging pocket of her cardigan. 'Would you like some coffee?' she said lamely.

When she returned from the kitchen a few minutes later, carrying mugs of a beverage she knew Georgiana could not drink, Georgiana had shed her coat and fur. She was standing by the window, and her mood was very different. 'You have a lovely flat, my dear.' She gestured to the thickets of overgrown roses entwined with bindweed and nettles, the virginia creeper, bare apart from a few dying red leaves, winding like rope over the collapsing garden walls. 'One thing I do miss is a garden.'

Chelsey's heart gave a painfully sharp beat.

'How sad that it's taken so many years for me to see your home.' Georgiana turned away from the window. Her face, now in shadow, was reflective; the line of her chin, touched by the rich light of vegetation, was delicate as a Flemish painting; her eyes were dark, unreadable pools. 'How sad that our lives are directed by accidents of history.'

Chelsey warned herself to be on her guard: from which play had Georgiana taken that soulful line? But the rusted chains of a very old love tightened around her heart. The spirits, ever watchful, hissed at her to be strong, to think of Lucy. 'Do you call it an accident of history, rather than fate –' Chelsey controlled the catch in her voice '– that this purse travelled such a circuitous route to find its way back to you?'

Georgiana laughed. 'An accident, and a minor one.'

Georgiana was lying. Chelsey knew this. Her prompt appearance at Frognal proved the importance of Chelsey's discovery. Her studied performance confirmed it. 'I thought it rather more than coincidence.' Chelsey drew a sharp breath and came out with it: 'It certainly has the mark of fate, since I got it right here, when Lucy and I were rolling on my settee.'

Georgiana didn't respond, not with a gasp nor any visible intake of breath.

Chelsey told herself to say no more, but the silence lengthened. 'She comes here quite often.'

Georgiana glanced away. 'I don't need the details.'

Even before Georgiana had replied, Chelsey was biting her tongue. Georgiana *did* need at least that one detail, and how else could Chelsey have conveyed it to her? Yet Chelsey felt not satisfaction but shame. She saw what Georgiana saw: a sordid little skirmish between two outcasts; Chelsey's soiled, dishonoured, envious waste of life. Chelsey felt her past rise up, thick as vomit. She couldn't look now at the powerful figure at her window, but she could see how utterly futile had been her ambition ever to be loved by her.

Georgiana watched, as if she followed Chelsey's every thought. Then, after a moment, she smiled kindly. 'Yet I am glad you got it, whether fate or accident brought it to you –'

she paused '– because it concerns something I would like to ask of you.'

Teeth clenched, Chelsey replied: 'Don't ask anything of me.' The spirits were still hissing in her ears, telling her to be careful, but Chelsey could barely hear them for the beating of her own heart. In spite of herself, she said softly: 'It's too late, Georgiana.'

Georgiana turned back to the window. 'Yes, I know. It's only just become too late, but it is so. You were faithful for a very long time. How unwise of me to think it was for ever.'

Tears began to burn at the back of Chelsey's eyeballs. 'Very unwise,' she muttered, while her torn heart cried out that it was not too late at all.

Georgiana, now smiling a different, sad smile which cut deep grooves into her cheeks, nodded. 'Perhaps you're right. Goodbye then, my dear. I must go, and take a good part of your life with me. I'm sorry.' She took a step towards the door.

'Georgiana, no.' Chelsey barred the way. 'I loved you dreadfully. I've never felt anything so deeply, ever, ever.'

'You did love me, once. Not now.'

'No?' Chelsey thought. She did still love Georgiana. She knew she always would. Love, great love, is for ever. 'No, I can't love you now,' she said bitterly. 'You've been too cruel to me.'

Georgiana spread her hands. 'Perhaps, my dear, you are right to disbelieve in accidents of history. Perhaps fate does have a part. If so, fate has been cruel to me too.'

'To you? Georgiana?'

'To me, an old woman, and a lonely one.'

Somehow, Chelsey was in Georgiana's arms, and Chelsey, a woman who never shed tears, was racked by hard dry sobs.

A few minutes later, they were both seated on the settee, and Georgiana's hand firmly enclosed Chelsey's. 'Chelsey, dear, there is still something I wish to ask of you.'

When Chelsey had nodded her agreement, Georgiana added, 'I'd like you to return the purse to Lucy at my next party; to do it when I give the signal.'

Chelsey agreed; at that moment she would have done the same if Georgiana had asked her to leap into a boiling cauldron.

A few more minutes, and Georgiana was gone. Chelsey cleared away the untasted mug of coffee, but Georgiana's last words still rang in her ears: 'We go back a long way, dear soul.' Yes, they went back a very long, very tortured way. Yes, Chelsey would do exactly as Georgiana had asked. She would, once again, be used by the woman she had loved for a quarter of a century, and who needed nothing from her but an act of deceit. She would do it. But this time the hired assassin would play the double agent.

Chelsey was determined to leave her script to the spirits but, in the hours that followed, she paced back and forth across the thin carpet, unable to eat, sit, or even make sense of her own motives. What did she want out of all this? To get Georgiana back? After 25 years of wanting, to climb into Georgiana's bed? The thought was laughable, if not obscene. Chelsey's drive was as powerful as sex or rage, but focused on no visible end. Though Chelsey (of course) relished the prospect of humiliating Fiona, its anticipation wasn't all that thrilled her. Something else churned in the darkness of her unknown soul. What?

And what, precisely, was the plot? Georgiana had been sparing in the extreme about details, but Chelsey was confident that the basis was to have the little purse returned to Lucy under Fiona's eyes: to present a double perfidy; Fiona's betrayal of Georgiana by giving the token of Georgiana's love to Lucy, and Lucy's parallel betrayal of Fiona. So that Fiona, out of disgust for both herself and Lucy, would be forced to end the demeaning liaison.

But, if this was Georgiana's plan, it had a weakness. Georgiana didn't know that Chelsey had the purse because she'd picked Lucy's pocket. Georgiana, lacking this essential information, was vulnerable and Chelsey, who had it, in a position of power. This was the only thought that gave a clear stab of excitement.

When darkness fell, around 3.30 p.m., Chelsey's nerves had been so jangled by wild imaginings and caffeine that, despite a thick scarf wrapped round the shoulders of her cardigan, she couldn't stop shivering.

Then her bell rang. She charged up the stairs and peered through the stained glass: the hood of a duffel coat. Chelsey wasn't ready for this yet; her body lurched with the impulse to run. But Chelsey Chamberlain was an actress, a professional. She steadied herself with a deep breath and opened the door with a casual: 'Well, guess who's here?'

Lucy hovered. 'I'm not sure I should be here.'

Chelsey offered no reassurance. She drifted towards the dark stairs and called, over her shoulder: 'I did say that whenever you ever needed anyone to talk to . . .'

Lucy stood, irresolute, for a moment, then pulled the big door to behind her and followed Chelsey down the half-flight and into her flat. Here again she was left to shut them in. 'Chelsey,' she began, 'in spite of what I did when I came here last time, I hope you understand that I'm not in *any* way after you.'

Chelsey reached into the broom cupboard and extracted a bottle of designer-label vodka, which she deposited on the coffee table. Lucy's eyes followed her progress. Lucy was still standing, coat buttoned, when Chelsey returned from the kitchen with glasses, tomato juice and Worcester sauce. 'I never thought you were, my dear.' With a sigh, she seated herself on the settee. 'That's not the issue.'

'No.' Lucy laid her coat over the back of the chair furthest from the settee. 'But I always seem to be making demands on you.'

'Any time, any time,' said Chelsey vaguely, as she mixed the drinks.

'It seems like I keep coming to you for help – which is an okay thing to do so long as you admit it – and then we get into a different space. I'm not quite sure how we get there. I mean, it isn't the real space.'

Again Chelsey smiled. 'It seems real to me. Limited, but real.'

'Maybe.' Lucy fidgeted slightly. 'But afterwards it feels like I've done something I shouldn't have. I feel like I've used you.'

Chelsey believed that many people used her, that life used her, that Georgiana had made her a footstool. 'I'm here to be used,' she said. Her voice was casual, but the wretched glass slipped in her hand, and slopped tomato juice onto her lap. She reached into her pocket for a paper tissue and her finger touched the envelope. She wiped the spill with her scarf.

Lucy looked at her sharply. 'Chelsey, is there something wrong?'

Chelsey raised her eyebrows. 'Yes, there is. For one, your Bloody Mary looks lonely.'

Obediently, Lucy slipped across to join Chelsey on the settee. 'I meant wrong with us. Somehow, you seem a bit off me.'

Chelsey laughed. 'Well that's a tough one: you warn me to lay off and then complain when I do.'

Lucy, head bowed low, studied her nibbled fingernails. 'It's all coming out wrong. I'm acting like a coquette. All I actually want is to keep things straight. I don't want to use you and I don't want to hurt you.'

'You'd be lucky to have that power, my dear.' As Chelsey spoke, it struck her that Lucy was the one person who had *not* used her. She looked at the small, hunched figure, at the baby-fine down which covered her head and ended in two neatly clipped spurs beside the sinews of her thin neck. Her shoulder-blades, un-coordinated as those of a new-hatched bird, shifted uneasily. Chelsey could not see her expression, but she knew that, although they were both game-players, Lucy was not playing with her. 'Your trouble is,' she added with something like tenderness, 'you think too much.'

Lucy raised her head, but didn't look at Chelsey. 'Do I? So do you.' Her glance now ranged over the flat – the high over-sized mantelpiece, the long narrow windows overlooking the precipitous wilderness of the garden, Chelsey's small escritoire, bare apart from a telephone, coffee mug and appointments book. Chelsey watched. As before, Lucy did not seem to notice the cracks in the wall, or how big, naked and cold the room was. 'You don't have a television,' she said suddenly.

Chelsey did not. It would be too painful to see how many actresses weren't resting. 'I loathe television.'

'Oh. I'd want a TV, if I was here.'

Chelsey looked at Lucy in astonishment. Could it be that the dear girl was thinking of a new second home, should Gospel Oak prove less than satisfactory? 'I'd have one,' she said gaily, 'if anyone was around who wanted to watch it.'

'Oh,' said Lucy again, 'that's good.' Then her glance darted back to her hands. 'Chelsey, have you ever been in love? Agonisingly in love? A bad love, the kind that eats you up like a cancer?'

Chelsey smiled. 'I guess not: I'm still here.'

'Lorraine said it was like that with you and Georgiana.'

'Was it? It was awfully long ago.'

'Yes, Lorraine's always shooting her mouth off. Chelsey, can I say this to you?' Dropping her head, Lucy continued: 'Something scary is happening to us – I mean us three in The Situation. We're all mad about each other – maybe even more than at the beginning, but we don't seem to be settling. Somebody's always having a turn. We're sort of chained by each other, and chained to each other.'

Chelsey didn't laugh. She looked long at the ceiling, then said, thoughtfully: 'Be careful of Lorraine. She's a weak woman with strong emotions. I suspect a violent streak, even if she isn't herself aware of it.' Then, after noting Lucy's knowing nods, she added, 'And be careful of Fiona.'

'Why?'

'Well. Many reasons.' Chelsey thought for a while. Fiona was loved by Georgiana. Fiona was about to be betrayed by Chelsey. Fiona was a goddess, utterly without scruples, and dangerous when crossed, as the gods were. But this was not something for the ears of a poor deluded child. 'Mainly for the wrong you thought you were doing me: Fiona may be using you.'

'I don't see it,' cried Lucy. 'Fiona loves me. She said so.'

Chelsey was careful. 'I hope she does. I hope she loves you better than all the others she's said that to.'

'What others?'

'Haven't you asked?'

'I never thought of it. Or of telling her about mine. Odd that. I guess with her I always felt like the only one – apart from Lorraine, of course.'

'Well, I won't tell you. We were all very loose, and very young, once.'

'Yes, don't tell me,' added Lucy hastily, 'it isn't important. We can all do sex with anyone we like, so long as we're honest, and tell each other.'

Chelsey gave Lucy a close look, trying to determine if Lucy had told Fiona about the afternoon spent so very recently on this very settee. She could read nothing from Lucy's profile, but did get a sense that this girl was subtle enough to have won points whether she told or not. The spirits, however, were of the opinion that Lucy had, for once, been afraid to tell – about her little indiscretion and likewise about the lost purse – and if they were right, it was all to the good.

Chelsey topped up the drinks – Lucy's was barely touched – and, as Lucy's hand reached towards the glass, to within an inch of her own, Chelsey's heart, bruised and raw from the morning's encounter with Georgiana, thudded against her ribs. Chelsey shot to her feet. What on earth was happening to her? Chelsey was deep in a plot against Lucy, yet the words had flown into her head, almost into her mouth, to say that Lucy could be what she wanted to be – an honest person – with Chelsey, but could only be a scarlet woman in the Fiona ménage. An honest person! Protected by Chelsey the hired assassin?

Chelsey took herself firmly in hand. She marched over to the curtains, drew them close and said: 'Honesty should be in your life, never in your mouth.'

Lucy seemed impressed. 'I think *you* are honest. I respect you for that.'

Chelsey laughed as she returned to her seat beside Lucy. 'Do you? I'm touched. I am the most deceitful person you're ever likely to meet. But then,' she added, smiling easily, 'I do know that my lies are lies, some of the time.'

Lucy laid an uncertain hand on her arm and said, 'Do you think I'm honest, Chelsey? I used to be so sure I was. Now I just don't know.'

Chelsey still smiling, shook her head. 'I think you are deep and profoundly devious by nature, my dear. I don't think you are honest at all.'

'What am I?'

'Opportunistic,' said Chelsey. 'You'll make off with whatever you can out of this business.'

Lucy didn't reply for a moment. Then, shifting to face Chelsey, she said: 'Thank you. That's what I was afraid of.'

'It's nothing to *fear*, for heaven's sake. It's self-preservation. It's a natural virtue, even if it didn't make it into the Ten Commandments.'

Chelsey knew what was going to happen next: and it did. Lucy wrapped Chelsey's hand in both of hers and, with the ardent gaucheness of an adolescent, kissed it. Chelsey loved chivalrous attentions; she associated them with the delicious utterly safe flirtations of a Noël Coward world. But the touch of Lucy's ice-cold hands had quite a different effect. This sweet, naïve, incongruous gesture sent her blood roaring, and for the second time that day, she could feel tears pricking painfully at the back of her eyes.

She withdrew her hand coolly, but could not deny that this curiously unformed and far from elegant person was becoming important to her in a way that was not entirely comfortable. They sat for a moment in silence. Lucy was thinking whatever she was thinking, and Chelsey made an effort to concentrate on strategy. Whatever was to come, it was vital that she played her game very carefully. Lucy would be a slippery little fish no matter what you wanted to catch her for. Chelsey had known defeat too often to believe she could get someone already on Fiona's hook but – for once in her life – there were signs that her luck was turning. 'Apropos of this openness you set such store by,' she said dryly, 'do you want to have another try at forcing Georgiana to apologise? We could get Midge to take you to the December party.'

Lucy grinned. 'I don't need Midge. I've been invited, by Georgiana herself. So I'm going with both of them, unless they chicken out. Isn't that the oddest thing? In ourselves, we're getting nowhere, but Georgiana's crowd seems to take us for a threesome.'

Georgiana had evidently wasted no time in setting the scene. 'Excellent,' said Chelsey. 'You're forcing Georgiana to accept you. That must cause her more than sufficient humiliation.'

Lucy seemed inclined to linger, but Chelsey was too wise to tempt the girl into another indiscretion. When the church bells at the top of the hill chimed seven, she sent her back to Gospel Oak, having extracted a promise that Lucy would, in any time of need, come direct to Frognal.

For an hour after, she paced up and down her living room, arms clenching and unclenching around her ribs. From time to time, she picked up Lucy's still half-full glass and ran her finger over the faint imprint, in tomato juice, of Lucy's lips. Occasionally she laughed out loud – at herself, the great fool. Chelsey had always believed that if she fell for anyone, it would be someone with a great deal of money, twice as much class and a very powerful position. And what little runt was creeping under her skin? She was, by this time, longing to consult the Tarot. But she didn't. The spirits could be mischievous, especially if you were in real need. And so she paced in a futile effort to still the agitation in her breasts and belly, for she also, terribly, wanted Lucy in her arms.

Part III

26

Saturday, 9 December, Georgiana's party

The December party was an issue. It had been for years. Georgiana had no patience with issues, which were not, of course, to be confused with problems. A problem was that species of difficulty amenable to resolution by a magnificent win on the horses, or the death of one's estranged spouse 29 days after inheriting from a stinking rich aunt.

But struggle with an issue led only to yet another 'on the other hand'. Issues would ultimately dissolve; like life, slow attrition would dim and then extinguish them. In a few years, the December party would cease to have this tiresome aspect, because Georgiana's parties would have passed into the landscape of memory. A few years more, and there would be no memories to hold them.

But in the here and now, the December party issue was an issue – a vexation. It was held a fortnight early to avoid the horror of Christmas. But Christmas was leaching through the calendar. From the time of the October party until New Year, those loathsome creatures, children, took to the streets in a state of madness. The week after that party, they turned ghouls and witches clamouring for treats, threatening tricks. A week later, leaping out from behind straw men, they demanded pennies but expected florins. By December, they had swelled to a vast pushing, shoving, screaming rabble, and Georgiana would venture out only in the case of dire necessity. This day, the innocent ninth, presented such a case. For the sake of two ounces of parsley, Georgiana had to cover her ears against the piercing sirens of computer toys, and then hack her way through a forest of firs at the greengrocer.

Even in her own drawing room she would not be safe. Tonight, Sarah and Sophie would be importuning everyone to sing carols for the benefit of some decrepit hospice; Tim and Thelma would be speculating about whether their offspring would spend the dreaded day *en famille*, and Toby, having already endured half a dozen embassy receptions in addition to the attentions of Tommy, would be preoccupied by a serious dialogue with his liver. In December, Georgiana's people didn't pay attention.

Second, at the December party, things were out of balance. September, too, was awkward, since August was partyless, being the month for Biarritz (long unvisited in the flesh but still preserved in Georgiana's diary). But September had consolations. Everyone met with pleasure, to exhibit their suntans and examine their friends' new wrinkles. The December party came round too soon, gave too little ease of forgetfulness. There was a staleness to things.

Third – and this was personal to Georgiana – early December was when her bank account swelled with the annuity which her former husband had neglected to cancel. She feared the day on which the money was due in case it didn't arrive; equally, she feared that it wouldn't stretch to the overdue bills that awaited it. This year, it had arrived punctually, and increased by 3.25 per cent – a mysterious sum to Georgiana who knew from billboards that investments were supposed to increase in multiples of themselves – but none the less necessary. Georgiana would not have gone so far as to call it welcome: its presence filled her in equal parts with relief and an awful sense of frailty.

Consequently, each year the Tempter whispered about the

relief of cancelling the December party. Each year, Georgiana steeled herself. Any one break with tradition – even in 1989, the year of so many endings in the wilderness outside of Georgiana's domain – would threaten the order of the universe.

So everything seemed perfectly normal as Georgiana telephoned her orders of vol-au-vents and angels on horseback, and was rung by the cellarman at Davy's of St James's, to arrange the delivery of wine ordered by the Hon. Toby Hume. She damped the creases out of her silver lamé top, and threaded a line of sequins around the surviving rhinestones on her chignon clip. She narrowed the waist of her long black skirt (having, alas, lost yet more weight). She switched on the hot water at 4 p.m. in preparation for her bath at 5, and reminded herself to turn on the heating at 6.

In fact, she did these things with notable despatch, because the little *entr'acte* planned for tonight's party filled her with formidable energy.

Although a party, even in its enfeebled December version, was an end in itself, Georgiana had no scruples about the propriety of using this one to expose the beast in sheep's clothing. Georgiana would sacrifice anything – even her own most precious creation – for Fiona. With vigour, her hair wrapped in a scarf in deference to the Mrs Mop she could not afford, Georgiana dusted the little parchment-shaded lamps before her windows, each swipe of her cloth inferring a sharp 'take that!'

In Kilburn, preparations began almost as early as in St John's Wood. Within minutes of awakening from her afternoon nap – somewhat extended by a miscalculation over her lunch-time allowance of Red Stripes – Midge began to panic. Her blue silk shirt was inexplicably buttonless and all her smart clothes, which had remained on the floor since the furious preparations for Lucy's visit, smelled of doggy anal glands. Unwisely, Midge washed the least doggy of these outfits – her Tyrolean trousers and their poppy-embroidered braces – but no amount of wringing out and rearranging over the bath could bring

them to a wearable state of dampness. So, in desperation, she
rifled her father's wardrobe, emerging with a tailed morning
coat and striped trousers. A dozen safety pins took care of the
surplus lengths of leg and arm, but nothing could counter the
overall effect – of the cock sparrow in a pantomime.

Midge would have found it a relief to phone Georgiana,
pleading a cold or a broken leg, but Chelsey had told her that
Lucy was coming, and Lucy would need a champion. Midge
donned the outfit, reducing the overly formal look as best she
could by adding a yellow-spotted floppy bow tie. As she
clipped this to her throat, Midge solemnly warned Raffles
that her mistress's clockwork was unwinding, and only a
loving hand with fingers (unfortunately not provided to dogs)
could re-coil the spring.

Chelsey began her preparations at around the time that
Midge, dressed but full of doubt, was contemplating steadying
her nerves with a small advance on her evening allowance of
Safeways Blended. Chelsey too paid close attention to her
costume. She put on her long chiffon gown in the most subtle
shade of eau de nil. Her hair fell gracefully about her half-bare
shoulders but, wisely choosing not to reveal too much throat
or collar-bone, she looped an Isadora Duncan scarf around
her neck, allowing its trailing ends to offer subtle glimpses of
the deep *décolletage*. Momentarily, she regretted the lack of
her Givenchy III scent, but perhaps the jasmine cologne she
used instead was more appropriate: its oriental ambience
would enhance the effect of the long velvet cape, patterned
fortuitously with moon and stars, which she would wear into
the room, and throw off at the appropriate moment. Dressed
and ready, she rehearsed her gestures before the mirrors,
noting with pleasure the billowing of skirts as she stepped to
and fro, the delicate tumble of sleeves as she raised in her
hands, high as a priest raised the Host, a small purse of fine
silver mesh.

Chelsey looked wonderful. This made it the more difficult
to counter the wicked little demon that had so blinded her

judgement that a duffel coat too seemed an object of beauty. She tried not to think of the famous medium's prediction, or to ask herself if Lucy's swift and fleeting gestures approximated to the flight of a sycamore seed. But the wicked spirit tricked her into parading her costume before the empty seat of the settee, and put into her mouth the ridiculous words: 'Try to believe, my darling, that I have something to offer.'

Chelsey knew her spirits. So she rounded on the seat, and added fiercely: 'Or don't, since I definitely do not have anything to offer. It's all the same to me.'

Anyway, Chelsey abhorred coupledom and would never become one half of one of those double-headed garden gnomes. Sarah-Sophie, Tim and Thelma, Ulric and Steven-John had done it, and exchanged what might have been souls for this mess of pottage. Even Toby was joining in the game. Surely these poor fools could look on Fiona and Lorraine, and see what horrors lay ahead. Out of nowhere, the touch of Lucy's hands enclosing her own shivered through Chelsey's memory. Whatever – if anything (but surely nothing) – was in store, Chelsey told that wicked spirit, with real ferocity, that she and Lucy would never, ever, become a couple. They would never use the word 'we', never make each other's tea, and never be in the same group at a party.

Anyway, Chelsey would doubtless never have to deal with such problems: the spirits sported with her, but were not and had never been her friends. Nor was anybody else. Chelsey was preparing to fight, whether or not in a field of stricken and headless angels, and she would rely only on her wits.

None the less, out of habit – and in slight irritation – she telephoned Steven-John, just in case the boy had once again been restored to Toby's favour and gleaned snippets of the machinations of Toby and Georgiana.

Steven-John had nothing to tell. For once allowing himself to be advised by Ulric, he had not even telephoned Toby.

Steven-John put down the phone and returned immediately to his interrupted talk with Ulric, which had an edge of matrimonial tartness about it, as if the process of discussion was providing its own answer.

'It is nobody's business but ours, Steven-John.' Ulric's voice boomed from the bathroom, where he was lining the floor with newspaper and topping up a water bowl. 'This is my settled view. There is nothing further to discuss.' Grandly, he returned to the bedroom, and squared up to Steven-John, who was squatting on the petit-point footstool.

'Okay,' said Steven-John.

'Humph,' replied Ulric. Then, his face softening, he scooped the wriggling blond bundle of a retriever puppy out of Steven-John's lap and kissed its wrinkled forehead and floppy ears. 'The matter is now closed.' Firmly, he shut the beast into the bathroom.

'But then, Ulric,' said Steven-John thoughtfully, 'marriage is a public thing. Friends have a part in it. And the marriage bond is respected. Don't you want that?'

'There's no point in wanting,' wailed Ulric, 'nobody will respect a marriage between you and me.'

'We don't have to tell them everything. They don't need to know we don't have sex. Sex isn't obligatory in marriage.'

'Steven-John! If you dare mention that word!'

Steven-John giggled. 'Promise. Even when Chelsey grills me.'

'Chelsey! Oh my God.' Ulric, in a Steven-Johnish gesture, covered his face with his hands. 'If you're going to talk to Chelsey, I'm going to plead a headache.'

'No headaches, earaches, anyaches. From now on, you're going to be well, so well, and we'll both be so happy.' Steven-John wrapped his arms about the great barrel of Ulric's ribs.

Ulric made one last stand. 'Stevie, they'll mock and scorn; they'll call us unnatural; they'll think we're perverts.'

'I don't care what anyone thinks.' Steven-John looked up through ruffled brows. 'I'm just so terrifically proud to belong to you.' The puppy began to whine and scratch at the door. 'To you and to our little Jonquil.'

Ulric laid his open hands on Steven-John's head, and

sprightly curls popped up between his fingers. 'How can I refuse this boy anything,' he intoned, 'when for all the tosh that pours out of his mouth, my senses are reeling from his utterly delicious coconut-scented hair oil? Oh, well, I suppose we could just about bear to have them at the ceremony. Even – oh my God – Chelsey.'

Then he pulled back from Steven-John's embrace. 'Are you quite sure Jonquil will survive three or four hours on her own? Shall I put out the green rabbit; you know she's bitten the squeak out of the frog?'

At Gospel Oak, preparations for the party were delayed by a quarrel. Nobody wanted to go. Everybody knew they had to go. They dressed hurriedly – Lorraine plucking something from the heap on the bathroom floor – and in silence.

At eight on the dot, Martina arrived, followed, of course, by Hugo. So far, things were absolutely as they should be. Hugo opened the door to Sarah and Sophie. They, aggrandised not only by vast winter coats and the usual wine, chocolates and flowers, but parcels suspiciously wrapped in crinkly paper, charged in like the mail train. Georgiana led them, with a mincing step, to deposit their luggage – encumbrances beyond the scale of her lobby – in the bedroom, and returned immediately to the kitchen to struggle with a cork. Seconds later, hearing Hugo exclaim, she peered out. Sarah and Sophie had re-emerged, bright as glow-worms in satin shirts (Sophie's ruby-red, Sarah's nativity-midnight blue), and the quiet of the drawing room yielded to excited chatter about nothing in particular.

Tim and Thelma arrived next, the first of the nine o'clock rush. They, with more sense of their dignity, had left their outer layers downstairs with the concierge, but Tim wore a sprig of mistletoe in his buttonhole, which he exposed to Hugo with a truly dirty-raincoat titter.

Allowing Sarah to take the wine tray, Georgiana joined Hugo in greeting Ulric and Steven-John. Chelsey followed.

Georgiana embraced her fiercely. 'Relax,' muttered Chelsey into her ear, 'it's all under control. Your purse is right here, on a chain round my neck.'

So far, so good. Chelsey didn't linger at her side, and Georgiana turned to watch Sarah's progress. Yes, so far, all was well: Sarah could be trusted to keep everybody's glass filled to the brim.

Midge had meanwhile slipped in unannounced, and made her way to the kitchen to help. Georgiana followed. Noting the eccentricity of Midge's garb and the puffiness of her face, she set her to doing something about the flowers, at the sink and out of range of the wine. The clatter of voices from the drawing room was enthusiastic but indistinct and a little nervous, quite as it should be at this stage. Only Ulric's voice sounded like itself as the words came to her, rich and strong: 'No, I really won't have more wine just now, thank you.' Then, in response to some indistinct mumble, doubtless from Hugo, continued, 'Oh, recovering wonderfully from a bothersome staphylococcal infection, though working too hard, as usual.'

Steven-John's gravelly rumble was more than usually clear as he added: 'I've been working too. I'm learning to read music. Ulric's agent has him booked for a massive concert next year, and I'm going to be allowed to turn the pages when he practises.'

Chelsey, standing now at the windows, called out: 'He can turn them himself, Steven-John. He holds his instrument in his throat, not his hands.'

'Well actually,' Steven-John blushed, 'I'd really like to accompany Ulric – I'm also learning to play the guitar, but –'

'– as it happens, in practice I accompany myself,' Ulric cast a fierce look in Chelsey's direction, 'on the piano. I've chosen a selection of Beethoven pieces and need help with turning the pages.'

'They're great songs, you know, Chelsey. There's one called *"Questa tomba"* – about the spirit world – that's as good as the Song of the Volga Boatmen.'

'Wonderful.' Chelsey pulled her cloak tighter about her. How absolutely typical of Steven-John to waken her demons with a brutally tactless reference to Ulric's 'massive concert'. 'Do put me down for the opening night.'

Her old bitterness rising with its familiar bilious tang, Chelsey noted that Ulric and Steven-John were burying themselves in a slush of coupledom as thick as Sarah-Sophie's. Chelsey had a particularly strong aversion to couples that evening. She turned to the window, and wiped a peephole out into the night.

Outside it was beginning to snow. She suddenly, desperately, wanted to be able to say: 'Oh, Lucy, look: it's snowing.' This was ridiculous; Chelsey didn't even like snow, while Lucy and her two lovers, running notably late, might well be in it right now, pelting each other with snowballs. Chelsey bit her lip. 'I say,' she called out to nobody in particular, 'there's something queer going on.' Steven-John and a few of his acolytes came to her side. 'What do you make of that?'

'Ah, the first fall,' said Steven-John with feeling. 'Every year it's like something you've never seen before.'

Ulric drew up beside him. 'Yes, strange,' he said, 'no other inanimate force – not rain, sun, wind, running water – expresses itself with that light and surprised touch, like fingering a harp.'

Chelsey glanced sharply at Ulric. Coupledom was doing something peculiar to his brain.

'Not inanimate, Ulric. Snow is alive. All the earth is alive.'

Chelsey's glance swung round to Steven-John's radiant face. 'Not for long it won't be,' she said. 'The fingers on your harp will have tightened round a few green throats before morning.'

As she spoke, a taxi materialised out of the night and sloshed to a halt below them.

Out stepped Fiona, her hair and camel coat bleached by the light from the porch, an aureole of white flakes hanging in the air about her. Lucy scuttled after, took Fiona's hand, and the two of them darted under cover and out of sight. Lorraine, shoulders hunched and stamping her feet, hovered in consultation with the cabbie, then stood to watch the vehicle slide and slither up the drive and into the night. She too entered the building, and their footprints slowly widened into slushy black holes.

'I think, Stevie,' said Chelsey *sotto voce*, 'that your earth has a mind for slaughter tonight.'

Steven-John fixed Chelsey with a look. 'I won't let anyone get hurt,' he said manfully.

Midge, at the sink, was elbow-deep in flowers, while pelted by anxieties that felt more like hail than snow. Standing there with her back to Georgiana, she had been so discomforted by the tails of her coat that she planned (at an appropriate moment when Georgiana's attention was diverted) to chop them off with the kitchen shears. In the meantime, she had pulled them up tight between her legs. Consequently, when Sarah and Sophie came in, she was unable to turn to greet them, her front view being quite unpresentable. They hadn't spoken to her. Midge, at first relieved, soon found this troubling. Were they angry with her? Had they taken her for the servant? Then they all went out, though Georgiana hadn't finished giving Midge her instructions.

Midge straightened up and viewed the matter sensibly. Surely she was glad to be left in peace for a few minutes? Hadn't she rather been wishing that Georgiana would let her make her own decisions about how many quarter-inches to snip off the ends of the stems? Shouldn't she be grateful that Georgiana had tactfully protected her from an encounter with those two inquisitive women? As these thoughts progressed, an unpleasant lump formed in Midge's stomach.

While endeavouring to ease this with a few forced burps, Midge returned to the flowers – everybody seemed to have brought flowers – which she'd laid out on the draining board around Georgiana's three large vases. There were roses with stems a yard long and straight as rulers, chrysanthemums the size of sunflowers, lilies that reminded her of the crucifixion, and a little spray of freesias, which she knew instinctively came from Steven-John. First she grouped them by colour, next by size, but found both arrangements too mechanical. So she began to stuff them in randomly, until each vase was packed. In the crush, one of the freesia stems broke, and Midge was left with a few drooping buds in her hand. She stroked the velvety petals. How lovely it was; how brave to issue such a rich scent when its neck was broken. A spasm of grief for the freesia took Midge, and tears flowed. Her burps turned into heaving sobs and then into hiccups.

Midge absolutely *had* to be on form that evening. Lucy must not again be allowed again to see Midge disgrace herself. More important, Lucy would be in need of protection. Midge had come to this party to fight. She needed strength. Lucy needed her strength. It was necessary for Midge to stiffen herself with one small drink. Neat as a thief, she reached up to the overhead cupboard and extracted the cooking brandy.

The lift clattered to a halt six inches above the level of the first floor and Lorraine yanked at the handles of the metal gates. Lucy hung back. 'Just brazen it out,' Fiona whispered hoarsely to her, 'to Georgiana, nothing ever happened between you, so you play it the same, okay?'

'Okay,' replied Lucy palely. They approached the door, and it opened wide.

'Darlings!' Georgiana, her once-famous smile spread from ear to ear, swooped on them. 'Darlings, you've brought the snow and – how delightful –' she stepped back and opened her arms wide '– you've brought the Snow Fairy.' Lucy shuddered as long fingers dug into her shoulders and Georgiana's jawbone collided with her temple.

Georgiana appeared not to notice. One hand still trailing over Lucy's shoulder, she stroked Fiona's cheek with the other. 'There are flakes in your hair, my love.'

Fiona's face, till then set hard, instantly melted. Georgiana took Fiona in her arms. The two women clung tight for a full minute, while Lorraine, with a grin printed across her mouth, took the duffel coat, shook it outside the door and hung it in the lobby.

Lucy fled into the room, her eyes darting to avoid curious glances, and edged her way towards the windows, in search of Chelsey. *En route*, she was captured by Sarah, who was dashing from group to group, having taken possession of Tim's mistletoe. 'We haven't formally met, but you're quite a celebrity after the last party,' said Sarah gaily. 'Welcome, little one, to the World of the Dead.' Lucy's grim face was engulfed by an avalanche of nativity-midnight blue.

'Good evening, friends.' Toby stood in the still-open doorway.

Georgiana released Fiona and grasped him warmly by the hand.

'Toby!' shrilled Sophie from across the room. 'So early!'

Toby stepped aside, and a most amazingly handsome man appeared beside him. 'This is –'

'– Tong Wi Li,' said Tommy, clipping his heels lightly together and giving a deep bow. As he bent forward, his gleaming hair surged over his brows; as he righted himself, it fell back, every hair in place. His smiling eyes ran easily over the assembly; he turned to take in the room from one end to the other, presenting a honed jaw, cheeks creased in a muscular smile, and a superbly sculpted head on very proud shoulders. The two men were of similar stature, but Tommy, younger, deeper-chested and glowing with health, looked the more substantial.

Chelsey, observing from the windows end, was satisfied. The spirits had drawn a near-perfect portrait of Tommy – though, for herself, she would have preferred somewhat more of the look of the inscrutable oriental. Equally pleasing was the shocked silence that now possessed the room: not only was that most confirmed of bachelors accompanied, but Georgiana appeared to welcome a stranger at her party. And most pleasing of all was the flash of something dangerous in Tommy's eyes as they passed lightly over the small figure half swamped by a blue satin shirt.

But joy, for Chelsey, was always brief. Between Toby and Tommy, standing formally but easily side-by-side, without touching, without gestures of any kind, ran an electrical charge that, even at this distance, she could feel. How perfect, complete, invulnerable, how arrogant these princes were.

Chelsey watched closely as Georgiana led the gorgeous Tommy into the room and surprisingly – suggesting perhaps a touch of nervousness – presented him first to Tim and Thelma.

Fiona and Lorraine were left, awkward as strangers, together at the door. Their eyes avoided each other and Lucy's desperate glances.

'Is it always so loud?' muttered Lorraine. 'It has the blare of a foxhunt.' She glanced round. 'And it looks like something painted by Goya.'

'You're talking about your friends.' Fiona's glance measured the distance to the nearest unattached glass of wine.

'Your friends, not mine.'

'Who are your friends in that case?'

Lorraine shrugged. 'I had a friend once. I thought she was all I needed.'

Fiona turned away. 'If I have to listen to you, I'd rather hear you talking to these people who are not your friends. There must be someone you can impress with your adventures in Malawi.'

'You don't have to listen to me at all. I can go home now.'

Fiona raised her eyes to the ceiling.

'But I don't expect I will leave just yet. I don't want to miss your couple act with Lucy.'

'Ah, Hong Kong. Good show,' said Tim bullishly. 'I'm in management training myself. We much admire what you chaps are doing over there.'

'We do well.' Tommy gave a nod of acknowledgement. 'We benefit from a century of British training.'

'In skills we British are rapidly losing,' added Tim.

'We have the advantage of a little fear for the future,' Tommy raised one perfectly shaped eyebrow, suggesting the far distance, perhaps China. 'It concentrates the mind wonderfully.'

Chelsey was delighted. This man was at least as clever as he was beautiful.

Thelma delicately smoothed down her skirt, stretched close over belly and thighs, before she extended a wrist to Tommy. 'Such a pleasure.'

Tommy, without a second's hesitation, brushed his lips against the multiple stones on Thelma's fingers.

'I say, Mr Tong, may I call you Tommy? Steven-John appeared at Tommy's elbow. Can you tell me about traditional Chinese herbs?'

Tommy's eyes glazed. 'Not a subject within my range.'

Steven-John pressed his point. 'Isn't there a special herb, or perhaps it's a flower, traditionally used for weddings?'

'Thinking of rhinoceros horn?' quipped Tim.

Steven-John blushed furiously. 'No.' He gestured to Ulric, who rather stiffly drew nearer. 'You see,' he said awkwardly, 'Ulric and I are planning –' Steven-John's hand disappeared into Ulric's great paw '– actually, we've already made the booking, at the Metropolitan Community Church for a cere-mony, as a matter of fact it's a blessing ceremony, and I rather wondered if –'

Tim hooted with laughter. 'You're not saying you two are planning to get *married*?'

'So!' Ulric fixed him with a hard eye. 'People of the same gender have been known to make lifetime commitments.'

'But that's the point: you *aren't* –' Thelma was incoherent with mirth.

'That's it on the nail,' added Tim. 'Just drop that sex-change business, and we'll have the patter of little feet.'

'That would be wonderful,' interposed Ulric grandly, 'but, sadly, at fifty, I fear I am past childbearing.'

Steven-John, standing quietly, his hand engulfed in Ulric's, looked utterly crushed. He dared not mention the dog. By degrees, the laughter gave way to a general sense of embarrassment.

Then Tommy turned to Steven-John. 'I'm a policeman,' he said rather formally, 'so my knowledge of herbs is limited to certain varieties. But I will enquire about the wedding herb.' He made the gesture of a vestigial salute, 'And, please accept my congratulations.'

Toby, taking the cue, extended a hand to each of them. 'Health and happiness,' he said.

Steven-John turned on Toby eyes that were swelled with tears. Toby clapped him firmly on the shoulder. 'You're the best thing that's happened to Ulric in a very long time.'

'Oh Toby.' Steven-John fell into Toby's arms.

Over Steven-John's head, Toby and Ulric exchanged a long look. 'This is not the moment to discuss it,' Ulric said quietly, 'but nobody tells my boy to "bugger off".'

'Oh please.' Steven-John flew from Toby to Ulric, and his face was crushed against the great hoop of bone and muscle of Ulric's chest. 'Don't fight. I needed to be told. I was infiltrating. I do that sometimes.'

With the point of his index finger, Ulric raised Steven-John's face and looked gravely into it. Then he straightened and turned a similar inexpressive gaze on Toby. 'Happiness to you too. As for health – and time – we both now have reason to hope for better than is our due.'

Toby nodded. 'Tommy returns to Hong Kong in three weeks. That suits me. My planning tends to be short term.'

Chelsey turned away from this slushy scene with a sense of disappointment. But her hopes soon rose again for Georgiana and Fiona, Sophie, Martina and Lorraine, and, from the other side, Sarah (with Lucy still in her grip), converged on the group. The flutter of congratulations from the new arrivals drowned the stammering cover-up noises from Tim and Thelma.

'My word,' said Georgiana, 'in all this excitement, I'm forgetting my social duties: introductions.' Raising her voice, she called out, 'And wine, Midge dear.'

She touched Tommy's elbow. 'Now, we all know who Tommy is?' She glanced about, acknowledging the nods of confirmation. 'Well, Tommy, here we have: Fiona Douglas –' (Fiona inclined her head and Tommy responded with a bow) '– you've already met Tim and Thelma Broadbent, and Steven-John and Ulric have introduced themselves.' There were further nods all round. 'The glorious ruby glow is our good friend Sophie Clerides, and beside her Lorraine, um, Struthers.' Midge, tray clanking dangerously, tottered into the room. 'And Margaret Winters.' Sarah took possession of the tray, and hands reached forward for more wine.

As they raised their glasses, Sophie slipped an arm around Midge. 'You're looking a tidge stressed, Midgeling my dear,' she said softly. Midge made noises like someone with a chicken bone in her throat.

Chelsey, still at the window, debated joining the group. It would, at the least, increase her chances of getting some wine. But she remained where she was. A slight distance gave cleaner air and a wider perspective. And, when the appropriate moment came, it would strengthen the reverberation of her opening lines. The time might be soon: the crowd was gathered, and Georgiana had drawn herself up to her full height. Deftly, Chelsey unhooked the little silver purse from her neck-chain and tucked it into her palm. But she still didn't know what she would say, or even what she wanted to say.

'Now, let us continue,' said Georgiana. 'You've met Sophie. This is Sarah, this Martina, this Hugo.' She scanned the group. 'Over there, our Cassandra, Chelsey Chamberlain.' Chelsey opened her cloak and the chiffon skirts flared as she made a full curtsey.

'Now who have I left out? No, not Lorraine. Ah!' Georgiana reached out her hand, and with a firmness of wrist worthy of Madame Defarge, pulled Lucy out from the depths of the crowd. 'You must meet Fiona and Lorraine's little friend –' she gave Lucy's hand, firmly gripped in her own, a slight shake '– Lucy.'

Lucy, exposed like pig-in-the-middle, responded with a wan and distinctly nervous smile.

Tommy bowed low. 'Pleasure to meet you, Lucy.'

Lucy stared at her Doc Martens.

Georgiana's grip on Lucy's wrist did not loosen. 'Lucy is the new girl in school,' she said cheerfully, 'so tonight, I suppose, is her formal initiation.'

As Lucy mumbled: 'An honour, I'm sure,' and Fiona grinned broadly and Lorraine's brow puckered in doubt, Georgiana gestured to Chelsey to draw nearer.

'Though young Lucy has, in a sense, initiated me,' she continued with a charming smile. 'At our last party, Tommy dear, Lucy crowned me queen – Persephone, no less, the Queen of the Dead.'

Fiona's head jerked. 'Georgie! Don't.'

'You misunderstand me. Persephone is also the Queen of the Earth, the rain, the crops – the goddess of fertility. Isn't that what you meant –' she gave Lucy's hand a shake '– my child?'

Lucy blushed furiously. 'Um, a great queen, yes. No, sorry; I've never heard of her.'

A titter of unease ran through the group.

'Well, dear, it is Persephone who sets the deer to rutting; it's she who spins the merry-go-round among friends like ourselves.'

'In that case,' interjected Toby, 'you, Queen and Goddess, gave Steven-John to Ulric, and our friend here to Fiona and Lorraine.'

Lorraine, in a clearly audible aside, hissed at Toby: 'What's this about?'

'About you, *inter alia*, Miss Struthers.' Toby's voice was arch, but he dusted himself down as if he'd been spat on.

'In that case –' Lorraine raised her voice '– if there's anything you want to say about me, or Lucy, cut the innuendo and come out with it.'

Chelsey released the deep breath she'd been holding since Toby's first words. Lorraine, being Lorraine, was interfering with the script. Despite another sharp glance from Georgiana, Chelsey was curious to see how much damage Lorraine could cause, and didn't pick up her cue. But Georgiana, Lucy's hand still bound in her own, merely reached out with her other for a glass of wine, passed it to Lucy with a beatific smile, and waited for Lorraine's squib to burn itself out.

But Lorraine wasn't through with her meddling. 'Perhaps we'd best give you a moment to think about it. Come, Lucy.' Pulling Lucy from Georgiana, she marched her into the kitchen, and shoved the door to with a thump that reverberated through the room, rattling the windows and tinkling the chandelier.

'Well, well,' said Toby, as the echoes died away, 'your friends seem a little sensitive tonight, Fifi darling. You must be feeling rather shaken.' Deftly, he took Fiona's glass out of her hand and exchanged it for a full one from the tray still held by Sarah. 'Shame! All poor Georgie wanted to do was to present a gift to the girl, to show no hard feelings.'

'The night is still young,' said Georgiana gently, planting a little kiss on Fiona's puzzled brow. 'Tommy dear, do tell us about jewellery fraud in high places. Start with the Romanov treasures.'

'Jewellery,' began Tommy with a small bow, 'is one of the oldest and most powerful currencies of corruption, although narcotics are now the American dollar of international crime . . .'

Chelsey smiled. Fiona had now been isolated, so full points to Toby on that. But, as far as the moral high ground was concerned, Round One, she thought, went to Lorraine – though there would doubtless be a different outcome when Lorraine next faced Toby over his desk at the Foreign Office. But Lorraine, she well knew, was past caring.

Lorraine drew Lucy into the centre of the kitchen with a grip like rope burn. 'Bullies, fascists; I hate them,' she muttered.

'You didn't have to rescue me.' Lucy's face and ears were hot red. 'I knew it was some horrible game, but I can handle being trussed up by Georgiana; I wanted to see it through.'

'You don't *know* them, Lucy. You don't know how they enjoy cruelty. This is a game, to pluck a live chicken – you.'

'You don't know what the game is.'

'No.' Lorraine didn't know. But she could smell a plot. She could also sense that Fiona suspected something, but willed herself to believe that the game was well intended – that all the horror of the last party would just cease to be when Georgiana, like a conjuror, flicked it away. She could sense, too, Lucy's excitement at the prospect of a fight. Lucy knew how to fight, and to fight dirty. And Lorraine knew well that Lucy's squeals of pain were, to Fiona, a mating call. 'You think you can ingratiate yourself with Georgiana's crowd,' she said bitterly. 'That's a laugh! I haven't been able to do it in ten years.'

'Lorraine,' said Lucy in a low, studied voice, 'this is between me and Georgiana. It doesn't concern you. Let me go.'

Lorraine released her, but placed herself squarely between Lucy and the door.

'Lorraine, be careful. This is Georgiana's flat – no place for you to have one of your turns.'

The now so familiar gush of anger swept Lorraine, leaving her breathless. She struggled for control. She breathed deeply. She picked up bottles and put them down. She pulled at her hair. She turned on her heel, then turned back to Lucy. Lucy held her with a look of weary reprimand. Anger came in another rush, and Lorraine let it take her. 'All right,' she hissed, 'go to them. Run to them, with your tongue hanging out. Crawl, lapdog. Have them all – Georgiana, Toby Hume, Fiona. Have them; have the bloody lot.'

'Lorraine, please try to listen. I'm not taking anyone away from you. I'm trying to get us accepted as a threesome. Please trust me.'

'You?' Lorraine's voice squeaked, then broke out in a roar: 'I'd rather trust the devil.' And, as had been happening with increasing frequency, and now seemed to happen of itself, Lorraine threw herself at Lucy, both hands extended to push at her shoulders. But this time, Lucy was not the one to topple. She stuck out her fist and it caught Lorraine full in the stomach. Lorraine crashed to the floor like a shot elephant, and the table, with all its winebottles, went flying.

The door flew open and Midge barged in, yelling, 'I'll protect you, Lucy!' Through the wide-open door beyond, a sea of faces stared.

Only Sophie followed Midge. She knelt over Lorraine, touched her forehead and wrist. 'Winded.' Rising to her feet, she looked hard at Lucy. 'Did you hit her?'

'No, she didn't,' croaked Lorraine, *I* hit *her*.'

Toby peered over Tommy's shoulder. 'With a boomerang, Miss Struthers?'

Georgiana put her arm around Fiona and turned her away from the distressing scene. Fiona, eyes blank as the victim of a car accident, allowed herself to be led. Sophie gave Lorraine some water, helped her to her feet, and by degrees they all drifted away from the wreckage of the kitchen. Lucy, ignored, hovered at the edge of the circle.

'Well, my dears,' said Georgiana, 'no hope now of any more wine, so I suppose, as we still have dregs in our glasses for one small toast, I'd better speed things up. Chelsey has something for young Lucy.' She nodded in Lucy's direction, then turned to Chelsey. 'Chelsey? Chelsey, do get *on* with it!'

'But take care,' added Toby, 'not to step too close.'

The circle widened as Chelsey moved slowly forward, extended her arm in Lucy's direction, turned her hand palm upwards, and opened her fingers. Crushed, and shiny with body heat and sweat, the little purse lay exposed.

'Oh, God.' Fiona started. 'My purse. Thank God. It's safe.'

Chelsey tensed her mouth and said nothing.

Fiona took the purse from Chelsey's hand and pressed it to her lips. Her eyes were full. 'Chelsey, thank you, thank you.'

'Chelsey got it,' said Georgiana calmly, 'from a common little thief, your trollop, the street-girl who punched Lorraine in the stomach.'

The purse was crushed small in Fiona's hand as, mouth wide, she stared at Georgiana, at Chelsey, and then vaguely at everything. 'From – who?'

'From Lucy. Who stole it.' Georgiana raised a hand. 'Tommy!' Tommy stepped smartly to her side. 'Tommy, value this, will you?'

Solemnly, Tommy took the purse from Fiona, weighed it in his hand, probed the mesh, prised open the clasp, then, taking a magnifying glass from his pocket, examined the hallmark. The crowd watched every move. 'It's from the Ghent workshops,' he said, returning the purse to Fiona. 'The type is not uncommon, though this is a fine example. Say thirty guineas.'

Georgiana's expression darkened. 'How would the courts deal with this in Hong Kong?'

Tommy made a disclaiming gesture. 'Our sentencing policy is severe, so it could be a custodial sentence, perhaps two years in gaol.'

Fiona gasped. 'Please stop. Please, all of you. I can't bear this.'

Georgiana's hold on Fiona was gentle. 'Do you want to send her home, Fifi darling?'

'I don't know. Oh, let her go.'

They all turned to Lucy, who had backed away and was now hovering near the hall doorway, her fist pressed against her mouth. 'Perhaps, Georgie,' whispered Toby, 'first, we'd better check your teaspoons.'

'I'm going,' Lucy mumbled. She took a step, then stopped and stiffened. 'I did steal it, Fiona, but I didn't steal to steal.' Her mouth opened and closed, as if words were dying in her throat, before she continued: 'I wanted to have something of yours, something precious to you, to hold close to me. I would have given it back later. But I lost it. I searched everywhere. I didn't know it was valuable.'

'Aha!' cried Georgiana in triumph. 'A liar as well as a thief, as well as a brute who punches people in the stomach. We know how you "lost" it, my dear.'

'No, please leave her alone,' said Fiona palely. 'Lucy, oh

God, don't *tear* me like this.' Head low and hands pressing the sides of her head, Fiona whispered, 'Just let her go.'

'Not yet,' snapped Georgiana. 'Don't you want to know what Lucy did with this purse that was so precious to you? Jewellery is, as Tommy said, currency. Currency she used to purchase a new lover.'

Fiona's head shot up. She laughed, a harsh bark of utter disbelief.

Again Georgiana gestured, this time with real irritation, to Chelsey.

Chelsey couldn't understand herself. She'd had so many openings, and been so feeble. It couldn't be stage-fright; Chelsey had never been afflicted with that horror. Yet she had stood there like a nellie, waiting for the voice from the prompt box. Even now. Mouth open, she stared at Georgiana.

'Come on,' hissed Georgiana. 'Speak, you idiot!'

Chelsey flinched, as if Georgiana had struck her in the face. She could feel the slap, across her cheek; the slap Georgiana had given Lucy at the last party. Chelsey, Lucy: the dispossessed, the despised, rejected. Chelsey's mouth filled with bitterness warm and thick as venom, and she wanted to spit.

But Chelsey, every moment of her life, was a professional. She took a deep breath, positioned herself centrally before the blackened central window, its panes now running with slushy snow, and drew herself up. She waited till all eyes were on her. She threw off her cloak, and her long, gauzy robe filled out, and slowly settled. Then she spoke.

'Lucy didn't exactly give it to me,' she said with quiet and even emphasis, 'I took it out of her pocket.' Chelsey turned to look directly at Lucy. 'At the time, Lucy was on my settee, making passionate love to me.'

Lucy's face, till then spotted with bright scarlet, turned the colour of a snail's belly. Chelsey felt Lucy's pain as if in her own breast, and with it came a renewed shock of energy at the thought that she was teaching Lucy the true character of deceit.

As Fiona stood, mutely gasping like someone about to be sick, Chelsey's excitement mounted. After twenty-five years of suffering, her moment had come: this was her great performance. Spreading her hands gracefully, she surrendered to her role: 'Does it shock you so much, Fiona, to hear that Lucy has her little secrets? Haven't we all had our little secrets?' Chelsey paused, and her stare met one pair of eyes after another, but met them blindly, since she saw only a field of stricken and headless angels. 'Sarah? Have you forgotten Fiona? Tim, any recollection of pleasant times with Sophie? Sophie; do you remember Midge? And Midge, dear, who exactly – apart from our dear Ulric – have you *not* been to bed with? All forgotten? But it happened. Perhaps Lucy has learned something from you.'

Chelsey, at last, turned her gaze on Lucy, and Lucy, with a shudder, burst into tears.

'Will it shock you even more, my friends –' Chelsey's voice, still perfectly controlled, was rising in sonorous power '– to hear that someone actually *loves* Lucy, against whom you laid this cruel plot this evening; the woman so many of you have abused? Fiona, is this so hard for you to understand?'

Georgiana gave Chelsey a glare of pure revulsion. Chelsey smiled back.

'Get out, Chelsey,' Georgiana muttered, 'and take your thieving little tart with you.'

'Ah, Georgiana, how sad.' Chelsey allowed her smile to fade slowly into a soft glance of compassion. 'You've forgotten too. You've forgotten your time with me. Yet a few days ago, you were reminding me of it. That too was sad; it left me grieving. To be importuned by an old woman who was once beautiful, alas, brings a shiver, for flesh draped loose over bones, a *mons veneris* thinly sprinkled with cactus hairs. It has the taste of decay and I, poor Georgiana, am not yet ready to be embraced by the Queen of the Dead.'

As Chelsey let her voice die away into a thunderous silence, there came what felt like a rush of wind from the kitchen.

Midge flew in and shoved the bottle of cooking brandy up under Chelsey's nose. The back of her jacket was hacked to about the level of her waist, as if she'd had a close scrape with a mousetrap.

She hissed: 'Take this,' and sloshed brandy across Chelsey's face. 'Swallow. Swallow your evil words, every one.' Midge was very drunk.

Chelsey, still dazed by the amazing performance the spirits had scripted for her, wiped her face slowly with the trailing ends of her Isadora Duncan scarf, but didn't push Midge away. Midge's fist once more swung up towards her, this time to rub the little spray of freesias against her mouth. 'Swallow everything, destroy everything that's clean and innocent, even the *flowers*.' Then, staggering, she swung round, flung her arms around Georgiana and howled: 'We love you, Georgiana. We all *love* you.'

Midge might as well have thrown herself at a statue. Georgiana didn't even blink.

Chelsey wiped her mouth. She began to get the sense of what was happening. Well, she could have asked for a more dignified conclusion, but this was adequate. She waited until Midge's wailing had died away. Then, raising her head, she said: 'Lucy: do you wish to add anything –' then, with a boldness that left her shocked '– before we go home, to Frognal?'

Lucy, tears streaming, shook her head. Chelsey moved gracefully over to her side, and took her hand.

'Yes, I do,' said Lucy with a tremble, 'I'm sorry, Fiona. It is true. I am involved with Chelsey. We did sex only the once, but what happened between her and me was more than just sex.'

Fiona brushed at the air near her ear.

'Though I love you, Fiona, with my life.'

Fiona leaned towards Lucy and whispered, in a dry, grating voice: 'Goodbye. For ever.'

'No,' howled Midge, 'stop. You've hurt her enough already.'

Fiona ignored this. 'Go. You little rat.'

Chelsey squeezed Lucy's hand, to give her courage. It seemed to work. Lucy took a deep breath, and said, her voice still shaky, but hard edged with irony: 'Do you know, you've just used the exact words Georgiana used when she phoned me. Well, Georgiana's done it now. She's got rid of me. She had to do that, you know, Fiona, because she can dominate Lorraine, but she can't dominate me.'

Chelsey gently led Lucy towards the door.

Chelsey was satisfied. She added nothing further until they were in the final doorway. Then, throwing her cloak around her shoulders, she said: 'Remember this, Fiona: you couldn't love Lucy, because you didn't trust her. Not because she is not worthy of trust, but because you and Lorraine, poor souls, cannot trust each other.'

With a sob, Lucy made a dash for it, her Doc Martens clattering as she stumbled down the stairs.

Chelsey, waited for silence then said, bowing low, 'How brave you all were; what courage to take up arms against Lucy, with your army of twenty against one.'

'Two,' called Steven-John. 'You forget Midge.' But Chelsey had already quietly closed the door and was gone.

'Well,' said Toby, 'I suppose this one minute's silence is appropriate. We have, unpleasant though it may have been, had a successful exorcism. But now, my angels, we should celebrate. Stevie, run along and fetch the bottles in the far rack of my cellar. Careful not to shake them.'

There was a rumble of agreement, but conversation didn't flow. Sophie and Sarah did their best, breaking out into an unaccompanied rendition of 'Do they know it's Christmas?'

But Midge stayed where she was, huddled on the floor, now beating her fists against Toby's patent leather shoes. After an exchange of glances with Tommy, the two men gently raised Midge, and Toby took her like a child into his arms.

Midge did not resist. 'It's not only Chelsey,' she sobbed. 'You were all so cruel. How could you hurt Lucy so horribly?'

'Not all. You stood by her, Margaret,' said Tommy.

'I couldn't help her, or anyone. I can't help myself.'

Toby patted Midge on the back. 'We have nothing against Lucy personally,' he said. 'But we have to protect our friends. Remember, Midge dear, that we have nobody but each other.'

'But what about her? We've thrown her to that wicked Chelsey, poor Lucy, poor freesia with its neck broken.' Midge opened her hand. In it lay the remains of the little flower scooped up from the floor, crushed and trodden-on but still giving a rich scent. 'It's still alive,' she said suddenly. 'Somebody take it and make it better. Lorraine. Yes, Lorraine and Fiona. Let them take it.'

Toby, shaking his head at this new madness from Midge, rocked her, making soothing noises. Lorraine took the crumpled mess and solemnly arranged its stem and petals against her palm in the semblance of a living flower. Midge, hiccuping in Toby's arms, watched. The violence ebbed out of her and, tears still oozing, she clung to him. Gently, he tucked the ragged ends of her jacket into her trousers.

Fiona was by the door, fumbling indecisively for the camel-hair coat when she felt a familiar presence behind her. 'Want to go now, Fifi?' said the voice, once so familiar, now bodiless as an echo.

'You knew,' whispered Fiona, without turning, 'that she'd taken Georgiana's purse, didn't you?'

'I knew she was searching for it. I didn't know why.'

'And you knew she was carrying on with Chelsey?'

'It crossed my mind. She was spending a lot of time at Frognal.'

'God, I've been such a fool.'

'She wasn't cheating, Fifi. She loved you. She really loved you. It was the real thing. But it couldn't go anywhere, because you wouldn't abandon me.'

'"Abandon you?"' Fiona snorted. 'That was never an option.'

'I know, you told me. I'll try to believe it.'

'Yes, try.' Fiona's hand reached back and touched Lorraine's. It encountered something slimy. She started, and swung sharply to face her.

Lorraine looked down at her hand. 'Midge wants us to heal this thing; it is, or was, a flower.'

'Heal *that*?' Fiona laughed. 'No chance. Well, I dunno, Lorrie. I suppose we can give it a try.'

Steven-John was back, with the wine, within half an hour, thanks to his recently acquired expertise in hailing taxis. But the party was over. Fiona and Lorraine had left quietly. Several others followed them. Sarah and Sophie were still singing, as they swept up the mess in the kitchen, and Hugo, one cloth tucked into his belt and another in his hands, was drying glasses handed to him by Martina. Midge had passed out in a corner. Georgiana, Toby's arm about her waist, was standing at the elegant, long, but blackened windows of her drawing room, staring out into the night.

Epilogue:
Lucy

I saw them today. I was sitting in the park, with my sandwiches and the pigeons, and they walked by, like people do in a park. They didn't speak. Nor did I. I disintegrated.

Weird. It's been ten years, for heaven's sake, and I've moved on. But it could have been ten seconds. If it was ten centuries it wouldn't be different. What happened then is still happening.

There I was, not looking for anything except a quiet space in my day, and they came, straight out of a dream: three old women. First they were strangers somehow sickly familiar, then all at once they were *them*. I must have blanked out because I only knew it when they were almost gone.

Why does this bother me? Nobody could be afraid of them now. Bit by bit, I put it together. Lorraine was behind, heavier, but walking like she always did, as if her shoulders lifted her feet. She actually looked at me, and at the sandwiches in my lap. She could have been going to say something – 'Are you Lucy?' 'Go to hell', whatever. I remember the face, craggy, like an old lion, like someone who doesn't listen any more. But maybe she never did.

Georgiana passed the closest. She wasn't wearing that terrible old fox-fur, but whatever she was wearing came out of the same closet. She did speak. She was looking at the lake. She said: 'I have rather a fondness for the cormorants.' She had a skull for a face and was walking without a stick on legs like sticks, but her voice – my God – it hasn't changed; it went into me like a knife.

Then this woman she was leaning on turned, and her look, out of those big vague wet eyes that couldn't smile, swept me, and before I know who she was, all my insides were crying out: 'Fiona!'

Fiona. My Fiona. I can't believe how she is now: so white, bare, frail and weathered. It was like seeing my own death. But it was still there, the magic. Even more so, as if ten years had stripped the flesh to let out more of the soul. There aren't eyes anywhere like her eyes. There's no head that can turn and make that line of throat. No other mouth can say nothing, and leave nothing to be said.

Then they were gone, and I went hollow inside, as if a mugger had grabbed my wallet. But they were the big losers, Georgiana's wicked angels. There are no more parties; they have funerals instead. Midge's first, then Toby's. They died of themselves, those two, like Chelsey said they would. Being was their poison. Tim and Thelma faded out after becoming grandparents, and the nurses disappeared to Norfolk. Ulric is holding on, in that awful flat full of dogs (Chelsey says Steven-John even feeds the starlings) but it won't be for much longer. Chelsey thinks she's the one that got away, but she'd lost herself years before, trying to become them.

And me? It doesn't matter to anyone except me and Chelsey that I can't forgive, but I do desperately want to forget. Or do I? What's it worth that it tells me that, for one moment in my life, I touched on something that was real, and for ever?

Now you can order superb titles directly from Virago

☐ Alias Grace	Margaret Atwood	£6.99
☐ Little Sister	Carol Birch	£6.99
☐ Fair Exchange	Michèle Roberts	£6.99
☐ Stuck up a Tree	Jenny McLeod	£6.99
☐ Like	Ali Smith	£6.99
☐ Pandora's Box	Alice Thompson	£6.99
☐ Cowboys are My Weakness	Pam Houston	£6.99
☐ The Cure for Death by Lightning	Gail Anderson-Dargatz	£6.99
☐ Brittle Joys	Sara Maitland	£6.99

Please allow for postage and packing: **Free UK delivery.**
Europe: add 25% of retail price; Rest of World: 45% of retail price.

To order any of the above or any other Virago titles, please call our credit card orderline or fill in this coupon and send/fax it to:

Virago, 250 Western Avenue, London, W3 6XZ, UK.
Fax 020 8324 5678   Telephone 020 8324 5516

☐ I enclose a UK bank cheque made payable to Virago for £ . . . .
☐ Please charge £ . . . . . to my Access, Visa, Delta, Switch Card No.

Expiry Date ☐☐☐☐   Switch Issue No. ☐☐

NAME (Block letters please) . . . .

ADDRESS . . . .

Postcode . . . . Telephone . . . .

Signature . . . .

Please allow 28 days for delivery within the UK. Offer subject to price and availability.
Please do not send any further mailings from companies carefully selected by Virago ☐